The Ha'Penny Steps

Book 1: Maruska's Story

By CR Spencer

C R SPENCER

Book 1 of the Ha'penny Steps Trilogy

Copyright notice.

This book remains the copyright of the author, CR Spencer. You may not republish or use the material contained therein for any purposes without the express permission of the author.
Date: 2 July 2024

First published August 2024

This edition published October 2024

This book is licensed for your personal enjoyment only. This book may not be re-sold or given away to other people. If you would like to share this book with another person, please purchase an additional copy for each recipient. If you are reading this book and did not purchase it, or it was not purchased for your use only, then please return to your favorite retailer and purchase your own copy. Thank you for respecting the hard work of this author.

Prologue Part 1
December 1940
A parachute bomb

He looked up at the dark sky. Searchlights danced across the heavens, seeking out the enemy bombers. He should have been hearing the incessant crashing and booming of the anti-aircraft batteries in Regents Park, but all he could hear was the deafening ringing in his head.

He struggled to get up. He looked down at his white-coated hands that seemed to flash in rhythm with the light from the surrounding explosions. He shook his head, trying to rid the shooting stars that sparkled within his eyes. He kicked off a couple of broken tiles that lay on his legs. By the large fire that had broken out on the other side of Langham Street, he could see two uniformed men running towards him. Their mouths opened and closed as though they were shouting at him, but he still couldn't hear anything.

One of the men roughly pulled him to his feet; the other began the thankless task of attempting to brush the white dust from his clothes. He recognised the uniforms; they were police officers. He swallowed hard, looking down. He stammered, "Where's my bag?" but he couldn't hear himself.

One of the policemen shouted at him, "Never mind your bloody bag. What in the name of God are you doing here?"

"My bag; my bag; where is it?"

The other policeman shook his head and flung the large green army issue canvas bag at him,

"It's here. Now bugger off like the sergeant says."

The man put his fingers to his ears and shook his head.

The sergeant looked at his mate and rolled his eyes, "The bomb's made him deaf. Just get him over the other side of the line and see if he needs the ambulance girls to have a look at him." He patted him down.

"Looks like he's okay physically; not so sure about his brains, though. Heaven knows how he could have missed the cordoned off area."

The constable dragged the man across the square as more bombs rained down in nearby Portland Place. He clutched the heavy canvas bag to his chest. He was unceremoniously plonked in front of an ambulance in the porch of an abandoned shop. .

The constable shouted at him, "Stay there until the all-clear..."

Peter Porteous wasn't in a fit state to go anywhere...He closed his eyes; that was close; too close for comfort. What was he doing? Ah, yes, he remembered. That bloody parachute bomb...

Porteous sat there. His Air Raid Precautions' dark, navy uniform was almost white. God knows what the dust was. He felt his chest tighten. Someone tugged at his sleeve. He opened his eyes to see a pretty London Auxiliary Ambulance girl mouthing at him.

"Wake up! Are you hurt?"

He pointed to his ears and shook his head.

She nodded, "Oh, don't worry, your hearing will probably come back in a little while." She reached into her shoulder bag and took out some cotton wool. She rolled two small balls and shoved them into his ears.

"The ringing will subside soon, but your ears may be a little sensitive for a few days." She lifted his chin,

"Let's have a look at you; can't see a damn thing with all that dust." The accent was refined. She turned and lifted out a small flask of water from her shoulder bag and poured it over his face. The grit from the dust irritated his eyes. He tried to turn away, but she held his head firmly in her grasp.

"Keep still..."

The ringing in his ears was gradually subsiding. He smiled at her. Her long auburn hair was fiercely tied in a bun. Her hands were graced with long, slender fingers. He noticed the thin wedding band. She smiled and held up the hand,

"Yeah, so don't get any ideas..."

She turned as a large and rather fierce LAAS sergeant shouted at her,

"Felicity! If he's okay, leave him. There's an injured child in one of the flats across the road. Come on, girl, move it..."

She sighed, "I'll have to love you and leave you. Just sit there like the good constable says and wait for the all-clear." She held her wrist up to what little light there was coming from the burning buildings to view her expensive watch.

She looked up at the sky, "They'll be gone soon. I can't imagine they've got anything left to chuck at us..."

She was gone; she ran across the road to join her sergeant.

Langham Place went quiet except for the crackling of the burning buildings. He could just about hear the sound of fire engines as they approached; it was time to leave...

He looked up to see the sergeant and his constable pointing at him from across the square. Peter Porteous stood up quickly; a little too quickly, as his head began to swim. He steadied himself by reaching out to the glass window in the shop doorway. He pulled up the sleeve of his jacket and tried desperately to focus on the face of his watch. It was close to eleven; the night was still young for the great and good of Germany to return for a second wave of death and destruction. He needed to get home.

He picked up his canvas bag; it now seemed twice as heavy as before, but he wasn't going to let this precious cargo be wasted. He threw the strap over his shoulder, not caring if it got tangled with his gas mask carrier, and slowly made his way out of Langham Place. He didn't hear the pretty London Auxiliary Ambulance girl, Felicity, shouting after him to wait for the all-clear.

He came out onto Portland Place; it was chaos, with yet another land mine having gone off in Cavendish Square. His ARP uniform afforded him exactly what he wanted, complete anonymity. No one gave him a second glance as they went about their business in the roar of the fires from burning buildings. Fire engines were everywhere. Several ambulances were parked up on Regent Street with their crews awaiting the signal to get to work, either rescuing the injured or retrieving dead bodies or parts thereof...The makeshift morgues would be busy tonight.

Porteous reached Oxford Circus underground station. A policeman guarded the upper steps. Porteous lowered his eyes, not wishing to attract attention to himself.

A loud voice brought him up sharply.

"Hey! Where do you think you are going?"

Porteous looked at the constable, who must have been in his early sixties.

"I'm trying to get home."

"Not down there, you are not! The place is already ten deep. There's no more room."

Porteous sighed, "Look, I don't want to shelter. I want a tube train..."

The constable laughed, "You'll be lucky. The trains stopped over an hour ago when the raid started. They may start again when the all-clear is given." He paused, "What happened to you?"

"Parachute bomb in Langham Place."

The constable smiled, "Yeah, I heard there were two; one outside the BBC and one in Cavendish Square. The Jerries have been after the BBC for a couple of weeks now."

He looked at Porteous, "Where are you going?"

"Up the Harrow Road, if I can get there."

"Hmm, that's a long walk; good luck…"

Just then, the all-clear sounded. Porteous stepped back behind some railings as a growing tide of humanity suddenly surged up the steps. He sighed and sat down on his canvas bag. It would take a good fifteen minutes for the crowds to reach street level and disperse. He watched as what appeared to be half of London poured out of all four exits in a desperate attempt to get home before a second raid commenced. He put his head between his hands and tried to focus. He could feel his chest begin to tighten again. His medication was at home. If he had a bad attack, he would end up in some hospital waiting room whilst doctors and nurses attempted to patch up the war wounded. He didn't have time for this.

He needed to get home and relieve himself of his cargo before someone began asking questions. He felt a tug on his arm.

"Porteous! Porteous! What are you doing here?"

Nancy Keeling looked down at the dishevelled Porteous, "Are you okay? You look terrible."

"Oh, hi, Nancy, are you still working?"

"Nah, the party got cancelled, but I've got that job in Wembley. I don't want to go up there but it's good money and a damn sight safer than down here."

"Go home, Nancy, it's not worth it."

She sat down beside him on the canvas bag. He could smell her perfume.

"I don't have a choice, Porteous, I go where Mifty tells me."

She reached into her fake leather handbag and extracted a cigarette also of somewhat dubious provenance. A gold lighter appeared as she cupped her hands and lit the tobacco. She inhaled deeply. He looked at her. She was in her early twenties. She was tastefully made up, with her dark hair neatly tied to one side. Her long navy coloured coat fell to one side, revealing a bright yellow dress. She pulled her knees up to her chest and wrapped her coat around her bare legs. She shivered in the cold December night air.

Porteous snorted, "Michael 'Mifty' Mitchell; all class that gentleman."

Nancy Keeling blew out some smoke, "He's all right, really. Doesn't take too much off me."

Porteous shook his head, "Nancy, how many times have I told you to get yourself back to Norwich? Didn't he hit you once? You don't need Mitchell or his boss Charlie Maitland."

Nancy Keeling laughed, ignoring the domestic violence question, "Norwich? I'd end up back in some frozen field screwing beetroot." She stretched out her long, thin fingers. "How long would my hands last doing that kind of work?"

Porteous looked at her, "I told you I can get you a job up at Smiths in Cricklewood; they're always short of girls."

She took him by the arm and sighed, "I tried that once and as soon as the others found out what I was, they wouldn't work with me. Silly bitches. The only difference between them and me is that they give it away for free."

He looked down at her bare legs, "Have you got no stockings? Have you used up the last pairs I gave you?"

She shook her head, "Nah. That Stocking Strangler is still on the loose. All the girls have stopped wearing them until PC Plod catches him. Esther knew one of his victims from Piccadilly."

"Which one?"

"The nineteen-year-old. Charlie Maitland says he'll chop the bastard up when he gets hold of him."

Porteous sucked in some breath, "That kid from Manchester? She'd only been in London a month." He paused, "I suppose it's some kind of logic...if you don't wear stockings, he can't strangle you..."

Nancy Keeling laughed, "Yeah, I reckon you're correct. He leaves one around her neck and takes one as a souvenir. Must be some kind of fetish. Anyway, can you get me some?"

"I dunno, Nancy. Jimmy's got hold of some WREN stuff; I'll ask."

"The WREN stuff is too thick, but I suppose they'll do." She paused and looked down at the canvas holdall, "What's in the bag?"

"That'd be telling, Miss Nancy."

She pouted, "I bet it's for Maruska…"

"That's for me to know and you to guess."

"Anyway, what happened to you?"

"Parachute bomb in Langham Place."

"You were always a lucky sod, Peter Porteous. Anyone else would be in bits in some morgue."

He began to cough. She asked, "Is your chest bothering you?" She looked at him anxiously.

He nodded, "My meds are at home."

"Well, let's get you back there."

Nancy Keeling spent the next ten minutes flirting with a taxi driver who was out to make the most of the lull in the bombing and earn a few pennies. The driver agreed to take her up to Wembley via the Harrow Road and drop Porteous off at the Ha'penny Steps for an appropriate fee either in cash or kind…Porteous didn't bother to ask which…

They sat in the back of the cab. She put her arm inside his and rested her head on his shoulder.

He asked her, "Who's the client?"

"Some retired gentleman who needs his bed warming for the night; no big deal, really."

"You've been before?"

He felt her head nod on his shoulder, "He's okay. Not too demanding, and he tips generously. Besides, I swiped a full bottle of good Scotch whisky last time. Sold it to another punter for a few quid before Mifty got his hands on it."

Porteous snorted, "Be careful, Nancy."

The cab slowed yet again as it carefully negotiated fallen debris in the road that the council had not got around to removing. It was pitch black. The skilful driver could have found his way blindfolded...

She reached up and pulled his head towards hers. She kissed him deeply on the lips. "I'll be fine, Porteous, besides, I'm saving myself for you..."

He waved at her as the cab drove off. He walked slowly towards the footbridge opposite Second Avenue. The Ha'penny Steps were a fixture in this part of west London. They crossed the Grand Union Canal into the notorious Kensal Town. Shielded by the canal on the east side and the Great Western Railway on the west, Kensal Town was a law unto itself, rarely visited by the local constabulary except in pairs...It was presumed that the steps got its name sometime in the distant past, when pedestrians were charged the grand sum of one halfpenny to save them the long detour up to Ladbroke Grove to get into Kensal Town. Not that many wise souls thought it judicious to cross over on to the dangerous territory without just cause. The toll didn't last too long, as local residents, not noted for their charm and politeness, soon saw off these wide-boy chancers. The canal company thought it better not to pursue the matter.

The blackout was strictly enforced and unless you knew your local surroundings, you would be in trouble. Peter Porteous had lived in Kensal Town ever since he first came to London on the promise of a job some years previously, only leaving it temporarily to answer the call-up to the army. His time in the military was cut short when his severe asthma was finally noticed, despite his best efforts to disguise it. Running across a barren landscape in Wales carrying some forty pounds of equipment soon sorted the men from the boys and the fit from the unfit. His medical discharge from the army was swift...

Porteous reached into his official ARP bag and took out a small torch that only stayed on when the button was depressed. Wardens had been taught to use the torch sparingly, turning it on only for a split second at a time in order to get one's bearings.

He flashed the torch at the steps and walked towards them; once he was on them, he would feel a lot more comfortable knowing that his home, for what it was, was only a stone's throw away on Bosworth Road. He looked over the railings at the top of the steps. The dark waters of the canal swirled beneath him as they made their way towards the Paddington Basin at the side of the railway terminus. The canvas bag on his shoulder was beginning to feel very heavy. He flashed the torch once to pick out the descending steps. As he slowly made his way down, a sound caused him to freeze. He clicked on the torch again. The light picked up a man and a woman pressed against a smoke stained wall. A female voice called out,

"For Christ's sake, hit the bloody light..."

Porteous recognised the voice, "Edith? Is that you?"

A gruff male voice called out, "Whoever you are, piss off. Can't you see a man's busy here?"

Porteous shone the torch again in the direction of the voices. This time he left the light on. The man had the woman's leg hooked up under his arm, almost on his shoulder. His trousers were around his ankles. The woman smiled and winked at Porteous. Her arms were grasped tightly around the man's neck as she pulled him on to her. She spoke softly,

"It's all right, Porteous. We're nearly finished."

Porteous cut the light, "You'd better get back inside, Edith, there's another raid coming."

There was no reply as the thrusting and grunting recommenced. By the time he reached the top floor of his building in Bosworth

Road, Peter Porteous, was feeling decidedly ill. He needed his medication, otherwise he could easily die.

He pushed open the door. The sound of some late night music was playing softly in the background. There were lights on in each room. He dropped the large canvas bag. It hit the bare wooden floor with a loud thud. Fortunately, the flat below him had been vacant since the start of the bombing a couple of months earlier. He had turned it into a useful storeroom for his illicit goods...A female voice called out,

"Porteous? Is that you?" The accent was thick and strong, although the voice was delicate.

He sighed and walked slowly over to the bathroom door. He leaned on the door frame. The door hadn't shut properly ever since the large landmine had gone off some two hundred yards away, in fact, most of the doors didn't fit any more. The whole building had been shaken to its core.

He folded his arms as the eastern European beauty lay back in the old cast iron bath. He replied,

"Who did you think it was, Maruska?"

She didn't look at him and sighed, "I dunno, Porteous, maybe it was my handsome Prince Charming coming to take me away from this hellhole. My grandmama always used to say that every good girl has a Prince Charming..." She stopped suddenly; her eyes had found him, "Jesus, Porteous, what happened to you?"

She sat up in the bath; the water sloshed over the side onto the tiled floor.

"Nothing, really, just a little acquaintance with a parachute bomb in Langham Place."

She stood up quickly, "You don't look too good. Is your chest bothering you again?"

He nodded as she carefully stepped out of the bath grabbing a towel, "Come on; get your meds and sit down. I'll be back in a minute."

She reached for his dressing gown that hung on the back of the door and threw it on.

She opened the front door and ran across the top floor landing, leaving delicate, wet footprints on the wooden boards and into her flat. She reappeared just as Porteous was pulling off his dust-covered clothes. She helped him remove his shirt and pushed him forward. The metal of the stethoscope was cold on his bare back.

"Jesus, Maruska, could you not have warmed it up?"

"Shut up, Porteous, I'm trying to hear your chest."

He smiled as she furrowed her eyebrows and swore profusely in Czech.

"Jednoho dne budete mít útok a nebudete se zotavovat..."

"In English, Maruska..."

"I said you'll probably have an attack one day and not recover...Shh! I'm trying to see if you need to go to hospital."

He coughed, "Why would I go when I've got a perfectly good doctor here wearing nothing but my dressing gown?"

She snorted and grabbed his hand to feel for a pulse.

He continued, "Anyway, what are you doing?"

"Taking a bath, idiot. Do you need that translating?"

"I didn't mean that. I presume the gas came back on, then?"

She shook her head and swore again, "Where's your atomiser?"

He nodded at the bathroom.

He watched as she mixed up the Epinephrine. She wrapped the elastic bands around the back of his head and began to squeeze the rubber bulb gently as the medication was pushed into his face-mask.

She said, "It would be quicker if we injected it, Porteous." He shook his head...

He breathed in the mixture from the bronchial dilator, waiting for his airways to clear. She patted him gently on the back as he shivered.

"It's probably the dust that set it off. God knows what you breathed in. How many times have I told you to keep well away from burning buildings?"

The muffled voice replied, "I'm an ARP warden, Maruska, it's part of my job to go near burning buildings."

"I'll boil a kettle; the inhaled steam will help after you've finished the atomiser. Sit there whilst I finish my bath."

He watched as she threw off the robe and climbed back into the bath.

She called out, "You know, there's much better medication out there now. They were using Ephedrine at the University." She disappeared under the now lukewarm water.

He waited till she resurfaced, "I use what they give me at the surgery."

The kettle began to whistle. He looked at her and she submerged again.

Slowly, he stood up and went over to the two-ring gas stove. He poured some steaming water into a bowl as she emerged again. He put it down and leaned into it at the kitchen table with a towel over his head. He was already feeling better.

Five minutes later, his breathing much easier, he boiled up some more water and took it into the bathroom,

"Mind your feet…" She quickly drew her legs up as he poured the water into the end of the bath. He threw off the rest of his clothes and climbed into the hot water. He felt her legs up on his chest.

"Are you okay now?"

He nodded as he lay back, closed his eyes, and recounted his near death experience.

They sat at the kitchen table in dressing gowns, drinking ersatz coffee. Maruska Bergman grimaced, "Jesus, Porteous, where did you get this stuff from?"

"That's all I could get. There's some real coffee downstairs, but I'm saving that for a deal later in the week. Just drink it and be thankful."

She eyed the canvas bag, "Did you bring me a present, Porteous?" She batted her eyelids.

"Open it, I thought you might like it."

She slowly undid the leather and metal buckles. Her eyes lit up when she saw the mass of material tightly packed into the bag; she squealed,

"Oh! Where did you get this?"

"Jimmy acquired it; I didn't ask where he got it from."

She pulled out the rolled up, soft and shiny material. Her fingers glided over the cloth.

"You bugger! It's pure silk! Perfect!"

She rolled out the parachute material on the floor and bent down on her knees, smoothing out the silk. There was just a little damage where the cotton cords had been roughly cut in a hurry.

"Is it German?"

Porteous shook his head, "Dunno; it could be. I'd have said it was British, but the weave is too fine. The Yanks are mixing them with nylon these days, and I suppose that's the way they will all go in the near future. Silk is almost impossible to get hold of now in its natural state." He paused, "Will it do?"

She looked up at him from her position on her knees on the floor.

"Of course it will. I should be able to get at least three good sets from this lot." She looked at the silk again, "It's a pity it's only one third of the 'chute. I need some more lace..."

He sipped his hot drink, "Yeah, I thought you might..."

She stood up, her bare feet making little indents in the soft material, "Come on, Porteous, I think I can get Madam Collier to buy everything if I use the right lace."

"I hope you charge the old woman a fortune for them."

"Don't worry, she'll take anything I can make."

She began to roll up the silk, "Help me..."

The material was soon back in the canvas bag. He asked, "Do you know which stores have got lace?"

She shook her head, "That old man in the shop on the Harrow Road opposite the Steps has some, I heard, but won't serve me because I'm a Jew."

Porteous looked at her, "Maybe, but he'll serve me..."

She wrapped his dressing gown tightly around her waist, "What time are you on in the morning?"

"Six, as usual."

"Are you working tomorrow night?"

"Yes, down in Chelsea. They are two wardens short for the fire watch."

"Don't they give you a night off?"

"Only when the Jerries stop coming..."

She sighed and picked up his dusty ARP uniform, "I'll sponge this down for you. It will be ready for tomorrow night. I'll make a start on the silk in the morning. Leave the bag here; I'll come and collect it when I need it."

She leaned into him and kissed him on his lips, "Don't forget the lace..."

He watched as she scurried to the front door of his flat and left. He yawned; God, he was tired.

Prologue Part 2
December 1940
Pressing machines and a draper's shop

It was nearly nine the next morning before Peter Porteous had five minutes to himself. He sat in the makeshift canteen in Building Number 3 enjoying the peace and quiet away from the loud noise of the machines and the incessant chatter of the girls. He was only three personnel down today; one with a hospital appointment, one with a sick baby, and one claiming her husband was on special leave from the army. He shook his head; it didn't really matter because half of the machines were not working. He'd done his best to patch them up but, as he frequently told the building supervisor, they were FUBAR, as our American friends would say, (Fucked up beyond all repair...)

He stared ahead as he blew the steam off his mug of tea. At least it tasted like real tea...He felt the bench seat shake as someone sat next to him.

A soft voice asked, "Are you all right, Porteous?" The Liverpool accent was harsh.

He turned to see the smiling face of Alice Halpin. She was dressed in a navy blue all-in-one boiler suit. Her long, auburn hair was tied tightly under a turban-style headscarf. A few stray strands of the hair peeked out.

He asked, "What's up, Alice?"

"Number 8 has packed up again. The bearing is making a horrible sound and I think it's burning."

He swore quietly, "How are we supposed to meet this docket if the damn machines keep packing up?"

"Dunno, Porteous, but Walker is shouting for you."

He closed his eyes. His ears were still ringing slightly from the explosion the previous evening. His chest was still a bit tight, but at least the cycle ride up through Kensal Rise at five-thirty earlier in the crisp, frosty air had cleared his lungs. The odd whiff of burning embers had drifted up from the West End to remind him of his encounter with the parachute bomb and the devastation of the nightly bombing raids. He had been up on the roof of the University building in Great Portland Street with Jimmy Ryan when the searchlights caught the parachute as it drifted down in the gentle wind carrying its deadly cargo. The Jerries had been after the BBC for over a week. You can't have propaganda being pumped out over the airwaves, can you? Last night, they missed again...

Jimmy Ryan was a fixer. He could get you anything for the right price. Born in 1903, he was too young for the Great War, but a life of petty crime in his late teens and early twenties had deterred even the most optimistic of recruitment sergeants from enrolling him in the service of king and country. It was said he used to work in his father's shop on the Caledonian Road before the family disowned him. Now, he lived by his wits, dealing exclusively in hard-to- get items on the black market. To keep the Ministry of Employment happy, Jimmy Ryan volunteered as an Air Raid Protection warden. Knowing his background of petty larceny and other associated crimes, the Ministry registered him as unfit for work. Jimmy Ryan was very proud of his status, as it meant he couldn't be pressed into factory work. Besides, he had slipped the female clerk in the Government Office a couple of pairs of stockings...

Ryan and Porteous had been bargaining for the silk when the parachute appeared in the searchlights. When the bomb didn't go off after it landed Porteous thought nothing of it. Sometimes they exploded, sometimes they didn't. Even Jimmy Ryan wasn't daft enough to attempt to cut the silk away from an unexploded bomb. This lot had come from somewhere else. Porteous paid one pound and ten shillings for the silk. If Maruska could get three sets out of it, provided he could get some lace, they could make a pretty penny.

He was stirred out of his daydreaming by the sharp tapping on his arm

"Porteous! Porteous! Walker wants you down in the workshop."

He looked at her and smiled, "He'll have to wait, Alice. Even I can't do two things at once."

She took his hand, "Did you have a rough time last night?"

He nodded, "Yeah, damn parachute bomb."

She raised her eyebrows; "One of the girls was saying her old man told her they had a go at the BBC again last night."

"Yeah, tell me about it..."

"No, it looks to me like you had an asthma attack."

"Yeah, that as well as the bomb."

"What were you doing up in the West End? Your patch is Chelsea."

"Doing a bit of business."

She snorted, "Serves you right, then. What did you get?"

He leaned into her and whispered, "Not telling you, Alice..."

She giggled, "Whatever it was, can I have some?"

"Maybe, maybe..."

A voice boomed out from across the other side of the canteen,

"Porteous! Porteous! For God's sake, get over here, now."

Porteous looked at Alice Halpin and rolled his eyes, "I'm on my break, Mr Walker."

The voice got nearer, "Never mind your sodding break. Why are your girls idle?"

Porteous looked at the shop supervisor, whose podgy face was almost purple with rage.

"They are idle, Mr Walker, because the machine that presses the casings has packed up, again."

Walker was almost in his face. Alice Halpin moved subconsciously on the wooden bench. She looked up at the bullying supervisor. The veins on his nose were bulging. His nicotine-stained teeth bared as he spoke; his breath was none too fresh, either. He wore a threadbare old brown suit that had probably come from some pawnshop or other. The girls often wondered what he did during the shift.

Walker raised himself up to his full height; all five feet three of him.

"Well, go and fix it!" The voice echoed around the empty canteen.

Porteous took one last swig of his hot, sweet tea and noisily plonked down the tin mug, "Yes, sir, whatever you say..."

He turned to his companion, "Come on, Alice, you'd better give me a hand..."

They stood up slowly, extracted their feet from under the bench and walked arm in arm to the door, trying to suppress their giggles.

The workshop was quiet when they walked in. The girls were gathered around a bench, smoking and chattering. As soon as they saw him, they scattered to their benches and began moving components around, pretending to look busy. He stood looking at the defunct machine with his arms folded. He could smell the burnt out bearings. He had replaced one set about a week ago, but the replacement parts were so badly made he was surprised they lasted that long.

He sighed, "Better get my tool box, Alice, and let's see if we can resurrect this pile of scrap at least until the end of our shift. Send Pru to the tool shop to get another two and a half inch wheel bearings and some new casings, if they've got them."

Alice Halpin scuttled off.

It took him just under one hour to disassemble the outer casing of the machine to get at the bearings and replace them. He lay on his back under the machine as Alice Halpin passed him tools and parts. As the production line re-started, he examined the burnt out bearings on a workbench. He held a part up,

"What do you reckon, Alice?"

She took the burnt part and held it up to the light, turning it slowly, "It's way out of tolerance; who made this piece of rubbish?"

Porteous shook his head, "Probably some fifteen-year-old, who should be in school, up in Coventry."

Alice raised her eyebrows, "I could do better than that, Porteous."

"A blind man could do better than that!"

He shouted over the noise, "Ladies! Ladies! Let's see if we can get at least half of the order done before we clock off. I'll have a word with the supervisor on B shift to see if he can make up the shortfall. Remember, our lads can't fly their little planes without these instruments."

There was a collective nod of agreement as the ladies went back to their business of assembling altimeters for the War effort. He turned to Alice Halpin,

"Keep an eye on that machine and the girls, Alice. I'd better go and write a report for management. I'll be back soon."

Peter Porteous sat in a little dingy office at the end of the workshop. He wrote a short report on why the shift had failed to meet minimum numbers. He shoved the burnt and broken pieces into a little cardboard box and wrapped the note around, tied with a piece of string. Cedric Walker appeared at the door.

Porteous turned slowly and held up his hands, "Before you start shouting, I suggest you have a look at what we are working with." He rattled the cardboard box. "This is utter crap and that machine is worse than useless. You need to persuade the Ministry to sort out Coventry. How can I get the girls to do the business when you ask me to work with this?"

Cedric Walker rolled up a cigarette, "Dunno, Porteous. I put in a request to management last week to have that press replaced but was told there are none in the country with everything being turned over to the war effort."

Porteous was exasperated, "This is the bloody war effort."

"Don't you raise your voice at me, Porteous. Get out there and chivvy those girls of yours along. Perhaps you might want to stay on after the shift to help make up for the loss?"

Porteous snorted, "I'm on in Chelsea tonight, bad luck, old boy..."

He pushed past the overweight supervisor and out into the shop. Alice Halpin smiled at him as he walked over to one of the ladies who appeared to be struggling as parts piled high on her bench, "Come on, June, let's see if we can clear this lot..."

The bell sounded at two. There was a collective sigh of relief from the assembled workers. He shouted out,

"Okay, ladies, let's call it a day. Leave it to B shift."

Alice Halpin and Peter Porteous sat in the Crown Public House. It was nearly three in the afternoon. They were both nursing a half pint of warm beer pulled straight from the cask. The place was crowded. In wartime Britain, you did your drinking in daylight hours before the Luftwaffe ventured over the Channel to shed their deadly cargo. Porteous sat by the window. Smoky pubs are generally not the best place to frequent if you are an asthmatic, but he had cracked open the side window and so was breathing in the cold December air. They were still in boiler suits, although Alice had removed the turban headscarf. Her dark hair scattered over her shoulders. He asked,

"When's Phyllis next back?"

Alice shook her head as she sipped the bitter tasting liquid, "Dunno, exactly. She's training down in Hampshire on some new procedure or other. She won't tell me what it is."

Porteous raised his eyebrows, "Hush, hush and all that? Has she got her commission?"

"Not yet; she reckons it will come after her training, but that'll mean a stint down at Dartmouth, and I'll never get to see her."

"I thought you said she'll get a job at the Admiralty?"

"Yeah, but only if she's an officer."

Porteous shrugged his shoulders, "Only a matter of time. What about you? You can't stay at Smiths for the duration?"

"I can, as long as you stay."

"You don't fancy joining up like Phyllis?"

"Nah, I'd probably end up in the north of Scotland whilst she's being chatted up by some posh naval officer in Trafalgar Square."

"Could be worse..."

He got a playful punch for his remark.

She asked, "Never mind about me, what's with you and your Czech doctor, Maruska? I haven't seen her for weeks."

"She's not a doctor, at least, not here. They won't let her practise; something about her being an alien and not to be trusted."

"I thought there was a shortage of medical staff?"

"There is, but being a foreigner in times of war doesn't help, anyway, she doesn't care any more. She's making enough money as a seamstress. She says that as soon as the war is over, she'll head to America. They're all foreigners there!"

Alice put down her beer mug, "Does she not want to go back to Prague?"

"I doubt it, Alice. She thinks the Nazis took all her family. She has nothing left to go back to."

"Will she be able to practise in America?"

"Yes, I think so. I've seen her certificates. She's got more qualifications than I can throw a stick at."

She spoke quietly, "What about Nancy?"

He shook his head slowly. "I saw her last night after the first all-clear; she was on her way to a client in Wembley."

Alice leaned into him, "One of the girls has a friend who is employed in the typing pool at West End Central Police Station. She told me that they're about to crack down on the working girls."

"I know, I know; I've told her several times, but she won't listen, especially with that so-called Stocking Strangler on the loose."

Alice Halpin spoke in a whisper; "She said the police have got as many undercover officers on the streets as they can spare. They reckon he's a serviceman."

He nodded, "Yeah, she says it's been very quiet with the bombing and the police activity. Anyway, Charlie Maitland, or whatever he calls himself these days, will buy off the police like he usually does."

They paused as laughter rose up from a group of men by the bar. Porteous could see Cedric Walker in the gathering. War never seemed to dampen the British sense of humour. He sighed,

"Come on, Alice. I need to have some rest before I go down to Chelsea later. The Jerries will soon be back, bringing mayhem and chaos to the landed gentry of the Royal Borough."

Alice Halpin gulped down the remains of her drink. He asked, "Have you got something acceptable to eat tonight?"

"Yes, my landlady acquired some corned beef last week. There's still a tin left. She'll cook up something half decent, and I'll eat with her."

They were at the door, "She's alright, that one," he remarked.

"Yeah, she's not bothered about me and Phyllis in fact she quite likes her around the place dressed in her uniform; it impresses the neighbours."

They were at their bicycles, fastening up their coats as a fine drizzle started.

"Any word from your parents?"

She shook her head, "I write once a week, but they never respond."

He took her hand, "They will, I'm sure, Alice. They'll accept you and Phyllis sooner or later."

There was a note of defiance in her voice, "I'm past caring, Porteous. I am what I am."

She leaned over and kissed him on the cheek before she rode off and turned left towards her lodgings in Golders Green and he towards Kensal Town and the Ha'penny Steps but not before a little visit to the drapers on the Harrow Road

It was approaching four by the time Peter Porteous leaned his bicycle against the railings outside the draper's shop in between Second and Third Avenue opposite the Ha'penny Steps. The light was rapidly fading on this December day. Passers-by were hurrying to get home before the black-out took a firm hold. As he pushed open the door to the shop, the bell attached to the top sounded out a loud warning. The shop was cold and bereft of customers. Two naked light bulbs cast an eerie glow over the glass counters.

Ivor Bennett appeared from a darkened doorway at the back of the three-sided counter. He looked well into his sixties, with a completely bald crown and just a smattering of grey from his ears around the back of his head. He had a dirty pipe clenched tightly between his yellowing teeth. His brown cotton lab coat hung down to his knees. Underneath, Porteous could see a hand-knitted jumper that had seen better days.

Bennett cleared his throat and removed the pipe. He stuck it in the outside breast pocket of his coat next to a couple of chewed pencils.

"Yes, sir, what can I do for you?"

Porteous walked up to the glass counter. Inside, he could see a variety of garments neatly folded, complete with a handwritten price tag. The shop was carefully arranged so that the proprietor could lay his hand on any item quickly.

Porteous answered quickly, "Lace...I understand you have some."

Bennett looked at Porteous; he thought he had seen him before but couldn't swear on it. "Well, sir, it's very difficult to get at the moment what with all the factories turning to making uniforms."

Porteous stared at the old man, "Have you got some?"

"I might have; it depends on what you want if for."

Porteous sighed, "Edging on some lingerie. White and about three yards."

Bennett grunted, "I'll see what I've got."

He shuffled over to the other side of the shop, bent down, pulled out a drawer and extracted a flat cardboard container. He took the box over to Porteous and opened it. He lifted out two little packets that were buried in layers of tissue paper and placed them on the counter.

"This one is Nottingham lace and the other, I got from a dealer in the East End, originates from Belgium." He held up the little cardboard wrap that had the lace tightly bound around it. He continued, "There are two yards of that and I don't feel inclined to cut it. The Nottingham lace, I'll cut you as much as you want."

Porteous picked up the Belgium lace. It was beautifully embroidered and was perfect for what Maruska wanted.

"How much?" he enquired.

"You can have that lot for three shillings. If you take two yards of the Nottingham stuff, I'll let you have them both for five shillings."

Porteous slapped two half crowns on the glass; "I'll take them. Wrap them up for me."

Bennett swept up the money and rang it into the ancient silver coloured till. As he wrapped up the lace he spoke quietly, although there was no one in the shop,

"I managed to get some black material; perfect for ladies undergarments. Would you like to see it?"

Porteous nodded. A few minutes later, a bolt of the shiny material was carefully laid out in front of him. Bennett went into his salesman spiel.

"Got this from the same chap in the East End. He's had enough of the bombing, so he's clearing out before he takes a direct hit. It's a mixture of rayon and cotton. I think it's from America."

He flipped the bolt so that half a yard was laid out on the counter. He rubbed the soft material between his finger and thumb. "Feel that, sir. I understand it's going to be used as a substitute for silk parachutes. Can't get raw silk for love nor money any more."

Porteous felt the material, "How much?"

Bennett coughed, "Normally ten bob a yard, but I can let you have it for seven and six. How does that sound?"

Porteous shook his head, "No, sorry, too much for my pocket, but I'll let the seamstress know. She might want it."

Bennett sighed, "Well tell her not to wait too long otherwise it will be gone. What's her name in case she comes in?"

Porteous looked at the old man, "Maruska Bergman. She's my neighbour over the Steps. You might remember her. She came in the other day, but you wouldn't serve her. Something about her being an alien or a Jew, I believe?"

Bennett coloured up, "I-I-I don't remember that, sir, but I get a lot of funny people coming in trying to steal from me and them foreigners are notorious for it."

Porteous reached over to the shopkeeper and grabbed him by the lapels of his brown lab coat and pulled him over the counter. "Okay, listen carefully, old man. My name is Porteous. If you like, you can ask about me over the Steps; they all know me there. If Maruska comes in, try to be a little more civil to her..."

Bennett swallowed as he felt Porteous release his grip. "Sure thing, sir. Tell her to come in anytime..."

Porteous picked up his parcel and left the shop.

The White Horse public house on Kensal Road was crowded as Peter Porteous entered. The smoke caught his chest immediately. He looked around. Edith Bell was serving at the bar. She whispered something to her colleague, lifted the bar hatch and made her way through the drinkers.

"Porteous, what brings you here?"

She guided him to the doorway, stuck one foot in it so that the cold fresh air came in. A voice behind her called out,

"Shut that bloody door, woman. I've only just got feelings back in me fingers."

Edith Bell turned quickly, and swore loudly at the complainant, who coloured up, much to the amusement of his companions. She pushed Porteous out into the night air.

Their conversation lasted around ten minutes. Edith Bell pecked him on the cheek and bade him farewell, promising not to take customers to the Steps again during the black-out...

Maruska Bergman was nowhere to be seen when he got up the stairs to the top floor. He opened her door and called out. He went in quietly. The whole floor was laid out with cut patterns for the lingerie. The old treadle Singer machine was pulled out into the middle. He could recall how difficult it had been for the removal men to heave the heavy machine up the three floors and then at her insistence for him to fit four little wheels to the base legs so that she could move it around to catch the light during the day. She had also demanded he box in the underneath of the table so she could use it for storage…It took him ages to replicate the wood pattern and stain so that it all looked original…

His ARP uniform was hanging on the wire that straddled the entire room. The uniform was looking pristine, with no hint of the adventure with the parachute bomb the previous evening. His dressing gown hung on the back of the door next to one other she had purloined. He shook his head, left the lace on the machine table and made his way back to his flat. He made some tea and lay on the bed and fell asleep inside five minutes.

Later that night, as Porteous made his way down to his fire watching duties from the top of Saint Luke's and Christ Church, a man and a woman entered the draper's shop on the Harrow Road from the door in the backyard and removed two bolts of black, rayon and cotton material…

PART 1

Maruska's Story

Chapter 1

April 1939
Ashford, Kent, England
An Interrogation

The woman sat in the chilly room; she was tired. She had her head down on her hands on the battered table. She felt dirty and unkempt. God knows how long she had been kept there. She needed to go to the toilet, but she hadn't seen anyone for at least an hour. She could hear the female guards chatting outside the locked door as though they didn't have a care in the world. When her interrogator had left her some time before, she had looked out through the dirty glass window onto what seemed like a courtyard. She could just see the roof of the old gymnasium where she had been accommodated with about fifty other women all going through the same process as her.

A key rattled in the door. She opened her eyes. She couldn't be bothered to raise her head. The guard came in and shouted

"Stand up, Fräulein!"

The woman ignored her, pretending to sleep.

She felt a rough tugging on her sleeve.

"I said stand up; are you deaf?"

The woman slowly lifted her head. She looked at the guard who was dressed in some sort of uniform that consisted of a navy blue skirt, and tunic, white blouse and flat black shoes. The guard looked as though she could lose a few pounds.

She stood up, "I need to go to the toilet, please." She spoke quietly.

The guard rolled her eyes, "Jesus, what's the matter with you people?" She shouted at the door, "Price, this Fräulein needs the heads..."

There was some muttering as a half smoked cigarette was extinguished. The woman was frogmarched down the corridor. Officer Price gripped her arm tightly, even though there was nowhere for the woman to go; every door seemed to be locked. The female guards went everywhere with keys dangling from a chain on their waist.

The woman was pushed into a toilet. "You've got two minutes and leave the cubicle door unlocked..."

The woman slowly walked to the last cubicle. She caught a glimpse of herself in the mirrors that were above the hand basins. She didn't like what she saw...

She sat on the pedestal. She was still wearing the same clothes in which she had been detained as soon as she walked off the steamer. When was that, a week ago?

The door creaked open...She looked up to see Officer Price staring at her with a smile on her face.

The woman spoke quietly as she lowered her eyes, "I'm not German."

The guard licked her lips and stared at the woman, "Do I look like I care?"

There was a loud knocking on the door, "Price! What are you doing in there? Mr Brown is waiting. Get her back, pronto!"

Price straightened up smartly, "Come on, stop messing around."

The woman slowly stood up, wiped herself and adjusted her clothes. She turned around and pulled the chain. She pushed past the guard, went to the sink, and rinsed her hands in the cold water.

Five minutes later, she stood at the door of the room facing the interrogator she knew as Mr Brown, although she doubted that was his real name...There was a pale coloured Manila file laid out in front of him. Her carpetbag lay open on a chair. It contained all that she had managed to bring with her.

Brown spoke first, "Please sit down, Doctor Bergman. I have a few more questions to ask you."

Maruska Bergman sighed...

He laid out some papers that contained her earlier statements; "Tell me again how you managed to get from Vienna to Zurich."

Maruska Bergman began slowly. "I was studying at the University Hospital..."

Brown interrupted, "What was the course?"

"Paediatric illnesses..."

He continued, "When did you start the course?"

"September 1937."

"Who put you on the course?"

She shook her head, "I don't know. I just applied for it. It was on a list at the hospital and as I had already completed my initial training in Vienna, I was entitled to apply."

"So, you were employed as a junior doctor back in Prague?"

She nodded...

Brown again, "So, let's recap, shall we? You were born in Karlsbad in 1910. Your father is a local doctor and your mother is an American citizen, although she was born in Prague."

Maruska nodded as he continued,

"She went to New York when she was three and came back in 1900 to marry your father."

Maruska stared ahead, "Yes..."

"You have two brothers, Lukas, who is three years older than you and David, who is eighteen months older than you. Where is David?"

"David is in Prague with his wife and children. Lukas is in New York; he married an American."

A pen scratched. "How did you manage to train as a doctor? It must have been unusual for a woman."

"My father helped. I did well in my school. The authorities in Vienna had no reason to reject me, as my father has connections. There were several other women on the course."

"Why did you not train in Prague?"

"They didn't admit women."

"But they employed you after you qualified?"

"Yes..."

Brown spoke quickly, "How many languages do you speak?"

He was firing questions from all areas at her. She knew this was a tactic...

"Czech, English and German."

"Who taught you English?"

"My mother. She always spoke English to me as a child. My father spoke only Czech to me"

"Where did the German come from?" enquired Mr Brown.

"You know, Karlsbad is in what the Nazis now call the Sudetenland. All my neighbours are ethnic Germans. I had to speak German to get along at school."

"How is your Hebrew?"

Maruska shook her head, "Not good. My family is not very religious. We only went to the synagogue on special occasions."

"Do you consider yourself Czech or a Jew?"

This was a blunt question, put rather bluntly.

"Both, I'm a Czech and a Jew therefore, I'm a Czech Jew," Maruska replied, a little too forcibly.

Brown cleared his throat, "So, how did you get from Vienna to Zurich?"

"I took the train."

"What date was that?"

"13 March."

"Who arranged that for you?"

"I arranged it myself. I just went to the Hauptbanhoff, showed my papers and got a ticket."

"What happened when the train crossed the border?"

"Nothing. The guards came on and checked my documents. I had an introduction for the local hospital."

"Who arranged that?"

"My father. The Swiss authorities are always looking for paediatric doctors."

"Why did your father send you to Switzerland?"

"I told you. The Nazis are looking to invade my country. Seeing what they have done to the Jews in Germany, my father thought it better that I should leave until all this trouble is sorted out."

"What about your family?"

"They are making arrangements to travel to America. The Germans allowed many of their own Jews to leave."

"So, you arrived in Zurich on the 13 March. Where did you stay?"

"I was recommended a small pension in Gottthard Strasse down by the Quai."

"Who recommended it to you?"

"A colleague in the hospital in Vienna."

"When did you leave Zurich?"

"March 27; it took some time to arrange for a ticket through France."

"How did you pay for this travel and accommodation?"

"I had some money saved from my work in the hospital, and my father wired me some."

"So you had two weeks in Zurich. What were you doing?"

"Nothing much. I had to go to the French Consulate several times to arrange for the correct papers. I spent my time walking down by the Quai, but mostly I stayed in my room."

"Did you meet anyone in those two weeks?"

Maruska looked up, "Yes, several people. I went to the local synagogue, and they made me welcome."

"Did you have any contact with a German official?"

"Not that I know of, but Zurich is an international city. There are lots of Germans there."

Brown asked, "Tell me about your trip across France."

"It took a long time. I had a delay in Geneva. With war threatening, there is much disruption to the rail network as priority is given over to the military."

"You stayed in Paris for two days?"

"Yes, there was a problem with getting a passage on the steamer. The authorities wouldn't let you board the train to the port without written confirmation of a berth. There are so many people trying to get off mainland Europe."

"Did you meet anyone in Paris?"

She shook her head, "No, I spent most of the time at the railway station in Gare du Nord waiting for my ticket."

Brown leaned in a little closer, "Did anyone give you anything to bring to England?"

"No, sir. All I have is that bag." She nodded at the carpetbag.

Brown stood up and carefully unclasped the woven bag. It had little navy patterns stitched into the seams that were beginning to look a little frayed. He laid out the contents on the table in a neat row. He spoke quietly,

"Let's see what we have, shall we?" He already knew what was in the bag.

In about two minutes, the entire possessions of Maruska Bergman stared up at her. There were two sets of underwear, three blouses, all of which had been worn on the journey, some assorted hosiery, a rather grubby white towel, a leather toilet bag, the contents of which were emptied across the table, and three hardback books together with her medical certificates.

White picked up one of the books, "You like Charles Dickens, Doctor Bergman?" It was a copy of Nicholas Nickleby.

Maruska shrugged her shoulders, "Yes, I suppose. My father gave it to me for a birthday, but I haven't got around to reading it yet."

He opened the book and read the inscription out loud in perfect Czech,

"Mé úžasné dceři u příležitosti jejích 18. narozenin, tati."

Maruska Berman's eyes twitched..."Yes, it was my eighteenth birthday."

Brown fingered a very old copy of some Hans Christian Anderson fairy tales; "Tell me about this, please."

"I don't know, I've had the book since I was a little girl. I think my mother gave it to me."

"It's in German."

"Yes, I know."

"Do you read German well?"

"Yes."

"You like poetry?" White was flicking through the third book, a copy of Heinrich Heine's *Reisebilder.*

"Sometimes."

Brown interjected, "You know the Nazis have burned this author's works. They say he's a decadent Jew. Why would you have a book like this?"

Maruska smiled, "Perhaps because he is a decadent Jew."

Brown laughed out loud, "Very good, Doctor Bergman." He sat down. "You may repack your items."

He gathered the papers as he began to speak, "I am minded to admit you to Britain pending formal approval from my superiors, but you must register an address with the police and report to them every two weeks. An alien registration process is being set up as thousands of refugees are arriving having escaped Nazi persecution. When that system is established, I require you to comply fully with the terms of your admittance. At the moment, I do not expect you to have any restrictions. You have no recourse to public funds, consequently, you must provide for yourself, but we will give you the sum of one pound and ten shillings to help you on your way. With your qualifications, I don't see a problem with any hospital employing you in some capacity."

Maruska breathed a sigh of relief.

"There is one more thing, Doctor Bergman, you would be well advised to avoid contact with any other German refugees, be they Jewish or not."

Maruska Bergman had no intention of consorting with any German.

Brown picked up the carpetbag, "You'll get this back when you leave. Officer Price will take you down to the office, where you will be issued with a temporary identity card. In the meantime, stay in your quarters. You will be informed when all the formalities have been processed. Good day to you."

With that, he was gone.

Maruska Bergman was escorted down to a basement office. Officer Price pushed open the door and called out, "Another one for you, ladies…"

There were collective groans from the assortment of copy typists and filing clerks. She was photographed, fingerprinted and made to sit on a hard chair for over one hour. Her tummy rumbled especially when another clerk brought in a tray of tea and biscuits. The office staff sat around a desk and gossiped as they had their refreshments. She was totally ignored.

Back in the detainees' quarters, Maruska Bergman lay on the bottom of a triple bunk, listening to the cacophony of languages around her. Dinner that evening consisted of a thin soup of an indeterminable variety and some lamb stew with potatoes and cabbage. She sat quietly next to a Polish girl who couldn't stop talking about her rich boyfriend...

Chapter 2

April 1939
London
Precious Cargo

Maruska Bergman watched the green fields and pastures of Kent flash by as the train to London Waterloo sped across the peaceful countryside. She felt grubby. The washing facilities in the Ashford Detention Centre for Aliens left a lot to be desired. The best she had managed to do was to rinse a few undergarments in tepid water in an old rusty metal bucket. Most of the female detainees were not interested in personal hygiene, just being very glad to have escaped the dark clouds descending over Europe.

She had a third class compartment to herself. She examined her carpetbag. Someone had opened all the main seams and rather clumsily tried to re-stitch them. She raised her eyebrows and removed the three books. These, too, had been taken apart in an attempt to see if there was anything hidden in the hardback covers. They had wasted their time. There were finger marks on the corners of her medical certificates as though they had been repeatedly examined. She sighed.

Victoria Station was busy. She pushed through the crowds of commuters standing in front of the big departure board awaiting their train home. It was as though the impending threat of turmoil in Europe was of no consequence to the clerks, solicitors, stockbrokers and shop assistants who thought of nothing but ensuring their journey home was smooth.

She stood looking at the big map of the Underground Railway System, trying to recollect the route for her journey. A railway official came up to her,

"Are you all right, Miss? Do you need any help?"

Maruska Bergman smiled at the man, "Yes, please, it's all so confusing."

"Where do you want to go?" he asked.

"Paddington Station, please."

The official stuck a finger with a dirty nail on the map.

"Right, Miss, you can go a number of ways but given the time of the day you'd be better doing this." He traced his finger as he spoke,

"Easy, Miss, just take the northbound Bakerloo line to Paddington; should take you about thirty minutes...You see the trains all go north, south, east or west...Just follow that arrow to the station concourse." He pointed at a sign, tipped his hat, nodded and disappeared into the throng.

The light was fading by the time Maruska found the Bayswater Synagogue in Chichester Place, Paddington. The large double wooden doors were locked. She tugged at the bell pull. She stood back as she could hear the top and bottom bolts being drawn.

Rabbi Isaac Levy slowly opened the door. Maruska spoke quietly in Hebrew. She slightly bowed her head in a mark of respect,

"Good evening, Rabbi Levy."

The Rabbi was surprised to see a very beautiful, dark-haired woman in front of him. He responded in Hebrew, "Good evening, my child, how can I be of assistance."

Maruska Bergman spoke in fluent Hebrew as she related her story as a refugee. He stopped her halfway through,

"You'd better step inside, out of the cold."

Maruska walked into the gloomy entrance room of the Victorian building. A single, naked bulb cast an eerie yellow light on the surroundings. He took her into a side room and said, "Would you like some tea?"

She nodded.

A short while later, a thin, gaunt female in her fifties, bustled in carrying a tray. The woman also spoke in Hebrew,

"Good evening, Doctor Bergman, my name is Rebecca. I am Rabbi Levy's wife. I understand you have just been released from Ashford?"

Maruska smiled at the woman, "Yes. I just need a recommendation of somewhere suitable for me to stay for a few days until I get myself sorted out."

Mrs Levy poured some tea, "Oh, don't worry, Isaac will help you out. We have some spare rooms in the old house behind the Synagogue for good Jewish girls."

Isaac came back into the room carrying a large, leather-bound notebook. He waved away his wife. "Now, let me take some details, Maruska. Is it all right if I call you Maruska?"

She smiled at him as she repeated her story again. It seemed as though she had said these words a thousand times since she had been detained in Dover. His pen scratched on the paper of the notebook.

After about ten minutes, he sighed and sat back as she sipped the hot tea. Her belly rumbled; she hadn't eaten since the pitiful meal yesterday evening.

This time he spoke in heavily accented English.

"You are the third refugee we've had in as many weeks. I fear for our brethren in Europe. I think a lot worse is to befall us. I thank the Lord that we are safe here. I'm sure Rebecca has told you we can let you stay for a few days until you find somewhere more suitable." He nodded at his wife who stood up.

As Maruska went by, he reached out and took her arm.

"I will pray that your family remains safe. In the meantime, you are welcome to our house."

Maruska nodded at him.

Rebecca Levy chatted away as she led her through the back of the Synagogue, across a courtyard and into an old house that had seen better days. Mrs Levy pointed out a small kitchenette near the back door. "You can make a hot drink in there, but you'll have to provide your own tea or coffee."

They climbed some wooden stairs. Maruska could smell damp in the old building. Mrs Levy pointed to a large bathroom on one of the landings,

"You may have a bath whenever you want, but you will need to put some money in the slot meter to heat the water. Do you have any money?"

"Yes, Ma'am, they gave me some money when I was discharged from the centre this morning."

"Good, good. Sixpence will give you plenty of gas for a nice, long hot soak. I'm sure you will be needing one. I've heard those centres are not very nice."

She opened a door on the top landing. "You can have this room. There's a gas fire, but again you will need to use the meter." Mrs Levy shrugged her shoulders, "It's not so cold at the moment."

She went to the window and drew back the curtains. There was still enough light for Maruska to see down into the courtyard behind the synagogue. The room was sparsely furnished with a single bed, a chair and desk and an old wooden wardrobe.

"You must be hungry. I'll bring you some more tea and something to eat. I'll leave it outside your room. I'm afraid it's not much but some cold meat and bread, but it will see you through until tomorrow."

"How much do I pay you, Mrs Levy?" Maruska asked, she reached into her pocket for her purse.

"Oh, don't worry about that. Just pay what you can when you leave. Isaac is very good at getting money out of the community." She paused for a second, "Do you know where you are going to work?"

"I have a recommendation for St Mary's Hospital on the Harrow Road. Is it far?"

Rebecca Levy shook her head, "No, no. You can get a bus from the main road to take you there." She moved to the door, "I'll leave you now to get settled in. We don't have many rules here, but please remember there are no visitors allowed, especially men." She smiled and winked...

Maruska nodded.

She fed a sixpence into the slot meter in the bathroom and turned the lever. She had eaten the cold meat and white bread and lay on her bed. She waited until all was quiet. A nearby church bell sounded out ten o clock as she quietly went down to the bathroom. She carried all her belongings with her in the carpetbag. She ran the bath. Although the room was initially chilly, the steam soon made her feel more comfortable. She took off her clothes and laid them on an old wooden chair. She sat on the end of the cast iron bath, and waved her hands in the hot water. Numerous thoughts went through her head. She was thinking about her family, her friends and her old life back home; it all seemed such a long time ago.

She put some cold water into the bath waved it around and then stopped. She went to the door, put her ear to it and listened. She checked the bolt to make sure it was still closed, and then turned the key in the lock one more time.

She went back to the bath and squatted down with her legs apart. She opened her vagina and probed her long fingers inside until she found what she was looking for, a tiny, white silk bag with a thin cotton drawstring...

Maruska Bergman lay in the bath until the water began to cool down. She must have dozed off. A loud banging on the door wakened her.

"Hey, you in there! You've been in there for nearly two hours. I need a quick wash before I go to bed."

Maruska shook herself and levered herself up out of the bath. The water sloshed over the tiled floor. She reached for the thin, cotton towel that she had found in her room.

"Okay, yes, I'll be out in a couple of minutes; sorry."

She heard some mutterings as heels sounded on the bare boards on the landing. Next, she heard a door slam...

She quickly grabbed her bag, threw her clothes into it and gingerly unlocked the door. She peered around. There was a faint light coming from under the door at the end of the corridor. She could hear some music playing softly from the room.

She ran up the stairs back to her room, locked the door from the inside, and dried herself off. The gas fire was still burning in the hearth. She shook off the towel and sat close to the fire, allowing the heat to radiate into her skin. She reached over to her bag and extracted the precious cargo that she had secreted in her body for nearly two weeks. She sat cross-legged with a handkerchief laid out in front of her. Very delicately, she pulled on the thin, cotton drawstring and opened the little pouch. She poured twelve diamonds onto the white handkerchief. The sparkling jewels glistened in the light of the fire as the church clock sounded out midnight. She used her fingers to move the stones around. There were five large and seven smaller stones. She knew exactly what they were worth. Maruska was satisfied that the gems were none the worse for their little trip. Having tied up the four corners of the handkerchief and placed it in her purse, she went to the Victorian washstand in the corner of the room. It was filled with cold water. A large matching jug sat next to it filled to the brim with more water.

Maruska Bergman carefully rinsed out the silk bag several times. She laid it next to the fire to dry. She yawned, pulled back the worn blankets on her bed and climbed in between the sheets. At least they were clean. Maruska fell into a deep sleep, the sleep of those who believed they had achieved something...

Chapter 3

April 1939
London
A rejection of sorts...

Maruska Bergman woke just before seven the next morning. There was a lot of noise below her as some of the other lodgers shouted and laughed at each other as they prepared to leave for work. Doors were slamming as the church bells chimed. She lay there for some time as, gradually, the noise dissipated. The room was cold. She cursed herself for not turning off the gas fire before she went to bed. She would need to find another sixpence to put into the meter.

She threw a coat over her naked body, slipped on her shoes and peaked onto the landing; all was quiet. She went down to the bathroom and scrubbed herself in cold water. The other girls had used what was left of her gas. Back in her room, she carefully re-inserted the gemstones and got dressed. She needed to purchase some more clothing, but first she needed to dispose of one of the smaller diamonds.

Maruska walked down Praed Street. She glanced up at St Mary's Hospital; this one was on her list. In Star Street, she barely looked at the old Victorian School as hordes of noisy children ran around the front yard. It was nearly ten in the morning when she pushed open the glass front door of Adelman's Jewellery shop.

The shop was old and dusty. Swirls of tiny particles danced and sparkled in the sunlight of the cold spring morning. Zev Adelman looked up from his counter. He was in his early sixties, bald with a pair of half-moon reading glasses stuck to his forehead. He had a pair of magnifying spectacles on his nose as he examined a small, golden coloured watch. He had on a white coat over a brown, threadbare suit. His tie was crooked. His appearance belied his wealth. Maruska greeted him in Hebrew,

"*Shalom.*" She bowed almost imperceptibly, but he noticed it.

He put down the watch and responded, "*Shalom Aleichem...*"

She spoke quietly in Hebrew, "I understand you purchase jewellery?"

He stared at her, trying to work out the accent, "Are you German?"

"No, sir, Czech, but we can speak in German if you want."

He smiled, "No, I don't think that would be a good idea given the present circumstances. Do you speak English?"

Maruska answered in English, "Do you purchase jewellery?"

"Yes, if it is worth purchasing. Do you have something you would like to sell?"

"I have a small diamond, but I don't know what it is worth," she lied.

"Can I have a look? I'm not promising anything, mind you, because we've had such a lot of fakes brought in recently, especially by refugees from Europe."

Maruska carefully placed a quarter-carat diamond on a black mat that sat on the counter.

Zev Adelman's eyes opened wide. He could spot the real thing from a distance...He called out, in Polish,

"*Shira, czy możesz tu przyjść i przez kilka minut zajmować się sklepem?*

Maruska knew he was summoning his wife...

A much younger woman, more than half his age, appeared at the door behind the counter. She had dark eyes and very long, black, curly hair that hung loosely from her head. Maruska noticed how strikingly beautiful she was.

Adelman said, "This is my wife, Shira."

Maruska greeted her in Polish, "*Dzień dobry, pani Adelman.*"

Adelman raised his eyes at that...

Shira Adelman nodded and yawned but said nothing.

Her husband lifted the counter and led Maruska to a small back office. In one corner was an enormous ancient safe.

He sat her down, "Can I take a look at this?" He was eyeing the gemstone, hoping he could make a pretty penny from this woman.

Maruska passed over the stone. He picked it up in a pair of special tweezers

He flipped over the examination glasses, switched on a desk lamp, and proceeded to examine the stone as though his life depended on it. He pulled over an old microscope and went through the same process. Maruska looked around; the place was just as dusty and untidy as the outer shop. It appeared to her that neither of the Adelmans had much in the way of domestic skills. She shook her head, well, she mused, I don't suppose Mr Adelman married the present Mrs Adelman for her domestic abilities...

She was awakened from her thoughts. She looked up to see Zev Adelman sitting back with his arms folded.

"It's real all right, but not the best." He dropped the stone onto a precision weigh scales. "It's about one quarter carat."

Maruska asked, "How much is it worth?"

He pursed his lips and wrinkled his nose, "Hmm, I'm not sure. There's a glut of these about at the moment. Would you be looking to sell it?"

"Yes, for the right price."

He stood up and walked to the back of the office. He pretended to flick through a book, muttering to himself. Maruska watched this performance; she had seen many similar, too many times before.

He sat back down, "I suppose I could buy it. Do you have any identity?"

She produced the temporary Alien card, and he examined it, "Hmm, says here you are Doctor Marusuka Bergman."

She said nothing.

"Okay, Doctor Bergman, shall we say twenty-five pounds?"

Maruska smiled, "I was thinking more like thirty."

He shook his head, "No, I don't think so. I'm going to have to send this to be cut and then mounted in a piece of jewellery. There's a lot of work in that, and even then I don't know if I will be able to sell it. People are being very careful with their money. Besides, there are plenty of stones of this quality around at the moment." He paused and then asked, "Where did you get it?"

"My father gave it to me to help me on my journey; I'm going to America to join my brother."

"Twenty-seven pounds and ten shillings; how does that sound?"

Maruska gathered the stone, "Thank you for your time, Mr Adelman. I'm sorry to have troubled you." She stood up to leave.

He held out his arm, "No, wait a minute. I'm sure we can come to some arrangement."

"Thirty pounds, Mr Adelman, no more and no less."

He sighed, "Okay, okay. If you'd like to wait back in the shop, I'll draw up the paperwork."

Maruska stood in the shop as Shira Adelman eyed her. She could hear the sound of the old safe as it cranked open on its rusty hinges. Shira beckoned her over silently, she whispered in heavily accentuated English,

"Go up to Benowitz in Hatton Garden, you'll get a much better price than here. Tell him I sent you..." She smiled at Maruska. "There's a café at the end of the street, I'll meet you there in twenty minutes."

Zev Adelman came back into the shop. He was carrying some paperwork and a bundle of used paper notes. He laid the money on the counter and carefully arranged the papers. He asked, "Do you have an address, Doctor Bergman, or shall I just make one up?"

"Whatever you think best, Mr Adelman."

He wrote something on the papers and then passed them over to her with his silver and gold fountain pen, "Please sign here." He pointed to a space at the bottom of the page. Maruska quickly skimmed the receipt, "It says here the value is only fifteen pounds."

"Oh, don't worry, that's for the authorities. I have your thirty pounds here. Please count it if you like."

Maruuska counted out the thirty pound notes; it was all there. She signed as he tucked the notes into an envelope.

"If you have any more stones, please come back. It would be a pleasure to do more business with you."

"I thought you said it was not of good quality?"

He coloured up...

Maruska bade him farewell, nodded at Shira Adelman and left the shop with the envelope carefully secured in her handbag. She breathed the air outside the shop, glad to be out of the oppressive atmosphere. She could feel the sweat and dampness under her arms and between her legs. She sucked in deep breaths through her nose and out through her mouth, slowing her beating heart.

Her tummy rumbled as she came back to her senses.

She was only seated for about five minutes in the café before Shira Adelman bustled through the door. She was carrying a wicker shopping basket. Maruska pushed over a cup of strong tea, "Would you like something to eat?"

Shira shook her head, "No, I don't have much time. The old fool questions me if I'm out too long. I have to go to the market every day to get fresh food. If I'm out too long, he gets cross with me."

She reached over and touched Maruska's hand, she leaned in and spoke quietly; "Do you have more gems?"

Maruska nodded.

"Don't come back here. Eventually, he'll tell the police. They turn a blind eye to his shady business in return for information. He thinks I don't know, but I see everything he does."

Maruska sipped the tea, "It's okay; I just needed some quick money to help me get settled." She patted her handbag, "I have enough here for the time being until I can get work."

Shira looked at her, "Do you have anywhere to live?"

"I'm staying with Rabbi Levy in the Synagogue for the next few days while I try to get work in a hospital, but I'm sure it will be difficult."

Shira nodded, "Yes, I know the Rabbi; I go there sometimes. Zev refuses to attend any synagogue. Do you have a pencil and some paper?"

Maruska passed over a scrap of paper from her handbag and an old pencil. Shira wrote quickly. "This man will take care of you. You can trust him. I'll get word to him to meet you the day after tomorrow outside the hospital at six in the evening."

"How will I know him?" Maruska asked.

"Oh, don't worry, I'll make sure he'll know you." She gulped down the rapidly cooling tea.

Maruska asked, "Why are you with Adelman? He must be twice your age."

Shira shrugged her shoulders, "My father owed him money for a bad deal. Adelman's wife had just died, so I paid the price."

"What?"

"It's what they call an arranged marriage. Don't worry; I manage. He's not very demanding. I can cope with his attentions once a week. Besides, I can get it elsewhere..." She winked at Maruska and smiled.

Maruska eyed the scrap of paper and noticed a man's name, "Are you getting it from him?"

"Ask him...Thanks for the tea." She was gone...

Maruska ate a plate of eggs and fried bread. Although the bacon frying on the large hob behind the counter smelled delicious, she thought she'd better not indulge.

After she had eaten her fill in the café, Maruska Bergman crossed over to a bank and changed one of the dirty pound notes for some loose change. She took the number 18 bus from Praed Street up to St Mary's Hospital, just over the canal on the Harrow Road. The unmistakable hospital smell assailed her nostrils as she entered the old, crowded building. It took her some time to find the right office. An officious looking prim woman with her hair tightly tied back in a fierce bun eyed her up and down.

"You want to see someone about a junior position here?"

Maruska nodded, "I have a letter of recommendation from the University Hospital in Vienna together with my certificates."

The woman slowly and carefully perused the embossed qualifications. She pointed at a chair. "Please sit there. I'll see if Professor Statham can see you. You should have called in advance for an appointment. He's a very busy man."

Maruska waited for over half an hour until a thin, white-haired man bustled in carrying a pile of paperwork. He called out, "Doctor Bergman?"

Maruska stood up, smoothing down her coat. "Sir?"

He cast a glance over at her, "Follow me, please."

He led her into an untidy office, "Please sit down."

He threw the files onto the top of another pile and sat down. He picked up her papers and carefully examined each one. Periodically, he peered at Maruska over his half-moon reading glasses, muttered to himself and then went back to the papers. She sat and stared impassively at him.

He spoke up, "So you were in Vienna when the Germans came?"

"Yes, sir."

He raised his eyebrows, "I do believe you were lucky to get out, Doctor Bergman. We hear some horrendous stories concerning people of your..." He paused, seeking the right word... "Faith. I do hope the British authorities made you feel welcome."

Images of the Ashford Detention Centre came into Maruska's head...

He picked up the letter of recommendation. "It says here that you are a good but inexperienced doctor."

She smiled, "Sir, the only way I can get experience is by working..."

"Hmm, I suppose you are correct. What are you looking for?"

"I want to specialise in paediatrics, but I would be willing to accept any position in your hospital, sir."

He went quiet for a few minutes, "I think you would be suitable for us here; we are always looking for good paediatric doctors, but there is a slight problem. You would have to get registered with the General Medical Council, and to do that they would need to check your qualifications. With the situation in Europe as it is at present, I think that would be difficult. We would need to contact the authorities in Vienna to verify your credentials, and that is simply impossible at present."

Maruska was expecting this.

He continued, "What I can do, given the imminent threat of war across Europe, is write to the Medical Council and see if they will grant you a temporary registration to work under strict supervision. There's plenty of routine medical work for you to do, thus freeing up more experienced doctors to do the more challenging cases." He stood up, indicating that the meeting was over.

"Now, if you'll excuse me, Doctor Bergman, I have some other duties that require my attention. Give your details to the chief clerk in the office, and I'll see what I can do."

He offered her his hand. She took it.

Maruska Bergman smiled at the chief clerk as she walked past her not saying anything ...

Chapter 4

April 1939
London
Church Street Market

Maruska Bergman was nearly three hours in the children's hospital in Praed Street. She got passed from pillar to post before being finally told the same thing she had by Professor Statham two days before. Yes, we'd love to have you but first, the General Medical Council needs to approve your registration. This time, however, Maruska left her contact details with one of the clerks. When she moved, she would let the authorities know of her new address. In any case, she determined that she would write directly to the Medical Council herself.

It was still light as it approached six in the evening. She stood on the steps to the hospital on Praed Street. It was blustery with a hint of rain in the air. She watched as commuters of all shapes and sizes rushed towards the station to catch a train to the outer suburbs. She glanced over at a newspaper seller. The printed board told of the latest crisis to befall Prime Minister Neville Chamberlain who was doing everything in his power to avoid a war with Germany and Adolf Hitler, at whatever cost, it seemed.

She knew it was Chamberlain who had signed away her homeland to the Nazis and allowed them to annex the whole of Czechoslovakia. She was about to cross the road to purchase a newspaper when she felt a gentle tug on her arm. She looked across to see a handsome, tall good-looking man who smiled at her.

He asked, "Are you looking for someone, Miss?"

She rummaged around in her purse for the scrap of paper, "Yes, a Mr Porteous."

He offered his hand smiling, "Yes, that's me." He looked around at the ornate entrance to the hospital, "This is a good place to meet considering you are a doctor."

She blushed, took his hand and looked down, "I understand you can help me with some things, Mr Porteous."

"Call me Porteous, everyone does." He looked up at the sky as rain began to fall. "Come on, let's get out of the rain and find somewhere more comfortable to talk."

He took her arm and led her to the Great Western Hotel that was opposite the station. The main bar was crowded, but there was a little snug room to the side. He pushed open the ornate glass door and indicated a table with two upright red leather chairs. "Take a seat. What would you like to drink?"

Maruska hadn't tasted alcohol for some months, "Gin and tonic, please." Her mother used to drink it from time to time.

Porteous returned with the gin and a small glass of beer. He remarked, "I have something to do later so I'll just stick to a small beer."

She undid her coat. He could see her slim figure for the first time. "Shira says I might be able to help you with a few things."

Maruska looked at him. He was in his early thirties. His eyes were dark brown and his jet-black hair betrayed not a hint of grey. She watched as he sipped the lukewarm, cloudy liquid.

"I'm looking for somewhere more permanent to live, somewhere not too expensive but safe and where I can mind my own business."

Porteous raised his eyebrows, "That's possible. I know of some places but it depends where you want to go and how much you would like to pay."

She was direct, "How do you know Shira?"

"I've known her for a long time ever since she moved in with old Zev Adelman." He smiled, "Why do you ask?"

"I just like to know with whom I'm doing business."

He noted the precise language, "Your English is very good..."

"I had a good teacher, my mother."

He leaned into her, "Look, Miss, I'm here to help you if I can. I can do a little of most things and I can usually get you items that can somehow be a little difficult to obtain. For a start, I don't even know your name."

Maruska Bergman sighed and repeated the story she had told her interrogators at Ashford several times. It was like the script of a play to her; one that she had memorised until she could repeat it in her sleep. He sat and listened as she hardly touched her drink.

He spoke quietly when she had finished her monologue. "How was Ashford?"

"Not very nice. You sleep twelve to a room in triple bunks if you are lucky. I was in a big hall with about fifty other women. There is no privacy. They lock the door after lights out. You have to use a bucket in the corner to relieve yourself."

He nodded, "I've heard it's not very pleasant. Shira was there for nearly two months before old Adelman bought her out. It seems most female Jews are sent there."

She asked, "Do you see Shira often?"

"When circumstances allow. I manage to get her some personal items that her old man won't pay for. Which reminds me; don't go back to his shop. He has already informed on you to the police. He thinks you have a hoard of precious gems stolen from some European aristocrat."

Maruska Bergman burst out laughing, "He is just annoyed that I wouldn't let him get away with stealing from me."

"Do you have more to sell?" he whispered.

"Yes but Shira said something about a jeweller called Benowitz in some place called Hatton Garden. Do you know of it?"

Porteous nodded, "I do, but he won't see you without an introduction."

Maruska added quickly, "Which, no doubt, you can arrange for a small fee?"

Porteous shook his head, "No, there is no fee. Shira asked me to help you so I will, but if you don't trust me, that's fine, we'll leave it at that." He stood up to leave. "I have to go now. It was nice meeting you, Doctor Bergman."

He was gone before she had time to say anything...She picked up a copy of the evening newspaper and read it as she sipped her drink, more than slightly annoyed with herself.

Maruska lay in bed later that evening, listening to the lodgers chattering away outside her door. She overheard one say that the new girl was a German Jew. She heard a few giggles and stifled laughter. She waited until the church clock sounded out midnight. She popped down to the bathroom, but there was no gas, and she had decided she wasn't going to provide free hot water for the other women.

Maruska emptied out the cold water from the jug on the night stand and went quietly downstairs to the kitchenette. She filled up the jug with two kettles worth of boiling water and went back to her room. She lit the gas fire as the water in the jug cooled. She stripped off her clothes and lay in her bed. When the water was sufficiently cooled, she spread some newspaper on the floor, placed the big metal basin on top, stood in it and gave herself a thorough wash. It was almost as good as a bath.

She dried herself by the fire and climbed into bed, remembering to save the gas and turn off the fire this time. She lay there thinking about her day. She was annoyed with herself for questioning Porteous. By this time, she had convinced herself that he was only trying to assist her. She turned to one side as the clock sounded out one in the morning. She wanted to know what was his relationship with Shira Adelman. Was she jealous? She decided it was none of her business, but then it was, wasn't it, if he was going to help her? She convinced herself that she didn't care if he was Shira's lover. Given her current domestic arrangements, somebody had to be, didn't they?

She had no idea when she had finally drifted off to sleep. The noisy girls outside her room disturbed her just after seven. She pulled on her coat and opened the door. Three women in varying states of undress were leaning against the banister. Two of them were smoking. They were in their early twenties and looked like typists or telephone exchange operators. They stared at Maruska.

She brushed past them and said in a loud voice, "*Guten Morgen*," in her best Germanic accent. She heard them snigger as she walked down to the bathroom.

There was some hot water, so she took her time washing at the sink. She looked at herself in the mirror; her hair needed a good wash and brush, but she wasn't too bothered. She was done trying to convince the authorities that she would be useful as a doctor. It was time to move on to other things. She stood still with hairpins gripped in her teeth as she tied back her long, black hair. By the time she had finished, the house was quiet. It was time to go and find Shira Adelman again...

She waited until nearly eleven o'clock in the café, hoping to see the woman. The waitress smiled at her as she refilled her teacup. Maruska was sitting by the window. From there, she could see down the street to the front of Adelman's shop. She was surprised to see a constant stream of customers entering and leaving. She noticed that some went in carrying items but exited with nothing in their hands.

The waitress interrupted her thoughts, "Would you like anything else to eat, Miss?" The accent was very London.

Maruska looked up, "I was just noticing that the jeweller is very busy."

The waitress looked through the window, "Oh him? The old Jew is a fence, Miss."

Maruska looked confused, "I'm sorry, a fence?"

The waitress snorted as she leaned in, "You know, Miss, he fences peoples' stuff what he ought not to. You know, stuff that has a dodgy past. Fell off the back of a lorry an' all that."

It dawned on Maruska what the waitress was saying, "How do you know that?"

"Miss, everybody knows that. If you've got something that might be a little 'ot, he's the man but don't expect a good price. He's in with the local gangsters and as for his wife, that trollop; she's got a fancy man up the 'Harrer' Road. Bold as brass, that one."

Maruska asked, "Have you seen her today?"

"Nah, today's Thursday. She'll be up the market flashing her knickers at some trader trying to get a bargain and whatever else is on offer."

Maruska stood up, reaching into her purse, "Where is this market?"

"Church Street. You can get almost anything there. Just walk up to the Edgware Road, turn left. It's just past the 'Harrer' Road, you can't miss it." Maruska knew she meant the Harrow Road...

Maruska asked for her bill. The waitress had trouble adding up the costs of some eggs, fried bread and two cups of tea on a little white notepad. "One and a penny, Miss."

Maruska tossed down a two-shilling piece, "Will that cover it?"

"I'll get your change."

Maruska called back from the door, "Don't worry, you can keep it..."

The waitress pocketed the coins with a smile on her face....

Church Street market was crowded. It looked as though people were determined to buy whatever they could before trouble set in. She looked around her, not knowing where to start. There were men in various coloured uniforms all over. Many had dyed blond women on their arms. The stalls were crowded as the traders cried out their wares. There was everything on sale from lingerie to overcoats, shoes and stockings and cardigans, blouses and dresses. Down the far end, a whole range of second hand furniture was available, as well as some antiques. The top end of the market was all vegetables, meat and fish. The police seemed to turn a blind eye to the drinkers who spilled out of the Hall Arms public house.

Maruska wandered up and down looking at the clothes and for Shira Adelman. She felt an arm slip into hers.

"Are you looking for me, Doctor Bergman?"

Maruska blushed up, "No, no. I've come to purchase some clothes."

"You upset Porteous."

Maruska could smell gin on her breath. It reminded her of her mother...

"Yes, I know, I'm sorry. I didn't mean to. I'm just a little nervous, that's all."

Shira linked her arm, "Shall we speak German just to upset the locals?"

Maruska shook her head, "No, Shira, let's not draw attention to ourselves."

Shira pulled her towards the pub, "Come on, I need a drink."

Two neat gins appeared on the table. Shira ignored the leering remarks of a drinker by the bar. She swore at him in German.

Shira Adelman opened her purse and took out a silver cigarette case and matching lighter. She crossed her legs and lit a cigarette.

Maruska asked, "Why are you not back in the shop? I thought your husband didn't let you out."

She smiled, "It's Thursday. He does his other business on Thursday. He tells me to stay away until late in the afternoon. I don't mind, it gives me a chance to have a few drinks and maybe see a certain person."

"That wouldn't be Porteous, would it?"

"Now, that would be telling, wouldn't it?" She tapped her nose.

Maruska took a sip of the bitter-tasting liquid, "Look, Shira, I need his help. Can you get him to see me again? I was a little too hasty in my rush to judgement. He says he knows of a place for me to stay, and he'll help me with other things."

Shira snorted, "You mean the gems?"

Maruska looked down, "Are you going to help me or not?"

Shira knocked back the gin and pushed over the glass, "Your turn, Doctor Bergman. I'll have a large one this time." She drew deeply on the thin cigarette and blew the smoke in the direction of Maruska.

She went to the bar and got Shira's drink. Upon her return, she spoke abruptly, "Are you going to help me? If not, I'll leave you now. I have some things to purchase."

Shira Adelman burst out laughing, "Oh, sit down, silly girl. Of course we are going to help you. You Czech's are too serious. Relax and get yourself another drink. I know what it's like after arriving in a foreign country when you know nothing. I'll tell Porteous to come back and meet with you. He only wants to help. There's nothing in it for him. He's got plenty of other irons in the fire."

Maruska had to work hard to decipher that phrase. She reached out and took Shira's full glass and took a drink, "Will you help me buy some things on the market?"

Later that evening, Maruska sat on the end of her bed. The clothes she and a slightly inebriated Shira Adelman had bartered for on the market were laid out on the bed. She had managed to acquire a new dress, three blouses, a cardigan and three pairs of French knickers and matching brassieres made of a silk and cotton mixture together with a white suspender belt and five pairs of black nylon stockings for the price of four, thanks to Shira. Under the light of the bulb she found several imperfections from faults in the manufacture of the lingerie, but she wasn't bothered; it was market stock after all. Shira had told her go back to the Hospital on Praed Street on Saturday at three o'clock. Porteous would be there.

When all had gone quiet, she went down to the bathroom only to find there was no gas. She sighed and washed herself again in hot water purloined from the kitchen. She slept through the night, with the gin having done its job...

Back in the flat above the jeweller's shop in Star Street, Shira Adelman lay on her back and stared at the ceiling whilst her sweaty husband grunted on top of her for about five minutes. He lay still after he had finished. She could hear him snore. She pushed him off the bed and went to the bathroom to clean herself, cursing that she had not had the chance to remove her silk stockings before he started on her...

She found her way back to her room in the dark, took a swig of gin from a bottle under the bed and fell asleep...

Chapter 5

April 1939
London
More bargaining

Maruska Bergman slept late on the Friday. She didn't hear the girls as they left for work. She went out at about ten in the morning to find a café for some breakfast. Rebecca Levy was waiting for her in the kitchenette. She greeted Maruska in Hebrew,

"How are you getting on, Maruska?"

Maruska smiled back and bowed slightly, "Oh, I'm fine, Mrs Levy. I've been to two of the hospitals, and they are going to contact me. I may have to write to the Medical Council to see if they will accept my credentials."

Mrs Levy frowned, "I thought there was a shortage of doctors with many having gone into the services?"

Maruska shrugged her shoulders, "I don't know, Ma'am."

"What will you do in the meantime?"

"I have some other skills that I can use." She paused for a second or two, "I may have found an apartment. I'll find out over the weekend. I hope you don't mind?"

Rebecca Levy reached out, "Of course not, my child. This accommodation is really only supposed to be temporary, but heaven knows, some of these girls have been here for months. Anyway, you'll be much better off away from them. They are only interested in clothes, drinking and finding a suitable husband."

Maruska was about to take her leave when Mrs Levy said, "Today is the start of Shabbat. Rabbi Levy always marks the beginning with a lighting of the candles before dinner. It's the one evening of the week when he likes all the residents to sit together for our evening meal. I do hope you will join us?"

Maruska nodded, "Of course, Mrs Levy; I'll be there."

There was a communal room to the side of the synagogue. Maruska was surprised to see the other five ladies of the house sitting quietly and dressed very modestly; some had covered their hair in little head scarfs. Rabbi Levy lit the candles and said the opening prayer of welcoming the arrival of Shabbat. He then spoke for about three minutes reminding those present of the importance of living a pure life. Then, they all sang a song praising the women of the house for all their hard work during the week.

Mrs Levy served up a meal of roast lamb and potatoes. Maruska struggled to eat the tough meat. The wine was bitter. After about an hour, the girls all left carrying with them their dishes. Maruska could hear them clattering about the synagogue kitchen laughing and joking.

Maruska got up to leave. Rabbi Levy waved her to sit down. Mrs Levy left to organise the kitchen clear up.

He asked, "How are you, Maruska? I do hope these girls have not been bothering you too much. They are not exactly well-endowed in the brains department. I keep them here only because their fathers insist on it."

"They are fine, Rabbi. They don't trouble me."

He nodded, "Good, good. Rebecca tells me you might be leaving us?"

"Yes, sir, I am hoping for some good news about some accommodation over the weekend."

"Do you know where this is?"

"No, not exactly, but a friend of a friend has put me in touch with it."

Rabbi Levy put his elbows on the table and steepled his hands; he peered over at her, "I think you are a sensible girl, but London can be very daunting for a newcomer like yourself. I would not want to have to contact your father to tell him of some misfortune that has befallen you. Just beware of false friends."

She thought about Shira Adelman...

He spoke quickly, "Off you go, child..."

Just before eight o'clock, she went down to the little kitchenette to make some tea. The girls were all lounging around smoking, dressed to the nines, some of them trying to straighten their stockings. They stopped talking when she went in.

She greeted them in German...

One of them spoke slowly to her, "Maruska, we are going out for a drink and there's a dance later at the Palais. Would you like to come with us?"

Maruska smiled and answered back in perfect English, "That's very kind of you, but I think I'm going to have an early night, but thank you for asking me. Do enjoy yourselves."

The girl's mouth opened wide...

Later that evening, Maruska lay back in the cast iron bath and soaked herself until her skin began to wrinkle. She closed her eyes, held her nose and submerged under the water. She counted to twenty; it was a game she used to play when she was a little girl. She used to dream of being a mermaid; one that could breathe underwater and in the air. She had read some fairy tale or other and become obsessed with the idea. She came up quickly with the water splashing over the side. She sat up, reached for some soap and thoroughly washed her hair. It was as though she was still trying to rid herself of the lingering smell of Ashford especially the smell of unwashed female bodies in her room.

Her mind was full of disconnected thoughts. What was she doing here? Should she have stayed in Prague or gone back to the safety of her family? She looked over at the tiny, white, silk bag that sat on the edge of the roll top bath. It had taken her several minutes to learn how to insert it at the beginning. She initially feared it would never come back out...She would be glad when she wouldn't need to do it again...

She heard footsteps on the wooden stairs. There was some stifled laughing and giggling and a loud "Shhh...you'll disturb the German girl..."

She thought she could hear a man's voice.

She got out slowly, dried herself and threw on her coat and ran back upstairs. She paused by a door and listened in. She could hear the bed squeaking rhythmically...She froze. There was heavy panting; the man's breathing was loud, and then she heard the girl, "Oh God! Oh God!....Now!....." There was a loud grunt as the man expended...

Maruska smiled as she ran back up the stairs. She closed her door quietly. She sat naked and cross-legged in front of the little gas fire whilst she brushed out her hair. She weaved her hair into two thick plaits before she got into bed. She shoved the little silk bag under her pillow and snuggled down under the covers, thinking about the lucky girl downstairs...

Peter Porteous was waiting for her on the steps of St Mary's Hospital. He smiled at her as he greeted her.

She took his arm, "Porteous, I'm so sorry about the other day. I didn't mean to offend you. It's just..."

He interrupted her, "No, stop, please. I understand perfectly. It must be very difficult for you. I believe Shira has been bending your ear?"

She smiled, "You could say that. She'd had a bit to drink before I met her."

He nodded, "Yes, she always does that when her husband wants something..."

She was confused, but she let it go. "Can we see the apartment?"

He laughed, "It's not exactly an apartment; just a little kitchen, a lounge and a bedroom. I'm afraid the bathroom is downstairs. Is that okay?"

"Of course."

He continued, "I spoke to the landlady. She wasn't interested in who you are, but she was impressed when I told her you are a doctor. She just wants the money for the rooms. Do you want to go and see it now?"

"How about Hatton Garden first, and then we can go after?"

"Sure, but I need to make a phone call first. Benny doesn't like cold callers. Come on, there's a 'phone box in the foyer of the hospital."

He led her into the hospital. There was an old red kiosk to the side. He pulled her into the box with him; she blushed, being in such close proximity to this handsome man. He shoved four pennies into the slot and dialled for the operator.

He waited for the connection and pushed the button when the call was answered. "Benny? It's Porteous. I might have something for you."

There was a pause. "Yeah, it's good. Put it this way, Adelman wants a look at them."

Maruska could hear laughter on the other end of the phone.

"Yeah, okay, about an hour...." Porteous replaced the receiver; the pennies dropped further into the box.

He said, "He'll see us if we go now. Is that okay?"

She nodded, "Can we take the bus? I haven't seen much of the West End yet."

He smiled...

They took the bus down to Oxford Circus. She sat and stared at the crowded shops, thinking about how quiet Vienna was since the Nazis had taken over. He grabbed her hand, "Come on, we have to change."

They waited a few minutes for the bus that took them down through Holborn and onto Chancery Lane. He led her up Hatton Garden. She had her arm in his.

Benny Benowitz had owned the large shop for nearly twenty years. He'd left Germany shortly after the end of the war in 1919. He told his wife he couldn't see a future for the country. Whilst England hadn't exactly welcomed the thousands of Jews rushing to escape mainland Europe, Benowitz was able to smooth his way through the bureaucracy, thanks to his wealth.

Porteous knocked quietly on the door. The light was beginning to fade as dark clouds appeared in the sky.

Benny Benowitz opened the door. He was a small man with a big stomach. He had on a three-piece, pin-striped navy suit. A chunky gold watch and chain were strapped across his waist. He looked at Maruska and smiled as he addressed Porteous,

"You didn't tell me she was that good-looking?"

Maruska looked down, blushing again...

Porteous shook his head, "Pay him no attention, Maruska, he does that to all the pretty ladies who come in here."

Benowitz led the two of them into a large back room. Four men of varying ages, shapes and sizes were bent over their desks. Bright lights illuminated their workstations. Each had an array of magnifying lenses on swivel stands. The air was hot with the heat and smell of the little blowtorches used to fashion the precious metals into desirable jewellery. The workers barely looked up at her. The Jewish Sabbath didn't seem to apply here. Benowitz beckoned her to sit down at a desk. He sat opposite her.

He asked, "What have you got for me, my dear?"

She answered in German, "I have a half-carat stone that I might be willing to sell."

The workers stopped...They looked up...

Benowitz smiled as he answered in German, "May I see it, please?"

Maruska dug into a little pocket in her leather purse and produced the stone. She carefully laid it on the black, felt mat in front of her.

Benowitz raised his eyebrows as he peered down at the sparkling gem, "Ah, I see you are serious about business, Doctor Bergman."

He flipped down the magnifying glasses that were perched on his head, and picked up the stone in a pair of wide-bladed tweezers. He turned it this way and that way looking to see how the light reflected from the precious stone. He dropped the gem onto his scales, waited until the balance stopped. He said quietly,

"It's a little over half a carat, Doctor." He had the stone back between the tweezers. He called out, "Moshe, come and see what we have here."

A little fat man waddled over to his boss, picked up the stone and examined it carefully. He went back to his workbench, and consulted an old and battered book. There was silence in the room for a few minutes.

He spoke in Hebrew, "It's good, Boss, but you need to ask where it came from."

Maruska intervened; again in Hebrew, "My father gave it to me as a birthday present."

The fat man tossed down the reference book, "You'll have to do better than that, Miss. This diamond is almost certainly from the old German colony of South West Africa. I thought I recognised the hue. I'd say it was from the Kolmanskop Mine. It was probably extracted more than twenty years ago, since that mine played out some time ago. I used to see them a lot in Berlin. Aristocrats were always bringing them in to sell when times got hard."

Benowitz held up his hands, "Yes, yes, all right Moshe. You can return to your duties."

Moshe muttered something under his breath and went and sat back down. Benowitz winked at Maruska, "Don't worry about him, he just doesn't like Germans. They stole everything off him during Kristallnacht last November, but I suppose he asks a valid question. How has a German stone of this quality come into your possession?"

Maruska spoke in English; she raised her voice, "I told you my father gave it to me as a present."

The workshop went quiet. Maruska could feel Porteous's hands on her shoulders. He whispered, "He's just being careful, that's all, Maruska. Benny doesn't deal in stolen diamonds.'

She looked at the jeweller, her eyes flashing, "Do you want it or not, Mr Benowitz?"

He looked over at Moshe who nodded. "Yes, I think we can agree a price. I can make a couple of really nice engagement rings once Moshe has cut it."

He picked it up again, "Shall we say seventy pounds?"

Porteous nearly choked…He'd never imagined it was worth so much…

"I was thinking more like ninety," replied Maruska. Porteous swallowed hard.

Benowitz sat back and smiled, "Eighty."

Maruska reached for the stone, "Ninety, Mr Benowitz, and that's it…"

"Come on, Doctor Bergman, give a little, I have a family to feed."

She smiled and shook her head, "Ninety…"

He looked up at Porteous, "Who is this hard lady, Porteous? You bring me a beauty well-versed in business." He laughed and held out his hand. "I'll write up the paperwork. Where are you staying?"

Maruska relaxed, "At the Bayswater Synagogue with Rabbi Levy."

"Ah, how are Isaac and his lovely wife Rebecca? I haven't seen them in a long time. Has he still got that brothel at the back of the synagogue?" He roared with laughter.

Maruska sat stone-faced, "I'll be sure to tell him you were asking after him..."

Benowitz left to complete the paperwork. She signed the papers as Doctor Maruska Bergman of Karlsbad, Czechoslovakia.

Benowitz called out, "Porteous, can I have a brief word?"

Moshe walked up to her as she sat there. He spoke quietly in German, "Where are you from, Doctor Bergman?"

She shrugged her shoulders, responding in German, "Karlsbad in Czechoslovakia. If it's anything to do with you."

He said, "I lived in Austria when I was young. You have a trace of Viennese in your accent."

She raised her voice; "I trained as a doctor in Vienna so it's hardly surprising since I spent nearly seven years there."

Porteous looked up. Benowitz called out, "Moshe! Leave our guest alone!"

Benowitz sat down in front of her and carefully counted out eighteen five-pound notes. He put them in piles. She swept them up and tucked them into her purse. He said, "If, perchance, your father gives you any more of these stones, I would be pleased to appraise them for you..."

Maruska smiled sweetly.

Moshe glared at her as the owner escorted them out of the shop.

Benowitz shook her hand and then Porteous's. He said, "See what you can do for me, Porteous, I'll make it worth your while."

Porteous nodded.

They were on the bus going up the Edgware Road, just past Marble Arch when Porteous finally asked,

"What was all that about with Moshe, Maruska?"

She stared out of the window as the rain began to pour down.

She didn't answer. He asked again, "Come on, Maruska, help me out a little."

She turned to him, "What are you doing for Benowitz?"

"Arranging a meeting for him, that's all."

"What kind of meeting?"

Porteous sighed, "A meeting with an acquaintance of mine."

"For what purpose?"

"He needs some things that are getting very hard to obtain."

"I thought you said he didn't deal in stolen things?"

"Diamonds, Maruska, he doesn't deal in stolen diamonds."

She rolled her eyes..."So, it's alright if he deals in other stolen goods?"

"That's up to him and none of our business. He asked me to arrange a meeting, so I will."

The bus was approaching Praed Street. She stood up to get off.

He looked at her, "I thought we were going to look at the flat?"

"I've changed my mind for now. Let me off, please."

He was exasperated, "Sure, sure...If you reconsider, tell Shira."

She pushed past him as the bus slowed to a halt. She hopped off behind several other passengers.

By the time she reached the synagogue, she was completely drenched. She went up to her room, pulled off her clothes and sat naked on the rug in front of the gas fire, allowing the heat to dry out her skin. She would sort out the washing in the morning...She glanced over at her bag. There was now more than a hundred pounds in cash tucked away in there.

She looked down at the dark patch between her legs...there were still ten diamonds remaining, but these would keep for important business later.

Chapter 6

April 1939
London
The Intruder

Maruska Bergman didn't sleep very well. She finally managed to get off just before dawn. There were too many things going through her head. Yet again, she had managed to fall out with Porteous. She was cross with herself but maybe expectations are different here in London? It was something she would have to learn.

She was awakened just before nine. There was a quiet tapping on the door. It took her some time to come to her senses. Those bloody immature girls again? Probably one of them wanting to borrow something.

She threw on her coat, went to the door, drew the top bolt and turned the key. As soon as the door half opened, Shira Adelman pushed in; she was battered and bruised around the face.

Maruska stood there open-mouthed. Shira flopped onto the bed and started to weep with her face buried in the pillow. Maruska sat on the bed gently and put her arm on Shira's back, feeling the heaving and sobbing. She sat there, knowing that the crisis would eventually pass. She pulled the coat more tightly around her naked body. She shivered in the early morning chill of the spring day.

She glanced up at the window; the rain had gone, and a weak sun peeked through the sky to help dry London's wet streets. The church bells cried out, summoning worshippers for the first service of the day. She had a slight headache; one of those you get when you haven't had enough sleep. She ran downstairs to the kitchenette. The house was quiet, with the residents sleeping late on a Sunday.

She quickly made some tea, and carrying two cups, she went back up to her room. When she opened the door, Shira Adelman was sleeping soundly in Maruska's bed. There was a pile of clothes on the floor.

Maruska pulled a chair up to the fire, lit the gas and sat down, occasionally staring at the sleeping woman. She sighed and she sipped her tea. She felt her eyes closing with the heat of the fire. She stood up, tossed off the coat and climbed back into her bed. Shira instinctively moved over, giving her just enough room. Maruska turned her back on her. As she drifted off to sleep, she felt Shira's arm come over her shoulder and pull her closer...

It was nearly midday before Maruska felt Shira Adelman stir. She gradually came out of her deep sleep, enjoying the warmth of Shira's body. It seemed such a long time since she had slept with someone.

Shira sat up, "I'm sorry Maruska...I shouldn't have come here like this."

Maruska propped herself up on one arm. She touched Shira's face, "Who did this?" She already knew the answer.

"How does it look?" she asked.

Maruska sat up and turned Shira's head towards the light, "As my father used to say, you'll live. You should have put a cold compress on that bruise soon after you got it." She paused as Shira looked down, "What did you do to deserve this?"

The Polish girl looked away, "He came looking for it last night. He was drunk, celebrating some big deal or other. I wouldn't give it to him, so he hit me several times. I don't know why I resisted because he took it anyway; he always does."

Maruska responded, "Sometimes it's better to give a little away in the beginning than something bigger in the long run." She hopped out of bed, not worried about her nakedness. "Come on, let me see what I can do with these bruises. Come over to the night stand, there's some cold water here."

Maruska looked at the woman as she got up. Already, Maruska could see red welt marks on her arms, inner thighs and back. She tried not to say anything as the girl sat down.

Maruska chatted away as she skilfully wiped down Shira Adelman. The marks were largely superficial and she could find no cuts. The bruising would go down over the next few days and with some carefully applied make-up; she wouldn't look too bad.

Maruska watched her, as she started to get dressed, "Do you want to have a bath downstairs? It will make you feel better."

Shira shook her head, "No you did a good job with the flannel. I feel much better already. I'll have a long soak when I return home, whenever that will be."

"Leave him."

Shira smiled, stood up and reached into her coat pocket. She lit one of her long, thin cigarettes. "I can't leave him, Maruska. Zev got me out of Ashford, and he paid off my father's debts. I married him willingly, even though he's an old man. I swear he must have bumped off his first wife." She giggled at the thought.

"What happened to her?"

"Cancer, I think. She was close to his age but she didn't bear him any children. Zev is hoping I will some day."

"Will you?" Maruska asked.

"Not if I can help it. At least not with him."

Maruska took a deep breath, "What is Porteous to you?"

Shira eyed her, "Somebody who has helped me out several times."

"Is he your lover?"

Shira snorted, "Oh, you poor girl. Of course, he's not. I just like to tell everyone he is so that uninvited men keep away."

"Your husband thinks he is?"

"Yes, but he won't mess with Porteous. He knows which side his bread is buttered. Zev does business with the Ladbroke Grove gang. Porteous works out of Kensal Town."

Maruska looked confused, "What is that?"

"Kensal Town; over the Ha'penny Steps. You could have seen it last night if you hadn't got stroppy with Porteous on the bus."

Maruska looked down, "How do you know about that?"

"We have a telephone, you know...Porteous is a good soul. He really likes you, but you keep messing him around. He has a flat for you and once he introduces you to his friends and neighbours, you'll be perfectly safe. Nobody will trouble you."

Maruska blushed again. "But everybody asks too many questions."

Shira laughed, "Of course they do. You can't just waltz in here and not expect people to want to know about you. The whole of London is suspicious of everyone, especially us foreigners. There's bloody war around the corner. Look what the Germans have done to your homeland. Do you think they'll stop there? They hate us Jews. They want to kill us all. My father is desperately trying to get out of Warsaw before they invade. If the Germans don't get us, Stalin and his merry band of Russian peasants will. I don't know who is worse."

"So I should just keep quiet?"

"Yes, in the beginning. You have to trust someone otherwise you'll get nowhere. There are enough spivs and crooks out there to clean you out. Zev has already told a few people that you have more diamonds, and it's known that you paid a call to Benny Benowitz yesterday. The Jewish community is very tight. Everyone knows everyone's business."

"I don't have any more diamonds," Maruska spoke quietly as she looked down.

Shira stubbed out the end of her cigarette, "You see what I mean? Trust, Maruska, trust...Oh, you'll learn soon enough. Go, go and get dressed, and we'll have some breakfast..."

They were eating a large helping of eggs, bread and butter washed down with hot, sweet tea in the café in Star Street. Shira had linked her arm with Maruska as they walked down Praed Street, which was quiet on this Sunday afternoon.

She asked, "Tell me about Porteous."

Shira looked up from her plate, "Oh, early thirties, well-educated, very good- looking, of course, and very astute."

"Does he have a lady friend?"

"As far as I know, he's had several, but he keeps himself to himself." She forked a large helping of scrambled eggs into her mouth. "He has two special friends that I know of."

"Women?"

Shira nodded. "You'll get to meet them soon enough, so take them at face value. Don't go off on one of your high and mighty fits."

Maruska looked confused, she was enjoying the breakfast. "What do you mean?"

"Well, there's Nancy; lovely lady except for her profession, and then there's Alice. Now she's an interesting one."

Shira leaned in and whispered, "Nancy's a prostitute, works up in the West End for that Maltese gangster, Charlie Maitland. Keep away from him and his boys. Porteous met her after he was booted out of the army. He kind of takes care of her."

"What about Alice, is she a prostitute as well?"

Shira giggled, "No, she's one of them."

Maruska shook her head. Shira went on, speaking even more quietly, "One of those funny ones, you know, prefers to take her pleasures with another woman..."

Maruska sat back and smiled, "I think you mean a lesbian, Shira. I saw lots in Vienna. It was quite fashionable before the Nazis invaded. Married women often took a female lover, especially if their husbands were too busy to satisfy them. There were a couple on my initial training course. The Germans stamped all that out. Now a woman is expected to bear lots of children for the Reich."

Shira put down her fork and stared off into the distance, "I had a crush on another girl when I was at school. I remember, during the hot summer of 1932, we spent all our time together. We used to swim naked in the lake. We discovered our bodies and how to make them work for you. We swore undying love for each other; we were never going to let a boy touch us..."

Maruska smiled, "We've all had those experiences, Shira, I know I have. What happened to her?"

Shira carried on eating, "Dunno. When school restarted after the summer, she disappeared. Her mother thought I was a bad influence on her when it was she who made all the running...Never saw her again..."

They ate in silence for a few minutes.

"You said Porteous had to leave the army?"

Shira nodded, "Yes, he's got really bad asthma..."

Just before eight in the evening, Maruska Bergman and Shira Adelman entered the White Horse public house on Kensal Road. Maruska was hit by the noise of the crowded hostelry. The blue fug in the air, caused by cheap tobacco, made her chest tighten and her eyes sting. Shira pulled her through the crowd towards the bar. She acknowledged the greetings of many of the male and female drinkers. Edith Bell looked up from the bar. She smiled at the Pole and gave Maruska the once over.

"Two questions, Shira, who is this rather pretty lady, and how did you get those bruises?"

Shira ignored the remarks, "Two large gins, Edith..."

Edith Bell snorted and turned to get the drinks. Shira slapped a half-crown on the bar counter. She turned to Maruska. "Now that they've seen you in here with me, you'll be perfectly safe. Kensal Town has a certain reputation. The police only come here in pairs and during daylight hours. They leave us alone, provided we don't kill each other too often."

Edith Bell plonked the drinks on the bar, "Well, we do occasionally but only those who deserve it..."

"Do what, Edith?" Shira looked at her.

"Kill each other. If we do, we do it discreetly...Come on, Shira, who have you brought with you, tonight?"

Shira took Maruska's arm. This is Doctor Maruska Bergman. She's a refugee from Czechoslovakia."

"Oh, she's the one Porteous has been talking about. You must be something special for him to spend so much time talking about you. I couldn't get a look in last night."

Maruska was embarrassed.

"What happened to your face, Shira?"

Maruska intervened, "She fell down the stairs last night at my lodgings. I'm afraid we had too much to drink."

Edith burst out laughing.

Shira asked, "Where's Porteous?"

"He's at home, I presume, he wasn't very well earlier."

"Is he okay?"

"Yeah, I think so. It was just another asthma attack." She went off to attend to another drinker.

When they were alone, Shira whispered, "You didn't have to say that."

Maruska sipped her drink, "I didn't think you'd want anybody to know your business."

Shira sighed, "Come on, drink up. Let's go and see Porteous."

"Will he mind us coming unannounced if he's not well?"

Shira shook her head, "Jesus, girl. Didn't they teach you anything normal at that fancy university of yours?"

Shira walked noisily up the wooden stairs of the three-storey house on Bosworth Road. The bells of the church on the corner chimed nine o'clock. Shira pushed open the door to the flat. Porteous was sitting at the table with both hands wrapped around a cup of hot tea. He looked pale. He made to get up.

"Sit down, Porteous. I've brought you a doctor."

He smiled at Maruska Bergman. She looked at him. He was half the man she had been with the previous day. She went over to him and took his hand. Her fingers were on his pulse. She turned to Shira,

"Go and boil some water, please, Shira. Make sure it's steaming."

She turned to Porteous, "What do you take, Epinephrine or Ephedrine?"

"The former," he wheezed, " and I've already taken it."

She put her hand to his forehead, "There's no fever." She bent down and tried to listen to his chest. She shook her head. "I can't hear a thing..."

She turned to Shira, "Pour the boiling water into a bowl and fetch a towel to cover his head."

She pulled up a chair and watched as he inhaled the steam under the cover."

Shira asked, "What are you doing?"

"It's an old trick we used to use in Vienna. The steam helps to dilate the bronchial airways. That's what asthma does. It..." She paused to find the right word in English, and shook her head, "*Stahuje*...I don't know the English word." She used her hands to show what she meant."

A muffled voice spoke out from under the towel, "Constricts, Maruska, constricts."

"Yes, yes, I knew it really..."

Shira rolled her eyes. "Don't ever swear at him, Maruska, he knows all the words...Go on with the asthma lecture and stop interrupting, Porteous." She poked him on the arm.

Maruska went on, "Yes, sorry, okay, the airways to your lungs get constricted making breathing difficult. Patients often get a build up of a thick fluid in the lungs, I think it's called mucus, sliz, in Czech. We called it *Schleim*, in German. Cough for me, Porteous."

He coughed. She could hear the rattle in his chest. She began to slap his back. He coughed even more. "That will help clear the muck from his lungs. Here, Shira, carry on doing this whilst I find something for him to spit into."

Shira went to her task with relish.

Porteous held up his hands, "Jesus, you're supposed to be helping me, not killing me..."

An hour later, Porteous was feeling much better. Shira found an open bottle of gin and was sitting next to an old wireless fiddling with the dials, trying to find some modern music.

Porteous and Maruska were in the flat opposite. He was showing her around. He stood at the door whilst she moved from the sitting room to the bedroom. There was a single gas ring on the hob with a water heater situated over the white, chipped sink. She turned the tap and the geyser flickered into life. Porteous called out,

"There's a gas meter under the sink. I put several sixpences in it already."

She smiled at him. She sat on the worn armchair in front of the small gas fire and looked around.

"This will do nicely."

She got up and went into the bedroom. A double-sized brass bed frame stood against one wall.

He called out, "I'll get you a fresh mattress tomorrow. I have plenty of bed linen."

She could hear Shira singing loudly across the hall.

She said, "So you want me to move into an empty flat that just so happens to be across the hall from you?"

Porteous shrugged his shoulders, "In my condition, I thought it might be a good idea to have a doctor close by…"

She laughed, "Tell the landlady I'll take it. How much does she want for rent and a deposit?"

"Don't worry about that, I already paid it. You are good for it…"

Maruska Bergman allowed Porteous to escort her back over the Ha'penny Steps and onto the Harrow Road to hail her a taxi.

She asked, "What are you going to do with Shira?"

He sighed, "I'll put her to bed when she passes out. She doesn't want to go home tonight. Her old man will give her another beating; he's probably been drinking all day. She's better off staying here. Shira will be fine tomorrow, and then she'll not touch another drink for a week or so. He's done this before. I might need to have a word with him."

A black taxi appeared. Porteous held up his hand and partially stepped into the road. He leaned into the driver,

"Take the lady up to Praed Street, please."

The driver nodded, reached up and turned off the light.

Porteous opened the door for her. Just before she entered, she turned, grabbed him and kissed him on the lips. He watched the taxi disappear off into the gloom of the night and then turned to go and sort out Mrs Shira Adelman...

The back door to the jeweller's shop on Star Street wasn't locked. Zev Adelman had had too much to drink to even care. He wanted his young wife, and she was nowhere to be seen. He'd sort her out when she returned. She was due another slap and, as the master of the house, he had the right to take her whenever he wanted. It is the duty of a good Jewish wife to bear her husband many children...He'd give that Shira what for, when he saw her. He might even tell her father; he wouldn't be pleased to learn that his daughter was not obeying her husband...

He had only just made it to the bed in his room before he managed to collapse, face down. He'd just have one more swig from the bottle...

The dark-clad figure cast a shadow on the grubby backyard. The church clock chimed four in the morning; there was a cold wind in the air. The streets were just about deserted. A solitary policeman whistled as he slowly walked down Praed Street on his beat. He didn't see the person who had ducked into a darkened shop doorway on the opposite side of the road. The person waited until the whistler of the mournful tune was one hundred yards away...

A gloved hand silently turned the doorknob. The catch slipped. The door creaked slightly as it was pushed open. If there had been any light, the intruder would have seen that the storeroom was untidy, as though no one ever bothered to pay it any attention.

The intruder went to the office and turned the knob; it was locked. Thick carpet masked any footsteps. At the top of the stairs, the intruder stopped, breathed in deeply and waited until the thumping heart slowed down. The intruder listened carefully. The loud snoring was coming from the large front bedroom that was above the shop. After a few silent footsteps, the visitor stood in the doorway. The door was pushed open gently.

The outside street lights bathed the room in a dull glow. There was a pause...

The first thing Zev Adelman knew was when the icy cold water from the jug on the washstand hit the back of his head. It caught his breath. He tried to get up, but something was pressing sharply against his back. Whatever it was, it pinned the man firmly to the bed. He felt a hand grab what was left of his hair and force up his head. He could see the brass railings of the bed. He was about to cry out when he felt something come over his head and fasten tightly around his neck. The ligature was smooth and silky; his nostrils caught a distinctive scent as it passed over his face. The weight shifted as two knees pinned his arms to the bed as he lay face down. He felt the material around his neck tighten. He coughed as he fought to breathe. His eyes began to bulge. A cacophony of silent noises mixed up with disconnected images filled his brain. So this is what it was like to die?

He wanted to be sick. He felt bile come up from his stomach and stick in his throat as the ligature tightened. The acid from the vodka he had been drinking all day, burned inside his gullet. Little stars began to flash before his eyes and then....the ligature went slack.

He gasped for air...the colour came flooding back into his face. He felt the hot breath of some person against his ear. He thought he felt some hair brush against his skin. He heard a whispered voice,

"Mr Adelman, can you hear me?"

There was no answer. The ligature tightened again. He nodded vigorously.

"I'll ask you again, can you hear me?"

He couldn't place the voice or the accent.

"Yes, yes. I can hear you, he gasped." The ligature loosened.

"Listen carefully to what I am about to tell you. If you ever lay a hand on Shira again, I'll come back and kill you. Do you understand?"

There was another vigorous set of nods.

"Say it!"

"Yes, yes I understand..."

The voice whispered again, "This is what it feels like to die, Mr Adelman." The ligature began to tighten again.

"I hope you never forget it..."

He coughed and choked again. He felt the bed move as the weight on his back was eased. The whispered voice again,

"I'm not here to steal anything, Mr Adelman, so stay here and count out loud to a thousand. I'll be watching you from the door. If you stop counting or try to get up, I'll kill you. You may start now..."

"One, two, three..." The voice was hoarse.

The assailant walked quietly back down the stairs as the count continued in the silence of the night.

Doctor Maruska Bergman climbed the stairs of her lodging house. Her footsteps could hardly be heard. If anyone had seen her, they might have noticed that she was wearing only one stocking...

Chapter 7

April 1939
London
Moving in

Maruska lay in bed listening to the noise of the girls as they moaned about having to get up and go off to work on Monday morning. She hadn't had much sleep. She reached under the pillow. Her precious little silk bag was still there. She finally got up when the church bell sounded out nine o'clock. She pulled her coat on over her naked body and went down to the kitchenette to make some tea. She stood with her back to the sink, staring out of the grimy window. She was slightly startled by the sound of Mrs Levy's voice.

"*Shalom*, Doctor Bergman."

Maruska turned to the voice and bowed slightly as a mark of respect, "*Shalom alechem,* Mrs Levy."

"How are you today, my child?"

"Very well, Mrs Levy, thank you."

"Did you have a productive weekend with regard to flat hunting?"

Maruska nodded, "Yes, Ma'am, thank you. I'll be leaving later today."

"Oh, my husband and I will be sorry to see you leave so soon. Where are you going?"

"I have the offer of a small flat in Kensal Town."

Mrs Levy raised her eyebrows, "I'm not sure if that is a suitable place for a lady of your standing."

Maruska smiled, "Oh, it's fine, Ma'am. I met some of the residents, and they seem really nice."

"The place has a certain reputation. There are some unpleasant people living there." She paused, "How did you find it?"

"Through a friend, Ma'am."

"That wouldn't be Mrs Adelman, would it?"

Maruska looked puzzled, "Is there something I should know, Mrs Levy?"

"Zev Adelman's wife is troublesome. She goes around with some unsavoury characters."

"I thought her husband didn't allow her out of the house?"

Mrs Levy laughed, "He couldn't keep that wild cat at home if he tried. Rabbi Levy told Adelman not to marry someone more than half his age. It was bound to end in tears.

"Well, Ma'am, she managed to help me get a place of my own, so I'm eternally grateful for that. She's been a good friend to me."

She rinsed out her cup, "I'll stop by later and give you some money and a forwarding address. Thank you for your kindness."

She went to the door and turned, "Ma'am, I need to purchase some medical supplies just in case I get my registration sooner than expected. Do you know of anywhere I can purchase these?"

Mrs Levy replied, "Yes, yes, of course. Let me think. Yes, I know. If you go up to the British Museum in Bloomsbury, there are lots of shops that sell medical equipment. Just take the bus up to the end of Oxford Street and ask."

The shop doorbell rang loudly as Maruska Bergman walked in. It was nearly midday. She had taken her time in bathing and getting dressed. She put on the new dress she had bought with Shira the other day. She paid particular attention to her appearance, ensuring that the seams on her new stockings were straight. She folded up her remaining clothes and just about managed to get them into her carpetbag. She thought she would go straight up to Kensal Town after her visit to Bloomsbury.

She was greeted by a man in a three-piece pin-striped suit, "Good morning, Madam, how may I help you today?"

"I'd like to purchase both a stethoscope and a sphygmomanometer and some other basic equipment."

The sales assistant peered over his glasses, "Of course madam, we have a good selection of both. Are you purchasing for yourself or someone else?"

Maruska smiled, "For myself. May I introduce myself? I am Doctor Maruska Bergman from Vienna. I have just arrived in London and I have applied for registration with the General Medical Council. Unfortunately, in my haste to leave Austria, I was forced to leave all my equipment behind."

The assistant cleared his throat, "Certainly, Doctor. I'm sure we can help you."

He reached under the counter and produced an embossed card, "We have two offers that we usually make to medical students." He flipped the card around so that Maruska could read it.

"On the left, we have the basic list which will certainly do for starters. However, for more experienced doctors like yourself, I would recommend our superior collection."

Maruska ran her eye down the list of nineteen items ranging from a stethoscope to a catheter and some ethyl chloride to be used as a local anaesthesia.

The assistant spoke up, "Was your journey difficult, Doctor?"

"A little, but your authorities have been welcoming. Have you got an atomiser?"

He looked at her, "Yes, we have received some, but they are a little expensive. I believe they have been approved for use with Epinephrine."

Maruska nodded, "Can you add one, please?"

The assistant disappeared into the back of the shop, thinking that his commission would be good this week...

He came back and placed the implement on the counter, "You've used one before, Doctor?"

She ignored the question. He asked, "Do you have a receptacle for these items?"

"I'm sorry, what do you mean, my English is not too good?"

"A bag, doctor. A proper bag for everything."

An hour later, Maruska left the shop carrying over twenty items in a new leather doctor's bag that she had bargained down to a sensible price much to the consternation of the assistant who could see his commission rapidly evaporating...

Maruska Bergman decided she needed to at least act like a doctor, even though she was not licensed to practise in London...

The desk sergeant at Harrow Road Police Station looked at Maruska, "What can I do for you, madam?"

Maruska placed her Alien identity card on the desk, "I was told in Ashford to report to the local police every two weeks."

The sergeant sighed and picked up the card. He examined it carefully, his eyes flicking from the black and white photograph back and forth to Maruska to ensure the picture actually was her.

"Hmm, you're the third this week. Anyone would think there was a spot of trouble in Europe..." He laughed at his own joke. Maruska fixed her dark brown eyes on him. He cleared his throat,

"Yes, well. Is this your first time here?"

"Yes."

"In which case, you'll have to complete a registration form nominating this police station as your preferred one. This means you can't report to another station unless you formally change it. Do you understand?"

Maruska yawned...

The sergeant rummaged around in a pile of papers and slid over a form. "Go over there and complete the form." He looked up at the large queue of London's finest flotsam and jetsam and shouted, "Next!"

Fifteen minutes later, Maruska, was back in front of the desk sergeant. He ran his eyes over the form and checked the details against her identity document.

"Okay, Doctor Bergman, this looks all in order, although I do question the wisdom of living in Kensal Town. There are some really unsavoury characters there. Might I advise you that it would be better if you sought lodgings elsewhere?"

Maruska yawned again...

He cleared his throat again, "Right, report back every two weeks. You'll just have to sign the register, that's all. If you get a job, you'll need to enter the details on the form. If you move, inform us straight away. I might tell you, Miss, that there is a possibility that some aliens might be interned if war breaks out. Keep your ears to the news because I wouldn't want my officers to have to come and seek you out. Do you understand?"

Maruska nodded, "Is that all, Sergeant?"

Maruska paid off the taxi at the Ha'penny Steps. The driver didn't want to go into Kensal Town, anyway; too many bad experiences in the past... By the time she reached the house in Bosworth Road, she was breathing rapidly. The two bags seemed to get heavier with each step. She climbed the few steps up to the main door and dropped her bags. She tried the door but it was locked. She banged loudly on the rusty door knocker.

The old, rusty hinges creaked as it opened. An overweight woman in her early sixties peered out. She was wearing a badly stained housecoat. A dark- coloured headscarf hid her rapidly thinning grey hair. She looked up at Maruska.

"Yes?"

"I'm Doctor Bergman. I'm moving into the top flat today."

The woman took a drag on a cigarette that was clamped between two nicotine-stained fingers.

"Oh, yes, I remember. I hope you've got some money for me?"

Maruska ignored the question, "Is Porteous at home?"

She shook her head, "Nah, he went out about an hour ago. There's one of his fancy women upstairs. I'll call her for you."

The woman let the door swing open. She went to the foot of the stairs and called out in a very loud voice,

"Nancy! Nancy! There's someone here to see Porteous." She turned to Maruska, "Well, come on in, we don't stand on ceremony here. Drop your bags on the floor. Nancy will give you a hand."

Maruska hefted the bags into the hallway and dropped them at the foot of the stairs. She could hear some heels clumping down the bare wooden steps. She looked up to see Nancy Keeling walking down the stairs. What struck her immediately was the inherent beauty of the girl. She was immaculately made up. She had on a white blouse and a pair of fashionable beige trousers that went high up the waist. Her heels were of the chunky square variety. With her auburn hair, Nancy Keeling could pass for a minor film star. As soon as she saw Maruska, she called out,

"It's all right, Martha, I'll see to the Doctor."

The landlady turned to Maruska, "Don't forget the rent, will you? It's due every Friday by six o'clock at the latest. I have bills to pay, you know."

Nancy shook her head, "Martha! Leave Doctor Bergman alone. Porteous has already paid you a month in advance..."

The old woman muttered as she went back into her flat and banged the door.

Nancy held out her hand, "Take no notice of her. She doesn't even own the place. She just looks after it for the landlord. I'm Nancy. Porteous said you might be along today."

Maruska noticed her long, delicate fingers. "Come on, I'll take one of your bags." She reached down and grabbed the carpetbag. "Jesus, what have you got in here?"

"All my worldly goods..."

Nancy laughed.

Maruska's flat was aired out. Someone had taken a damp cloth to the window and cleaned away months of grime. She could actually see out of it now. Porteous had put a new mattress on the bed. Some neatly folded sheets and blankets were placed at the foot.

Nancy asked, "Where do you want this?" indicating the bag.

"Leave it there, I'll sort it out later."

"Porteous put some crockery in the kitchen. Would you like me to make you some tea?"

Maruska nodded.

Nancy lit the gas fire; she sat on the wooden chair while Maruska sat on the armchair.

Nancy asked, "Do you know who I am, Maruska?"

"I think so. Shira told me a little about you."

Nancy smiled, "Well, she would, wouldn't she? Well, you know what I do. I'm not ashamed of it. I send money home to my mum every week and I take care of my little sister."

Maruska looked at her, "It's none of my business, Nancy. You're a friend of Porteous; that's all I need to know. How did you meet him?"

Nancy sipped her tea, "Oh, that's a long story, Maruska, one for another time. Let's just say, he got me out of a very tricky situation. What about yourself?"

Maruska went through the tried and tested story...

"And your family?" Nancy asked when she had finished.

Maruska shook her head, "I really don't know. They'll get out if they can. Europe is not a good place for us Jews any more."

Nancy reached out and took her hand, "You'll be fine here. Porteous will make sure you'll be all right. What are you going to do for work until your registration comes through?"

Maruska smiled, "I can do a bit of sewing..."

Nancy left just before four. She said she had to go to work. Maruska busied herself around the flat wiping out cupboards and cleaning where she thought it was needed. There was a useful supply of household goods under the sink.

Just before six, Maruska lay down on the bed she and Nancy had made up earlier. There was so much going through her head; she almost couldn't make sense of it all; Prague, Vienna, the hospital, Ashford and now, finally, she was settled somewhere safe, for the moment...She turned her head towards the light of the newly cleaned window, trying not to think about what she had to do...

It was dark. She felt the bed move. Her instinct was to lash out until she heard the soothing voice of Peter Porteous.

"I see you've settled in?"

She stirred, shaking her head vigorously, "Do you normally enter a lady's bedroom uninvited?"

He snorted. She said, "Pass me my coat."

She sat up, not bothering that the bed covers fell away from her body exposing her naked breasts, She clicked her fingers, "My coat, Porteous, I want to get up."

He sighed, stood up and went to a hook behind the bedroom door. He turned and tossed the coat towards her, "I'll make some tea."

He was sat at her kitchen table sipping the hot tea when she came in with her bare feet padding softly on the carpet. She pulled the coat tightly around her waist, "You frightened me."

He blew away some steam from the cup, "Yes, sorry. I was just wanting to see if everything was to your satisfaction."

She picked up the cup in both hands, "Yes, yes, it's all good."

"He said, I gather you met Mrs Cunningham earlier?"

"Who?"

"The old woman who lives on the ground floor, Martha."

"Oh, her. She asked for more money."

He shook his head, "She's just trying it on. She knows I paid four weeks in advance for you."

Maruska made to get up, "I'll get my purse."

"Leave it. You can pay me later. It's not important." His hand was on her arm. "Have you eaten?"

"Not yet."

He stood up, "Make yourself decent. I have some beef stew on the stove. We'll talk later."

With that, he was gone. She smiled...

She got some hot water from the kitchen and washed herself all over standing in an old tin bath she had found hanging on a hook behind the door. She dressed carefully, making sure that all was in order before she knocked quietly on the door across the landing.

He called out from the kitchen, "Come on in. I never bother locking it..."

She pushed open the door. He had pulled out an old hardwood table into the middle of the living room floor. The table had been set for two. The smell of the beef wafted through the flat. Her tummy rumbled.

"Would you like something to drink? Look in the sideboard."

She walked over to a rosewood cupboard and opened one of the doors. She pulled out a bottle of whisky and a bottle of brandy. She poured two whiskies and added a splash of water from a jug on the table. He smiled as he came in carrying a large bowl of beef and vegetable stew that had been simmering on the stove for hours.

He glanced at her. She looked particularly beautiful this evening as she slowly sipped her drink.

The beef was tender and to her liking. Halfway through the meal, she asked,

"What is it that you do, Porteous?"

He looked at her, "I work up at Smiths making components for aeroplanes." He paused, "And then I do a bit of trading..."

"What do you trade in?"

He shrugged his shoulders, "Whatever will make me some money. People ask me to get them things and if I succeed, I take a small commission. I had to find something to do after I was discharged from the army. I didn't want to work in a factory, but we are facing a war. I suspect many will once it kicks off."

"Do you really think there'll be a war?"

He nodded slowly, "Yes, It doesn't matter what Chamberlain and the Government do. They are all afraid of Hitler. They'll give him carte blanche to take the whole of Europe as long as he leaves Britain alone. Hitler claims that the British and Germans are kindred spirits, but our government would be foolish to believe him. You can't appease a criminal. Look what he's done to your country. He simply annexed Austria and got Britain and France to agree to him taking the Sudetenland. You don't do deals with snakes..."

Maruska added, "Don't call it the Sudetenland. It used to be Czechoslovakia."

It was late. The gas fire and the large brandy she had consumed after dinner had made her sleepy. She was sat next to him on the couch. He felt her head on his shoulder as the breathing became steady.

Slowly, he eased her off and lay her down. He spread a blanket over her.

He was sound asleep in his bed when a naked Maruska Bergman lifted the covers and slid in beside him. He turned to her. She pushed him away,

"I've come to bed to sleep, Porteous..."

He smiled....

When he woke up the next morning, she was gone. He shook his head, smiled and went about his business...

Chapter 8

June 1939
London
Routine...

Maruska Bergman had settled into a simple life in Kensal Town. Knowing that she was close to Peter Porteous and being a doctor, local residents treated her with respect. She was now sleeping regularly with Porteous, although she very rarely spent the whole night with him. He couldn't quite work out why she would always leave him for a few minutes before they made love. Whenever he queried her, she would respond,

"Women's business, Porteous..."

He figured it was something to do with her personal hygiene, but he had long given up trying to fathom out the Czech woman. He just knew that she was special and that he was probably falling in love with her.

Not long after she had moved in, she was playing cards with Porteous, Alice Halpin and Nancy Keeling in his front room. They were drinking whisky. There was a knock at the door,

Porteous answered it to be confronted by two local women. Both were in a state of distress.

One of them said, "Porteous, will the doctor come?"

Porteous looked across at Maruska; she shook her head.

He looked at the two women. He knew them from Southern Row near the White Horse public house. They were neighbours. He asked,

"What's wrong?"

"We need the doctor. Those stupid husbands of ours have had a silly disagreement and cut each other with knives."

He looked at the silent one; her face was red from crying. He turned back towards Maruska. Again, she shook her head.

Alice Halpin reached out and touched her arm, "Come on, Maruska, they might need your help."

She sighed, finished off the last of her drink and stood up, her chair scraping on the boards, "Get my bag, Nancy."

She went up to the women, "Where are they?"

The women took her arm, "Come, doctor, they are bleeding out."

The house in Southern Row was a mess. There seemed to be crying children everywhere. One of the wounded men was sat in a chair, oblivious to the fact he was bleeding all over the wooden floor. The other was laid out in a pool of blood. His breathing was shallow. He had a chest wound.

Maruska quickly examined the one in the chair; he would keep. She shouted to Alice, "Make some bandages and press on his wound hard." She nodded and shouted at the wives to bring hot water and sheets to tear up.

Maruska turned to the injured man. She ripped open his shirt and swore in Czech. She turned to Porteous, "He needs to get to a hospital. I'm not sure if I can do very much for him here."

One of the wives cried out, "Please, Doctor, we can't afford the hospital."

Porteous touched her arm and said, "If he goes to the hospital, the police will want to get involved."

She shook her head and went to work on the injured man.

She called out, "Nancy, rip his shirt off him." She turned to the women who were busy tearing up a sheet. "Where's the hot water?"

She worked on him for about one hour. She managed to staunch the bleeding by packing the wounds with the cotton material. She poured half a bottle of whisky in the wound. This woke up the man, who swore at her profusely. He got a slap for his pains from his wife.

Maruska smirked, "This will clean the wound..." She turned to his wife, "He's lucky. Another fraction of an inch and his lung would have been punctured."

Alice grabbed the bottle and poured the remainder on the seated man's wounds. Both men were drunk.

Maruska sat cross-legged on the floor and sewed up the man using some silk thread. She bandaged his chest tightly. Porteous and his wife carried him upstairs to his bed.

Maruska said, "He needs to rest for a few days. He's lost a lot of blood. Change the bandages in the morning and pour some more alcohol on the wound. He's lucky. I'll be back to check on him in the afternoon. If there's any sign of infection, he'll have to go to hospital. Do you understand?"

The wife nodded vigorously.

Alice had patched up the other man, but Maruska sewed up a couple of cuts. Porteous brought the two wives together and had a quiet word with them...

Later that night, Maruska stood in Porteous' bathroom and peeled off her clothes. They were covered in blood. He watched as she submerged herself several times. He sat on the edge of the roll top and held her glass. She asked,

"What did you say to them?"

"I told them not to be so stupid in future and could they please not tell everyone you helped."

She held her nose, closed her eyes and submerged again. He stood up, finished off her drink and left her to it.

She came back into the living room towelling her hair. She was wearing one of his dressing gowns. Porteous was listening to a late night radio broadcast from the BBC announcing that the King and Queen were dining with President Roosevelt at the White House.

She blew him a kiss and went across the landing and into her own flat. She couldn't be bothered to fix her hair. She threw off the dressing gown and climbed into bed, glad for the peace and quiet of her own company...

Over the next four weeks, she delivered two babies, patched up several victims of fights, reset a broken arm in a makeshift splint and extracted a bullet from a leg wound...Porteous told her not to ask any questions...

Chapter 9

September 1939
London
Rose

War was in the air.

It was one of those early September days. Summer was technically over, but Mother Nature had other ideas. The day broke balmy and humid. The elegant female walked nonchalantly along the road, glancing from time to time at the terraced houses that lined the streets of this part of north-west London. The woman could feel the perspiration trickling down from her back and between her legs, even though she wore a thin dress and no stockings. The slightly elevated heels of her open-toed shoes showed off her smooth legs. A light brown bag, slung over a shoulder, swung in a rhythm as she walked. Her long, dark hair was tied back off her face. There were little beads of perspiration on her forehead and top lip. From time to time, she dabbed them away with the white lace handkerchief she carried in her free hand.

It had taken her nearly twenty minutes to walk from her home. It was approaching nine-thirty; she didn't want to be late for the encounter. Her mind was occupied with procedure...

Leash in the left hand meant all is well. Leash in the right hand meant return twenty-four hours later...

The female had no idea who her contact would be. It could be either male or female. Her heart quickened slightly as she turned off Harvist Road and into Milman Road. She looked over at the park. It was busy with early morning mums pushing their offspring in prams. She could see the occasional nanny, distinguished by a pretend uniform, together with a smattering of dog walkers.

She walked past Kempe Road keeping her eyes on the park. She glanced behind to check if she was being followed, but quickly dismissed the idea. She would only need to concern herself with that issue once she had made contact...

She crossed over the road allowing a milk cart, pulled by a rather bored horse, to pass her. The driver tipped his hat at her...she blushed...

She went through the green iron gates of the park entrance. She could see the bandstand over on the northeast corner of the park. She walked slowly as her heartbeat quickened.

Leash in the left hand meant all is well. Leash in the right hand meant return twenty-four hours later...

She spotted the bench opposite the bandstand. An old gentleman sat on one corner reading a newspaper with an ancient briar pipe clenched between his teeth. He had no dogs...

She walked past him and up towards the entrance on Chevening Road. She could feel the slight incline in her calf muscles. She stopped to admire a bed of late flowering plants and then did an about-turn. She could see the old man walking off in the distance, aided by a stick. She quickened her step and reached the bench before anyone else had a chance. She sat down, crossed her legs and extracted a book. She held it in such a way that a passer-by could recognise the title. She pretended to read...The sun was beating down strongly; she felt her face burning. As she lifted a hand to cover her eyes, she saw the contact.

A rather glamorous woman with dyed blonde hair came towards her. The two small, white terrier dogs pulled at her left hand. She was talking to them as they strained on the leash. The dog walker glanced over. The seated woman raised the book slightly so that she could get an even better look.

She felt the seat move slightly as the dog walker sat down. The two dogs immediately moved to the side of the bench.

The woman took a deep breath, "Those are nice dogs. What breed are they?"

The dog walker looked over at her, "Why, they are West Highland Terriers. They call them Westies...Do you own a dog yourself?"

The woman shook her head, "No, but my brother has one..."

The dog walker smiled and took out two little treats for the expectant dogs. She spoke softly as she looked ahead onto the grass, where three little children were running around.

"It is time to go to work, Rose..."

The woman known as Rose nodded, "It has been a long time, what do I call you?"

"You call me Freda."

Rose slowly put away the book she was reading. Freda said, "They are displeased with you. You need to remember that you just don't know who is watching you."

Rose stared ahead; she knew what Freda was talking about.

"What were you thinking of?"

Rose swallowed hard, "I had to do something. The girl could be useful."

The voice became stern, "No. What's an old Jew and his whore of a wife got to do with you?"

Rose shrugged her shoulders, "There were no consequences."

"There's always consequences. Stick to what you've been instructed to do. Do you understand?"

There was a silence between the two. Freda eventually said, "Have you mastered the wireless?"

Rose nodded, "It's not difficult."

"Is it secured the way it is supposed to be?"

Rose sighed, "Yes, my neighbour constructed a box underneath the sewing machine."

"And the case the transmitter came in?"

"I left it by some bins outside a public house as instructed."

"Good, good..." There was a short silence.

"Listen carefully; you transmit five words tonight at midnight. Don't be late."

"What do I send?"

"The first sentence of the National Anthem."

Rose smiled, "The English one, I presume?"

Freda went on, "You have an interview tomorrow at midday in an exclusive fashion house in Chelsea. The mistress of the house is looking for a skilled seamstress. Take some samples down with you. This is your cover, as we agreed."

Rose looked up, "What does she want?"

"She's expanding into lingerie; you'll have no issues with that."

Rose raised her eyebrows, "That's fine. What's my backstory?"

"Keep it simple, Polish refugee and all that. Stick to the legend."

"Is there anything I should know?"

"The husband works for the Admiralty. He likes a pretty woman, but remember, you are here as the wireless operator. That is your priority. Do you understand?" She leaned in and whispered an address.

They went silent as a nanny walked past pushing a pram with two infants sitting up, staring out. The nanny smiled at Rose.'

Freda stood up, "You start picking up on Sunday. Check out your drops before then."

Rose swallowed and looked at the departing nanny and her charges...She stared ahead as Freda continued quietly; Rose had to strain to hear the words.

"The British Authorities are going to start issuing identity cards through the Census enumerators towards the end of the month. These cards are nothing; they won't even carry a photograph. When they call at your door, show them your alien registration card. They probably won't know what to do. As soon as the cards are issued, I will get you one in your English name. Even if they introduce a photograph, I can still sort that out."

Rose nodded; she had heard about this possibility.

"The biggest problem will be if they start interning what they call enemy aliens."

"But I'm Czech," replied Rose.

Freda shook her head, "They will categorise you as German through your connection to Austria and the Sudetenland, which is now technically part of the German Reich. Are you still reporting to the police station?"

Rose nodded again; Freda continued, "Good. If they introduce internment, they'll do it through the police station. You'll be called for interview before a tribunal. We'll make a decision about your future when that happens. In the meantime, carry on as you have been instructed. Do you understand?"

Rose didn't answer.

Freda untied the two dogs, who got to their feet, albeit reluctantly. They were enjoying the respite of the shade. Freda leaned in again,

"Keep to your business and we'll all get through this. Get it wrong, and we'll be dancing on the end of a rope...Next week, same time..."

Rose watched as the woman she had become to know as Freda, walked away.

Rose had no intention of dancing on the end of a rope...

Rose took out her book as Freda walked off into the distance. She had to admit she was a little surprised, but then again, she had no knowledge of her contacts. It had been drummed into her to keep it that way. She sat there for about fifteen minutes pretending to read her Charles Dickens novel, but she was checking out all the adults in the park. When she had satisfied herself that all was clear, she stood up and began to trace her steps. At the exit back out onto Milman

Road, she purchased a cold drink from a man pushing a cart of ice cream who was making the most of the last of the summer. He wiped his brow,

"It's a hot day, Miss."

She nodded as she slipped him a copper coin to pay for the drink. She stood in the shade of a tree and sipped the cold, watery orange juice that was in a little glass bottle. She dropped the empty container in a crate as he began to push the barrow away. He nodded at her.

It took Rose about twenty minutes to walk down to Kensal Green Cemetery. She entered through the main gate, just past the railway station on the Harrow Road. She could hear the chatter of a group of cemetery workers over by the canal. She walked slowly, taking in her surroundings. She approached the Anglican Chapel and turned left to walk down to the eastern side and the Dissenters' Chapel. On the right, she could see the gas works that bordered the top end of Ladbroke Grove. Opposite was a bench. She sat down. Apart from the gravediggers, there didn't appear to be anyone else in the cemetery. She reached behind her and let her fingers touch the old brick wall. Her hands moved slowly, feeling out the edges of the Victorian bricks. The fingers stopped when she found a gap in the mortar. She looked around quickly; one last final check, and stood up. She pushed on the brick; it moved slightly. Carefully, she pulled out the brick and peered inside. It was empty.

She turned the brick, replaced it and quickly left the cemetery. If the weathered side was showing when she returned, she would know there was a message.

She walked down Scrubs Lane and across Wormwood Scrubs. The second drop-off point was in a wall opposite the prison. As she approached, the unmistakable smell of confined bodies assailed her nostrils. She could hear the shrill whistles of the guards as they ordered prisoners about. She found the place easily enough in a wall that had seen better days. She performed the same procedure of turning the brick and left.

She waited in the early afternoon heat for a bus on Du Cane Road outside the prison. The bus dropped her near North Acton Cemetery on Park Royal Road. Ten minutes later, she walked past the entrance to the Central Middlesex County Hospital. She found what she was looking for near the old infirmary. At the rear of the building there was a little garden of repose, into which had been built several pergolas for patients to sit and take in the air. The third one from the right contained her drop off point... The place was busy with men and women in white coats and nurses in uniform. No one paid her the slightest attention.

As Rose walked back out onto the main road, she determined to get a bicycle...

Just before midnight, Rose closed the main door to her flat and slid across the top and bottom bolts. She went to the pedal sewing machine and moved it across the floor, thanks to the four wheels her neighbour across the landing had kindly put on the feet of the machine. It rolled silently across the boards.

The machine was about ten years old, but it had been well maintained, with the engineering as precise as it had been when it was first manufactured in the United States of America some time before. Rose remembered the cursing and swearing of the three removal men as they struggled to get it up the three flights of stairs to her apartment together with that locked suitcase. A one-pound note soon quietened them down...

She pulled up a chair and sat down. On her left were three books. She lifted the main needle and then removed the two screws of the sewing plate with a sixpence. It flipped up on a spring. Her long fingers reached into the plate and felt for a catch. They found it and she pressed a lever. She felt the table-top click and move very slightly. She reached over with one hand and heaved at the wood. The top flipped over revealing an enclosed, polished wooden box.

She unlatched the box top and pulled out the electric cable. She stood on a chair and unscrewed the light bulb. She connected the cable to the light socket and looked down to see the valves beginning to glow. Next, she lifted a thin antenna from the box and hooked it onto the length of wire that was already slung across the room, upon which were draped items of clothing Rose had been making. This makeshift device significantly amplified the signal. She sat down quietly and lifted out the key. It was still connected to the transmitters by a woven cloth cable. She sat back, folded her arms and closed her eyes. She checked that her silver stopwatch was fully wound for the tenth time... Next to her sat a piece of paper with blocks of numbers written in her familiar script.

The church bell on the corner began to chime midnight. She pulled on a pair of headphones so she could hear what she was transmitting.

Her hand reached over the key. She rested the palm of her hand on the edge of the box with her fingers poised...She began to depress the lever on the key desperately trying to bring back the rhythm that her counterpart somewhere in deepest, darkest Germany, would recognise...

After twenty seconds, she stopped...She had sent two words. She waited a further minute and then began again. She finished the final word of the message just as the second hand on the stopwatch reached twenty.

She pulled off the headphones and quickly disconnected the set from the electricity and homemade antenna. Rose had no real interest in knowing whether or not her message had been received...

Within less than two minutes, the sewing machine was back in its usual place up against the window and the scrap of paper was smouldering gently in an ashtray...Rose was sitting up in bed reading from one of the three books. As was her want, she was naked...

Cynthia Fleming was struggling to keep awake. She had been sitting in front of the wretched screen for over three hours. The flat line traced across in front of her, regular as clockwork. She glanced down at her script that contained her list of wavelengths; only five more to go before it all started again, but at least she would get a ten-minute toilet break in between. She turned the Bakelite knob; the signal danced before her eyes and then settled as it went out across the wavelength. She yawned and tried to make the uncomfortable Air Ministry headphones sit more easily on her head.

It had been a mistake to have that one last gin and tonic back at the boarding house. Whose birthday was it? She had no idea, but the offer of a free drink was too hard to refuse. The regulation thick black skirt, Barathea blazer and white blouse uniform was far too hot for the confines of this dark and stuffy listening room. And woe betide any wireless girl who arrived for duty not wearing regulation stockings...(thick, grey, Lisle variety...)

The room was presided over by an old spinster dragon drafted in from some dead end job in the Home Office. The old bat carried a wooden ruler, which was regularly slapped on a table to ensure her fifteen girls were all paying attention to their monitors. There was a general hubbub of noise as fifteen or so specially trained operatives eavesdropped on broadcasts emanating out of occupied Europe. Their job was to listen to transmissions in Morse Code and write down what they heard. An administrative assistant busied herself going around sweeping up the yellow chits upon which these messages had been recorded, as the operators rang their bell upon transcribing a message.

Cynthia Fleming sighed. How did she get roped into this so-called temporary assignment? Her job as a clerical officer in some run down office in Whitehall seemed paradise at the moment. What was it? Oh yes, a branch of the civil service that looked after ancient monuments. At least it was a regular nine till five job, (four on a Friday) with a lunch break between twelve and one and a chance to flirt with the service men and women in the Volunteer Arms just down the road from the office...

The line traced across the screen...She settled in her seat as the dragon walked past behind her. She didn't need to look up. The old spinster's lavender scent announced her presence from two yards away...

Cynthia Fleming looked up as the dashing young pilot officer entered the room carrying a clipboard. The girls cast furtive glances at each other and suppressed a smile. Cynthia was in the running to be the first wireless girl to bed the young officer...

The dragon coughed loudly. The girls returned to their monitors. Cynthia sighed again, trying to imagine running her long fingers through his thick, black chest hair as they lay in bed following a rigorous bout of sex...The pilot officer thrust the clipboard in front of the dragon...She placed her half-moon spectacles on her nose and began to read. She didn't approve of this young man as he disturbed her girls...Couldn't the Royal Air Force send down a more mature officer, at least one who was married?

She passed him the pile of chits. He flicked through them. At this time in the conflict, very little of what was being heard was of importance; this was yet to come.

The officer caught Cynthia's eye as she stared at him across the room. He winked; she flushed up...He was making her all hot and bothered...

Somewhere in the distance, she heard a faint pinging. What was that? She hadn't heard that since initial training in Collet Court months ago. Was this something going out as opposed to coming in? Her eyes returned to the screen. The little white dot was dancing to the sound of regular signal. Her heart leapt. She took a deep breath; adrenalin coursed through her veins. Notions of tiredness disappeared, along with any slightly erotic thoughts about dashing young RAF officers. Her training kicked in...

Her hand reached over and banged loudly on a push bell. The dragon looked up from the clipboard. Pilot Officer Barton froze on the spot. Cynthia Fleming turned a series of knobs trying to get a better signal. The ping sounded loudly in her ears. She shook her head; *I need to get a fix...*'

Then, the signal ceased...The dot returned to its flat line; all was silent.

She glanced at the dials, grabbed her log pad and wrote down the wavelength and time to the second according to the large illuminated clock on the wall. She smelled lavender...

She pulled one of the headphones to the side of her head, "Signal, Ma'am, bearing 96 degrees."

Pilot Officer Barton said, "What was it, Cynthia?"

The dragon thoroughly disproved of this vulgar familiarity, "Telegraph Assistant Fleming, what was it?"

"Someone transmitting locally, Ma'am."

The dragon turned to the RAF officer; he shook his head, "There are no training exercises scheduled tonight, Miss Atkins." He turned to Cynthia, "How long was it?"

"Around about twenty seconds, sir. I may have missed the beginning."

She felt his hands on her chair as he leaned over her, "Keep listening, if it goes to pattern, there'll be another transmission." He looked up and shouted,

"Pay attention, everyone. We have an outgoing transmission on bearing 96 degrees. Listen out for any other broadcasts but keep recording the usual from Europe. If you catch a similar transmission, make sure you record it accurately."

There were shouts of acknowledgement.

Sure enough, the dot began dancing again after sixty-one seconds. Cynthia began to write down the numbers…The transmission stopped just before twenty-seconds. Barton swept up the note pad and studied the writing,

"It's all numbers," he called out, "Does anyone else agree?"

There were nods of approval from two other operatives. He muttered quietly, "Well, bugger me…" much to the consternation of Miss Atkins, chief dragon of the listening station…

They waited half an hour; there was no other transmission. The girls of The Uxbridge Listening Station returned to their regular sweep of the airways and recording whatever came out of the Third Reich and occupied Europe.

Pilot Officer Norman Barton and Wing Commander William Jenkins were in the map room. They had a series of charts laid out in front of them. At the top of the table sat fifteen telegraph logs taken from the girls. They all said the same thing, more or less.

Jenkins checked the bearing for the tenth time; 96 degrees. He placed the drafting T-Square hard up against the edge of the table and drew a thin pencil line across the large-scale map of London from the basement office in Uxbridge all the way to Essex.

He turned to his junior officer, "Call them again, Barton. God knows what they are doing. They either have it or they don't."

Pilot Officer Barton lifted the heavy receiver and tapped impatiently on the call button,

"Is there anything from Hendon?"

"What? No? Get them for me immediately."

He slammed down the phone and shook his head. The telephone called out again. He snatched it up,

"Yes? Oh for goodness' sake...We got a clear double transmission just after midnight, one minute apart, and you got nothing?"

Squadron Leader Jenkins didn't bother to look up. He just shook his head.

"What do you mean, you had a power cut?"

Barton slammed down the phone. "You wouldn't believe it, sir, main fuse box blew just before eleven. They are still waiting for the electricians to arrive..."

Jenkins looked up and smiled, "Not to worry, Barton. At least we know the system works. Tell the girls to keep an extra attention to this wavelength. Get an account from the girl and write it up. I've already informed the Ministry. They want a full written report first thing in the morning."

Barton asked, "What about the code, sir?"

"Oh, I don't know, we'll let the boffins in Whitehall make that decision. In the meantime, wire the details to listening stations in Merton, Bexley and Hornchurch; together with Hendon, that should cover it."

The Squadron Leader lit a cigarette as he stared at the map. "Could be anywhere along that plane." He traced the line right across London. "Let's hope the bugger transmits again and soon. I reckon it was just the first; maybe a test of something or other."

Pilot Officer Barton joined him at the table, "What kind of transmitter, sir?"

Jenkins shook his head, "Could be something we've not seen before. It's going to have to be small, so it will be limited in the wavelength used. The Dutch tell us they picked up a German with one in a small suitcase. It couldn't receive, just send, but that's the whole point, isn't it?"

Barton straightened up, "I'll go and get that report, sir."

He pushed open the listening room door. The airless room was heavy with feminine sweat and adrenalin. He looked over at Miss Atkins, who nodded. He called out,

"Miss Fleming! Can you come with me, please?"

Cynthia Fleming stood up, straightened her skirt and pulled on her jacket. She had a smirk on her face much to the annoyance of the other girls. She wasn't going to let this chance go begging...

Just after one in the morning in Hamburg, the offices of the Abwehr, Germany's secret intelligence service, were quiet. Gefreiter Rolf Bauer was sitting at a desk reading the evening newspaper. Wehrmacht Auxiliary Jutta Meyer was glued to her receiver. At twenty-one, she was one of the youngest volunteers to the service. She relished the status that her post gave her. The additional clothing allowance that came with the job made it even more worthwhile.

She adjusted the earphones as the transmission came through. She called out, "Corporal, my friend is on the line..."

When the transmission was finished, Rolf Bauer rushed out, clutching the paper on which she had carefully transcribed the message. She sighed and sat back, salivating at the thought of meeting this lady of mystery one day...

Chapter 10

September 1939
The Admiralty Offices, Whitehall, London
Rosemary McCumiskey

Cynthia Fleming was nervous. The excitement and adrenalin of the previous evening had made it very difficult for her to sleep when she had finally got into bed just before eight in the morning. Her room mate in the lodging house was already out on the six o'clock shift; she had the room to herself for a few hours before Pilot Officer Norman Barton and his driver would come to pick her up just after midday. A few hours sleep would be in order.

When she had got back, her roommate, Henrietta Forbes-Carlton was still trying to find some clean underwear for her shift... Her side of the room looked as though it had been hit by one of Mr Hitler's bombs...

Cynthia breathed out slowly, "Jesus, Hetty, did your mother not teach you how to tidy up?"

Forbes-Carlton smiled, "Where I come from, dear Cyn, one simply doesn't clear up. One gets the maid to do it..."

Cynthia tossed her jacket at her...

"Lend me that nice dark blue dress, old girl. Rupert's going to pick me up after shift to go off for a spot of luncheon in some delightful country pub out beyond Amersham."

Cynthia sighed, "Are you hoping to get lucky?"

"Rather, old bean. I haven't seen him for over a week..."

Cynthia waved at her cupboard space, "Help yourself, but I want it back laundered and pressed."

Henrietta squealed, "Oh, you are such a brick. What would I do without you?"

Cynthia shook her head, "Go to work in dirty underwear, I suspect."

Forbes-Carlton laughed, "Oh no, one could never do that. Much better to go without..."

Cynthia Fleming took her time changing into her pyjamas. She sat up in bed as Hetty pulled on a pair of silk stockings, certainly not the regulation ones so beloved by the old dragon Miss Atkins. She stood in front of the full-length mirror and admired herself.

"Will I do? Cyn?"

Cynthia nodded, "Go on, get out and let me sleep. I've got an appointment in Whitehall at one-thirty. Got a lift with a certain Pilot Officer..." She smirked.

Hetty froze in her tracks, "What, the dishy young man we've all been wetting our knickers over?"

"Yes...enjoy Rupert or whatever his name is..." She turned to the wall, closed her eyes and ignored the barrage of questions from Henrietta Forbes-Carlton...

She was disappointed to find that Pilot Officer Norman Barton was not in the car when it pulled up in front of the lodging house just after twelve. A young corporal hopped out and opened the door for her.

"Where's the pilot officer, Corporal?"

"Sorry, Miss, the Squadron Leader took him off earlier for a briefing. It seems there was a flap on in one of the listening rooms last night. I don't suppose you know anything about that, do you?"

Cynthia ignored the question. The Corporal manoeuvred the vehicle at speed towards central London. She stared out of the window and yawned.

The heavy blackout curtains were drawn, keeping out what was left of the weak September sunshine. Cynthia Fleming blinked to try to get her eyes adjusted to the dim light of the briefing room. She looked up and down the table. She had never seen so much braid on so many uniforms before. It seemed as though all three services were represented. Two men and a fierce-looking woman sat silently in civilian clothes. The female had on a twin set and the obligatory pearls. A familiar voice stirred her,

"Ah, Cynthia..."

She looked up to see Pilot Officer Norman Barton standing up. He said,

"This is Telegraph Assistant Cynthia Fleming. I won't bother to introduce everybody but you know Wing Commander Jenkins and the others are from the services with an interest in our business. The three at the front are from the security services. You may address the lady as Miss Smith. Do take a seat. We'll call on you when necessary."

Cynthia looked around. There were two empty seats at her end of the table. She sat down and placed her regulation handbag on the table.

The senior officer said, "Right, Barton, let's hear it again..."

Norman Barton began. He related the incident of the previous night, from the first transmission to the last. He went over to a chart and his finger traced the line of the bearing 96 degrees.

The woman held up her arm; Barton cleared his throat and sat back down. She looked over at Cynthia Fleming,

"How long have you been a wireless operator, Miss Fleming?"

Cynthia looked briefly at Barton. He nodded almost imperceptibly,

"Just under six months, Miss Smith," she replied.

"Where did you train?"

"Collet Court, ma'am."

Smith flicked open a Manila file, "It says here you were top of the class."

Cynthia blushed.

"Was it a male or a female?"

Cynthia looked at her quizzically, "Sorry, ma'am?"

"The transmitter; was it a man or a woman?"

"Oh, a woman, ma'am, definitely. The keystrokes exhibited all female characteristics."

There was a collective sigh in the room. Someone said, "I told you so..."

Smith held up her hand to silence the audience, "Name a couple of those characteristics."

Cynthia closed her eyes recalling her training, "Even spacing, light depression of the key and a recognisance of timing."

One of the male security officers asked, "How can you be sure it wasn't a man pretending to be a woman?"

Cynthia shook her head, "Never seen that before, sir. It's not covered in the training manuals."

"It's possible, though, isn't it? After all, you don't have much experience."

Cynthia looked at him, "Anything's possible, sir, I just know what I heard."

"What exactly did you hear, Miss Fleming?" It was Miss Smith again.

Cynthia stood up and looked at her interrogator, "May I?"

The woman waved her arm and sat back.

As Cynthia went past a seated Norman Barton, he held up her original log; she took it deftly. She went up to the board, picked up a piece of chalk, and began to write the string of sixty-seven numbers into a five blocks. She said,

"There were two distinct transmissions one minute apart."

She was interrupted by a question,

"How do you know there are separate blocks?"

"Sir, you learn to recognise the keystrokes. There were tiny breaks between the blocks. A skilled operator can disguise these, especially when the receiver recognises the sender."

"So, whoever sent this transmission is relatively new to the game?"

"I would say so, sir. She should have changed wavelengths before the second transmission."

Wing Commander Jenkins spoke up, "It could be a test transmission, sir. After all, we've been listening for months and never heard a thing." He nodded at Cynthia, "Thank you, Cynthia, please sit down."

She was glad to be dismissed. Little beads of sweat began to trickle down her back...

Smith stood up, gathering her papers, "We'll talk to Bletchley Park. In the meantime, find that damn transmitter..."

Cynthia Fleming sat as the three clattered out of the room. There was almost a sense of relief in the room. Two hours later and after copious amounts of good quality tea and biscuits, a strategy of sorts was agreed...

The woman known as Rose pushed open the door to an upmarket ladies shop in Chelsea just before midday. The doorbell sounded loudly. An assistant looked up, her spectacles perched on the end of her nose.

Rose looked around the shop. There was an assortment of tailor's dummies, suitably attired in expensive haute couture clothing. She could hear laughing from a room behind the counter.

"Madam, do you have an appointment?"

Rose looked at her, "I'm not here to purchase. I have an interview for a seamstress position."

The assistant looked her up and down, "Wait here. I'll see if Madam Collier is available."

Rose smiled and leaned back against the glass counter. The place even smelled of money. War or times of strife seem to have little or no effect on certain classes of people. Thus, it ever was...

Rose was surprised to see a very attractive forty-something lady come bustling in. She was dressed in a crisp white blouse, tight skirt and a pair of black court shoes with a modest heel. Madam Collier's hair was neatly tied up on the back of her head. She looked like she had spent an inordinate amount of time in front of the make-up mirror that morning. Her accent was refined and very Home Counties.

"Are you the seamstress?"

Rose nodded, "Yes, ma'am, Rosemary McCumiskey, but everyone calls me Rose."

Collier looked her up and down, "Polish, I understand?"

Rose nodded. Collier added, "Follow me, please."

She addressed Rose as she walked, "I hear you are very good...You can see we operate a very exclusive service here. There are no ready-to-wear items in the shop. Everything is made-to-measure. We have a very discerning clientele."

She led Rose through an extravagantly furnished fitting room, complete with easy chairs and a sofa. There were three changing cubicles on one wall. A middle-aged slightly overweight woman, dripping in furs and jewellery, sat on the sofa with a long cigarette in one hand. She smiled at Rose.

Collier pushed open a door to the sewing room. It was bright and spacious. Two assistants looked up at her and then went back to work. She stood by a large sewing table, upon which sat a bolt of expensive black silk and several thin wooden patterns. She said,

"We've never gone into lingerie before but my clients keep asking for it. That lady outside is your first commission. She wants a full set. I've got a shop in Bishopsgate that is making her corsets from the same batch of silk. Your task is to make her French knickers, a matching brassiere and a suspender belt. You can use any lace that's in the workshop or anything else you think would be nice. I don't care how long it takes, but do try and finish it today. If you are as good as they say you are, it should be no trouble." She clicked her fingers,

"Mildred will assist where necessary." She pointed at one of the assistants.

A small, mousy woman looked over and smiled.

Collier clapped her hands, "Well, get to it, then..."

Just before five in the afternoon, Lady Patricia Highsmith left the Sloane Avenue shop with a smile on her face, clutching a box of the finest silk lingerie carefully wrapped in tissue. She paid just over fifteen pounds for the service, on account, of course.

Madam Collier, took Rose's arm and said, "Well done, Rose. How about a drink back at my place? I have some ideas I would like to discuss with you."

Just before eight that evening a certain Miss Smith of the Security Services and MI5 in particular, sat at her desk smoking a long cigarette. Opposite her sat a tall well-groomed man in pin-striped trousers and a dark-coloured jacket. His shoes were highly polished. He pushed Cynthia's log back over the table,

"Sorry, old girl, really can't help you." The accent was cut glass public school and Oxbridge.

Smith looked at him, "What do you mean, John? It's a bloody cypher. That's what HM Government pays you and those boffins at Bletchley Park to do."

He smiled, "Look, you send me sixty-six letters copied down by a slip of a girl in Uxbridge and expect me to make sense of it?"

She turned to one side and put her brown shoes up on an upturned regulation civil service waste paper bin. She blew out some smoke.

"Come on, John, you can do better than that. We know the Abwher is about to send agents to Britain. This could be one of the first."

"I'm sure of it, old girl. But I need more than that to make head or tail of it…"

"Look, John, in a few months the whole service will be up to our eyes in rounding up so-called enemy aliens. Each bloody one has to be interviewed and categorised in front of a tribunal. We don't know where to start. If we can get a jump on Miss Hitler here, we might be able to persuade our lords and masters to give us a few extra resources."

He shook his head, "No can do. We're desperately trying to work out the codes that Jerry's using. We haven't got a clue what's coming out of Berlin at the moment, just garbled messages. The Cabinet Secretary is having kittens."

He paused, "Look, I'll tell you what. Bring me a decent transmission, and I'll get some of the chaps to look at it. That's about the best I can do at present. In the meantime, get Jenkins and those girls back on tracking German Military transmissions, especially those from the Luftwaffe. That's more important than some amateur spy planted in London by the Abwehr. For goodness' sake; we're still in the middle of some phoney war. There's nothing for German agents to report back to their bosses, and there won't be until the show kicks off. But if your boys get the radio, we wouldn't half mind a look at it…"

Smith sighed…."Pour me another drink, you old rascal."

A naked Maruska Bergman was propped up on one elbow looking at Peter Porteous as he snored gently. The church clock on the corner chimed one in the morning. She yawned as she traced little circles on his chest with her long fingers.

"Porteous," she spoke softly, "Porteous, wake up." She pressed a finger in more firmly.

He grunted, "Yes, yes, Maruska, I'm awake." His eyes were clamped shut.

Her hand went down below his waist, "Can you get me a bicycle?"

Chapter 11

September 1939
London
Rose

The cemetery was still very busy. It was a Sunday afternoon. Friends and relatives of the dearly departed were making the most of the unseasonably warm late September weather. It wouldn't last too much longer. The woman looked up at the dark clouds that were rolling in from the west; a sharp thunderstorm was definitely on the cards to remind Londoners that it wasn't just the war that was turning on them. She had been sitting on a bench that had an unobstructed view of the Dissenter's Chapel and its immediate surroundings. Her newly acquired Saxon ladies' bicycle was leaning against the side of the bench. A quick coat of paint disguised its origins from prying eyes. Her neighbour had kindly given the machine the once over and installed a front and rear carrier together with a set of battery-powered lights. If the actual owner of the bike happened across it purely by accident, she would never recognise her pride and joy upon which she had put one pound down and the rest at one pound a month for twelve months...

Rosemary McCumiskey looked up at the darkening skies. She had been on station for nearly two hours. She needed to relieve herself but was reluctant to vacate her vantage point. She was looking for the contact that would drop off a message in the dead letter box...

Protocol insisted that any message should not be left at the drop site more than two hours before pick up, although it didn't matter if the item was not collected for days. The handlers at training insisted on a rigorous adherence to rules, whatever the circumstances.

Rose squirmed on her seat. The clock on the Anglican Chapel, some two hundred yards away, chimed the three-quarters. The contact was late...She would have to abandon pretty soon and report back to Freda.

She watched as the visitors began to thin out. There had been a smattering of genuine mourners remembering some loved one from the past but most were couples glad to take in the late summer air away from prying eyes of families. Ladies clung on to their menfolk. Some were dressed in uniform as able-bodied men and women were taking up the call to arms. Rose watched as the occasional couple disappeared into the thick undergrowth and bushes for some amorous clinch or other.

She would give it till five o'clock and call it a day. She still had some items to sew at home for Madam Collier. A few minutes later, she spied her target. The contact was dressed in his Sunday best suit that was a little too short on the length. He had mutton chop greying whiskers and a pair of wire-rimmed glasses. Rose wondered what on earth had brought him to this position in life. It could be a mixture of incentives. For most, it was the promise of money. For some, it was ideological. They were the most dangerous, Rose thought, as the man hurried past her without even a glance in her direction.

She raised her eyebrows at his casualness trying to work out what had driven this man to fall into the arms of the madman, Adolf Hitler...

Rose stared down at her book but out of the corner of her eye she watched as the contact made straight for the drop-off point. He sat down, extracted a folded copy of The News of the World and began to read about vicars misbehaving with choirboys and the like...

He waited till the clock struck the quarter and then nonchalantly turned around to the wall behind the bench and removed the brick. He threw in an envelope, turned the brick and stood up, refolding his newspaper.

Rose felt the first drops of rain on her head...

There was a lot of movement in the cemetery as couples headed quickly for the main exit on the Harrow Road, not wishing to get completely soaked before supper. She tossed the hardback book into a basket bag that was placed on the front carrier and readied herself for leaving just as the man walked past her. His hands were thrust deep into his pockets. His head was down sharing eye contact with no one. She let him get fifty yards in front of her and then mounted the Saxon. Fortunately, her neighbour had found an old factory overall somewhere in the house. She had quickly altered it, shortening the sleeves and trousers. A leather belt wrapped around her slender waist disguised the man's size. Her outfit was completed by a headscarf wrapped as a turban. If anyone were to pay her any attention, they would see a factory girl out for some fresh air either before or after her shift. London was now teeming with similar factory girls as the war effort got into an extra gear.

The contact turned right at the Anglican Church and headed for the main exit on Harrow Road. She followed him at a safe distance as he went quickly up College Road. She watched as he turned up his collar in a vain attempt to keep out the rain. By this time, Rose had dismounted from the Saxon and was pushing it with one hand. In the other, she held a large umbrella that her lovely neighbour had loaned her for such eventualities as London's inclement weather.

He walked left onto Purves Road and crossed over to the side that borders the railway. She watched from under the umbrella as he entered building number 105. She gave him a minute and then pushed the Saxon past his house. It was a typical Victorian two-up two-down terraced house with a small front garden and, no doubt, a toilet in the rear yard...She went along to the end of the road and turned into Ravensworth Road. She walked back to the Harrow Road before she remounted the Saxon throwing the drenched umbrella into the back carrier bag. By this time, she was pretty much soaked through, but she wasn't bothered. The storm passed quickly. It took her about twenty minutes to get along to the Central Middlesex County Hospital. The evening turned warm as she pedalled along ignoring the catcalls of passing workmen.

She smiled at the gateman who was pretending to guard the main entrance to the hospital and managed to persuade him to mind her bicycle whilst she went to retrieve her precious cargo. The Garden of Repose was deserted. She quickly extracted the brown envelope from its place. It was slightly wet. She popped into the old infirmary and found the nearest toilet just before she added to the general dampness of her clothes...

The light was fading by the time she reached Wormwood Scrubs. The lights on the high, prison perimeter fence had come on illuminating the surrounding area. She pulled out the envelope from behind the brick, turned it casually glancing behind her.

The main gate to Kensal Green Cemetery was firmly locked by the time she got back. She wasn't bothered... She pushed the Saxon back down Ladbroke Grove and went along the towpath to the canal. Halfway along, she hid the bike in some bushes, removed the front light and climbed over the railings into the Cemetery. She was thankful for the comfort the dim lamp provided. Now, Rose was not normally a superstitious person, but there is something definitely disconcerting about walking through a deserted graveyard in the dark especially in sodden clothing...

She quickly located her envelope, turned the brick and departed for the warmth and security of her home.

She pushed the Saxon into the hallway and leaned it against the stairs. The house was quiet with the occupants mostly in The White Horse on Kensal Road at this time on a Sunday evening. She skipped up the stairs with the two carrier bags under her arm. She put an ear to the door of her neighbour's flat across the landing from hers, no sound; he wasn't in. She gently opened her front door and looked down to see if the hair had been moved from its place at the bottom of the frame indicating that someone had entered. It was still intact. A quick glance told her that all was well. She breathed a sigh of relief, went into the kitchen and boiled up some water on the gas stove.

She peeled off her wet clothes. She was sodden to the core. She stood in the old tin bath and poured hot water over her head several times scooping the water back up from the container. She dried herself off and pulled on the old overcoat that she used as a dressing gown; she really must get one of her own.

She flicked on the gas fire to help her dry off. Her wet clothes were slung over the wire gently steaming as the room warmed up. She tore open the envelopes. Her heart sank. It would take her a good two hours to code the messages before she transmitted them at midnight...

The house was quiet. Rose had heard some of the tenants return from the pub just after eleven. Most had work to go to in the morning. Rose listened to hear if her neighbour from across the landing had returned. She silently slid across the bolts of the door. Privacy is what she needed. Just before midnight, she rolled out the sewing machine and went through the process of setting up the radio. She wrapped the coat tightly around her body and sat on the chair. She flexed her fingers and waited for the church bell to chime...

This time, she broadcast for thirty seconds before stopping and selecting another wavelength. She managed to send five words in the allotted time. Halfway through, she paused, got up and made some tea. She went again to the door and listened; all was quiet.

It took her another fifteen minutes to complete her task. She watched as the paper with the handwritten code burned brightly in the hearth and sighed. This was not how her life was meant to be....

Over in Uxbridge, Henrietta Forbes-Carlton was not amused. After her amorous adventure with Flying Officer Rupert Hayes, she had been summoned to see Squadron Leader Norman Barton and been assigned to work with Cynthia Fleming for the foreseeable future. Now, Henrietta Forbes-Carlton didn't object to working with her roommate, it's just that the old dragon, Miss Atkins, really didn't like her and seemed to enjoy finding the slightest fault with either her work or her appearance. In addition, the shift change meant that she wouldn't be able to spend time with Rupert for a couple of weeks and there was that lovely party to attend down in Cobham...

The two of them sat in a corner of the Listening Room 3. Cynthia was locked on to the original wavelength and Hetty was working the airwaves, plus and minus ten degrees. Bletchley had told them that the transmitter was likely to be small and limited in what it could do. So, could they please listen carefully?

Since the original transmission, there had been nothing. Cynthia was getting bored. At least with the other work, messages from the German Reich were coming in all the time as the Nazi war machine got into full gear. The work of the telegraph girls was of national importance as Britain prepared itself for invasion...She had decided that it would be better to go back to normal duties.

The girls were deep into the eight-hour graveyard shift on the Sunday night. Cynthia looked over at Hetty who raised her eyebrows. Cynthia smiled. It was unusual to see her friend dressed in full regulation clothes. No chance of wearing silk stockings with the old dragon on the prowl.

At about one minute past midnight, Cynthia heard the first bleeps of the transmission. Her hand shot up to adjust the headphones. Hetty froze and looked at her. She instinctively sounded the warning bell, reached for her log and picked up a pencil. Miss Atkins looked up, nodded at the administrative assistant, who quickly ran off to fetch the officer of the day...

The first blast lasted thirty seconds. Cynthia quickly wrote down the numbers. Yes, it was definitely the same hand as before. This time, the keystrokes were much quicker, as though the operator had been practising. The blip on the screen stopped. Hetty looked up and mentally recorded the position of the second hand on the big wall clock. She moved the waveband dial, desperately trying to locate the next bandwidth, as the wireless operator would surely switch channels this time.

Sure enough, Hetty located the next signal at minus eight. This time, Cynthia sounded the warning bell. An aroma of lavender pervaded the air. Miss Atkins was behind them, she hissed,

"Don't miss anything, the pair of you, otherwise there'll be hell to pay."

Cynthia swallowed and thought, *'Just clear off, you old bat, we know what we are doing...'*

She felt Hetty's leg rub up against hers under the desk...a gentle wave of pleasure went through her body...

Whoever was transmitting was doing a good job. The thirty-second bursts were followed by a move to a new channel. The girls had to be quick to locate it and begin to transcribe.

After fifteen minutes, it all went quiet. Squadron Leader Norman Barton stood behind them reading the yellow chits, as Wing Commander William Jenkins flicked through them. He shook his head,

"Same as last time, Barton. Seemingly a random set of numbers."

Barton nodded as the transmission recommenced...

An hour later, Cynthia Fleming, Henrietta Forbes-Carlton, and Squadron Leader Norman Barton stood in the map room with Wing Commander William Jenkins. The Wing Commander asked,

"Cynthia, are you sure it was the same hand?"

She nodded, "Positive, sir. The operator is very competent. The bursts were much quicker, as though more information was sent to be within the allotted time."

He looked at the recently transcribed signals, "Are you sure these are blocks of numbers?"

"Definitely, sir. Whoever is transmitting is good but, I can read her."

He lit a cigarette looking at the digits, "I wonder what it all means?"

The girls shook their heads. This question was way beyond their pay grade. They were tasked in recording the messages, not decoding them. That was someone else's problem.

The door knocked and a young RAF corporal entered, smartly saluted the senior officers and said, "Sir, Hendon says they got a partial fix." He handed over an official note.

"Go back and check on the other stations."

The corporal saluted quickly and disappeared. Jenkins and Barton leaned over the large map on the table. Jenkins triangulated the signal from Hendon. He stubbed his finger on the chart,

"The bugger's somewhere here..."

His finger was on a very rundown part of northwest London known as Kensal Town...

In Hamburg, in the darkened offices of the German Military Intelligence, known as the Abwehr, a very hot and bothered Wehrmacht Auxiliary Jutta Meyer handed over a copy of some jumbled up letters to Gefreiter Rolf Bauer who immediately ran out of the room to go and talk to his bosses. It took some time for the tingling in her spine to subside…She would have to have a look at this lady's file…

The following Wednesday, The Honourable John Porter, lately of Corpus Christie College, Cambridge and now of Bletchley Park, sat in the MI5 office of the woman known as Miss Smith. He was sipping a large gin and tonic. His feet were up on the adjacent chair. He was clad in regulation, pin-striped trousers, crisp white shirt and golden cufflinks and a dark and very expensive jacket. A red silk handkerchief peeked out of his front breast pocket. The handkerchief matched his tie.

Dorothy Smith sat opposite him with her feet up on the upturned grey standard issue civil service wastepaper bin. She tapped the ash off her long, thin cigarette.

"Come on, John, the suspense is killing me…"

He snorted, "We know what it is, but we haven't a hope in hell of telling you what the messages are."

Smith shook her head, "Well?"

He sighed, put down his drink and pointed at the large sheet of paper on her desk. "Right, one of the boys cracked it. He's some kind of nutter with one of those super brains. He broke the record for the Times crossword on his application."

She snapped her fingers, "John, I don't want a potted history of one of your cypher boffins…"

He smiled, "Okay, Miss Smith, I'll try and explain in words of no more than two syllables…"

She laughed, "You're an incorrigible rogue, John Porter, just tell me.

He leaned over the sheet. "The beginning of each message has one of three common numbers. We think this is telling the receiver which code reference the number relates to. In our experience, this usually refers to a book. You see each of the transmissions, and there were nineteen in all, commences with a three digit number that contains either one, two or three."

He pointed to a transmission, "You'll note this one starts with 33, yet this one commences with 304. Likewise, all the other bursts start with a 1 or 2 somewhere in the number. Are you following me?"

She smirked at him. He continued, "The first subsequent number is a page number, the second is a line number and the third is the position of the word."

He picked up a copy of a Penguin edition of *Murder on the Orient Express* that lay on her desk and examined it with disdain, "Did you actually read this?"

She shook her head and smiled.

He went on, "So for example, if I wanted to send any word, I would simply find it somewhere in the book and write the page number, the line number and then the word number on the line. Here, let me show you."

He flicked through the paperback, stopped at a page, ran his finger down the side and quickly wrote 116, 23,and 7. He pushed over the paper. "What's the word?"

She found the word in less than five seconds, "*Morning*. It's that bloody simple?"

He shrugged his shoulders, "Yes, so simple that a child could master this. You don't need months of cypher training for this operation."

"So, without the books, it's virtually impossible to decode it?"

He sat back and sipped his drink, "Afraid so, old girl. Not a cat in hell's chance. Even if we figured out the books, we would need to know which edition was being used. The Abwehr could have set the agent up with thirty-odd books for all we know. The day or date of the month could determine which three are being used for the transmission."

"What language are we in?"

"I'd say English. Not too many German books knocking about these days, and you wouldn't exactly go into your local bookseller and order a copy of *Mein Kamph*, would you? But it is worth remembering that the agent could have slipped in with some books in her native language."

Dorothy Smith stared off into the distance, "Our best bet is to get the agent."

"Hmm, that's your bailiwick, I think. We'll just play with the code when you get it. There's enough of the other stuff coming in from Uxbridge to keep us busy for the next two years."

She raised her eyebrows, "Is that similar?"

He shook his head, "Nah, that's proper code; much more sophisticated." He paused as he took another sip, "What's your intelligence telling you?"

"We have a general area that we'd like to search, but it's presenting us with some difficulties. The tracking beacons are only accurate to within a couple of square miles. I'm trying to persuade our lords and masters to stump up the money for a mobile tracking van. If we could get one in the area, we'd have a better chance of a more accurate intersection."

She stood up and went to a map of London; he joined her. She poked a finger at Kensal Town and asked, "Do you know it?"

He shook his head, "Sorry, I only ever frequent the West End and Knightsbridge when I'm not in Whitehall."

"Well, it's not exactly a nice area." She traced her fingers along the map. "You see it's sandwiched between the Grand Union Canal on one side and the Great Western Railway on the other. The line runs down to Paddington. They have dogs in there that eat policemen."

He raised his eyebrows, "Hmm, as nice as that, eh?"

"Yes, we could swamp the area with security personnel, but it will only antagonise the locals, and we'd have a riot on our hands. The Permanent Secretary has instructed a softly, softly approach."

She stared at the map, "We do have an opening, though..."

"What's that, Dorothy?"

"The Census."

"What? I understood that it would be cancelled?"

She nodded, "Yes, but the enumerators have all been recruited and trained. I shouldn't be telling you this, but HM Government wants identity cards issued to every adult in the country."

He smiled, "Good luck with that..."

She continued, "There's no reason for the enumerators not to be out and about in the area. Even the fine, upstanding residents of Kensal Town will need an identity card to get a job, claim the dole or, when rationing comes in, which it surely will, buy their eight ounces of meat on a Friday. We can get a good idea about who is living there."

She said, "Pour me another drink, and I'll tell you my thinking."

They sat down; she continued, "There's one other thing that you should know. They are going to introduce a system for aliens, and that's falling to my boys and girls. Once the enumerators have done their initial sweep, we'll have an idea where all the foreigners are residing."

He interrupted, "I thought that was the responsibility of the police?"

She shook her head, "It is, but most of them can't be bothered. We did a check on one local police station and there's not one recorded visit of an alien since January." She leaned in, "Internment is coming."

He sipped his drink, "Quite right, we can't have these bloody foreigners wandering around without a care in the world when there's a war on."

She sighed; she could never tell when he was joking, "Every one of them will be categorised by a tribunal. Category C; no restrictions, Category B; some restrictions as to jobs, movements etc. and Category A; we lock 'em up in some faraway camp for the duration."

He raised his eyebrows. "You are presuming the person doing the transmitting is actually a foreigner." It was more of a question than a statement.

She nodded and went on, "Current thinking is that our elusive agent is a recent immigrant, so we are checking all the records in Ashford. He or she, and according to the girls in Uxbridge, it's probably a she, may have come through there, so there'll be a record of some sorts."

He snorted, "How many have passed through those pearly gates since it opened?"

She shook her head, "Too many, John, but we've got to do something. If we sweep up all the aliens in Kensal Town, we can sweat them. Given the nature of the area, we don't think there'll be too many. We are doing a cross-check with the local police stations."

"Hmm, makes sense. What are you going to do if you get this person?"

"Current policy is to turn them. They could be very useful."

"I'd put them on the end of rope...Bloody cheek. Coming over here and sabotaging our war effort."

She spoke quietly, "Word from up high is that if the Germans invade, we've got little chance."

He nodded, "Yes, we've got contingency plans in place to blow up everything at Bletchley."

He drained the last of his drink, "Come on, old girl, fancy a spot of dinner down at Luigi's before he gets interned?"

She laughed, "Let me get my coat..."

Chapter 12

September 1939
London
Rose

Rose was late for her meeting. She cycled furiously up the hill towards Kensal Rise. The day was still young; the Indian summer was still casting its benevolent warmth on this part of London. She turned right onto Harvist Road and on towards the park. She would get an ear bashing if she was late.

She wheeled the Saxon towards the bandstand and sat down on the bench. She extracted her book and pretended to read. If anyone noticed her, she was just an ordinary factory girl taking a break.

Freda approached, what was it? *Leash in the left hand meant all is well. Leash in the right hand meant return twenty-four hours later...*

The dogs were pulling at her left hand...

The woman sat down and stared ahead, "You were nearly late..."

Rose nodded as she turned a page in the book. "I'm here and not late."

Freda hissed, "Keep to your agreed schedules..."

Rose turned another page.

The tone softened, "I like the outfit. Very fetching..."

Rose tried hard to identify the accent. "Thank you, I didn't give it much thought. Most of the girls where I live dress like this."

There was a pause in the conversation as two women walked past, chattering away.

Freda spoke quietly, "The transmissions all went well on Sunday. Now, keep radio silence until further instructions. Check your drop points as per normal. If anything comes in, I'll give you instructions. Do you understand?"

Rose nodded imperceptibly. Freda went on, "Return here every week as agreed. I'll only come if I have instructions for you, otherwise carry on with your life. I've seen a copy of the new identity card. It's nothing we can't deal with."

She stood up, pulling the dogs towards her, "Wait for fifteen minutes and check your surroundings."

With that, the woman known as Freda was gone.

Rose watched her out of the corner of her eye as she went back up past the bandstand and out through the exit on Kingswood Avenue and Chevening Road. As soon as she had exited the park, Rose stood up, grabbed the Saxon and walked quickly after her. Rose followed at a safe distance as Freda went onto Willesden Lane. Rose nearly lost her on the crowded Kilburn High Road, but Freda's red hat singled her out. Twenty minutes later, Rose watched as Freda entered a mansion block on Abbey Road in St John's Wood.

Rose stood there for a while pondering the next course of action. Eventually, she wheeled the Saxon into the driveway of the block and up to the outside door. On the left of the entrance was a range of doorbells. Each number had a name typed next to it. She ran her fingers down the nameplates and shook her head. There was nothing that could identify Freda. A voice sounded in her ear. She turned to see a General Post Office deliveryman in his uniform. He was pushing a regulation Post Office bicycle. The front rack was heavy with a brown sack of letters.

"Can I help you, Miss?" he asked.

Rose thought quickly, "Yes, the lady with the two dogs, I have a message for her and I can't remember her number."

He leaned his bike against the wall and rummaged in his sack, "Oh, that'll be Mrs Cranford, flat number ten on the top floor. I just love those two dogs."

He held out his hand, "I can take it up for you if you like?"

Rose shook her head, "No, it's all right, I was told to hand it to her personally."

The postman shook his head; "Suit yourself. Make sure you pull the door closed when you come in. The lift is on the right. Leave your bike next to mine; no one will trouble it. I'll start on the ground floor and work up." He looked at his sack, "Too many bloody letters today..."

With that, he was gone inside. Rose entered the vestibule and waited till the postman had disappeared down the corridor. She quickly went back out and rode away.

The woman known as Rose, went up to Queens Park every week at the allotted time for the next few weeks, as the Phoney War gathered pace. She never saw Freda once. The dead letter boxes were checked religiously on a regular basis; nothing new materialised.

Rose turned her attentions to sewing and making decent money for her future...

In late September, early one morning, the Census enumerator knocked on the door. Rose was down in Chelsea trying to fit a size fourteen woman into a size twelve set of pure, silk lingerie.

Martha Cunningham, the landlord's appointee gatekeeper to the tenement block, stood in the doorway with her arms folded. A cigarette was stuck to one corner of her mouth. The enumerator, a small, mousy looking female in her early forties looked at her, nervously. She held out a printed card.

"Good morning, madam, I am sorry to bother you, but I need some details about who lives in the house."

Cunningham looked bored, "I tell you what, sweetie, I'm a little busy at the moment. Can you come back later?"

The enumerator was taken aback. She hadn't really wanted Kensal Town as an assignment, but you get what you are given, don't you?

She stammered, "It-it-it won't take long. I just need some information so that we can issue the identity cards. I have the details of who was here ten years ago during the last census, if that will help?"

Cunningham leaned against the door and blew out some cigarette smoke. She knew the identity cards would be important for getting rations.

"Oh, very well, then."

The enumerator smiled; she flicked through the papers on her clipboard. "I'll only be a few minutes; let me see. Ah, yes, I've found it. Last time there were six occupants in residence here. If I call out their names we can just tick them off and that's all we'll need."

Cunningham sighed, "Go on then."

"Right, Mr Marsden?"

"Left five years ago. Got a job on the railways in Swindon."

"Mr Prentice?"

"Ran off with his fancy lady after her husband threatened to kill him...He owes a month's rent."

The enumerator swallowed as she ticked the name off the list... Miss Proctor?

"Died of alcoholic poisoning, sorry."

"How about Mr Webster, Alfred Webster?"

"Got five years in Wandsworth for grievous bodily harm. His stuff is still in the basement...He owes rent as well..."

The enumerator sighed, "Who is living here now, Mrs, Mrs....?"

"Cunningham, Mrs Cunningham; me husband passed away four years ago. Fell in the canal one night, pissed as a lord...silly old fool..."

"Yes, well, I'm sorry to hear of your bereavement." She traced her pencil down the paper, "I see you are still on the list?"

"Yes, although I'll bugger off toutey suitey if the Jerries start bombing. Got me sister down in Penzance."

"Who is here then?"

"Let me think, okay. There's old Mrs Hardcastle next to me on the ground floor. Not much use in talking to her; she's deaf as a post. I'd have to knock to see if she made it through the night..."

The enumerator cleared her throat.

"And then on the first floor, there's Mr Blunt and Mr Watson..." The enumerator scribbled furiously. "And on the top floor there's Porteous and a new lady; a doctor, so I've heard, one of them refugees. I believe she's a Jew."

Cunningham folded her arms and looked at the enumerator who asked, "Are any of the tenants at home?"

Cunningham shook her head, "How should I know?"

"Would it be all right if I came in and knocked on their doors?" the enumerator asked timidly.

Cunningham shrugged her shoulders and stood to one side. She flicked the cigarette end out onto the street. "Sure...help yourself. I'll go and see if Mrs Hardcastle is still alive..."

The enumerator left about twenty minutes later having identified four out of the six residents in Bosworth Road and left forms for the two missing residents on the top floor to complete, promising to bring the new identity cards back at a later date...

The following week, Rose sat with the woman known as Freda on the bench in Queen's Park. Freda asked, "Is it all going well?"

Rose stared at two young children playing about fifty yards in front of her, "Yes although Madam Collier's husband is getting a little too familiar."

"Hmm, that's to be expected...Is there anything in the house?"

"I'm not sure. When I'm there, I work with the madam in the sewing room. She's actually very good at what she does; she has a keen eye for detail, but I did notice that he carries a brown leather briefcase with him wherever he goes."

Freda thought for a moment, "He's something in the Admiralty, but we're not sure. If you get a chance then have a look but don't take risks until we find out exactly what he does. Transmitting is your prime job."

She paused as an elderly couple went past.

"You have a pick-up on Wednesday afternoon after three o'clock from the hospital. Don't transmit it; just bring it to me. There'll be the usual drops on Sunday, don't transmit those either. After your last long transmission we have instructions to stay silent. I'll get these messages sent by another way. Do you understand?"

Rose nodded. Freda reached into her bag and handed over a new brown identity card with her name, age, address and occupation. Rose examined the card discreetly. The folded front cover announced that it was the National Registration Identity Card. It already had the authentication stamp...Her first name had been anglicised to Rosemary.

Freda whispered, "Make sure you sign it when you get home. When the enumerator returns, you may get one in your other name, but I think they'll leave you with your alien card. Use this one when you are out and about. There will be less questions from the police."

Rose tucked it into her handbag. Freda stood up pulling the dogs with her, "Next week..."

Chapter 13

October 1939
London
Belina

Belina Candido was not happy. She was not used to this cloak and dagger work. It was so far removed from her daytime job back in Lisbon at the German Embassy where she had been employed as a local interpreter. She had been officially transferred to the Portuguese Embassy in London under the orders of some high-ranking government official anxious to please their German friends and partners.

Unfortunately, not many of the other diplomats in Belgrave Square, the home of the Portuguese London Embassy, appreciated Belina Candido. She was mistrusted by nearly everyone, partly because of her connections to the German Embassy in Lisbon, but mostly because she hadn't come up through the usual diplomatic channels. Her nominal position as Assistant Cultural Secretary meant little, if anything, to the ambassador. It did mean that he was not to question her or query her role. It was just as well because Belina Candido didn't really have a role that could be defined. It also allowed her to spend little time in her pokey office somewhere in the attic in Belgrave Square.

However, her diplomatic status and passport allowed her to go where she wanted and when she wanted, in the guise of promoting cultural exchanges between British and Portuguese universities and other academic organisations.

It was Wednesday. She had returned late the day before from Southampton on the south coast of England. It was fortunate that she had a good memory because her handlers had drummed into her the need to memorise and not write anything down until the last minute and then get rid of the incriminating document as soon as possible.

The weather had turned. She lay in bed in her flat in Bayswater. She hadn't slept well with her mind full of details. The house was quiet as it was after nine and the other lodgers had long since departed for work. She took a deep breath and forced herself out of her bed. She went up to the window. She could see activity in Kensington Gardens; little matchstick men and women going about their daily business. She walked over to the mahogany wardrobe and looked to see what she could wear.

'Be smart but casual. Try not to bring attention to yourself...'

'What does that mean?' she thought. '*Smart but casual*?'

She sighed and closed the door as the kettle whistled on the two-ring gas stove. She turned it off and poured some boiling water on the last of her Portuguese coffee. She would have to drink that muck the English called coffee for now or at least until more came into the Embassy.

She dropped a sixpence into the gas heater and ran water into a deep bath in the adjacent bathroom. That had been her only stipulation; the accommodation in London had to have its own bathroom...

She lay in the bath with her arms resting on the side. A radio played on the little shelf just above her under the window. She was only supposed to listen to broadcasts from the BBC but the temptation to listen to some of the swing music from America was too great. Her toes moved up and down to the beat of the song.

Today was the day. She sighed again. There would be many more of these assignments before they would let her back to Portugal and her family unless she did something about it...

Keeping to protocol, Belina Candido exited from the taxi outside the Central Middlesex County Hospital just before one o'clock. She had finally decided to wear a dark blue dress with some black-laced shoes and tan stockings. Her beige raincoat made her unremarkable as per the instructions from her trainers. She had spent about thirty minutes writing down her message. She was trained well. She could précis one hundred words down to thirty and not lose any of the salient facts. Who needed adverbs or adjectives? Her talent for languages had earmarked her out for this particular assignment.

She walked past the gatehouse and smiled at the uniformed attendant. He doffed his hat at the pretty woman and watched her as she walked confidently off towards the hospital building.

She glanced up at the old clock tower; she was well within the time frame. She walked up the steps into the entrance hall to be hit by the strong smell of disinfectant; she wrinkled her nose. Hospitals had never been on her list of favourite places to visit. She had been trained to walk with an air of confidence; no one would challenge her during the afternoon visiting hours.

She walked on through the building and out into the garden of repose. She looked around. A few of the pergolas were occupied with white-coated men and nurses in full uniform out to grab a quick smoke. Her destination was occupied. Two women in their early thirties were engaged in a deep, furtive conversation. Berlina walked past them; they stopped talking. She sat down under the next pergola and took out a hardback book and began to read.

As soon as the two women left, Berlina changed places. The garden began to empty out as a hand bell sounded the end of visiting. Cigarette ends were carelessly tossed onto the paving stones of the semicircular pathway. She waited until the garden was nearly empty before she stood up and put her foot on the bench as though she was retying her shoelace. Quickly, she inserted the envelope and turned the brick as per instructions. She straightened up, smoothed down her skirt and walked slowly back towards the building. She entered through the rear door and went up the back stairs to the third floor.

She pulled a chair up to the window and sat down. She had a perfect view of the garden and all who visited...

Rose

Rose had been sitting in the garden for nearly an hour before she spied her target. She had on a white laboratory coat that she had donned during a brief visit to the ladies' toilet when she had arrived earlier. She had a book on her lap pretending to read. Although her eyes skimmed over the words, few, if any, had meaning. She stifled a yawn, cursing that she had not had much sleep the night before. Her lover had been quite demanding, although she secretly enjoyed every minute of the encounter. She heard him as he left just after dawn in the morning, whistling as he went down the wooden staircase and off to wherever he did his business.

After he departed, she dozed off before the church clock demanded she make something of her day; she had important work to do...

Rose spotted the well-dressed woman as soon as she entered the garden. She sank further down into the seat and raised her book up closer to her face. She had to admit, the handlers were good at selecting their operatives

The woman in the dark blue dress and beige coat flicked her long, dark hair as she looked around furtively. Rose thought she was good but not that good. Rose watched carefully as the woman slipped over to the drop-off pergola. She raised her eyebrows as the letter was inserted into the space behind the brick.

Rose stood up and went back into the hospital. There was only one way out and that was along the main corridor and back out through the main entrance. Rose straightened her skirt under the laboratory coat and stood pretending to read the notices on the old pin board. These were familiar to her. She noted lists of professors asking for volunteers and the usual array of courses for doctors and nurses alike together with rooms to let or requests for accommodation.

The female came up the steps into the entrance hall. Rose expected the woman to walk past her and along the corridor towards the main entrance. Her plan was to follow the operative and establish her identity and location for future reference. Instead, the woman tuned immediately left and began to climb the stairs. Rose looked up to see her pause on the landing between the ground and the first floor. The woman peered out of the window and then continued.

Rose went to the staircase with her hands deep into the pockets of the laboratory coat. She silently went up the stairs following the operative. By the time she got to the third floor landing, the woman was sitting by the window on one of the chairs that was used by staff on a quick break from the wards.

Rose didn't look at her as she passed by and along the short corridor and through the swing doors. She looked back through the porthole windows of the door. The woman had not moved as she continued to stare out of the window and onto the garden.

Rose swallowed nervously; this was not what she had expected. Why had the operative not simply left the hospital grounds as soon as she had deposited the envelope?

There could only be one reason; the person who was to be hunted had turned into the hunter and Rose had no intention of becoming the prey. She looked again through the porthole. The woman had extracted a cigarette. Rose watched as her immaculately manicured fingers and hands used a gold lighter. A matching case was in her other hand. She slipped the case back into her handbag and breathed out the smoke. Rose sat down on one of the chairs that appeared to be a waiting area for some clinic or other.

Rose waited until two men each wearing the obligatory white coats approached her, chatting away. One of them nodded at her; she smiled back coyly. She quickly followed them as they pushed through the swing doors. Their voices echoed on the stairwell. The woman barely glanced up from her book as three white-coated individuals went past. She didn't even notice the woman trailing closely behind.

Rose turned left onto the second floor, leaving her two guides none the wiser as they continued their animated conversation. She stopped by the doors. There were three chairs carefully stationed under the stairs. She went into the comparative darkness of the place, brushed away some cigarette ends and sat down and began her wait...

It was close to five o'clock in the afternoon before the woman left her observation post. Numerous cigarette ends had been carelessly stubbed out on the floor. Rose watched her as she went back down the stairs, along the corridor and out through the main entrance. The light was beginning to fade and there was a chill in the air. Rose quickly removed her white coat, folded it and placed it into her bag. She would return for the message in the pergola tomorrow. She didn't need it until her meeting with Freda on Friday, as there was to be no transmission. Rose fastened up the buttons of her navy jacket. The woman was fifty yards in front of her along the drive. Rose quickened her step. She was thankful that she had left her precious Saxon at home.

As she turned out into Acton Lane, Rose slowed. The woman was waiting patiently in a bus queue. Rose walked on past her and joined the line thankful that the queue was busy with chatting office girls having just been released from their secretarial duties for the day. The bus came along a few minutes later. The woman climbed the steps to the top floor so that she could smoke. Rose sat on a bench seat by the step.

Two buses later, Rose walked along Bayswater Road thankful that the journey had occurred during the busy rush hour, the threat of war or not...She stood against the railings of Kensington Gardens and watched as the woman went up the steps of a Georgian terraced house in Lancaster Gate. Rose quickly crossed the busy road and ran along the pavement. The house was in darkness. A light came on the top attic; Rose sighed. She approached the house and went up the steps. She looked at the nameplates. There were several. Fortunately, the bells appeared to be in descending order. She stuck her finger next to the top name; Miss Berlina Candido...

Rose turned as three women came up behind her,

"Are you looking for someone?" asked one of them.

Rose smiled, "Yes, Miss Candido."

The woman raised her eyes, "Her? You'll find her on the top floor, the attic flat."

She held the door open for Rose. The women entered and stood chatting at the bottom of the stairs. Rose quietly climbed the stairs as she could hear doors to the flats closing noisily.

Rose was breathing deeply as she reached the top flat. The door was highly polished. She wondered who was paying the rent on this upmarket flat. She slowed down her breathing and leaned her ear against the door. She could hear the faint sounds of some American music in the background.

She tried the doorknob. It turned slowly and silently. She stopped, letting the knob return to its resting place. She reached under her skirt and unclipped a stocking. She rolled it down her leg, shook off a shoe and pulled it off. The hosiery went straight into a pocket of her jacket. She extracted a pair of fine, white cotton gloves from her handbag. She polished the brass door with her hand, removing any traces of her fingerprints.

The door opened silently. Rose could hear the soft voice of a woman singing along to the words of the swing song. She could also hear splashing of water...

Rose looked around her. Berlina Candido's clothes were carelessly strewn across the living room floor. Her foot touched some expensive, silk underwear. Rose bent down and picked up the French knickers. She raised her eyebrows; the lingerie was of good quality. The intricate design of the lace trimming was impressive...

Rose peered through the bathroom door. Berlina Candido was laying back in the roll top bath with her arms outstretched on the sides. Her eyes were shut tightly. Rose could see her fingers tapping to the rhythm of the music of the electric radio that was sitting above the bath on a shelf under the frosted window. Slowly, she approached the woman. She could see her full breasts bobbing in the warm water. The breasts had protruding dark nipples. Rose could see a mass of dark hair below her waist.

She sat on the edge of the bath, calmly took off her white cotton gloves and reached over and placed her hand firmly on Candido's head. She pushed violently. The woman submerged and began to struggle. Rose reached over and placed her other hand on the naked womam's head. Candido's legs began to thrash about as water splashed over the side and onto the tiled floor.

Rose released the pressure. The woman came up gasping and spluttering for breath. She looked at Rose with wild eyes.

Rose put a finger to her lips, indicating that the woman remain silent. The woman opened her mouth to speak. Rose pushed the head down again and this time held it for longer.

The woman came up; she didn't look too well. Rose reached over to the radio and turned up the volume slightly. She put a finger to her lips. The woman nodded violently.

Rose spoke quietly in German...

"Who are you?"

The woman swallowed nervously; she began to answer in English.

Rose sighed and shoved her back under the water.

The woman gasped again as she came up for air....Rose hissed, "German, please..."

Berlina Candido nodded vigorously.

"Let's try again, shall we, Berlina?"

Candido closed her eyes. She had been told it might come to this. She answered in German.

"You know my name already. I work at the Portuguese Embassy."

Rose asked, "What is your work?"

"I'm-I'm-I'm an assistant cultural secretary," she stammered.

Rose smiled, "What does that mean?"

"I help to arrange visits between British and Portuguese universities."

Rose snorted, "What's your real job, Berlina?"

The woman stammered again, "I-I-I don't know what you mean?"

Rose stood up and pushed the woman back under the water with both hands. As she held the woman under, she thought she recognised the tune. Her lover was always listening to this music, although she couldn't see what all the fuss was about. She released the pressure. Berlina Candido emerged from the water gasping for breath.

"Okay, okay. I'll tell you but don't push me under the water again."

Rose smiled; this was easier than she thought.

"I watched you plant the envelope. You were supposed to leave but you didn't. Instead, you thought you would lie in wait for someone to collect it, and then what, Berlina? What are your instructions?"

Candido shook her head, "I don't have any instructions; I-I-I just wanted to see who would pick it up."

"Well, Senhorita Berlina Candido, you are looking at her."

The woman's eyes opened wide in alarm, "Look, I meant no harm."

Rose's eyes blazed, "You broke protocol and by doing so you placed me in danger. Now you might like working for the Nazis, but I don't. Do you know what the British do to agents of the Third Reich?"

The woman shook her head; Rose went on, "Well they don't take kindly to spies. I hear they are very good at extracting information from a pretty girl like you. Do you think it's just our mutual friends in the Gestapo that don't care about the Geneva Convention? The British are masters of it. If they take you, you'll disappear into the system never to emerge again." Rose paused.

The woman began to cry. Rose shook her head and spoke more softly in English, "How did they get you?"

The woman sobbed, "I was working as a translator in the German Embassy. They took my little sister. They are keeping her in a convent outside Lisbon. They will release her upon my return."

Rose asked, "Why did you not go to the authorities? Portugal is supposed to be neutral?"

"A senior member of the Portuguese government is a Nazi. I was told he could make life difficult for my family if I didn't cooperate. We don't have much, and my mother is ill. She requires expensive hospital treatment."

Rose could understand this; "What was your plan today?"

"I-I-I don't know. I just wanted to see who would pick up the message."

Rose asked, "What's in the message?"

"Information about the building of the British fighter plane, the Spitfire."

Rose nodded, "Ah, yes. The plane that's going to save the British from the oncoming slaughter...Where did you get it?"

"I went down to Southampton. There are some factories down there, but they are clearing them out in case they are to be bombed. The new dispersal factories are dotted around the town in converted premises. I managed to locate three of them."

"Do you know why the information is not to be transmitted?"

"I-I-I don't know..."

"Who's your handler?"

"Some woman. I meet her every Thursday in Kensington Gardens."

"What's her name?"

"She calls herself Mirna."

"Describe her..."

"About my height, glamorous with dyed blonde hair; always well-dressed. She never goes anywhere without her two dogs..."

Rose stiffened up, "What do you know about her?"

"She's Ustaše."

"What? Those fascist fanatics from Yugoslavia?"

"She is Croatian. Her husband is a big noise in the army. They are planning to let Hitler take over so they can impose their warped ideology. They are intent in killing all the damn Jews in their country."

Rose stiffened, "How do you know this?"

"She came here once bringing her dogs and a bottle of brandy. She drank herself into a stupor and fell asleep on my bed."

"Why is she in London?"

"She claims it is all a result of her husband's mistress who wanted to get her out of the way. Her husband believes she'll never make it through the war."

Rose stood up and walked around the small bathroom.

Berlina Candido asked, "Can I get out of the bath, the water's cooling off."

Rose shook her head, "When did you last see her?"

"Thursday, she always turns up."

"Where are your notes from your visit to Southampton?"

"I burnt them."

"When is your next drop?"

"When I have some more information. I'm supposed to go to the main factory in Birmingham next week, but it's getting more and more difficult to travel."

Rose sat back on the bath, "What happens if you get taken or you don't make it?"

"They told me my family would be well looked after."

Rose snorted, "Okay, Senhorita Berlina Candido, is that all the information you have for me?"

"Yes, yes, I swear."

Rose leaned in, "Do you have an issue with Jews?"

"Well, they've trying to take over aren't they?"

Rose shook her head...She reached into her bag and took out the stocking. She calmly sat on the end of the bath and rolled it back over her leg. She stood up, lifted her skirt and clipped it back into place. She peeled back on the white gloves. Berlina Candido looked on; her arms were firmly crossed over her chest. She shivered. She was beginning to get cold.

Rose sat back on the edge of the bath and sighed, "I was going to strangle you with my stocking, but they are never the same after; they seem to stretch out of shape and silk ones are getting harder to obtain"...she thought of her neighbour across the landing who always seemed to be able to lay his hands on anything she requested...

Berlina Candido began to shake whether it be through cold or fear, Rose couldn't tell. Either way she couldn't be bothered.

Rose reached over and tipped the electric radio into the bath. Berlina Candido thrashed about wildly as two hundred and forty volts of angry electricity coursed through her body. The hot radio valves hissed in the water as the plug shot out of the socket with a bang.

Rose stood up as the fizzling water subsided. Berlina Candido slowly sank into the water with her eyes wide open... She stood over the bath looking down at the woman whose hair floated out behind her head. Rose sighed; this was a good-looking woman. What a waste...still, she mused; her family would now be safe...

It was nearly midnight before Rose left. She carefully looked through the apartment. She found some jewellery and some natural pearls. These went into her bag along with a yellow pad upon which Candido had transcribed her latest message. More importantly, she had found the stationery that the woman had used for the message drops. She lifted the pad and envelopes. She had waited until all the residents had either gone to bed or were safely tucked away in their rooms. She crept down the stairs and out onto Bayswater Road. It took two attempts to hail a taxi. None of the drivers wanted to go up to the Ha'penny Steps...

Chapter 14

November 1939
London
Rose

Rose didn't see Freda for nearly a month, although she had the envelope from the deceased Berlina Candido. Curiosity got the better of her and, sitting up in bed late one night, she slit open the message. It was, as she noted, a couple of hundred words of detailed notes regarding the transferring of Spitfire manufacturing to smaller workshops in the Southampton area. She stared at the typescript, pondering whether she should make some subtle alterations but decided it would be too dangerous. She slipped the note back into one of the envelopes she had removed from the flat in Bayswater.

Rose could feel the cold wind snapping at her legs as she rode up to Queen's Park for her regular Friday rendezvous even though she had on the factory girls' uniform which she much preferred when on the bicycle.

Freda approached her and, throwing caution to the wind, sat down immediately and began talking.

"Did you get the message from the hospital?"

Rose snapped back, "I've been carrying it around for weeks. Where have you been? I nearly destroyed it."

Freda stared into the distance, "There's been a problem."

"Yes, the problem is that I've been carrying around a death sentence in an envelope."

"We've lost an agent."

Rose went quiet, waiting for Freda to continue.

Freda continued, "There won't be any more pick-ups from the Hospital."

Rose smiled to herself, "Oh, that's a pity. I quite liked going up there."

"The stupid idiot electrocuted herself in the bath..."

Rose raised her eyebrows as Freda went on; "It took us months to get that silly girl into place, and now it's all been wasted. Our masters are not at all pleased."

Rose asked, "What do you want me to do? I'm only trained as a wireless operator."

Freda shook her head, "Nothing, nothing. Stick to what you know best."

Rose shrugged her shoulders; "It's just as well, as I'm not clear about what else I could do."

Freda took the envelope and it disappeared into her bag. Rose asked, "Are you sure you don't want me to send this message?"

"I'm absolutely positive. We have other ways of communicating. Maintain radio silence."

Freda leaned in, "You have a pickup at Wormwood Scrubs tonight. Ten o'clock; don't be late. Bring the message back here tomorrow..."

With that, she was gone, pulling her reluctant dogs with her. Rose sighed; she had been hoping for an evening of peace and quiet with her lover across the landing...

The smell emanating from the prison was particularly unpleasant that evening. Blustery showers rained down from on high. Rose hid in the darkness of a disused building across the playing fields. She tried to brush off as much of the rain as possible, but it seemed a lost cause. The Saxon was resting just inside the dilapidated building that was once a changing room for the footballers on the playing fields of the Scrubs. The wind couldn't seem to be able to make up its mind as to which direction it was coming from. Riding up a small incline with the rain driving into your face is certainly not something to be recommended. The scarf on her head was sodden; she pulled it off and flapped away some of the moisture. Her hair was damp. She tied it back and smoothed out the wrinkles before she replaced the scarf.

Some movement in the alley between the prison and the hospital attracted her attention. She peered into the gloom. It looked like two people clamped together for some nefarious reasons. The female was wearing a white headscarf that stood out in the yellow street light. She sighed; longing for the warm bed she shared with her lover.

Just before midnight, Rose had had enough. The two hours had allowed her to observe the same woman with three different customers...She raised her eyebrows thinking there must be some good trade to be had in the local pubs.

She wheeled the Saxon over to the drop-off point and leaned it against the wall. She pulled out the brick and felt inside; there was nothing. Rose's heart skipped a beat...

She replaced the brick, and spun around looking to see if there was anyone else in the vicinity. She swallowed hard as her mind began to race. She reached for the bike when she heard a voice,

"Stay where you are!"

The voice was female, "Don't move!"

Rose breathed in deeply as the white-scarfed female came into view. She hissed, "You've been set up..."

Rose's eyes darted from side to side, desperately trying to work out what she should do. She felt a hand on her arm.

"It's okay. They are waiting for you in the alley between the prison and the hospital." The accent was definitely Irish.

Rose asked, "Who are 'they?'"

"Local thugs. They have no idea who you are. One of the warders from the prison hired them to get rid of you. You'll end up in the canal before the night is through, slit from head to toe, that is, after they have had their fun with you and, looking at you, they'll have lots of it…"

Rose looked at her, "How do you know?"

"Jesus; just feckin listen. I spend my life servicing those bastards from the prison. I don't know who are the biggest criminals, the warders or prisoners. I work the Prince of Wales public house."

"Who is the warder?" asked Rose.

"Big, old, ugly bastard with a chrome dome."

"What?"

"Chrome dome, bald man…"

"What's his name?"

"Charles Wilson, senior officer and a bully as well, especially when he's drunk."

Rose looked over at the alley, "How many of them?"

The woman looked back, "Three. They carry flick knives and coshes. If they don't cut you, they'll crack your skull before tossing you into the canal."

Rose asked, "Why are you helping me?"

The woman shrugged her shoulders, "Dunno, really. Wilson owes for the beating he gave me recently. I don't mind a bit of rough, it's to be expected in my line of business, but he goes too far. Damn near strangled me. If it wasn't for one of the girls rescuing me, I'd be pushing up daisies in some feckin field…"

Rose had to work that one out…She asked,

"What do I do?"

"Walk across the Scrubs. It's pretty dark and they'll never find you. Head straight towards the railway line; when you reach it, turn right and follow the tracks. There are some steps up onto Scrubs Lane. You can find your way from there."

Rose nodded, "Thank you. Do they know who I am?"

"Nah; they were just told to look for a woman dressed in a boiler suit wheeling a bike."

Rose reached over, "What's your name?"

The woman laughed, "Marie, at least that's what I tell my customers."

"Well, Marie, I owe you..."

"For fecks' sake get on your way before they come lookin' for yer."

"What about you?"

"Don't worry about me. I can take care of myself." She lifted her skirt; a large knife was strapped across her thigh just below the top of her stocking.

Rose smiled, "Thank you...I'll see you soon..."

"I'm countin' on it...."

It took Rose nearly twenty minutes to push and half carry the Saxon up to the railway line and off the open space in the dark. By the time she reached the road, she was covered in mud and looked a sorry sight. She mounted the bike and rode home; she had had a near miss, and she didn't like it.

After a good soak standing in the tin bath, Rose retired to bed. She found it difficult to sleep with all the thoughts going through her head. There would be no romance that night. She had to formulate a plan of action and carry it out to protect her future.

Rose kept clear of Queen's Park on Friday. After all, she was supposed to be dead and the woman known as Freda would not be expecting her. Rose had other plans...

It was gone midnight when Rose approached the mansion block in St John's Wood, the home of her contact, Freda. She had made an excuse to her lover and left on the Saxon. He wasn't too bothered;

she never actually stayed the whole night with him, preferring to sleep in her own bed. At least, that was what she told him...

Abbey Road was quiet, as though the world favoured staying behind closed doors in an attempt to prepare for the onset of real war and not the phoney one that was going on at present. As she rode past a parade of shops, she caught sight of a policeman shaking hands with some of the shop doors. She noticed he was surreptitiously smoking a cigarette that was cupped in his hand. He glanced up at her and then went back to his futile pursuit.

The night was cold but dry. She had on her overalls. A navy silk scarf covered her head and part of her face. A black, leather bag was strapped across her shoulders. She leaned the Saxon against the railings of the block opposite where the woman she knew as Freda lived. The bike was hidden under some unkempt bushes. A passer-by could not have seen it...

Rose walked up to the mansion block. There was a small light over the door. Rose was surprised it had not yet been removed under the rigorous blackout regulations, but these rules only ever impacted upon the rich when they were absolutely necessary. During her previous visit, Rose had noticed that there were some steps at the back of the ground floor. She didn't bother to try the front door. She walked quietly around the side of the building. Her shoes crunched on the gravel. At the rear of the building, she found what she was looking for. The back door was sandwiched between two large dustbins. She pushed gently on the door; it opened.

As she went up the stairs, she could hear music and other signs of life from the flats. She leaned into the door of number 10 on the top floor. She couldn't hear anything. She tried the door handle; it was locked. She bent down and slowly opened the letterbox. She started back suddenly. One of the dogs was peering up at her with its tail wagging furiously. Its mate quickly joined it. They started whining and looking up at the door as though they were expecting something pleasant.

Rose pinned herself to the side of the door. The woman known as Freda stirred from the couch with a drink in her hand, She spoke in Croatian.

"What is the matter with you two? Is that cat from across the way teasing you?"

The dogs looked up expectantly. They would enjoy nothing better than to chase the feline around the top floor...

Rose heard the bolts of the door slide back; she braced herself as she slid on a pair of white cotton gloves.

The door opened halfway. Rose quickly barged against it. One of the dogs yelped as its foot got caught in the ensuing melee. Freda's glass went crashing to the floor. The crystal shattered into thousands of tiny pieces. Rose had her hands around the neck of the woman as she pushed her back through the door. She stopped and used her foot to shut the door behind her. The dogs ran for cover; they were not used to this. Rose shoved the woman back along the hallway and into the living room. The smell of cheap alcohol was in the air. She pushed the Croatian back onto the sofa and hissed in English.

"Stay there and don't make a sound..."

Freda looked up at her and sighed, "I thought you were dead?"

Rose smiled, "Obviously not, much to your disappointment, I presume."

Freda shrugged her shoulders, "I don't care either way. They'll come for you regardless of what happens now."

"What do you mean?"

Freda laughed, "Not so clever, are you?"

Rose straightened up, "I located you, didn't I?"

"I let you, my dear. If I'd have wanted, you would have been dead not long after our first meeting, but I was told you have a purpose and, so far, you've delivered, so, they let you live."

"You're not making any sense…"

"My dear, they are all playing games. We are just like pawns that they move around the chessboard and pieces have little worth, so they are expendable. Can I pour another drink?"

Rose nodded; she was unsure of what was actually happening. Freda reached over to the tray at the side of the sofa and poured a large one into another crystal tumbler. The dogs appeared at the door looking forlornly at their mistress.

Freda raised her arm and pointed, "Bed!" The dogs sloped off, whimpering with their tails between their legs.

Freda knocked back the clear liquid in one go and refilled the glass.

Rose said, "Tell me about Charles Wilson."

"Huh? Him? He's just one of life's great losers who are still hanging on to a lost dream."

"And what dream might that be?" asked Rose.

"British Union of Fascists; Mosley's lot."

Rose nodded, it made sense; it always did in the long run.

"What's his job?" asked Rose.

"Information on leading political figures who might be interested in helping our cause."

Rose raised her eyebrows as Freda continued. "There are a significant number of British politicians who are opposed to fighting Germany. Wilson is the link, as many of them were and still are closet supporters of Mosley. He thinks he'll get some important job after the invasion."

She stopped and took another large gulp from her glass. "I told him to kill you personally."

Rose looked at her; she wasn't so glamorous any more. She was sitting there in a worn housecoat with her hair in a complete mess, drinking herself into a stupor.

"So, why now and why me?"

"I want out of this, you stupid girl," Freda snapped.

Rose nodded, "So you thought the easiest way is to remove me?"

"Well," Freda smiled, "What's a Jew doing working for the Third Reich?"

Rose sighed, "Preserving my life and that of my family."

Freda laughed, "They aren't going to let you live once your usefulness is finished. The bombing will start soon, and I don't aim to be around to see it happen. I've already sent lots of information back about London docks. The Luftwaffe will have a good time pounding that to pieces."

"So," asked Rose, "What do you plan to do?"

"I'm going to Ireland until I can find a way back to my home."

This time, Rose laughed, "Will that be after your husband has grown tired of his mistress?"

Freda stirred at Rose; her eyes blazed with anger, "What do you mean? How do you know?"

"You don't think Berlina Candido's death was an accident, do you?"

There was one of those silences...Rose continued, "You know it's very dangerous to have an electric wireless playing near a bath...She told me everything before she boiled in the water."

Freda made to get up, but a combination of too much alcohol and the strength of Rose, held her down. "Stay there..." she hissed.

Freda sank back into the sofa. The housecoat fell open. She was naked underneath. "Drink up," said Rose. "It will make things easier for you."

Rose sat there for the next hour whilst the woman known as Freda wallowed in self-pity regaling stories of how much she loved her husband even though he had spent his whole married life cheating on her. But, no matter, once the war was over and all the communists and Jews had been slaughtered in Croatia, a new, cleansed country would rise from the ashes, free from racial impurity.

She would take her place as the wife of one of Croatia's leaders. The Abwehr was training more agents, and soon they would not have to rely on a Jew like Rose to do their work. She had only been spared because of her ability with languages and her fine brain.

Rose took all this in and thought...

She watched Freda's eyes close slowly as the alcohol took effect. Soon, Freda was snoring loudly. Rose quietly searched the place from top to bottom being very careful not to disturb anything. She couldn't find a radio. This meant that there must be at least one other wireless operator in London. She found some fake jewellery but left it in situ; she still had enough of the real stuff to worry about. There was about two hundred pounds in cash. She stuffed that in her bag. She found the envelope that she had retrieved from the hospital. Freda had not yet passed it for transmission. This went into her bag as well.

She stood looking down at the woman known as Freda who was comatose on the sofa. Rose lifted up her chin; it flopped down as soon as she let it go. She parted the housecoat and looked down at the white body. There was little to indicate she was in her forties. The skin was clear and unblemished with no tell-tale signs of ageing. Only the dark patches in her armpits and groin betrayed the fact that her hair was dyed.

Rose went back into the bedroom and picked up a pillow. She stood over Freda and pressed the pillow into the woman's face. She held it there tight. There was no struggle. Eventually, the chest stopped moving. Freda became still, as her life ebbed away.

Rose picked up the bottle of spirits and poured the remainder over the dead Croatian. She watched as little rivers trickled down between her ample breasts and sighed.

There was just one loose end to tie up; she would do that in the next few days...

There was disarray the following evening in Uxbridge as Cynthia Fleming and Henrietta Forbes-Carlton desperately tried to copy a transmission from somewhere in west London. The operator, whoever she was, took no time in submitting the hundred words or so. The changes in the wavelength were so rapid that the two operators had to be quick so as to not miss the first numbers. The gaps between the transmissions were getting shorter. Pilot Officer Norman Barton leaned over Cynthia Fleming making her even more hot and bothered especially as the stocking clad legs of Henrietta Forbes-Carlton were rubbing discreetly against her...

The main bar in the Prince of Wales public house on Du Cane Road, not far from Wormwood Scrubs Prison, was packed and very smoky. The walls and ceiling were yellow through decades of cigarette tar and the bare floorboards were littered with ground-in-dog-ends. Rose soon found the female she knew as Marie leaning against the bar chatting away to a woman who appeared to be polishing glasses. Rose caught her eye; Marie nodded and spoke to the barmaid.

Rose made her way through the crowds to a quieter corner. Marie appeared clutching two glasses of a clear liquid. She said,

"I was half expecting you this evening." She offered Rose a glass, "Compliments of the house."

Rose looked over at the barmaid and raised her glass. The woman nodded. Marie spoke,

"That's Miss Hilda; she runs the girls. If you want to work from here she takes twenty per cent. I told her you were new to the game."

Rose nodded, "Where are you from, Marie?"

"Little place outside Cork. But let's not be askin' each other questions...Do what you have to, and then we can be about our own business." She smiled.

Rose shrugged her shoulders, "Where's Charles Wilson?"

Marie nodded her head to one side; "You see that group of bastards over there. He's the one with the bald head."

Rose looked over to see five men all dressed in regulation navy blue trousers and collarless white shirts. Each clutched a beer glass. By the looks of it, they had already consumed several drinks.

Marie leaned in and asked, quietly, "Do you want him tonight?"

Rose nodded...

"Have you come prepared?"

Rose patted the top of her thigh, "Same as you."

Marie whispered, "Tell him it's two pounds for the night. He'll knock you down to thirty bob then get him to take you back to his place. He lives just up the road on his own. His wife disappeared some years ago."

Rose sipped her drink.

Marie said, "Take him quickly before he gets started. If he starts on you, you'll be sorry." She patted her backside, "He likes the rear door...He's a feckin big bastard and strong too." She paused, "Once you leave here, you're on your own. I won't be able to help you."

Marie went over to the group of men. She tapped Wilson on the shoulder. He turned. She began a furtive conversation. Occasionally, he looked over at Rose; she smiled back at him.

Marie went back to the bar and to Miss Hilda.

"What's your name?" Wilson asked Rose. She could smell the prison off him. He towered over her.

She looked down, "Virginia"

"How much, Virginia?"

"Two pounds for the night."

He finished his drink, "Make it thirty bob."

She shook her head, "Sorry, two pounds, or I'll get someone else."

"Are you worth it?"

She smiled at him, "Try me..."

He unlocked the door to his terraced house in Norbroke Street. The house smelled the same as the prison. He grabbed hold of her and pulled her to him. She could smell the beer on his breath.

"Patience, big boy. I don't want my clothes torn, especially my stockings..."

She turned away from him, lifted her skirt and extracted the knife. The blade was razor sharp; her neighbour across the landing had sharpened it...She held it behind her back and began to undo the top buttons of her dress with her other hand. He came towards her; his expression had changed. She held up her free hand,

"Wait a minute, let me surprise you. Turn around and let me get undressed."

He grunted and licked his lips...She stared at him...He sighed and turned around...

He felt a sharp scratch in the small of his back as the blade pierced the skin. She felt the knife scrape against his vertebrae. His eyes opened wide in horror as his legs gave way. She twisted the knife just as her handlers back in Vienna had taught her. He tumbled to the carpet in front of the fireplace in his front room.

She was on him in a flash. She held the knife against his throat.

"Why did you send three men to kill me?"

It took him a second or two to work out what was going on, "You? They told me they had taken care of you..."

She shook her head, "Well, it seems you just can't trust anyone. Now, answer my question because it looks like you don't have much time." She shifted her knees as she sat firmly on his chest. Blood started to seep from the corner of his mouth.

"Mirna sent me. She's going to wait for me in Ireland when this all kicks off."

Rose shook her head, "Yes, but why me? I'm just the messenger."

"You could lead them to us." He began to cough. She moved away slightly to avoid his blood.

"She played you just like she played the rest of us," she said, quietly.

He began to shiver, "Well, you're only a Jew; no one cares…"

Rose sighed as she stood up and straddled over him, "Are you just a deluded fascist hoping that everything will turn out right for you and your lot in the end?" She bent down and wiped the blade on the man's white shirtsleeve, "Are you a religious man, Wilson?"

He nodded. She said, "Well, prepare yourself to meet your maker."

She quickly bent down and plunged the knife into his chest piercing his heart. As she pulled it out, blood spurted up. She had to move quickly to avoid being covered.

Rose didn't bother to search the house. The police would find any incriminating evidence linking him to his other life in the service of Hitler. She left quickly having rinsed the knife out in cold water from the kitchen sink and tucked it back into the sheaf strapped to her thigh. Rose pulled a scarf over her head as she walked quickly down Du Cane Road. She glanced up at the Prince of Wales as she passed by wondering how many clients Marie had serviced in the time she had been with Charles Wilson…

The knife went into the canal as she crossed the Mitre Bridge on Scrubs lane. Her lover would always get her another…

She washed herself off thoroughly, standing in the small tin bath, pulled on a coat and went quietly across the landing. Porteous was sleeping soundly. She cast off the coat, lifted the covers and slid into his bed. She heard him say sleepily,

"Is that you, Maruska?"

"Who else do you think it would be, Porteous?"

Chapter 15

December 1940
London
The Blitz

Maruska Bergman was busy. Her skills as a seamstress were in constant demand. She had to juggle the requests of Madam Collier and her rich clientele in Chelsea with her unofficial work... She was down to one agent; that of the man who worked for the railways. She made a habit of checking the dead-letter box in the cemetery every Sunday. She varied the days and times of the transmissions. She knew she was being monitored. During training, Hamburg had told her that the British were getting very good with their tracking equipment. She kept a close eye on the neighbourhood looking out for any signs of activity that was out of the ordinary. She knew that the census enumerators were spending a lot of time in the area on the pretext of issuing the new identity cards.

The landlady, Martha Cunningham, had left to join her sister in Penzance at the first sign of trouble. There had been dogfights in the sky as the Luftwaffe attempted to knock out the RAF before any invasion but nothing serious. The old lady on the ground floor, Mrs Hardcastle, had been removed to an old persons' home when Mrs Cunningham had departed. Messrs Blunt and Watson on the middle floor had been called up to the army. That just left Porteous and Maruska Bergman on the top floor. No one came to collect the rent...

When the census enumerator returned, Maruska assured her that there was no doctor living in the house. She showed her the identity card issued to Rosemary McCumiskey. The enumerator scratched her head and said there must have been a mistake but not to worry, she would sort it out...

By April, Porteous was busy at Smiths in Cricklewood where they were ramping up the war effort and producing cockpit instruments for aeroplanes. Although he tried, he could never persuade Nancy Keeling to join him; she preferred to make her money in a different way.

Maruska attended Harrow Road Police Station every two weeks and signed the Aliens' register. She noted that she was employed as a seamstress in Chelsea. The desk sergeants got to know her and paid her little attention as she came in smiling. She always presented herself well on those days.

Porteous was at Smiths on 15 September when the first major daylight raid commenced. The air raid sirens sent the factory girls into a panic as they scuttled for the makeshift shelters. Porteous sat with the girls clutching at him as the Royal Air Force did their best to deter the Luftwaffe. The daytime raid was not successful and by October, London and other big cities were the subject of constant night bombing. Porteous signed up as an air raid protection warden, not through any altruistic reason but because it gave him carte blanche to wander through the deserted blacked out night-time streets of London without any difficult questions being asked of him. His unofficial business was thriving. The residents of Kensal Town looked to him to obtain the unobtainable...He was doing a roaring trade in ladies' stockings especially the finer cut ones, care of Jimmy Ryan, of course.

Maruska's client, the one who lived in Kensal Rise, was supplying the Abwehr with a lot of information regarding the movements of materials and machinery vital for the war effort. Maruska patiently decoded the messages and transmitted them at various times in the day and night but only when Porteous was absent. Miss Smith of the security services never did get the authorities to stump up the money for a mobile wireless detector unit, although Kensal Town residents did notice an increased police level as it went from one patrol a day to two, but never after dark...Miss Smith was told to be patient because by the end of the year, the Uxbridge listening station was going to be upgraded. The tracking beacons would be accurate to within one hundred yards. As soon as this happened, the area would be swamped with security personnel. The Nazi agent wouldn't stand a chance...

London slowly emptied out. Many children were evacuated and those who had the resources, disappeared out to the suburbs where one were less likely to be hit by a bomb. The woman known as Freda was correct. The east end of the city, especially around the docks area, took a real pounding. Casualties were high. Porteous was sometimes drafted over to the docks to assist in the fire-watching duties. This gave him even more opportunities to go about his business. There was often something to be had after a particularly heavy raid. Porteous' friend, Jimmy Ryan, was well in with the local lads who always had something illicit to sell on. He seemed to specialise in tobacco, alcohol and ladies clothing. The gangs, having broken into warehouses during the night-time raids and blackout, were keen to move the stuff as quickly as they could.

Porteous always had a stock of hard-to-get items stored in the now vacant flat below his and Maruska's. Sometimes, customers would even come to the door looking for that elusive pair of stockings or a packet of coffee...

Maruska had to fight off the attentions of Madam Collier's husband who seemed to be around when she was at their home in Chelsea. She had decided that it wasn't worth the effort to try and find out what it was that he did in the Admiralty. With no more Freda to worry about, she reckoned that her masters in Hamburg would be satisfied with what she was sending to leave her alone for the time being...

A week after Porteous' encounter with the parachute bomb in Langham Place, Maruska Bergman presented herself at Harrow Road Police Station to sign the Alien register. The fat desk sergeant looked at her with a certain amount of disdain; he looked over her shoulder as she signed the register.

"You're next..." That was all he said,

Maruska looked up at him; his teeth were yellow from years of smoking extra-strength cigarettes.

"I'm sorry, next for what?"

He snorted, "Interview in front of the Alien Tribunal Board." He paused and his finger ran down a list of names... "Ah, yes, Doctor Maruska Bergman, tomorrow at eleven in the morning. It says here you are Austrian. I don't know why you weren't picked up before along with the Germans and Italians."

"I'm not Austrian. I'm Czech."

He shrugged his shoulders, "All the same to me...Anyway, make sure you are present at the town hall on Paddington Green. Bring your Alien Registration card and any other documentation given to you when you entered Britain. If there is an air raid, find the nearest shelter and then present yourself at the Tribunal as soon as the all-clear is given." He sighed, "You are the tenth Alien this week..."

Maruska stared him out as he completed his paperwork. He handed her a copy of the summons to the town hall and his clipboard, "Sign here to say you have accepted the summons."

She scrawled something.

"Good day to you, Miss. If you don't turn up, I'll be very cross, do you understand?"

She nodded as she made for the door.

Outside, she took a deep breath to slow down her heart rate. Although she had been expecting this, it was still a bit of a shock to her system. It meant that her plans would now need to be brought forward.

She got back to Bosworth Road in Kensal Town about an hour later. She could hear Porteous' radio as she climbed the stairs. She pushed open his door. He looked up from the newspaper he was reading. He was dressed ready for a night of fire watching in his uniform.

She asked, "Are you going out so soon?"

He nodded, "Yeah, there's a briefing at four. They are struggling with all the bombing. We lost two wardens the other night when the school in Chelsea took a direct hit."

She pushed away his newspaper and sat on his lap. Her arms went around his neck. "I've been summoned to a tribunal tomorrow."

He raised his eyebrows, "Well, I'm a little surprised they haven't got to you sooner."

She buried her head on his shoulder, "They might lock me up."

He shook his head, "Nah, that's reserved for Germans, Austrians and Italians. I'm sure they'll grade you as a C especially as they need more and more doctors with so many being called up for active service."

"The sergeant at Harrow Road said they have me listed as an Austrian."

"That's a mistake, I'm sure. Just go along and tell them your story. Just because you came via Vienna doesn't make you a spy."

Maruska's eyes opened wide at that point...

She asked, "What will happen if they make me Category A?"

"They'll lock you up, I suppose but don't worry, I heard from Jimmy that they give you a few days to sort out yourself."

There was a pause in the conversation.

She asked, "What time are you back?"

"Not sure, I think it could be an all-nighter. They are expecting multiple raids tonight as Jerry's got the bit between his teeth smashing up the docks and the surrounding areas. They are after the railway stations as well trying to disrupt train movements. Paddington keeps getting hit but, so far, only minor damage."

"I'm scared, Porteous."

He sighed, "Nothing to be scared about. If they lock you up at least you'll be safe from all this mayhem. Which reminds me, make sure you go to the church as soon as the air raid siren goes off. That crypt is so far underground you'll be very safe."

Maruska turned up her nose, "It's damp down there and that priest gives me the creeps."

Porteous smiled, "He's a bit touchy-feely, especially with a pretty young woman. Just go, do you promise me?"

He felt her nod on his shoulder. She whispered in his ear, "What time are you leaving?"

"In about half an hour."

She stood up pulling at his arm, "Good, come and make love to me before you go..."

It was pitch black by the time Maruska Bergman was awakened by the sound of the air raid siren. It seemed very loud this evening. She couldn't remember when Porteous had left. She got up, threw on his dressing gown and ran across to her flat. She pulled on the boiler suit over her naked body and grabbed an old coat, trying to make herself as unattractive as possible. A pair of black hobnailed boots completed her outfit. She wrapped the scarf around her head, tucking in as much of her hair as possible.

She clumped down the stairs not bothering about the noise; there was no one else in residence. She crossed over the road and felt for the railings in the dark. She followed them until they ran out at the entrance to the church. Since the real outbreak of hostilities, the church bells had ceased. She felt an arm in hers. Edith Bell smiled at her,

"Come on, Maruska, we don't want to let the Jerries get you after all you've been through..."

She half pulled the Czech up the steps and into the gloom of the church. Maruska thought that all these places of worship smell the same; a mixture of old ladies, moth balls and burnt wax...

The priest stood at the entrance to the crypt in a side chapel; he beckoned them over. Maruska hesitated,

Edith whispered, "Don't worry, I'll sort the old lecher out..."

Maruska responded, "I can't abide the man, he makes me shiver."

Edith sniggered, "Where's Porteous?"

"Out watching for fires."

"Tell him I have something that might interest him..."

They reached the door. Father Dermot O'Brien reached out an arm. Edith took it before he could touch Maruska. She said, "Father Dermot, I have something to show you..."

Maruska pushed past her and joined a group of residents and their offspring sitting on an old church bench chatting away. They nodded at her as she sat down wrapping the overcoat around herself. The crypt was cold. She could see breath steaming out of her mouth. She shoved her hands deep into the pockets of the old coat. The lights of the crypt were on, but they were very dim and seemed to flicker with each explosion as the bombing grew nearer and nearer. She looked around for Edith, but she was nowhere to be seen.

A large explosion seemed to rock the church. The woman sitting next to Maruska whispered, "They are going for the railway line tonight..."

Maruska nodded; her messages to Hamburg were all from the railway worker. She knew there was a shipment of precious machine parts due out to the converted car factory in Coventry sometime soon...

Edith came through the door; the priest was nowhere to be seen. She smiled at Maruska, "That's him sorted out for the next twenty-four hours or so, or at least until he reloads. It just needed a flash of my knickers and a quick tug, that's all."

Maruska smiled, "I wish I had your confidence."

Edith shrugged her shoulders, "It's just practice, that's all. The old bastard should know better. Porteous has already had a word with him about fiddling with the youngsters. Us older ones can take care of ourselves. He thinks his cassock gives him carte blanche to do what he wants." She smiled, "Never mind, I got a ten bob note out of him for my troubles."

Maruska laughed, "No doubt he took that from the collection plate as well."

A really close explosion shook the whole church. The lights flickered and then went off. This time, they did not come back on. Someone lit the three candles situated up on the walls; they gave off an almost religious light. Maruska had not noticed them before. She looked around her. Edith was snuggled up to her close. She could feel her body heat. Sometimes she wished she were as thick-skinned as the other women in Porteous' circle. But wasn't that why he chose to spend his time with her because she was different?

She felt Edith's head rest on her shoulder and sighed. Edith said, "I hope my pub is okay."

"Is it yours, Edith?" Maruska was surprised.

"Well, it's technically the old man's, but I haven't seen him for nearly five years. He went off with some floozy from Maida Vale. They have a couple of kids now. He's somewhere down across the river. He never got around to transferring the tenancy. The brewery's not bothered as long as I keep paying the rent and selling their beer. I smiled at the magistrate and gave him a promise when the licence was up for renewal. It's amazing what you can get sitting on some man's lap in the room behind the court with your knickers around your ankles."

Maruska smiled, "Is your money safe?"

She felt the head nod, "Yes, locked up in The Midland Bank in Marylebone. There are a few days' takings from the pub and my own little side business, but I could live without that. How about you?"

Maruska shook her head, "I don't have too much, but it's safe." She was thinking about the little silk bag of diamonds carefully secreted in its intimate place...

She could see Edith's big brown eyes stare at her in the gloom, "Yeah, right..."

Maruska playfully slapped her. She put her arm around Edith and pulled her close as another bomb shook ancient dust from the ceiling.

It was nearly two in the morning before the all-clear was sounded. Maruska fell into her bed thinking about what she needed to do to preserve her liberty.

Chapter 16

December 1940
London
The Alien Tribunal Board

Maruska Bergman gathered her documents and laid them out on her kitchen table. The house was empty. She had heard Porteous return not long after she had gone to bed after the heavy raid, but he didn't come to her. He left just after five-thirty for the early shift up at Smiths in Cricklewood. She looked at the papers and sighed. Her whole life was laid out on those few sheets. She had no certificate of birth to prove she was born in Czechoslovakia, but that was irrelevant now that it was the German Sudetenland.

She examined her medical certificates. These were beginning to show signs of wear and tear since they had been removed from the glass frames that had been so proudly displayed in the family home in Karlsbad. She smoothed them out and laid them carefully in a Manila folder she had lifted from Porteous' store downstairs. Porteous had also forged a reference from Madame Collier in Chelsea under the name of Maruska Bergman on some stationery that she had liberated from the Chelsea shop.

She threw off the dressing gown and poured lukewarm water over herself standing in the tin bath. She dried herself off, squatted and checked that all was well with the little silk bag. She looked around the flat; a flat that she had been happy in for over a year. Perhaps they might not let her return to gather some personal items before they interned her? Porteous' words were ringing in her ears, *'They give you time to get your affairs in order...'* She hoped he was right because her affairs were definitely not in order.

She stood next to the full-length mirror and examined her naked body. Her figure was still good, but perhaps her breasts were a little smaller. All that cycling was doing her good.

Maruska Berman walked into Paddington Town Hall just before eleven in the morning. An ancient commissionaire in full regalia greeted her. He asked,

"Good morning, Madam. How can I be of assistance today?"

"The Alien Tribunal Board, please."

His face dropped, "Oh, another one," he scowled and responded abruptly.

"First floor, take the left corridor; you'll find a lady seated at a desk. Register with her..."

He turned away to greet a couple before she had time to answer. She sighed and went up the ornate stone steps. A prim looking female was sat at a makeshift desk at the end of the corridor. Maruska walked up to her and said,

"Doctor Maruska Bergman; I have an appointment at eleven."

The woman never looked up. She raised her hand as if to silence her, "Have you got your paperwork?"

Maruska dropped the Manila file on the desk with a thump. The woman finally looked up and peered over her half-moon glasses,

"Take a seat. The clerk will come and get you when she is ready." She waved a hand at a row of chairs, picked up the file and began to look through it. She ticked off Maruska's name on a list attached to a clipboard.

Thirty minutes later, the clerk to the tribunal board opened the door and called out, "Bergman!" She went over to the desk where the receptionist held up Maruska's file.

Maruska stood up, smoothed down her skirt and followed the clerk. The receptionist had still not looked at her.

The room was stuffy. She could smell stale pipe tobacco. Three men sat at a desk. Every one of them was middle-aged or older, as though whoever organised this exercise had scraped the barrel in trying to find suitable people to undertake this work. The clerk took up her position at a desk to the right-hand side of the panel. A single hard wooden chair was placed in the middle of the room. Maruska stood and stared at them.

The clerk said, "Please sit down."

Maruska placed her handbag at the side of the chair and sat down. She pulled her skirt down to her knees and crossed her legs.

The clerk began, "Please confirm your name, place and date of birth and occupation."

Maruska answered slowly. The clerk continued, "The purpose of this tribunal is to assess your suitability to remain at liberty in Britain under Emergency Powers granted to the government. You will stay silent unless a member of the panel asks you a question. Mr Peter Hadley of the Home Office will chair the panel. To his left is Mr David Stuart also of the Home Office and the remaining member of the panel is Inspector Eric Everard, seconded from the Metropolitan Police." The clerk returned to her paperwork.

Peter Hadley addressed her, "Good morning, Doctor Bergman. I trust you are well and that your stay in Britain has been satisfactory?"

Maruska half-smiled; she opened her eyes and uncrossed and crossed her legs, "Yes, sir, thank you."

Hadley looked at her long legs and cleared his throat; "I have the paperwork from your interviews in Ashford. It seems you satisfied the authorities there as to your suitability."

Maruska nodded.

Hadley sat back and folded his arms, "It says here you are working as a seamstress in Chelsea and you have brought a good reference from a Madam Collier. Why are you not working as a doctor?" He looked up at her expectantly.

"Sir, I am waiting for my registration to be approved by the British Medical Council. Unfortunately, all my references are at the University of Vienna and there is currently no communication with Austria."

"Yes but surely one of the London hospitals can give you some medical work? Heavens knows there is a chronic shortage of qualified personnel."

Maruska stared at him, "I have been trying, sir."

Eric Everard spoke up, "Why are you living in Kensal Town, Doctor Bergman?"

Maruska shrugged her shoulders, "I had the offer of an apartment at a reasonable rent and as I may be employed by the local hospital I thought it would be a good place to stay."

Everard stared at her, "Do you like living with criminals"

Maruska stared at him, "I'm sorry, sir, I don't know what you mean."

"The place has a certain reputation for thievery, black marketeering and prostitution."

Maruska shook her head, "I've not seen any of that, sir."

"Perhaps you didn't want to."

Hadley intervened, "Have you had any contact with German or Austrian citizens?"

She shook her head, "No, sir, Mr Brown in Ashford told me to avoid them."

"What about fellow Czechs?"

She shook her head, "No, sir, I've not met any of them."

David Stuart leaned forward, "What about your colleagues in the Jewish community?"

"I stayed with Rabbi Levy at the synagogue in Chichester Place. He and his wife helped me find accommodation."

"Do you earn sufficient money from your work as a seamstress?"

"I have enough for myself," she replied.

"How does Madam Collier pay you?"

"I get a commission from everything I make that is sold. She puts it through the books, so I am assured."

Stuart looked down as he wrote, "Don't worry, we'll check that."

Hadley spoke, "How long were you in Vienna?"

"Sir, I did my course there, so it would have been seven years altogether."

"You then went to Prague?"

She nodded. He asked, "What brought you back to Vienna?"

"A paediatric course, sir."

He looked down her file, "Ah, yes I see. Did you finish that course?"

"No, sir. It was not possible. The authorities were beginning to crack down on Jews, especially foreign ones."

Stuart asked, "Have you had any contact with your family?"

"No, sir. It is not permitted to write letters to occupied Europe."

"What about your brother in New York?"

"I wrote to him when I arrived, but I don't know if he ever received my letter. I have not heard anything from him for nearly two years."

"What about your father and mother?"

"They were trying to get to America, but I don't know, sir. The Germans may have picked them up."

Everard asked, "Do you work every day?"

She shook her head, "No, sir, only when Madam Collier requests my presence."

"How many days did you work last week?"

"Just two, sir."

"Then how do you earn enough money?"

"Sir, I get some private commissions."

Everard snorted, "I bet you do…"

Maruska's eyes blazed, "What's that supposed to mean?"

The clerk piped up, "I told you to only speak when you are spoken to."

Maruska looked down and muttered in Czech.

Hadley held up his hand, "Doctor Bergman, tell us about your present circumstances."

Maruska looked at him, "It's nothing out of the ordinary, sir, I have enough money to live on until my medical registration comes through."

He asked, "What are your future plans?"

"My family has agreed that we will all try to meet in New York when the war is over. My father does not see a future for us Jews in Europe."

"New York is a big place, Doctor Bergman."

"My mother attended the Brooklyn Heights Synagogue before she came back to Czechoslovakia. We will meet there."

Eric Everard spoke up, "Who are your acquaintances in Kensal Town?"

"I just know the tenants in my house, that's all."

"Do you frequent the White Horse public house on Kensal Road?"

"Yes, I have been there once or twice."

"Do you know the landlady, Edith Bell?"

Maruska nodded.

"Speak up!" the clerk said.

"Yes, I know her."

"Have you ever seen her involved in illegal activity?"

Maruska wondered where this was going, "No, sir, I have not."

Hadley asked, "Do you intend to remain in London for the duration of the war, Doctor Bergman?"

"Sir, as long as I am able, but I don't know what I would do if the Germans invade. I've thought about Ireland, but we are not sure if the authorities would let us in."

"Who are 'we,' Doctor Bergman."

"Us Jews, sir. We don't seem to be welcome in many places." Maruska looked down.

Hadley cleared his throat, slightly embarrassed, "Well, let's hope for the best shall we? Do you have any relatives or friends outside London?"

"No, sir, I am on my own."

Maruska could feel a sense of sympathy in the air. She stared at Peter Hadley and uncrossed her legs again. Hadley said, "Are there any more questions?"

The remaining panel members shook their heads.

He went on, "Thank you, Doctor Bergman, that will be all for the present. A decision from this panel will be sent to the Home Office for confirmation. It will then be communicated to you in due course. If you are categorised as A, you will be expected to present yourself at Harrow Road Police station within twenty-four hours. Please bring only one suitcase. If this panel decides on category B, restrictions on your movements will be outlined to you together with the conditions for you to remain at liberty. If you are categorised as C, you may get on with your life. Any decisions will be reviewed automatically in due course. If you are to be interned, you will be allowed to appeal against this decision." He paused.

"In the meantime, carry on reporting to Harrow Road Police Station. The clerk will show you out and return your file. Good day to you, Doctor Bergman."

Maruska Berman was glad to leave the room. She could feel the sweat trickling down her back. She casually smiled at the clerk as she handed over her file without saying anything.

Thirty minutes later, she watched as the man known as David Stuart came bounding down the steps of the Town hall and into a waiting black car clutching a briefcase. The driver was wearing an army uniform...

At about five in the afternoon, the Honourable John Porter of Bletchley Park sat in the darkened office of Dorothy Smith of MI5 in the Old Admiralty Building. David Stuart had not long returned from the typing pool clutching a copy of the notes from his meeting with the Alien Tribunal Board. He nodded at Smith and Porter.

Dorothy Smith lit another long, thin cigarette and blew out the smoke, "Well, let's have it David."

"We have interviewed three possible agents all based around the area of Kensal Town. The first is a French citizen who managed to escape from France just after Dunkirk. He came on our radar because of his communist sympathies. You know the sort of thing, trades union agitator and all that. I doubt he's got the brains to work for the Abwehr. I think we can count him out, although he lives just across the Harrow Road so he is within range of the tracking beacons."

Smith looked up, "What did the Board recommend?"

"Category B, largely because of his political beliefs. He is going to be told who he can see and be with. We expect him to kick up a fuss because he has connections to De Gaulle and the Free French."

Smith snorted, "Let him. The Home Secretary has no time for these wasters. If they had defended their bloody country a little better in the first place we wouldn't be in this current predicament."

John Porter raised his eyebrows at that.

David Stuart referred to his file, "And then we have Mr Alphonse De Jong lately of Roermond in Southern Holland. He was originally arrested by the Nazis and then suddenly let go. He lives just outside the tracking beam sector, but he appears to spend a lot of time visiting a lady of ill repute in Kensal Town. He was originally kept in Ashford for nearly six months before they kicked him out largely because he's a qualified engineer and Lord knows we could do with a few more of them."

"We haven't got him working on anything sensitive, do we?" asked Smith.

"Good heavens, no, Ma'am. We've got him working for London County Council on some sewage upgrades and repairs. He'll be categorised C, but we'll keep an eye on him."

The Honourable John Porter leaned forward, "That leaves just one..."

Stuart nodded, "Yes, sir, a Jewish Czech doctor who goes by the name of Maruska Bergman." He referred to his notes, "Born in Karlsbad in the Sudetenland in 1910. She interests us because she lived in Vienna for more than five years whilst she was completing her medical training. Claims she was forced to train in Vienna because the medical authorities in Prague didn't admit women. Now we know that wasn't true by the time she entered the university. She says her father, who is a local doctor, pulled some strings to have her admitted to the medical school in Vienna."

Porter interrupted, "Bit far-fetched, old boy, to have a Jew working for the Nazis, wouldn't you say?"

Smith answered him, "Not really, John. If they've got her family in one of those ghastly camps she'd probably do anything to protect them."

Porter nodded thoughtfully.

Stuart went on, "Well, she possibly fits the bill. Very bright, speaks several languages fluently and is particularly good-looking and well-presented."

Dorothy Smith smiled, "Another Mata Hari, no doubt..."

Porter snorted.

"What is it about her in particular?" asked Smith.

"She lives right in the middle of Kensal Town..."

Smith and Porter sat up as Stuart went on, "She claims to be working as a seamstress down in some expensive shop in Chelsea. I've sent a couple of boys down to interview the proprietress who appears to have given her an impeccable reference. I'm hoping they'll be back soon." He placed her picture on the desk.

Porter raised his eyebrows, "Yes, good-looking all right."

Smith asked, "How did she get here?"

"Yes, well, that's the thing. She managed to get from Vienna to Zurich by train."

Smith said, "I thought the Swiss had virtually stopped admitting Jews for fear of upsetting their Germanic neighbours?"

"That's exactly it, Ma'am. Bergman claims she had a letter of introduction to a hospital in the city and the guards let her through. She was in Zurich for about two weeks; stayed in a small pension down by the Quay whilst she negotiated with the French Embassy. We have someone checking out her story, but the French Embassy is now virtually closed. Anyhow, she manages to get herself out of Switzerland and across France to Paris where she got on a train for the steamer. We picked her up in Dover."

He selected another file and flicked it open. "This is her file from Ashford."

Dorothy Smith asked, "Which Mr Brown interviewed her?"

Porter smiled again.

Stuart ran his finger down a sheet of paper, "Giles Deeprose."

Smith nodded, "Not many get past him."

Stuart continued, "Deeprose flagged her up as a possible concern, but he had no hard evidence to keep her and the centres were already full with refugees flooding in from Europe. He thought she might be useful in one of the hospitals. He also noted that she kept herself to herself and had virtually no contact with other detainees."

Porter asked, "What was she carrying?"

Stuart handed him a sheet of paper from the file, "Here's an inventory of her personal belongings; nothing out of the ordinary there. In fact, all she appears to be concerned about are her medical qualifications. She said she had used up all her money in getting here."

Porter began examining the list as Stuart went on, "They took all her belongings to pieces including the carpet bag but found nothing. She did over five hours of interrogation."

Porter sat up, "Wait a minute, it says here she was carrying an English version of Charles Dickens' Nicholas Nickleby and two works in German including a translation of Hans Christian Andersen and some collected poems of Heinrich Heine?"

Stuart shrugged his shoulders, "Yes, lots of refugees carry books to pass the time on their arduous journeys."

Porter looked at Dorothy Smith; she nodded. He stood up, "If you'll excuse me, colleagues, I need to get back to Bletchley Park. My lads and lassies have a pressing appointment with Charles Dickens..."

Stuart looked at Dorothy Smith who shook her head...

Smith's phone rang. She picked it up, listened for a few seconds and said, "Send him in, please."

Smith and Stuart both looked over at the window and the first air raid siren of the night began to wail.

A tall, thin man entered carrying a briefcase. He glanced at his boss, John Stuart, and then at Dorothy Smith, "Ma'am," he said with a formal nod.

"Matthew," she replied, "What have you got for us?"

Matthew Earnshaw was slightly breathless, "Ma'am, Madam Collier in Chelsea doesn't have a Maruska Bergman on her staff. She has a part-time seamstress named Rosemary McCumiskey."

"What?"

"A Polish refugee, allegedly. I showed her a picture of Bergman. She says that's McCumiskey..."

David Stuart stood up, "I knew it. That woman has been taking us for a ride ever since she entered Britain. Good God! How did Deeprose miss her?"

Smith spoke up, "Calm down, David, we've got sufficient evidence to intern her at the very least, but we would need to catch her with the damn radio to do anything more serious with her."

"Why has she given a false name to her employer?' asked Stuart.

Smith shook her head, "She could be a common criminal, for all we know, hiding from something."

Earnshaw commented, "Ma'am, Madam Collier says she saw an identity card with the name McCumiskey."

Stuart snorted, "Let's add the charge of a false identity card to the list." He turned to Earnshaw, "Run McCumiskey through the census list to see if one has been issued in her name. I would bet that the card she is carrying is a forgery."

Dorothy Smith extracted another long, thin cigarette from a silver case. She was about to light it when the first bombs of the raid began to drop somewhere over in East London.

Stuart looked over at the window and said, "Jesus, don't they ever have a night off?"

Smith lit the cigarette, blew out some smoke and said, "Mathew, get a team together and go and arrest her first thing tomorrow. I want that house taken apart brick by brick. Find that radio. Pick up any other residents. They might be able to shed some light on our Doctor Maruska Bergman. There's nothing we can do tonight with the raid."

He nodded. Stuart was more eager, "We can get her tonight, Ma'am."

She shook her head, "No, it's too dangerous especially with her lodgings being in Kensal Town. We don't want to upset the natives, do we? No, first thing tomorrow morning will do nicely. Have her taken to Chiswick. I'll get Deeprose and his boys over to interrogate her. Let's hope they do a better job this time. Now, bugger off and get the arrangements made. You can work from the shelter in the basement."

Stuart looked at his boss, "What about you, Ma'am?"

"I'm going home. I've got a cat to feed..."

Chapter 17

December 1940
London
A Parachute Bomb

Maruska knew that the best thing would be for Shira to drink herself into a stupor, fall asleep then all would be forgotten in the morning. It was the pattern of her behaviour.

She ran across the hallway and went into Porteous' flat. He always had a good supply of alcohol. She reached into a cupboard and took out a bottle of expensive gin. There was plenty in the makeshift store downstairs. When she returned to her apartment, Shira Adelman was tearing at her clothes. The dress was in shreds on the floor. She was pulling at her underwear. Maruska stopped. There was nothing she could do, so she poured a large drink into one of the glass tumblers that she had found in her small kitchen.

By the time she got back, Shira was ripping off her stockings. She grabbed the drink from Maruska and tossed it right back down her neck. She shook her head as the bitter alcohol burned her throat.

She said, "I'm tired of him, Maruska."

Maruska whispered, "I can see that, Shira. Maybe it's time to leave him?"

Shira took the bottle off the Czech doctor and took a hefty glug. Maruska watched as the drink spilled down the side of her mouth. She reached over and wiped away the gin, "Come on, Shira, that's enough." She pushed her to lie down on the bed, "Time for a little sleep, I think."

This time there was no protest from Shira. She lay back and closed her eyes. Maruska reached over and turned the drunken woman onto her stomach conscious that many a person has choked on vomit when in this particular state. She looked at Shira's bare back. It was covered in welts and bruises as though her husband had beaten her with a heavy leather belt. Maruska lifted the woman's arms so that they were stretched out at the side of her head as she lay on the bed. Shira Adelman began to snore.

Maruska picked up the pile of clothes that lay on the floor. The cheap, gaudy dress was ripped where she had pulled at the buttons. There were holes in the tops of her stockings where she had tried to pull them off without unclipping the suspender belt. The underwear was largely intact. Maruska sighed. Shira would just have to go home in something else.

The snoring got louder.

Maruska turned to the task in hand. She made sure that her guest was dead to the world and flipped over the sewing machine. She quietly unscrewed the radio and dropped it into a battered suitcase.

Maruska locked the case and buckled up the side straps. By the time she had lugged the case downstairs it was going dark. There had been ominous warnings all day about the possibility of heavy raids that night. She knew she didn't have much time. She wheeled the Saxon down the steps of the house and balanced the suitcase in the front basket. She pushed herself off. The bicycle wobbled slightly under the strain of the heavy load, but she was soon pedalling up Kensal Road. By the time she reached Ladbroke Road she was out of breath. She really should have changed into her boiler suit...

She crossed over the road and bumped the bike down the steps and onto the towpath. She remounted and rode furiously west along the path. The suitcase and the precious radio went into the canal on the side of Wormwood Scrubs. She stood and watched it as it momentarily floated before water gradually filled the inside and the case disappeared into the murky waters. Even if the authorities raided her flat, they would find nothing incriminating...

The warning sirens began to sound just as she arrived back in Bosworth Road. Maruska cursed. She wouldn't have time to bathe. She was hot and sweaty despite the cold, dry air. She climbed the stairs to her flat and shouted for Porteous. He still hadn't returned from Smiths. If he weren't home by now, he would be staying the night at the factory on some rush job or other.

She pushed open her door gently, not exactly sure what she would find. Shira Adelman hadn't moved. Maruska listened carefully. The snoring was still there. She froze as she heard the beginnings of the attack. From East London, the thuds were getting louder. It was time to get to the shelter.

She sat on the bed and shook Shira Adelman, "Shira! Shira. Wake up. We have to get to the shelter."

Shira Adelman swore in Polish. She didn't even open her eyes.

"For God's sake, Shira, we need to leave, now."

Maruska couldn't quite work out what she replied, but it sounded like, "Fuck off!"

Maruska stood up; Shira would just have to take her chances with the bombs...

She wrapped herself up in her coat and made for the stairs. She glanced back at the sleeping woman, remembering the promise she had made to her husband all those months ago;

'If you ever lay a hand on Shira again, I'll come back and kill you...'

Maruska Bergman leaned the Saxon against the railings of the church on Bosworth Road. She skipped up the steps to be greeted by Father Dermot O'Brien. He smiled at her. As she pushed past him, she felt a hand reach under her coat and skirt. Maruska turned sharply and called out in a loud voice, "If you touch me again, I'll kill you!" She had a knife pressed up against his throat.

He swallowed nervously as she extracted his hand. With her free hand, she grabbed his testicles and squeezed. His eyes opened wide.

She felt a hand on her arm, "Leave it, Maruska, I'll take care of him..."

Maruska Bergman relaxed as she turned to see a smiling Edith Bell. She let the priest go.

"Go on, Maruska, I'll meet you in the crypt."

Maruska sat on a bench. The shelter was crowded that night. The bombing got heavier. She felt the bench move as Edith Bell sat down. She put an arm through Maruska's,

"Don't take him too seriously, Maruska. As long as he leaves the kiddies alone, he's harmless."

Maruska sulked, "The bastard shouldn't be allowed to get away with what he does."

Edith Bell shrugged her shoulders, "He is what he is. He'll probably end up in the canal like many of his predecessors; anyway he's fine now."

"What did you do, give him one of your famous tugs?"

"Yeah, but he wanted me to kiss it better..."

They both laughed out loud...

They huddled up close as a loud bang made the old Victorian church shake with dust coming down off the ceiling. Father Dermot O'Brien appeared at the door with a flushed face. Maruska glared at him...

Just before midnight, there was a pause in the bombing. Maruska stood up,

"I'm just going to run back to the house."

Edith Bell grabbed her, "Stay here, whatever it is can wait."

Maruska shook off her arm, "No, I have to go. I'll be back in a few minutes."

Edith Bell shrugged her shoulders, "Oh, okay, just be careful. The all-clear has not yet sounded."

Maruska pushed on the heavy church door and peered out into the night. She could see the glow of burning buildings across the Harrow Road. She wondered how many houses had borne the brunt of German bombs that evening.

She bounded up the stairs to her flat and pushed open the door. To her surprise, Shira Adelman was sitting at her sewing machine dressed in her boiler suit. A glass of a clear liquid was in one hand.

"Shira, are you okay?"

Shira Adelman took another swig from the tumbler, "Of course I'm okay, Maruska, why wouldn't I be?"

Maruska took the glass off her guest and plonked it down on the side of the sewing machine, "Good, perhaps we can get to the shelter?"

Shira ignored her, "Can you teach me to sew? I think I need to learn a new skill."

"Yes, sure as long as you come with me to the church."

"Why did you take him from me?"

Maruska stopped in her tracks, "What? What are you talking about?"

"Porteous; you took him from me." The words were slurred.

Maruska shook her head, "Don't be silly, Shira, you're a married woman and the last time I looked neither Porteous nor I are."

Shira Adelman stood up. The top of the boiler suit was not buttoned up. The brass buttons were open down one side. Maruska could see her full and firm breasts. She reached over to do up the buttons, "Come on, Shira we can talk about this in the morning."

Shira pushed her away, "No! Leave me alone. You took the man I loved…"

Maruska sighed. In the background she could hear the distant droning of bombers. She reached out for Shira's arm, "Come on, let's go before the Jerries come back."

"Fuck off! I thought you were my friend…"

"Look, Shira, you can stay here and be blown to kingdom come all you want, but I'm going back to the shelter."

Shira took another swig and lay back on the bed, "Yes, yes, I'll be over in a few minutes." Maruska knew she wouldn't.

The bombing was getting nearer and nearer as Maruska bounded down the stairs. They were really going after Paddington Railway Station that evening. Burning buildings from the other side of Kensal Town lit up the road and pavement. A forlorn bomber flew overhead. She listened as its engines droned away into the distance as searchlights chased it vainly. The night suddenly became silent. She paused as she came to the steps of the church. She turned, looked up, and then she saw it. The loud fluttering of the parachute echoed in the still night air. A searchlight from over on Ladbroke Grove had it in its sights.

She stood transfixed as it slowly sailed down towards the earth. It got so low that the searchlights lost it. It was no more than four hundred yards away. Maruska's heart leapt. She made a lunge for the small passage under the church steps next to her precious Saxon. She had barely made it before a blinding flash of light preceded a very loud bang. The explosion engulfed her. She fell next to her bicycle and was immediately covered in dust. And then, blackness...

Maruska Berman had a buzzing in her ears. It was a loud buzzing, not like the sound that an annoying fly makes when it won't leave you alone. It was a much deeper sound. She tried to open her eyes, but somehow they wouldn't. Instinctively, her hand went to wipe away the dust, but her medical training kicked in and stopped her. She forced herself to blink; her eyes were sticky as though her body had produced sufficient mucus to prevent damage to the delicate organs. Gradually, her sight began to return as she blinked. The loud buzzing morphed into a piercing ringing. She tried to call out but all she could hear were muffled sounds like those you get when you submerge underwater.

She shook her head and felt dust fall from her face. She began to move. She could feel the cold metal of the Saxon's handlebars against her bare skin. She pushed off the bicycle and moved her legs. The light from a nearby burning building allowed her to see where she was. She remembered diving into the narrow passage below the church steps next to her bicycle. Slowly, she pushed herself into an upright position. She looked down at her legs. Apart from torn stockings and a bloodied knee where she had fallen, all looked well. She reached up and grabbed the edge of one of the old, worn steps. She pulled herself up and steadied herself.

She looked over at the burning building. It had taken a direct hit from the parachute bomb. The explosion had also taken out three of the houses on either side. She swallowed nervously and spat out some blackened dust. A coughing fit followed. She climbed up out of the recess under the stairs. The ringing in her ears began to subside. She thought she could hear the bells of an auxiliary fire engine as it picked its way through the debris on the Harrow Road over the other side of the Ha'penny Steps. She began to walk across the road. She looked down as she felt water sloshing over her shoes. A small torrent of water was pouring down the small incline of Bosworth Road. She looked towards Kensal Road to see a fountain of water shooting up into the night. The explosion had clearly ruptured a water main. There were smaller spouts all along the road where the pressure of water had burst through the pipes and up through the pavement. She stopped at one and washed the dust off her face. She drank greedily to rid herself of the bitter taste of acrid smoke that was beginning to engulf the area punctuated by little but regular explosions. She couldn't find her house in the wreckage. She walked up and down for a full five minutes finally deciding which one was hers. She stopped and stared as the searing heat warmed her blackened face. And then she screamed,

"Shira!"

She stood with hands on hips and looked at the carnage. No one could have survived that...Shira Adelman was long gone.

And then, she heard the familiar droning of more bombers. This roused her from her thoughts. She needed to act quickly. She could return to the safety of the church crypt, or she could make good her escape...

Maruska Bergman half carried the Saxon up the Ha'penny Steps. She was out of breath as she reached the top and wheeled her bike along the pathway. She bounced the machine down the steps on the other side. Harrow Road was deserted. She mounted the bicycle and began to pedal. She knew there was a church down at Desborough Street where the canal passes under the Harrow Road. That would do for a shelter.

She leaned the Saxon against the railings and pushed open the door. She could smell the crowd of people who turned to the door as it opened. A voice shouted,

"For Christ's sake, shut that bloody door..."

Maruska quickly closed the heavy wooden door behind her. The church benches were packed with adults desperately trying to comfort crying children. As she walked in she felt an arm grab her,

"Where do you think you're going? The crypt is full. Wait your turn like everyone else."

She looked up to see an old man with venom in his eyes.

She raised her arms, "Yes, yes, okay. I'll just sit in the corner."

He let her go. She stepped over prone bodies and made her way to the darkened corner. She sat down on the cold stone floor, brought her knees up to her chest and wrapped her arms around them. She lowered her head onto her knees and closed her eyes...

Chapter 18

December 1940
London
Keeping a promise

It was pitch black at four in the morning when the all-clear was finally sounded. Maruska Bergman had drunk copious cups of bitter tea. Londoners pride themselves on the amount of tea they can consume in times of stress. She wasn't quite the first out of the door, but she exited quickly as she didn't want some dishonest person relieving her of her precious Saxon. Suddenly, there were lots of people crowding along the Harrow Road, anxious to get home quickly. She watched as parents dragged sleepy children along the road and wondered why they had not taken advantage of the evacuation that had seemed to have preoccupied the city's residents during the so-called Phoney War. Indeed, Maruska had heard of those parents who had brought their unhappy offspring home after hearing tales of neglect and abuse at the hands of some middle class, country-dwelling citizens.

She clutched the Saxon and waited for the throng to disperse. Her brief pause was interrupted by the gruff voice of an Air Raid Precautions Warden,

"Move along, Miss. You can't stand here; get yourself home or wherever you are going."

She nodded at him and mounted the bike. She pedalled away, avoiding the debris of modern warfare scattered across the road.

She turned off the Edgware Road and into Praed Street. She hid the Saxon in a little side road next to Paddington Basin. Praed Street was busy with all manner of civil defence vehicles and personnel milling around, waiting for the Auxiliary Fire Brigade to douse the flames of the railway station and the yards beyond. Five London Auxiliary Ambulances stood by to tend to the sick and injured or to remove bodies to the numerous temporary mortuaries that had been set up around the capital. Maruska strolled past them all, anonymous and almost invisible. She walked out of Praed Street and into the connecting road to Star Street.

Adelman's Jewellers was completely dark; she expected nothing less after her last visit. She went around the back and tried the rear door. It was locked. She removed a shoe, waited for the noise of a passing emergency vehicle and then put the window through. She reached carefully through the broken glass and released the cheap lock. The storeroom was as untidy as she had seen it on her last visit.

Not caring too much about the amount of noise she made, Maruska went up the stairs. Her nose told her where she would find Zev Adelman. She entered the bedroom. He lay face down on the bed, snoring loudly. She walked up to the curtains and pulled them across. She went back to the light switch and turned it on. The room was lit from a naked bulb. The old man had still not stirred. She could see a cut on the back of his head where Shira had indeed hit him with a bottle.

He woke up just as the stocking tightened around his neck.

He spluttered, "What the..."

He couldn't get any more words out as the silk tightened across his throat.

Maruska leaned into him. Her knees pressed firmly against his back. He began to thrash around wildly. She began to whisper,

"Remember me, Adelman?"

He shook his head as she released the tension on the stocking.

"What did I say last time I paid you a visit?"

There was no answer; the silk tightened again.

He gasped for air as she released the ligature.

"Who, who are you?" he stammered.

"Shira's friend."

He snorted, "She has no friends but me."

The stocking tightened again. This time she held it longer. She felt the body go limp. She released it and thumped his back with a closed fist. He gasped and spat as life returned.

"God help me!"

Maruska smiled, "It's a bit late for that."

She held on to the knotted stocking as she slid off the old man. She placed her face next to his. He appeared to have difficulty in focusing. His eyes clamped shut.

"Did you beat your wife again?" she asked.

She felt him nod.

"What did I tell you last time?" she asked again."

"You told me you would come back and kill me."

"Open your eyes.

She shook him vigorously, "Open your eyes!"

Slowly, two rheumy eyes blinked as they opened. He jerked up,

"You! What's it to you? What do you want?"

"I always keep my promises, Mr Adelman."

He began to struggle. Quickly she mounted him again and pulled hard on the silk. She felt him go limp again. She released it and he began to stir.

"My keys are in the drawer; take what you want."

"I was going to..."

She sat back for a moment, "Do you believe in God, Mr Adelman?"

"Yes, of course." The voice was hoarse.

Maruska answered in Hebrew, "Start praying because you are about to meet him to answer for your crimes."

He began to intone some ancient prayer.

She breathed in deeply and then pulled hard on the stocking. He went quiet. She held it tight for a good few minutes. This time, there was no coming back for Zev Adelman. She got off him quickly as his bowels loosened. She stood back and looked at the lifeless body. At least he wouldn't be able to beat any wife in the future…She said a quick prayer over his body.

She spent the next few hours, until it got light, looking at Zev Adelman's hoard of ill-gotten gains. The key to the old safe was on the bunch. She quickly put the high value items to one side, as they were too easy to trace. She wanted to disappear into the chaos that was now wartime Britain. She had decided that the jewellery to was too risky, but she cleared it out anyway and placed it into an old linen drawstring bag. She pocketed about three hundred pounds of cash in low denomination notes. These would do nicely. She went back upstairs into Shira's bedroom and went through her collection of clothes. She packed a few items, enough to see her through the next few days, into a small bag she found on top of an old wooden wardrobe. She sat on Shira's bed and dabbed some cold water on her cut knee using a flannel she found in the bathroom. She found several packets of stockings in a drawer by the side of the bed. She smiled as she recognised them as coming from Peter Porteous.

She peeled off the other torn stocking and put on one of the new ones. She tossed the torn stocking and the one she had used to strangle old Adelman into a waste bin in the bathroom. She had no need of such a souvenir. She straightened the leather thigh strap and adjusted the six-inch blade…

Praed Street was still a melee of emergency vehicles and personnel as she retraced her steps back to Paddington Basin and her Saxon. She observed several corpses covered in regulation grey blankets awaiting transportation when the good ladies of the Auxiliary Ambulance Brigade had finished dealing with the live casualties.

As she walked along the side of the Basin, Maruska hurled the bag of jewellery into the dark waters.

For the police, the murder of Zev Adelman and the kidnap and suspected murder of his wife, Shira, was probably down to a straightforward robbery as evidenced by the broken rear door window...The police would get around to it when circumstances permitted. In the meantime, since Adelman kept a meticulous inventory of his precious items, a list was circulated to all similar shops.

Benny Benowitz of Hatton Garden raised his eyebrows and smiled when he heard the news of Adelman's demise. Little fat Moshe shook his head,

"Shame about the wife; good-looking woman that one..."

It was still early in the morning when Doctor Maruska Bergman wheeled the Saxon along Purves Road just north of Kensal Green Cemetery. She had cycled the long way around via Queen's Park and Kensal Rise to be on the safe side in case she accidentally bumped into any of her neighbours. Despite the cold of the late December day, she could feel the sweat on her back and between her legs. She was also annoyed that Shira had taken her boiler suit; it was much more practical when riding the bike.

The small suitcase she had purloined from the Adelman house was placed in the front basket. It contained just enough clothes for her journey. She was getting quite adept at balancing the Saxon with a load.

She opened the gate and bumped the bike up the step into the small front garden of house number 105. She breathed in deeply trying to slow her beating heart. A horse pulling a milk wagon trotted past. She looked at the driver who was dressed in his white outfit complete with a cap and striped apron. The empty bottles rattled as the horse plodded along, its breath steaming out of its mouth and nose. Even in times of war, the British demanded their early morning cup of tea laced with fresh milk. The milkman tipped his hat as he went past.

Maruska tried the front door handle. It turned. She pushed open the door and wheeled her bicycle onto the tiled floor. Her nostrils were filled with the smell of something frying in the kitchen. Somewhere in the house, a radio was playing the BBC. She recognised the Home Service. She leaned the bike against the banister to the stairs and quietly walked along the hall. The kitchen was directly in front of her. Doors to what the British called the front parlour and the living room were on her left.

She walked quietly up to the kitchen door. A man dressed in a pair of black trousers and a white shirt had his back to her as he stirred the frying pan. He was cooking eggs and what looked like bacon. Maruska's tummy rumbled. She hadn't eaten for nearly twenty-four hours.

She stood looking at the man. He spoke without turning around, "I've been expecting you. What took you so long?"

Maruska froze. He continued,

"Would you like me to serve you some? There's plenty."

The accent was broad southern Irish. Maruska had heard this often in Kensal Town where there were enough Irish labourers to dig out the canal twice over. He still hadn't turned around.

She walked quietly into the kitchen, pulled out an old wooden chair and sat down, "Not just yet."

The man turned around with a smile on his face. He was clearly about to go to work. His white shirt was collarless; braces hung down his sides. His hair was still a little wet from when he had washed and made himself presentable. His grey mutton chop whiskers were groomed perfectly.

"Would you like some tea?" he asked.

Not waiting for an answer, he poured the dark liquid into a white China cup. He placed it on the table telling her to help herself to milk. "I'm afraid I've got no sugar. Couldn't get any the other day and this is the last of the bacon; bloody war!" He laughed out loud.

Maruska clutched the cup between two hands and sipped the hot liquid. He sat down with a plate in front of him, "Are you sure you wouldn't like some food whilst it's hot?"

"Later, maybe."

She watched as he tucked into the food as though he didn't have a care in the world.

They were silent for a few minutes...

"What's your story?" he asked.

She looked at him.

"I figured you are the radio operator," he said.

Maruska nodded.

"You know I let you follow me all those months ago. You are not as good as you think you are."

Maruska smiled, "You only saw me because I let you."

He returned her smile and forked some food into his mouth, "What's your background?"

"I was going to ask you the same thing," she responded.

He shrugged his shoulders, "Nothing of significance, really, I just want the bastard Brits out of my country."

Maruska raised her eyebrows at that. She didn't know much about the situation in Ireland, but she knew it was a problem for many of those across the Irish Sea.

He sipped his tea, "You see the Brits killed my father and uncle in 1916 and that other bastard, Winston Churchill, has had a hand in all the problems in Ireland. So, I'll support any cause that agrees to rid them from my home country."

Maruska asked, "So, you think if Hitler invades Britain he'll agree to giving the whole of Ireland back?"

The man shrugged his shoulders, "That's what he's told De Valera, our President."

"I'm not so sure. Look what he did with my homeland. It's a very brave man who trusts the tyrant."

He paused in his eating, "So why are you helping them?"

"I have no choice. They took my family and locked them up. They threatened me that if I did not co-operate, they would end up in some death camp or other."

He resumed eating; "You do know the Brits built the first concentration camps during the South African Wars at the turn of the century?"

Maruska looked at him quizzically, "That's no excuse."

He went on, "For me, it's a means to an end. For you, it's a matter of expediency. So, we are no different."

Maruska could see the logic; he continued, "So what do they have over you and your family?"

"We are Jews..."

He stopped chewing, "Hmm, I didn't think they would stoop that low."

Maruska snorted, "Of course not, you have never lived among them. The Nazis will stop at nothing until they have murdered every Jew in Europe including Ireland. You are deluded if you think they'll stop at the Irish Sea."

He tilted his head to one side and shrugged, "It'll be worth it to get the bastards out of my country."

"So, you'll change one set of bastards for another?"

"The lesser of two evils."

"So you don't care if the Nazis kill all the Jews?"

He shrugged his shoulders.

She sipped at her tea, "How did they recruit you?"

"I just walked into the German Embassy and volunteered. Two weeks of training in some country mansion out in the back of beyond, and I'm here." He paused and then asked, "What's the purpose of you coming here today?"

Maruska looked at him, "The operation is finished."

He stopped, "What do you mean?"

"It's over. I no longer have a radio. Your friends from the Luftwaffe blew it to smithereens last night along with all my belongings including the house in which I lived."

She let the silence fill the air, "I was called before the Alien Tribunal Board. Somehow, I don't think they believed me."

He smiled, "Ah the joy of being a foreigner in someone else's country."

She asked, "What will you do, now?"

"I was planning on leaving anyway. It's getting too dangerous to keep passing on information. The Germans took out a train shipment of fighter plane parts on its way to Coventry the other night. They will have worked out that someone is assisting them. I've spotted some security types sniffing around the depot in recent days and asking the bosses all kinds of questions."

"So there wouldn't have been any more information for me to transmit?"

"You've still got your other agents."

Maruska shook her head, "They are both dead."

"What? I was told it was a cell of four agents."

"Well, strictly speaking there were five, if you include the handler."

"Okay, the handler can sort you out; maybe give you some more people to work with."

Maruska spoke silently, "She's dead as well..."

"Why are they all dead? Have you been compromised?"

"They are dead because I killed them before they could kill me."

He swallowed and breathed out and sat back, "Our masters won't be pleased. Maybe it's time for you to leave as well."

She nodded, "Yes, I think so. Where are you going?"

"Back to Ireland; the Brits can't get to me there."

He stood up and pulled out his silver pocket watch, "Much as I love sitting here chatting to you as you really are very nice, but I need to get on shift. I get my wages later today, so maybe it's a good time to disappear."

Maruska reached underneath the table and up her skirt. She located the knife tucked into its little holder next to her stocking top.

He became silent. He hadn't realised this woman was a killer. He turned around with his back to her and reached into his lunch box that was sat on a table next to the gas cooker. He put his hand into the flip top leather container and began to feel for the Webley Revolver. Maruska had the knife against his back with one arm around his throat in a flash.

"Drop it..." she breathed into his ear.

He was slow to respond. She pressed the blade into the small of his back. It pierced his crisp white shirt and punctured the skin. A little crimson patch appeared on the linen. He flinched...

"I said drop it..."

The hand slowly removed itself from the box, "Look, I know we can work something out..."

"Yes, I'm sure we can." Maruska pressed the blade a little further into his back and began to twist it.

"Jesus!" he screamed.

"Turn around slowly." She extracted the knife.

She stepped back. He was a little unsteady on his feet. He leaned back against the cooker. There was a lot of blood coming out of the gaping wound in his back.

He said, "You don't need to do this." His hands came up in submission.

"You were going to kill me, weren't you?"

He shrugged, "It's just business, that's all. Nothing personal. Like you, I need to protect myself. Can I sit down? I'm feeling a little faint."

She nodded at the chair. He slumped into it, breathing heavily.

She pulled out the old Webley Revolver, "Did they give you this?"

He nodded, "I'm supposed to use it on myself if I'm about to be caught, but I never could; I'm too much of a coward."

"So you thought you would use it on me?"

"As I said, business."

The blood began to drip down from the chair onto the tiled floor.

She leaned into him, "Listen to me, you old fool. You laid down with dogs and now you get up with fleas. You will slowly bleed out, unless I do something about it, which I could because I'm a doctor. I knew exactly where to cut you."

He looked at her; his eyes were glassy; he laughed, "You Jews are all the same. Having you lot murdered is a price well worth paying to get my country back."

Maruska raised her eyebrows at that, "I've heard it all before..."

She knelt down in front of him. His head lolled on his chest. She lifted his chin. His eyes opened, "Save me..."

She pushed the knife up under his ribcage and turned it slowly. His eyes bulged.

She stepped back and watched him die...She never did learn his name...

Chapter 19

December 1940
London
Interrogations

Peter Porteous was in shock. He stood across the road staring at the remains of the terrace of houses that once contained his home. There was nothing left except a smouldering pile of burnt bricks and charred timber. An acrid stench filled the air. Periodically, steam would rise from the rubble as the Auxiliary Fire Brigade sprayed the remains with a weak jet of water. That was all they could get with the water main having been fractured by the bomb the night before. Indeed, the whole of Kensal Town was without water and would be for some time until the authorities could get workmen over to sort it out. The residents wouldn't hold their breath.

Edith Bell slid an arm inside his. He glanced at her briefly. He was tired having pulled a double shift up at Smiths in Cricklewood.

He whispered, "Have you seen Maruska?"

Edith Bell froze, "No."

"Don't mess me about, Edith. Was she in the crypt or not?"

"She was, but she left during a lull to check on something from her flat. She never came back."

He looked at her and raised his voice, "What did she go back for?"

"I don't know, I don't know. She never told me." Edith Bell began to cry. "She just said she had to go back to the house, that's all."

He asked, "Were you in the shelter when the bomb went off?"

She nodded, "Damn near took the roof off the church. The place must have moved at least half a foot."

He looked around anxiously as two policemen approached.

The sergeant addressed Porteous, "I understand you lived in one of these houses?" He gestured at the pile of rubble that must have stretched fifty yards.

Porteous did not answer. Edith Bell looked at him.

The policeman said, "Come on, sir, we are trying to ascertain the losses here so we need to check on all residents."

Porteous looked at him, "Yeah, okay, I understand. There were just two tenants remaining in number 26. That's Doctor Maruska Bergman and me. All the other flats are empty."

The sergeant ticked off something on his clipboard, "Have you seen Doctor Bergman since the raid?"

Porteous shook his head. Edith Bell spoke up, "She was in the shelter, but she went back to the house during a quiet time in the raid."

The policeman looked at her, "Did she leave before the all-clear?"

Edith Bell nodded and looked down. The sergeant muttered something and then left.

Porteous was so transfixed by the site of the pile of smouldering rubble that used to be his home that he didn't notice that he was suddenly surrounded by a group of men dressed in suits with dark grey overcoats. If he had looked up towards the junction of Kensal Road and Bosworth Road he would have seen two vans, out of which poured several uniformed soldiers, complete with rifles, led by a non-commissioned officer. From the other end of the road at the junction of Southern Row, five police officers began walking smartly towards them led by Inspector Eric Everard of the Metropolitan Police.

Edith Bell felt a tug on her arm. She turned to see one of the security team standing over her. Porteous had still not noticed as he continued staring at the remains of his home. All thoughts about the stash of illicit goods stored in the vacant flat below his had disappeared. Where was his neighbour and lover, Maruska?

He felt two hands either side of him. They took a firm hold on his arms. Some of the residents of Kensal Town who had gathered to survey the scene suddenly melted away not wishing to get involved with anyone of authority. A voice with a clipped Home Counties accent whispered into his ear,

"Peter Porteous?"

The voice didn't wait for an answer, "Would you mind coming with us? We would like you to answer a few questions..."

In Chiswick, two hours later, Peter Porteous sat with his head in his hands in an unheated, bare, room. He had no idea where he was. The unremarkable brick building was situated in some nondescript semi-industrial estate. It was cold; he shivered from time to time not knowing whether this was because of shock or the late December temperature. He had said nothing as he was being led away from the ruins of his house. He barely looked up as he sat handcuffed on the uncomfortable wooden bench in the back of the unmarked van between two of the security officers who had surrounded him on Bosworth Road. It was as though the fight had gone out of him. He could think of nothing but Maruska Bergman.

On the other side of the building, Edith Bell was not so quiet as befitted the landlady of a public house in Kensal Town. She had to be led, half carried, kicking and screaming, by three Metropolitan Police Officers, much to the consternation of Eric Everard who really liked things done quietly. He had never heard such foul language uttered by a so-called member of the fair sex. She sat handcuffed to an old iron chair that was in turn bolted to the bare concrete floor. Her wrists were red with the chafing of the worn metal of the handcuffs. This didn't stop her struggling. A large female officer, in some uniform or other, stood anxiously by the door with her ample arms folded across her chest. What Edith Bell needed was the good slapping she would have got if she had been in a regular women's prison...

Giles Deeprose of Ashford, Kent, otherwise known as Mr Brown, came through the door noisily, clutching one of his manila files. David Stuart of His Majesty's Security Services, soon followed him, together with a guard. Porteous didn't bother looking up. He sat and stared at the battered, wooden table. He still wore the cuffs.

Deeprose spoke up; his cut glass Home Counties accent was pronounced,

"Who the devil handcuffed this man?"

Stuart shrugged his shoulders, "Normal practice, sir." He beckoned at a uniformed officer who stood guarding the door.

The guard unlocked the cuffs and stepped back, "Behave yourself, sonny..."

Porteous rubbed his raw wrists as blood began to flow freely back into his hands. The pins and needles were particularly sharp.

Deeprose shuffled his paperwork, "Mr Porteous, we haven't had the pleasure. My name is Michael Brown. One of my jobs to interview foreign nationals when they first enter Britain."

Porteous looked up, "I'm not a foreign national, as you well know and your name is not Michael Brown."

Deeprose cleared his throat, "Yes, well, that may be so, but you will address me as Mr Brown for the purposes of this meeting."

Porteous shrugged his shoulders, "Why am I here? I have committed no crime."

David Stuart intervened, "Don't make me laugh, Porteous. The Metropolitan Police has a file on you this thick." He made a gesture with his hands.

Porteous smiled, "So, charge me or let me leave."

Deeprose held up his hands, "Yes, yes, we'll come to all that later."

He laid the picture of Maruska Bergman that had been taken for her Alien identity card in Ashford before she was released. He asked, "Do you know this woman?"

Porteous nodded, "Yes, That's Doctor Maruska Bergman. She is one of my neighbours. Do you know where she is?"

Deeprose shook his head, "I'm sorry to have to tell you that she is currently listed as missing following the enemy raids last night."

Poreteous swallowed hard, "Have you searched the building?"

Stuart smiled, "You saw the state of the terrace. There's nothing left. We think it was a parachute bomb meant for the railway line but to ease your mind, there's a thorough search going on at present. If there are any survivors or bodies, they will be located."

Porteous looked down, "What's all this to do with me? I pulled a double shift at Smiths yesterday making cockpit instruments for the Spitfire."

Deeprose leaned in, "When did you last see Miss Bergman?"

Porteous looked at his interrogator trying to work out what was going on, "I didn't see her yesterday so it must have been the day before."

"Have you any idea where she was?"

"No, not really. She's often at her job in Chelsea. Have you tried there?"

Stuart sat back, "There is no one named Maruska Bergman employed at Madam Collier's fine establishment."

Porteous knew this, "Well, that's what she told me."

Stuart raised his voice; "Somebody forged a glowing reference for your doctor neighbour from Madam Collier to satisfy the Alien Tribunal Board. I don't suppose you know anything about that?"

Porteous shook his head and folded his arms, "Since this has nothing to do with me, I'd really like to leave. I haven't slept for nearly forty-eight hours, and I'm on shift again this evening."

Deeprose moved some papers, "It says here you are an Air Raid Precautions warden?"

"Yes, mostly fire-watching duties, but I do other tasks when required."

Stuart referred to his notes, "Peter Porteous, born April 15th, 1905, in Leicester. Left school aged fifteen and took an apprenticeship with the motor trade but quit after two years. Why did you leave, you could have had a good trade?"

"It was affecting my health. I'm sure your detailed notes will tell you I suffer from asthma."

"Which is why the army discharged you."

"Yes, I tried, but there are some things I cannot do."

Deeprose spoke up, "Yes, but you do good work for the war effort up at Smiths. You are serving your country in a different way, and the work you do as an ARP is highly commendable."

Stuart thought there had been enough bonhomie, "Where did you meet Bergman?" he asked aggressively.

"She was referred to me by a friend. Doctor Bergman needed a more permanent home. She was living at the Bayswater Synagogue when I first met her."

"Who was the friend?" Stuart had his pen at the ready.

"Mrs Shira Adelman of Star Street in Paddington."

Stuart scribbled on a piece of paper and clicked his fingers. He held up the paper as the uniformed officer came over, "Go and pick up this lady and bring her here."

The policeman scuttled out of the room. A similar looking officer replaced him adopting a similar pose.

Deeprose asked, "What do you know of Doctor Bergman?"

Porteous shrugged his shoulders, "Only what she told me."

Deeprose quickly flicked through his papers, "What did she tell you?"

"She said she is from the Sudetenland in Czechoslovakia. She qualified as a doctor in Vienna and escaped through Zurich after the Nazis took control."

"How do you know she's a qualified doctor?" asked Stuart.

"I've seen her diplomas."

"They can easily be forged."

Porteous sighed, "I've observed her treat people with serious injuries and deliver several babies. And what's more, she was able to give me the latest treatment for my asthma."

Stuart scribbled furiously, "So, she was your personal physician?"

Porteous ignored the jibe, "She told me she had applied for work as a doctor at St Mary's on the Harrow Road and Paddington Hospital on Praed Street. They informed her she would have to have her qualifications recognised by the General Medical Council."

"Did she make an application?" This time it was Deeprose.

"As far as I know. It was taking a long time so that's why she took work as a seamstress."

Stuart asked, "What exactly was she making?"

Porteous stared at him, "Lingerie, as I understand."

"That wouldn't be from stolen parachute material, would it?"

Porteous looked down, "I never saw her do any work at home, so I couldn't tell you."

"Did she have a sewing machine?"

"Yes, an American Singer, I believe."

"Where did she get it from? Those machines are priceless at the moment."

"I've no idea. Two workmen delivered it one day whilst I was at work."

"Have you ever seen her use it?"

Porteous shook his head wondering where this was all going. He was anxious not to incriminate himself.

"Did she ever talk about her family back in Czechoslovakia?"

"No not really...Look, what is all this about?"

Deeprose lowered his voice as though someone might hear a secret, "We don't think Maruska Bergman is who she says she is."

Peter Porteous knew she probably wasn't but then many people in Kensal Town were not who they said they were. He asked, "Well, who do you think she really was?"

Deeprose leaned in, "A German spy..."

Across the other side of the building, the large, female prison officer on detached duty to the 'Hush, Hush Services,' finally got to slap Edith Bell when she found herself unobserved by anyone else. From being a vociferous and uncooperative detainee, Edith Bell went into silent mode.

Eric Everard scraped the chair noisily as he sat down, "Are you feeling a little better now, Miss Bell?"

Edith Bell looked up, "It's Mrs Bell, you useless prick."

"Really? I thought your husband found some sense and finally moved out for a calmer life. I believe he's much happier with his new lady."

There was a short and terse response, "Fuck off, copper."

Everard shook his head and searched through his notes, "You were the last person to see Maruska Bergman."

She responded, "Is that a question or a statement?"

"The priest at the shelter says you and her always sat together, and last night was no different."

"Yeah, so what?"

"So, where is she now?"

"How the fuck should I know? Look, she left the shelter during a pause in the bombing. She said she had something to do at home."

Everard's brows furrowed, "Did she say what she needed to do?"

Edith shook her head, "No, I tried to tell her to stay but Maruska's a wilful lass. She does what she chooses to do. Anyhow, why are you asking me questions about her? You should be out looking for her."

Everard snorted, "Are you serious? Didn't you see the state of the row of houses? If she was in her flat when the bomb went off, she's bound to be dead."

Edith Bell looked down.

"Are you still earning money on your back, Edith?" Everard sneered.

Edith stared him out as he went on, "Your husband is technically the licensee of your pub yet he no longer lives there. So, how can that be? To be a landlady of a licensed premise, you have to be of good moral standing. Ladies who prostitute themselves can hardly be placed in that category, can they?"

Edith looked up at him and shrugged her shoulders, "You don't award the licence, do you?"

"No, but a quiet word with the magistrate would soon sort that out," he smiled and sat back. "Look, I know all about you lot in Kensal Town. You think you are a law unto yourselves and that rules and regulations that apply to the rest of us have no bearing on you. Well. I've got news for you. They do, and soon the police, together with the council, will start to clean up that cesspit, commencing with the closure of all the pubs in the area."

Edith Bell raised her eyes to the heavens and asked, "Do you have a cigarette?"

Everard muttered, "Jesus Christ..."

There was a knock at the door. He nodded at the female guard and she opened the door. A uniformed officer stood there waiting for him. Everard got up and went to the door. Edith could see them whispering furtively. The policeman unwrapped what looked like a dirty handkerchief and showed the contents to Everard. He nodded and then turned to Edith Bell.

"You'll have to excuse me for a moment, Edith. This guard will get you some tea and a cigarette..."

Eric Everard, Giles Deeprose and David Stuart stood in the corridor a little way down from where Peter Porteous was being detained. The shock of seeing his house and all the contents destroyed, together with news that his lover may be a Nazi spy had drawn the life out of him. He sat slumped at the table.

Everard showed the contents of the handkerchief to the assembled group. Four brass buttons, blackened with smoke and slightly out of shape owing to the intensity of the heat, sat forlornly in the palm of his hand.

Stuart was getting impatient, "What is this, Everard?"

"Buttons from what's left of a boiler suit."

"And?"

"The priest says that Maruska Bergman was always wearing an old, green boiler suit."

"Yes? So what?"

"The buttons were found next to the incinerated corpse of a human underneath the smouldering rubble. The ambulance girls say it's definitely that of a female, but the body has been shipped off to the mortuary for a more detailed examination."

There was a collective silence among the group...

Deeprose looked at his watch, "So, she's dead, is she?"

Everard replied, "Looks that way, sir. As far as we know, she was the only one in the building. The bombing was particularly heavy last night. Most of the residents were in the shelter underneath the church. If she left to return to her lodgings before the bomb went off, then you can more or less guarantee she didn't make it."

Deeprose sighed, "Well, that's us finished for the moment. Come on Stuart, we'd better report to our lords and masters. Everard, you can give Porteous the good news and then bail him until further notice. He knows even less than we do about our mysterious Czech."

Everard protested, "But, sir, I've got a robbery and murder down in a Praed Street jewellers that require my attention, plus all these wretched black marketeers. Can't one of the uniforms do it?"

Deeprose turned and called over his shoulder, "I'll have a full report on my desk by close of play this afternoon. Good day to you, Inspector."

Everard called out, "What about Edith Bell?"

"Civilian matter, old boy. Nothing to do with us..."

With that, he was gone, closely followed by David Stuart.

Everard walked into Porteous' detention room. Callously, he laid out the burnt buttons on the table.

"Do you know what these are, Porteous?"

Porteous shook his head.

"Have a closer look."

Porteous picked up one. He rolled the button between his finger and thumb,

"I'd say it's a brass button."

"Correct. And where would you find this type of button?"

Porteous was too tired to play a question and answer game.

"Well, I'll tell you. They are the brass buttons off a boiler suit. They were found beside the burnt body of a female under the rubble of what's left of your home. Your neighbour often wore such a green boiler suit, did she not?"

Everard did not wait for an answer, "So, I'm sorry to tell you that the body looks like your neighbour, Maruska Bergman. The corpse has been taken to the mortuary." He stepped back.

"I'm granting you bail on your own recognisance pending further enquiries. Go and collect that whore, Edith Bell, and get out of my sight. One word of advice, Porteous, if I were you, I would cease all activities relating to the black market. Because, by Christ, if I catch you at it, and I will, I'll make sure you spend the rest of the war locked away in some prison..."

With that he was gone...

Porteous put his head in his hands and wept profusely.

It was nearly six in the evening by the time Dorothy Smith of the Security Services had gathered her faithful servants in her grandiose office. She was resigned to the inevitable. She spoke quietly with a cigarette in her long fingers.

"Let's have the good news, David."

He shook his head, "She's dead."

Smith exhaled some smoke, "Are we sure?"

David Stuart nodded, "She had taken to wearing a man's boiler suit, like many females do these days." He laid the blackened brass buttons on Smiths desk, "These were found next to the corpse."

"But we don't know if it was her?"

"Ma'am, the only female remaining in the house was Bergman. She was often dressed in this attire."

"Where's the body now?"

"At Paddington mortuary. I've sent one of the boys down to check with the pathologist, but he says it will be days before they get around to any detailed examination. They have confirmed that it's a female, though."

Dorothy Smith sighed. She turned to Giles Deeprose, "What does Porteous know about her?"

"Nothing, Ma'am. He only knows what she told him."

"Are you sure?"

Deeprose nodded, "There's nothing doing there, I'm sure. He's just a common person supplementing his living with some unauthorised trading. Apparently, he's very good at his job up at Smiths in Cricklewood. We checked his army records for the short time he was enlisted before his medical discharge, and all is good there. We turned him over to the local police."

Dorothy Smith thought for a minute, "Any joy with the Dickens book, John?"

John Porter shook his head; "We've checked every known edition going back to the 19th Century at the British Library, nothing but mumbo jumbo like the original messages. We have no idea how many foreign editions there are, even if we could lay our hands on them."

Smith sighed, "Okay. I can't see this going anywhere at the moment. Uxbridge report no further transmissions for a few days, but they'll keep a close ear to the airwaves. I'll tell the minister that we think she's dead."

She stood up, signalling that the meeting was over. "Time to move on." She turned to Giles Deeprose, "Get your lads and lassies down in Ashford to get their fingers out and do their jobs properly. I don't want a repeat of this. If in doubt, lock 'em up..."

Deeprose flushed up. He prided himself on his ability to do the job. He wasn't paid enough to be given a dressing down in front of his fellow officers...

The officers sent to pick up Shira Adelman never did find her...

Chapter 20

December 1940
London
A train Journey

Doctor Maruska Bergman sat next to the body of the dead Irishman. She had helped herself to a plate of eggs and bacon. Well, he did offer, didn't he? She hadn't realised how hungry she was until she started eating.

She stepped over him and washed up all the crockery, including the frying pan. She carefully dried the items and stowed them away in their correct place. She went upstairs to the two bedrooms. The Irishman was an orderly individual. The front bedroom, where he slept, was neat and tidy. The bed was made. She spent some time rummaging through his meagre belongings, but she could find no reference to his name or family. She did find a little tin that contained about sixty pounds in notes. She emptied the money into her bag. The bedroom at the back of the house overlooked a small tiled yard. A brick outhouse at the end appeared to be an outside toilet. As it was daylight, Maruska decided that she would use the chamber pot that was stowed under the bed.

She laid down on the neatly-made single bed and closed her eyes...

The light was beginning to fade when Maruska woke up. She looked out of the rear window. She could see some movement from the next-door yard. A harsh female voice called out from the back door,

"'Urry up in there; yer tea's ready..."

She heard the toilet flush and the old wooden door opened. An old man with wisps of grey hair on his balding head came out trying to button up his trousers. Maruska stepped back from the window; it was time she left.

She smoothed down the bed and took the chamber pot down to the kitchen, where she rinsed it out in the sink. She took it back upstairs and wiped it out with a clean towel from a linen cupboard on the landing. Using the same towel, she carefully went around the house, wiping anything she had touched.

She paid the dead Irishman no heed whatsoever.

She pushed out the Saxon from the hallway and out onto the cracked tile pathway. She rubbed the door handle with the towel and stowed it into her basket. She quietly went through the gate, closed it behind her, mounted the bicycle and rode away.

It took her over an hour to pedal down to Euston. She flicked on the lights that Porteous had acquired for her. She was just another anonymous office girl making her way home before the air raid sirens sounded, although she much preferred being taken for a factory girl...

She turned into Melton Street and dismounted. Several bombs had hit the station recently, but some passengers were still hurrying in and out. She joined a queue at one of the ticket office windows, still clutching her bicycle; she wasn't going to let that go...

She smiled at the clerk, "Are there any trains to Liverpool?" she asked.

The clerk sucked his teeth and picked up a clipboard. He flipped down the spectacles that were perched on the top of his head.

"There's one scheduled at 10.30 this evening, but it's full and there's no guarantee it will leave if Jerry returns to bomb us again." He peered through the glass at Maruska's bike.

"If you want, I can give you a ticket for the goods wagon. You can take your bike in there?"

She smiled at him, "Yes, yes, I'll take it." She reached into her bag to extract some money.

"Hold on a minute, miss. You are not supposed to be travelling; there's a war on, you know?"

Maruska looked at him with her eyes wide open, "Sir, I need to get to Liverpool to take care of my sick mother. She's very ill and has no one to look after her..." A tear trickled down Maruska's cheek.

The clerk cleared his throat, "Alright, alright...there's no need to make a fuss. Do you have an identity card?"

Maruska pushed over the now slightly battered card.

The clerk picked it up, "Miss Rosemary McCumiskey, I see. This looks all in order." He punched his machine and a ticket came whirling out into the little brass recess that straddled the glass. "With the bike that will be one pound and fifteen shillings and there's no guarantee that the service will operate. Do you understand?"

Maruska sniffed loudly and wiped away another tear, "Thank you, sir."

She passed over two one-pound notes, not knowing if they came from Zev Adelman or the Irishman, not that she cared either way. She pressed the ticket into her purse and dropped it into the bottom of her bag. A quick glance at the large station clock told her she had over three hours to wait. She was concerned that any air raid could delay or even cancel the departure, and then she saw a couple of platoons of soldiers patiently sitting on their kit bags by one of the entrances smoking and playing cards. Two harassed corporals

were trying to corral them and stop them sloping off to one of the bars to partake of some alcoholic refreshment. She spotted a young one sat away from his colleagues. His face was buried deep in a book. She quietly went up to him.

She smiled at him as he looked up, "Which train are you getting?" she enquired.

He looked up, surprised to see such a pretty lady wheeling a bicycle. "Ten-thirty to Liverpool, Miss, although we are only going as far as Crewe."

"Do you think it will run? I need to get home to my sick mother."

He put down his book, "Yes, it will run alright, especially as it's carrying soldiers. You'll need to board about half an hour before it departs. Trains are known to leave as soon as all the passengers and goods are on board."

She nodded, "Thank you."

"And make sure you bring some food and water. I've been stuck on one of these for nearly twenty-four hours. Better still, go and eat something before you board."

She thanked him. He returned to his book as she wheeled the bike across the forecourt to Euston Square and onto Eversholt Street. She spotted a working-man's café just along next to Lancing Street. The windows were steamed up with condensation. She leaned against the door as it opened. The smell of greasy, fried food hit her along with the heat that was in contrast to the cold evening. A voice called out,

"You can't bring that bike in 'ere."

Maruska answered, "I just need some food to take with me on the train."

An overweight woman, who looked like she had eaten far too many of her own fry-ups, appeared at the door. Maruska could see the place was crowded.

"Take it around the side. There's a red gate. I'll go and open it; you can come in that way. If you leave it on the street, some tea-leaf will nick it for sure..."

Maruska didn't really understand but pushed the bike around and sure enough, the woman was waiting for her with a cigarette stuck between her lips. Her accent was very London,

"Come on in, love, we'll sort you out..."

Maruska leaned the Saxon against a brick wall, picked up her bag and followed the lady through a messy kitchen and out into the dining room. The place buzzed with noise. She could see a smattering of women dressed in a variety of clothes who looked like they were about to go on a night out.

She sat down at a table. Two of the women sat smoking on the other end. They glanced at her and nodded. Maruska ordered the 'Dish of the day' not bothering to ask what it was. She just needed some sustenance before she boarded the train.

A hot plate of some indeterminate stew arrived, complete with some dumplings and covered in thick gravy. A large mug of tea was plonked down beside her. Maruska looked up at the lady who smiled at her, "Eat it all up, luv. If yer gettin' on a train, you'll have no idea when yer'll eat again."

Maruska tucked into the surprisingly tasty meal.

One of the ladies sat on the end of the table addressed her, "Where are you makin' for?"

Maruska looked at the woman who seemed definitely overdressed even though her ample bosom was peeking out of her partially unbuttoned blouse.

Maruska swallowed some food, "Crewe. My husband's got a few days' leave."

The woman laughed, "Got an 'usband have yer? I had one of them. Kicked the idle bastard out years ago. Now I have lots of 'usbands every night..."

Her friend burst out laughing. Maruska looked confused. "Take no notice, luv, she's only messin' with yer. How long have you been married?"

"A couple of years," Maruska replied.

"You forrin or somat?"

"I'm Polish," said Maruska.

The woman looked at her mate, "They get everywhere, don't they, Ivy?"

The woman named Ivy nodded as she drew on a cigarette. "What do you do, luv?"

Maruska responded quickly, anxious to end the conversation, "I'm a seamstress when I can get work."

Ivy moved a little closer to her, "I tell you what, when you return, pop back in 'ere and ask for me. I can get you lots of work with a face and figure like yours. I work for Charlie Maitland down in Soho. Treats us real good, he does, doesn't he Muriel?"

Maruska knew who Charlie Maitland was; Nancy Keeling had often spoken of the smooth-talking Maltese vice king.

"What's the pay like?" Maruska was trying to look interested.

"You can get ten pounds a night if you are not too fussy. Charlie takes his cut, and you have to give your minder some."

Maruska nodded as she ate, "I'll think about it. There's not much doing in dressmaking these days, and I don't want to end up in one of those factories.

The proprietress returned with a paper bag, "Don't be messin' with the lady, you two. Do you hear?"

Ivy smiled, "It's alright, Maude, just seein' if the lady is sorted."

The proprietress, plonked the paper bag down on the table, "Here you are, luv, just a little sommat to keep you goin' on your journey."

Maruska smiled at the kindness. She reached into her purse and asked, "How much do I owe you?"

"Call it one and six, luv, and you take care of yerself and yer 'usband."

She moved away, "Come on, I'll let yer out wiv yer bike..."

Maruska Bergman stood at the doorway to the last goods wagon of the ten-thirty to Liverpool via just about anywhere that had lines that were intact. A porter came along, "Hurry along, Miss. If you are going, then you'd better get on board…"

He walked past her as she was struggling to get the Saxon up into the carriage. She squinted in the dark, trying to get her eyes to adjust to what little light there was. She spotted some wooden railings that ran down the length of the carriage. She wheeled the bike over and leaned it against a polished one. She grabbed a strap and fastened the machine as tight as she could to the rail. She breathed out and looked around at the assortment of wooden crates that appeared to have been casually and carelessly tossed inside. She walked over to a single box that sat next to a grubby window just as the steam engine gave a few jolts and moved slowly off, huffing and puffing. In the distance, she could hear the first early warning siren; the German bombers were somewhere over the southern coast.

She glanced at her watch and held it up to the light. The train was seven minutes early. The driver had clearly decided he wasn't going to bother hanging around for the Luftwaffe. She had to hold on tightly as the carriage rocked and rolled as it gathered pace over the numerous points that littered the railway lines into the station. She made her way to the wooden crate and sat down, desperately holding on to the side rails. The train picked up speed as it made its way through northwest London, and the swaying began to subside somewhat. Maruska noticed how hard the box was. This would be a rather unpleasant, lengthy trip. She spotted some dark, grey blankets that were used to protect the more valuable cargo. The bundle was held together with a canvas strap. She unbuckled it and took out one of the coarse blankets. After folding it several times, she placed it on the box. This gave her a much more comfortable seat for her journey.

She sat down and watched the darkness of the blackout in London flash by. She thought about Porteous. Was he grieving for her, or had he moved on? Would he even look for her? She thought about her parents, wherever they were. Indeed, were they still alive? Her actions might hasten their demise, but what could she do? Hopefully, her handlers back in Hamburg would soon presume she was dead. No doubt they would send someone to look out for her. Given the fact that she had completely wiped out her cell, she couldn't think of anything less likely.

She pondered how she had got herself into this situation. She was a doctor, after all, sworn to protect life and not take it, as she had casually done in the interests of self-preservation. War makes for very strange bedfellows...She couldn't quite grasp how easy it had been to kill the members of her cell. She patted the blade that was strapped to the top of her thigh underneath her dress; it gave her a sense of security.

She shoved another folded-up blanket against the side of the rocking train, leaned back and closed her eyes. She was tired, but thankful to be getting as far away from Kensal Town and London as soon as possible.

She felt the prodding, but she was in a deep sleep. Was it Porteous? He used to poke her when her snoring kept him awake...A distant voice was in her ear,

"Miss, Miss, can I see your ticket?"

She forced herself to open her eyes. The light was harsh. The conductor was carrying an old-fashioned glass oil lamp as the train was in blackout. She opened her eyes. The man was in his late fifties with some grey hairs pushing out of his official hat.

"Miss, your ticket, please."

Maruska fumbled in her bag for her purse and then found the ticket. He held it up to the light, "Is that your bike over there?" he asked, pointing to the Saxon.

She nodded as he clipped the ticket, "It's funny," he remarked, "My wife used to have one like that only in a different colour. Some person stole it, and I'm still paying it off." He handed back her ticket, "You take care of it, Miss. There's some very dodgy people around."

As he made to go off to fulfil his duties; she asked, "Where are we?"

He looked at his watch, "Just south of Rugby. It looks like we are going straight to Crewe. Got to get these soldiers off at the right place but don't be surprised if we are delayed in Crewe."

She nodded, "Is there a toilet?"

He pointed to the exit door to the main train, "Two carriages along and don't use it if we are stationary, do you understand?"

She stared at him not knowing that train toilets deposited their contents out on to the open track....

She watched him disappear into the gloom.

She tucked her bag behind the box after removing the purse, stood up and made her way to the door.

The carriage was dark but was packed with soldiers, some sleeping, some smoking and some engaged in a card school. She had to make her way through the mass of legs and arms that were sprawled across the gangway. Just before she reached the door, the catcalls started. There's nothing worse than a bunch of testosterone-fuelled young men topped up with a few beers. She ignored them and pushed open the sliding door to the next carriage. She began picking her way along when she felt an arm on hers,

"Can I help you, Miss?"

She turned to see an ugly male whose beery breath made her gag. "No, no, thank you."

"The toilet is at the end of this carriage. I'll show you if you like?"

She shook her head, anxious to get away. "No, I can manage."

He leered at her, "Don't worry, I only want to help you."

She was about to swear at him and then thought the better of it.

"Okay, lead the way…"

He pushed past her. She got a whiff of an unwashed body complete with alcohol and cheap cigarettes; just what every young woman needs when she is being romanced…

There were some grunts as he kicked a few stray legs away from the passageway. He slid open the end door and held it for her. She smiled at him coyly as she went past.

"The toilet's just there," he said, pointing to a door that was marked in bold letters, 'WC.'

She went in, but his foot prevented her from closing it. She pressed up against the blacked-out window as he squeezed in behind her.

"Okay, okay, take it easy. I'm not giving it away for free, you know."

He looked down at her, "I knew you were a tart. What self-respecting woman gets on a night train without her husband?"

She tilted her head, "Thirty-bob, or else go and get one of your soldier boyfriends to tug you off."

He began unbuttoning his trousers and snorted, "Me? I don't pay for it. I take it when I want."

She shook her head, "Okay, sonny, let's see what you've got and then I'll tell you how much you are going to pay. The bigger it is, the more you pay, but I'm telling you I don't do anything for less than ten bob."

He had his penis out in a flash, "Is this big enough for you? I've had no complaints in the past." He laughed.

She looked down at the organ, suspecting that it hadn't been washed in a long time.

She shrugged her shoulders, "It'll do, I suppose. Shall we say a pound?"

"You'll be lucky. By the time I've finished with you, you'll be begging for more."

He moved closer to her and put an arm around her waist. He pulled her to him. She lifted up a leg and propped her foot against the lavatory bowl.

She pushed him back, "Let me just remove my knickers; I don't want them torn."

She reached up her skirt and grasped the handle of the long blade. He didn't see it as she quickly pressed the cold steel against his penis.

"Don't you fucking move," she growled into his ear. "One slip, and I'll have your prick in two pieces on this dirty floor." She lightly drew it across the flesh, drawing blood. He yelped. His erection was subsiding rapidly. His eyes widened and flashed from side to side in terror.

She brought a knee up into his groin just managing to remove the knife before she connected. As a doctor, she didn't fancy having to clear up this mess...

He screamed as he crumpled to the floor. She aimed a kick at his groin and connected with the point of her shoe. By this time he was squashed up against the side of the toilet, not caring that he was lying in some other man's urine. She kicked him again, this time to his head. His eyes lolled as he briefly lost consciousness. A trickle of blood began to seep from the wound over his left eyebrow. She raised her foot and stamped on his groin...

"Explain that to your mates, you bastard..."

He groaned.

She closed the door behind her and quickly made her way back to the goods carriage. She was breathing heavily by the time she arrived and flopped down on the blanket-covered box. She smiled; her father couldn't possibly have foreseen that his beloved daughter would be capable of doing this...

The proprietress of the café on Eversholt Street had done her proud. The paper bag contained two bacon sandwiches, a sausage roll and two pieces of bread and butter or at least what passed for butter in these times of shortages, and a hard-boiled egg. She reached into her bag and took out a small flask that she had liberated from the Irishman, into which she had poured some fresh water.

The train stopped as she ate. The violence had given her an appetite...

She wiped away some of the grime on the darkened window and tried to peer out, but she could see nothing. The conductor came hurrying back to check the lights at the rear of the train.

"Nothing to worry about, Miss. Just some drunken soldier who seems to have fallen in the WC and cracked open his head. I don't know where they get these people. We've made an unscheduled stop in Birmingham so that they can get him to hospital. We'll be on our way soon."

With that, he was gone...Maruska leaned back and smiled; one less problem to worry about. Mr Big and Brave soldier would not be telling his mates that a little slip of a female had done this to him...

The train was stationary for nearly two hours...

Chapter 21

December 1940
London
Information, or lack of it...

Just as Maruska Bergman was sleeping in the goods wagon of the Liverpool-bound train, Peter Porteous sat on an armchair in Edith Bell's bedroom in the attic of The White Horse public house on Kensal Road. Edith was undressing. Porteous was still in the same clothes he was wearing when they were picked up by the security services as they were observing the ruins of his home. Porteous paid her no attention, even though this rather good-looking woman was removing her clothing.

"Tell me again..."

She looked at him, "Jesus! If I've told you once, I've told you a hundred times. Drink your whisky."

Porteous sipped at the expensive malt. She removed her skirt, folded it up and sighed.

"We were sheltering in the crypt during the air raid. It was bloody heavy. They were giving the railway a real pounding. There was a pause and Maruska said she needed to get back to the flat for something. And no, she didn't tell me what it was."

"Did you try to stop her?"

"Of course I did, you idiot. But you know Maruska better than me. Once she sets her mind on something, there's no changing it."

"Where was that priest?"

"I told you; he was curled up in the corner pretending to read stories to the children."

"He didn't leave after her?"

Edith shook her head, "No, he's too much of a coward."

Edith began to unbutton her blouse. He put his head in his hands, "Why would she go out in the middle of an intense air raid?"

She tossed the blouse into a linen basket in the corner by a washstand.

"I have no idea...Now are you coming to bed or what? You did say you were on shift early tomorrow, and I've got a delivery from the brewery at seven."

She propped one leg up on the bed and unclipped a stocking, rolling it carefully down her leg so as not to ladder it. That, too, went in the basket.

He said, "There's something not quite right."

She paused as she was peeling off the other stocking, "What do you mean?"

He stood up and began to pace, "Maruska is far too bright to do something as stupid as this. She was quite fearful of the bombing."

The other stocking went towards the basket. It didn't quite make it; it hung forlornly over one side. Edith went over the washstand and began to scrub her face with cold water and soap.

His face appeared behind her in the mirror, "Her bike! Where's her bloody bike? She never went anywhere without that."

Edith stopped and looked at him in the mirror with water dripping down the side of her face, "That's a point...Now that I come to think of it, she always used to put it under the steps to the church whenever there was a raid, and she was in the shelter."

He passed her a towel, "Well it wasn't there earlier today when the police and fire services were all over the place."

She shrugged her shoulders; "Maybe she wheeled it back to the house where it would have been safer?"

He looked at her, "Who in Kensal Town is going to steal the doctor's bicycle?"

She poured some of the water into a large basin, "Pass me my night dress." She pointed to a cotton nightgown that was folded on her bed.

She said, "If she did take it back to the house, there wouldn't be much left of it after that blaze. The bloody thing would have melted in the heat."

He nodded and sat back in the chair.

As she dried herself off, she said, "Leave it, Porteous. She's probably gone, like many of the souls in London, thanks to the Jerries."

He put his head in his hands and nodded, "You know, they said she may have been a German spy."

Edith had her face covered by the nightdress as she pulled it over her head, "What? What did they say?"

He shook his head, "Not much. More of an insinuation, really. They asked a lot of questions about her. I just repeated what she told me that she had escaped from Czechoslovakia. They even suggested that perhaps she wasn't even a real doctor."

Edith sat on the bed, "Well, that's a load of nonsense. How many lives has she saved in Kensal Town?"

"That's what I told them."

"They even suggested that might not have been her real name."

"You saw her certificates."

"Yes, but they said they could be forgeries."

"Hmm, they appear to have an answer for everything. Did they offer you any proof?"

He shook his head again, "No, of course not."

"Then it's all speculation."

"I'm beginning to wonder if she was even a Jew."

Edith lifted the bed covers, "Well, that's easily sorted; just ask Shira..."

She patted one side of the large bed, "Now get undressed and come and get some sleep."

When Edith Bell awoke before dawn the next day, Peter Porteous had already left for his job in Cricklewood.

He walked into Building Number 2 at Smiths and was immediately surrounded by his girls. Alice Halpin ushered them away, barked an order at them in her harsh Liverpool accent, and took him by the arm to the old canteen. She plonked him down on a bench and went and ordered two mugs of hot sweet tea.

As she slid in beside him, she asked, "What happened?"

He sipped the tea, "Parachute bomb; land mine. Whatever you want to call it. Took out a whole row of houses on Bosworth Road, including mine."

Alice looked at him, "Maruska, is it true what they say?"

He bowed his head, "She's officially listed as missing. They have a female body down at the makeshift morgue in Paddington. They presume it's her, but there's not really anything left that's recognisable apart from the brass buttons of her boiler suit."

Over the next twenty minutes, Peter Porteous told Alice Halpin the whole story. She sat there open-mouthed as he relayed the bit about her possibly being a German spy.

Alice stared ahead, occasionally sipping her tea, "I don't believe a word of it, do you?"

He shook his head, "I don't know, really. She was quite the girl of mystery at times. I never knew where she was half the time especially after I got her that wretched bicycle."

Alice took his hands, "Look at me, Porteous. You never saw anything that could be construed as suspicious, did you?"

He didn't answer; she continued, "Put yourself in her position; a young woman totally alone and far from her home and family. You were good to her, and she was good to you. Listen to me, unless you live with someone for a long time you'll never really know that person and even then, there are always some secrets. As far as you are concerned, Maruska was a doctor fleeing from Nazi persecution. I saw her treat sick and injured people, so don't let them tell you she wasn't a real doctor. And as for her not being a Jew, Shira will put anyone right about that. I meant to ask, where did you stay last night, seeing as you are now technically homeless?"

"With Edith in The White Horse."

Alice raised her eyebrows, Nancy won't like that..."

"I know. After the shift, I'll go up and see her. I'm not doing any ARP stuff for a few days until I get myself sorted. I also need to see Jimmy Ryan so that I can give him the good news about our burnt stock..."

Their intimate conversation was rudely interrupted by a booming voice, "Porteous!"

Alice Halpin and Peter Porteous both turned around and simultaneously shouted, "Piss off. Walker..."

The shift was long and arduous but Alice took over and chivvied up the girls whilst she left Porteous to his thoughts. When Cedric Walker, the supervisor, heard the news, he decided it would be better to leave Porteous to his own devices today, as long as the production line kept going.

It was dark by the time Peter Porteous got down to Paddington on his bicycle. As he turned into Star Street, he could see an elderly and very bored policeman flapping his arms and stamping his feet to keep out the cold. He was stationed directly outside Adelman's Jewellery shop.

Porteous hesitated. He would normally keep well away from the police, especially as he was not wearing his ARP uniform. He took a deep breath and walked boldly up to the officer as if he was about to enter the shop

"Can I help you, sir?" the policeman asked.

Porteous looked at this ageing officer, "Yes, I wanted to speak with Mrs Adelman."

"So do the Metropolitan Police, sir."

"What happened?" Porteous looked incredulously at the officer who must have been dragged kicking and screaming out of retirement.

The policeman looked suspiciously at Porteous, "What's your business with Mrs Adelman?"

"I told you, I want to speak with her or her husband, if he's available." Porteous looked at the boarded-up shop, "What's going on? Has something happened?"

The policeman cleared his throat, "I suppose it will do no harm to tell you, as Scotland Yard have finished their investigation here."

"What investigation?"

"Look, sonny, there's been a break-in at the shop and old Mr Adelman has been murdered."

Porteous' mouth dropped, "What?"

"Are you listening to me? I said, someone broke into the shop the other night, murdered old Adelman and cleared out the contents of his safe."

"What about Mrs Adelman?"

The officer shook his head, "Nowhere to be seen, I'm afraid to say. It looks like whoever killed the old man took Mrs Adelman. She's disappeared; no one's seen her since the night of the really intensive bombing. Detectives would like to get hold of her to find out if she knows anything, but they are saying the robbers have probably killed her after having a little fun. I hear she was a good-looking woman."

Poreous stepped back, finding it hard to take in what he had just heard; first Maruska and now Shira.

"What happened to Mr Adelman?" Porteous asked.

"Strangled with a lady's stocking as he lay in his bed."

Porteous backed away. The policeman inquired, "Who shall I say was asking after her?"

Porteous turned and walked away, ignoring the policeman's request for his name. He went into the bar at The Great Western Hotel recalling that's where he and Maruska had their first conversation. He ordered a large whisky, gulped it down at the bar, and then requested another. He slapped a coin down on the counter and took his drink to a small table in the corner, away from the other early evening drinkers.

He sat down with all sorts of thoughts going through his mind...

An hour or so later, he knocked on the door of the Bayswater Synagogue. Mrs Rebecca Levy answered the door.

Porteous stood back not wishing to intimidate the Rabbi's wife, "Hello, I'm sorry to bother you. I was wondering if you've seen Doctor Maruska Bergman in the last few days?"

Mrs Levy smiled at him, "Maruska? Oh no, sorry. What a lovely girl she is, not like some of those flighty types that are living here. My husband is far too lenient with them." She paused and a look of concern appeared over her face. "Has something happened to her?"

Porteous began to speak, but she stopped him and ushered him into a side room, "Would you like some tea, Mr...er...er?"

"Porteous, ma'am; I'm a good friend of Doctor Bergman."

She paused, "Porteous, that's an interesting name, Irish is it?"

He smiled, "No ma'm, Scottish, I believe. I think one of my ancestors was a lodge keeper to a wealthy lord or other back in the Middle Ages."

"Well, sit down, and I'll bring you some refreshment.

She returned with some fine bone china cups and saucers and proceeded to pour some tea, "Tell me about Doctor Bergman."

Porteous related the story of the bombing in Kensal Town as he sipped the hot liquid.

She said, "Oh, my dear. I do hope she's all right. The bombing was very heavy the other night. We heard that several parachute bombs had been dropped. They were after the railways."

"I take it you haven't seen her, then?"

Mrs Levy shook her head, "She'll be in our prayers."

"What about Mrs Adelman?"

Mrs Levy put down her cup, "Oh, that's just terrible. I fear for her. My husband always said no good would become of her and as for that husband of hers, a bad lot he was. The crowd with whom he was doing business determined his fate. He would only come to the synagogue when he wanted something. He brought Shira here to get his marriage blessed by the Rabbi. Isaac did so only because he saw it as his duty."

She paused and then added, "He used to beat her, you know."

Porteous nodded, "I know."

"She was a little difficult from time to time but what do you expect when there is such an age difference. Shira was young. She wanted to see the world and ..." Her voice tailed off...

Porteous reached over and took her hand, "I know Shira. She'll find a way to stay safe." He didn't convince himself.

"What do you know of Maruska?"

Mrs Levy shrugged her shoulders, "Only what she told us that she had escaped from Vienna when the Nazis took over."

"Nothing about her family?"

"Not much, come to think of it." She stood up and went to a drawer in an ancient dresser that stood by the window. She took out her husband's notebook and sat back down.

"When she came here first of all, my husband took some details from her."

She flicked through the book, "Ah, here it is." She passed over the notebook and Porteous scanned through the immaculate, copperplate script, befitting of a respected rabbi. The story was not much more than what she had told him.

"Was she an observant Jew, Mrs Levy?" He asked.

"Oh yes, very much so; such a good and pure girl. Her Hebrew is excellent. I was sorry to see her leave, but she is an independent spirit. Which reminds me. A letter came for her last week. I was going to send it back, but perhaps you can take it for her?"

She ran out of the room and returned with a plain white envelope marked St Mary's Hospital, Harrow Road.

Porteous placed it in his pocket...

He stood in the entrance to the hospital on Praed Street and carefully opened the letter. It was dated a couple of weeks previously.

Dear Doctor Bergman

Further to your application to work in this hospital, I am pleased to say that the General Medical Council have approved your application to work as a doctor's assistant. You will work under the supervision of an experienced doctor until it is deemed that you are a fit and proper person to practise medicine in this establishment pending the verification of your qualifications in Vienna, whenever that may be.

Please contact Doctor Richard Buchard, Consultant of Paediatrics, at this hospital to arrange a meeting.

Yours sincerely

Professor John Statham

Porteous smiled. If he ever found Maruska, she would be pleased...

Porteous arrived at West End Lane, in West Hampstead, about an hour later. He was hurrying; the early warning air raid siren was sounding across the capital. He was not alone. Fellow residents were making haste to either their homes or to a shelter. He knew Nancy Keeling would be at home if she weren't working.

He cycled up the lane and past the underground station just as staff were busy trying to shut the metal grills to close the station. The trains would cease for the duration of the raid. He turned into Crediton Hill and wheeled the machine up the short pathway to one of the Victorian terraced houses. He extracted a key and opened the door.

Closing the heavy wood and glass door behind him, he called out, "Nancy! Nancy! It's only me."

He threw his coat onto a hook by the door, where it joined several others. The warmth of the house hit his cold face. A sleepy Nancy Keeling appeared at the top of the stairs. She was dressed in a robe that was pulled tightly around her waist. She smiled when she saw Porteous,

"Hey! I'm glad you came. I was worried about you. Alice called in earlier, she said you might pop by." She skipped down the stairs with no sign of the deep sleep she had been in before her visitor arrived.

She put her arms around him and hugged him tight; she whispered in his ear, "Any news of Maruska?"

She felt his head shake, "Come, I'll make you some tea."

She led him into the kitchen, put the kettle on the gas and reached for her cigarettes. She opened the back door to get a better listen. It was like turning up the volume on the sirens. She poured the hot water, together with some milk and sugar, into a flask and told Porteous to grab his coat.

"What about you?"

She smiled, threw off the coat and stepped into a boiler suit that Maruska had shortened for her some months previously.

She did up the buttons, not bothering about putting on any underwear and fastened her coat. By this time, he was holding the door open for her. They made their way down to the bottom of the garden and Nancy opened a rusty gate onto the old recreation ground that used to stage amateur football matches before the Blitz. There was enough light from the full moon for them to pick their way about twenty-five yards to a brick building that had been turned into a makeshift air raid shelter by a couple of ARPs some time ago, not that it was used very much by local residents who preferred to huddle together in the larger shelter back towards the underground station.

She pushed open the door. The place smelled of damp, but at least the thick brick building and roof might give them some sort of protection against the enemy bombs. She pushed him into a corner and sat him down. She produced two tin mugs from deep in the recesses of her overcoat and poured some tea.

They talked for nearly two hours. Porteous explained all that he knew about his Czechoslovakian lover, which, as he rapidly finding out, was not exactly very much.

Nancy listened carefully; she always knew there was something not quite right about the girl who had taken Porteous' affections so easily, but she didn't say anything, preferring to keep her own counsel.

"Edith says you stayed with her last night."

He nodded, "There's a vacant house down at the bottom of East Row opposite the school. Edith is going to speak with the landlord tomorrow. There shouldn't be a problem."

"Why don't you just move in here?" She asked, looking straight into his eyes. "My housemate has cleared off back to Hampshire. You can help with the rent.

He smiled, "That's the tenth time you've asked me to move in with you..."

She shrugged her shoulders, "You can't blame a girl for trying...but, seriously, Porteous, we'd be good for each other. You never know, I might be persuaded to change my occupation if I knew I had a good man to come home to every evening."

She snuggled up to him, "You know I've always loved you, ever since you helped me when I first came to London."

He held her tight and stared into the darkness, as the sound of falling bombs seemed to get closer and closer.

They were silent for a few minutes; he said, "You know that Shira has disappeared?"

She sat up, "What? She's probably on one of her benders again."

Porteous shook his head, "I fear not, this time, Nancy, her old man is dead, and the shop has been robbed."

Nancy Keeling was wide-eyed, "How did he die?"

"Strangled with a stocking, so I'm led to believe."

"That doesn't sound like Shira. She would have plunged a knife through the old bastard's heart, if I know her. What are the police saying?"

He shrugged his shoulders, "Robbery gone wrong is how Scotland Yard are telling it with Shira kidnapped and murdered. All of his valuable stock has gone missing. God knows what they did to Shira."

Nancy put her head down on his lap. She knew he was hurting, but she didn't know what to do about it. She whispered, "You've still got Alice and me."

He nodded in the darkness. He realised he'd just lost two of the four women who meant the most to him. She felt him sob...

The all-clear was sounded just after two in the morning. Nancy led Porteous to her bed, where he slept fitfully until it was time for him to get back up to Cricklewood to make instruments for the war effort. She propped herself up on one arm as she watched him get dressed. He kissed her on the lips before he left...

Chapter 22

December 1940
Southport

The sunlight on this late December day in 1940 was harsh on Doctor Maruska Bergman's eyes as she exited from Liverpool Lime Street station. Christmas seemed to have gone without a trace. The journey from London had taken nearly twelve hours. She was tired, having only slept fitfully on her makeshift bed of woollen covers. Liverpool showed signs of recent bombing; this was not exactly what she had bargained for except that this city was not to be her final destination. She wheeled the Saxon over the road to St George's Hall, wondering what to do next.

She stood in front of the concert venue for a few minutes, trying to get her bearings.

"Can I help you, Miss?"

She turned to see the stern face of a Liverpool police constable.

She stammered, "No-yes, sorry. I'm a little confused. I was looking for a small hotel where I can rest up for a day or two."

"I take it you want respectable lodgings?" She didn't like his questions.

She nodded.

He sighed and pointed, "Just walk down to Skelhorne Street. There are a couple of decent places there." He paused, "Can I ask you what your business is here in Liverpool, seeing as you are a foreigner?"

Maruska was exasperated, tired and generally fed up; she looked at him as he held out his hand, "Can I see your identity card, Miss?"

She didn't answer him. She rummaged in her bag and produced the card. He examined it carefully after putting on a pair of reading glasses.

"Ah, Miss McCumiskey. Your address is given as London, so why are you here? You know you are not supposed to be travelling?"

"I have come to see my mother and take care of her. She's old and not in good health. I'm trying to get a connection to North Wales, but there are no trains until tomorrow." Maruska's tone was one of defiance. She hadn't endured the uncomfortable journey to be confronted by some provincial copper...

The Policeman pretended to examine the card, "Very good, Miss. You'll find a few decent hotels on Skelhorne Street but a word of advice, don't be hanging around the station with the other women otherwise the magistrate will put you straight back on a train to London, do you hear me?"

Maruska ignored him and walked away.

The sour-faced receptionist insisted on taking three days' rent for the small room, but at least it had a sink where she could wash. Maruska had to produce the identity card for a second time. The receptionist took down her details before delivering a parting shot,

"You can put your bike in the yard at the back. Please remember, no other guests whether male or female are allowed in your room."

After depositing the Saxon, Maruska trudged up to the top floor room. It looked like the hotel had been a family home, and Maruska's room was up in the old servants' quarters in the attic.

She locked the door, tore off her clothes, and stood naked by the sink, giving herself a thorough wash in cold water. It seemed you had to pay for hot water...

She climbed into bed and promptly fell asleep...

It was dark when she awoke. She dressed in clean clothes and slipped downstairs. There was a different receptionist on the desk.

"Are you the foreign girl in room forty-one?"

Maruska nodded, "Yes, I was wondering if you know of somewhere I can get something to eat?"

The receptionist pointed to the door, "There's a café across the street. They don't have much, but if you say you're from the hotel they'll give you a discount. Don't be out late. The Jerries have been bombing the docks for the last three nights. The sirens usually start at about ten. Come down to the cellar; we are normally pretty safe down there, and I always have a hot drink available."

The food was simple but plentiful and good. She sat back and breathed out just as the siren started. She looked at her watch; it was barely nine o'clock. She heard the anti-aircraft guns before the familiar drone of the Heinkel He111 planes began dropping their deadly cargo. She hurried across the road back to the hotel.

She spent another uncomfortable night in a cold, damp basement with some other residents including three Royal Navy junior officers, two travelling salesmen and what appeared to her as three ladies of the night cursing their luck at having to abandon punters around the back of the station. Maruska resolved to leave Liverpool as soon as possible and get as far away from enemy action as possible.

She was up early the next morning. The sour-faced receptionist was on duty. Maruska approached her.

"Could you tell me how to get to Southport?"

The woman looked up, "Yes, you need to walk over to Exchange Station and get the electric train. They run every fifteen minutes if the line is not damaged, but as it goes through the docks and there was pretty heavy bombing last night, don't be surprised if the trains are not running."

Maruska responded quickly, "I'll take my chances. One more thing, is there a ladies outfitters close by? I need to get some more clothes."

"You'll find some on Victoria Street on your way to Exchange if you have the right coupons. Are you checking out?"

Maruska dropped her key on the desk. The woman shrugged her shoulders, "Don't forget your bike..."

Maruska found what she was looking for; a boiler suit that had actually been made for a female. She smiled at the assistant and slipped into a changing room and put it on...

The sour-receptionist was correct. The main rail viaduct into Exchange station was damaged and trains were being diverted via a circuitous route to Liverpool Central.

Two hours later, Maruska walked out onto Southport's rather grand Lord Street still wheeling the Saxon.

The Jewish community in north-west England had expanded rapidly during the later part of the 1930s and early 1940s as Jews fled Nazi persecution in Europe, but even so, there were still less than one thousand in Southport. Maruska could blend in with the local community and wait out the war. If the Germans invaded, they would do so from the east, giving her plenty of time to get back to Liverpool and a boat across to Ireland. Well, at least, that was the plan.

The synagogue on Arnside Road was fairly easy to find. The locals appeared friendly enough as she asked the way. She walked down Lord Street, which seemed to have been immune to the war. Fashionable ladies paraded along the Victorian canopied walkways, in and out of expensive fur shops and bespoke dress emporiums. Maruska, as a plain factory girl, was totally invisible to them...

The office to the synagogue was situated in the adjacent house. Maruska knocked on the door. A little old man wearing a kippah appeared at the door. He spoke English with a German accent. He bowed slightly, not knowing what to make of this rather attractive factory girl with a bicycle,

"Good day, Miss. What can I do for you?"

Maruska returned the bow as a mark of respect. She answered in Hebrew.

"Good day to you, sir. I was wondering if I might speak with the rabbi?"

He relaxed when he heard his native language, "Rabbi Samuelson is in Liverpool today...perhaps I may be of assistance?"

Maruska, looked down, "I am a refugee from Czechoslovakia. My name is Doctor Maruska Bergman. I am looking for some simple accommodation. I understand there is a hostel for young Jewish ladies in the town?"

The man ushered her in through the old wooden doors; it was not often he had the pleasure of speaking with such a lovely looking doctor.

He offered her his hand, "My name is Reuben Frisch and I act as the Rabbi's secretary and assistant. Please sit whilst I make some tea for you."

Maruska sat down and looked around at the front room of the house that had a variety of Jewish symbols displayed. Mr Frisch came in carrying a tray of tea and some plain biscuits.

"Have you travelled far, Doctor Bergman?"

"I was staying in London, but I left a few days ago. The bombing is getting too intense."

He smiled, "Well there is very little of that here, although the Germans have managed to dump some ordnance over Ainsdale. I do believe that several houses were destroyed and some lives were lost, I'm sorry to say."

Maruska sipped her tea. He continued, "Where did you study to be a doctor?"

She looked at him, "Vienna, Mr Frisch."

"Ah, I thought I detected a Viennese accent." He lapsed into German, "We have need of a Jewish female doctor here. Many of the wives would prefer to be seen by one of their own kind."

Maruska stuck to Hebrew, "I'm sorry, Mr Frisch, but the General Medical Council won't let me practise until they recognise my qualifications. But I am a proficient seamstress and can work wherever needed."

He smiled, "My family is from Prussia, but they were able to get out at the turn of the century. We were in Manchester until the war started. You can speak to me in German if you wish. Walls do not have ears in this house."

Maruska shook her head; "I learnt not to use that language as soon as I came to England."

She told him a sanitised version of her life whilst he ate the plateful of biscuits. She even managed to produce a tear or two when she related the disappearance of her family. She didn't tell him of her double life.

He asked, "What brings you to this part of the world?"

"Sir, I fear that Britain will soon be invaded by the Germans. I had originally wanted to stay in Liverpool so that I could get to Ireland quickly enough, but that city is not safe."

He thought for a moment and nodded, "Yes, that is what we all fear. Rabbi Samuelson is in Liverpool exactly on that mission, hoping to find a ship's company that will take those who are able across the Irish Sea. However, there are some in our community who are too old and infirm to make that journey. They are resigned to their fate if the Nazis invade."

Maruska looked at him, "I heard that there is no guarantee the Irish Government will permit us Jews entry."

"Yes, but it is a land border. They would have a hard time stopping us if we so wished..."

He seemed eager to talk of Europe mentioning that he had visited Vienna as a young man and found it a vibrant and liberated city. Maruska became anxious to leave. She prompted him,

"Do you have accommodation in the hostel whilst I seek work, Mr Frisch?"

"Yes, of course, but you must first see the Rabbi. In the meantime, I'm sure you can reside with Mrs Gelber. She has a small boarding house on Gordon Street. I will telephone her to say that you are coming."

Maruska nodded.

Mrs Gelber was a plump woman in her late fifties. She smelled strongly of mothballs. She bustled around Maruska, very proud that she would have a doctor staying with her. The room was small but warm, clean and comfortable. Maruska collapsed on the bed for a couple of hours before she decided to change out of her boiler suit, put on some respectable clothes and go and see what there is to see.

The smell of the sea hit her as soon as she exited on Gordon Street. She walked along the Promenade before stopping at a tearoom. That night, the only sounds she heard as she lay in her bed were the distant thudding of bombing in Liverpool, some twenty or so miles away.

Southport would do nicely as a place to sit out the war before she was able to progress with the next part of her plan...

She never did get to reside into the Jewish Ladies Hostel, as Rabbi Samuelson persuaded her to move into the large home of an elderly widowed Jewish lady on Cambridge Road as a live-in carer. The lady was infirm and Maruska looked after all of her daily needs. The old lady was invariably in bed by eight in the evening listening to her wireless, leaving Maruska to do whatever she wanted. Maruska occupied a spacious room on the top floor next to a bathroom where a meter was not required for hot water.

She had no need for work. Mrs Janowicz paid her a decent enough wage that included food and accommodation. Maruska shopped and cooked for the old lady, who was not too particular whether it was kosher or not. Indeed, she was partial to the odd bacon sandwich from time to time, which she ate with a twinkle in her eye.

Every month or so, Doctor Hedges visited to give Mrs Janowicz the once over for which he charged an exorbitant fee. Maruska was frequently sent out to the local pharmacy to retrieve medicine, most of which she knew to be a complete waste of money. Maruska did like the old rogue, who was clearly trying to ingratiate himself with Mrs Janowicz and get into her will.

Over tea, they chatted about medicine. It seemed to Maruska that he was testing her to see if she really was a doctor. As it transpired, she knew more than him…

Chapter 23

1941
Maruska Bergman laid to rest

It was late January 1941 before Peter Porteous finally moved into the old house on East Row, exactly opposite the small Catholic primary school. The house was draughty and damp in the basement, but it had an inside toilet and a bathroom. The premises had once belonged to an aspiring middle class merchant. In order to impress his clients and neighbours, he had installed two rooms in the attic for his servants' use, together with the bathroom. The small paved yard at the rear did contain an outside toilet and a hand-operated water pump.

Porteous had decided that the basement could not be used to store his illicit goods, but the spare bedroom was good enough. After the bombing of his home on Bosworth Road and the subsequent interrogation, Detective Inspector Eric Everard of the Metropolitan Police was giving him a hard time. Porteous and Edith Bell had been bailed when they were released, but they had to report to Harrow Road Police Station every week. This was becoming a chore.

One Thursday evening, Edith Bell finally snapped. She shouted at the desk sergeant,

"For Christ's sake, either charge us with something or stop this nonsense! I've got a pub to run."

Porteous stood back and smiled; the desk sergeant could sort this out. He knew Edith...

The sergeant slowly put down his pen, pushed his half-moon spectacles to the top of his head, and looked at Edith.

"Now, look here, Mrs Bell. The inspector says you and your friend here have to report weekly and that's what you'll do otherwise, I'll get the magistrate to revoke your bail, and you'll spend a few nights in Holloway."

Edith Bell smirked, "Tell your fucking magistrate; see if I care."

Porteous knew that the local magistrate was eating out of Edith hands, and elsewhere, come to think of it. It was he who ignored all requests to remove her pub licence, probably because she demonstrated her appreciation in her own individual way.

The sergeant looked at Porteous, "Sir, if you wouldn't mind keeping Mrs Bell under control?"

Porteous shook his head, "Sorry, Sarge. It would be better if you just let us sign the register and leave, would it not?"

He indicated the growing queue of would-be bail jumpers, prostitutes, thieves and assorted miscreants from West London.

The sergeant cleared his throat as he picked up his pen, "Okay, you two, consider yourselves to have reported. I'll see you both next week."

Porteous took hold of Edith's arm. She shouted, "Get that fucking Everard to either charge us with some trumped-up crime or let us get on with our lives!"

Porteous pulled the still-protesting Edith out and down the steps. He remarked, "That doesn't help, Edith."

She put her arm in his as they walked, "I know, but I enjoy it."

"Why don't you go and see your friendly magistrate and ask him for some assistance? I'm sure he could do something with Everard."

"That's exactly where I'm going until opening time."

Alice Halpin and Nancy Keeling laughed at the story as they sat in Porteous' new home later that evening. Alice had cooked some stew from a Liverpool recipe called scouse, which was just some cheap cuts of lamb and beef with some vegetables and gravy. It had sat bubbling on the stove for a couple of hours whilst they polished off a bottle of gin. It was the first time Porteous had the two ladies in his new home.

Alice knocked back some gin, "Any news of Shira? She asked hopefully.

Porteous looked at her and shook his head, "I think she's gone. Knowing her, she could be anywhere."

Nancy looked at Alice, "She's normally back by now."

Porteous responded, "The police are looking for her. I heard that they are considering making her a suspect for her old man's death. They pulled in all the Ladbroke Grove crew; they have absolutely no idea what happened to Adelman. It's odd that neither her nor her body haven't turned up yet."

Alice said, "Even the canal eventually gives up the dead."

A silence descended over the dinner table. Nancy took his hand, "Are the police saying anything about Maruska?"

He looked down, "I haven't been down to the mortuary, but they'll just fill in a few forms and send her for burial. Rabbi Levi from Bayswater says he'll take care of her. I think he had a soft spot for her. I'll probably go to the service."

The ladies spoke up, "We'll both go, Porteous."

He ushered them out just before nine so that they could get home before the first air raid warning. They were both a little tipsy, but Nancy has always had a talent for persuading reluctant taxi drivers to take her home.

Porteous lay in his bed. He thought he could smell Maruska Bergman on his sheets. She was probably the only woman with whom he had fallen in love. Yes, he loved both Alice and Nancy in their own way and probably Edith and Shira, but Maruska was different. The accusation that she may have been a German spy troubled him. Not so much that she was actively supporting an enemy that was intent on blowing London to pieces every night, but that she had possibly deceived him. He prided himself on his ability to read people. Maybe she was what they suspected her of?

She did have unusual habits. She rarely spent the whole night with him after they had made love. There had always been an edge to their intimate moments. If they suddenly had the urge to make love, she would always disappear back to her flat before returning. Why was that?

And, he knew virtually nothing of her life apart from what she had told him. He sighed as the gin and sleep finally took him.

Porteous was back in his Air Raid Precautions uniform, but he wasn't on duty. He had been excused following the destruction of his home, but could he make sure he was back in a couple of weeks? Holborn was dark. The black-out was effective. It was just after seven in the evening. He tapped quietly on the glass door to the boarded up-shop in Red Lion Street.

He heard a voice, "Who's there?"

Porteous answered quietly as the bolts slid open. Jimmy Ryan greeted him,

"The kettle has just boiled. I've got some fresh tea; help yourself."

The light in the disused shop was weak, but Porteous could see some boxes stacked up in the corner behind the old wooden counter. Ryan was busy counting out packets of stockings and making notes in a little battered notebook with the stub of a pencil. The cellophane packets were laid out on the counter like a pack of cards.

Porteous sipped his tea, "How much did we lose, Jimmy?"

Ryan stopped and looked up, "We or you?" He had a smile on his face.

Porteous shook his head, "Come on, Jimmy, you're the bookkeeper."

"All told? About two hundred and fifty pounds. The scotch on its own was worth nearly half of the amount. That's a pity because I had already sold most of that to some lords and ladies in Mayfair. I'm going to have to return their deposits. It seems that the war only affects us lower classes." He laughed.

"Can we cover it?"

Ryan nodded, "Elphicke says we're good for it, but it would help if we can shift some of these nylons as soon as possible." Denis Elphicke controlled most of the distribution of illicit goods in Central London.

"What's demand looking like up your neck of the woods?" Ryan asked.

"Desperation, Jimmy, since I lost that last box of stockings. All the night ladies of Kensal Town are going around barelegged. An eyeliner pencil down a leg just doesn't cut it any more."

Ryan raised his eyebrows; "I thought there was a mandate for them not to wear stockings until the strangler has been caught?"

Porteous shook his head, "You know those girls, they think they are naked if they haven't got any stockings. Anyway, many of the other women of Kensal Town just want their regular supply back. I've got an order book as long as your arm."

Ryan threw the remaining packets back into the box, "Good, there's nearly fifty pairs in there. Got them from a chap down at the docks who said they were liberated from a burning cargo ship last week. He wants two bob a packet, but you can knock them out for two-and-six or three shillings. Here, have a look." He held up a stocking to the light.

Porteous shuffled over, picked up the item, spread his fingers into an open leg and examined it carefully.

"Where are these from?"

"Dunno, they came off a ship from South America."

Porteous, "These are good quality. Three bob a packet, I think."

"You know the market better than me. Get rid of them; I've got three more boxes out back."

Porteous smiled. "Any booze?"

"Just some cheap gin. It tastes disgusting, but throw a tonic in it and you'd never know. Here, have a taste." He tossed a half-empty bottle to Porteous.

Porteous cracked open the top and took a small swig, He grimaced, "Yeah, you're right. I'll make sure Edith has got plenty of mixers!"

"See if you can get her to take a couple of boxes."

He nodded, "She will. What else have you got?"

"Ten pounds of rolling tobacco."

"Jesus, Jimmy. I thought Christmas was finished?"

He shrugged his shoulders, "I get what I get. Just knock it out and we'll soon pay off Elphicke."

They sat for about an hour going through various items ranging from men's shirts to ladies' lingerie until the early warning sirens went off. Ryan pulled a battered old van around to the back of the shop, and they quickly loaded up the contraband. They just made it up to the White Horse Public House on Kensal Road before the sirens began blaring out their deadly warnings.

Edith Bell kissed Porteous and rubbed her hands, "Good, some gin. I was getting low."

"You haven't tasted it yet," replied Porteous.

"Don't worry, I'll tell the girls not to serve it until the customers have had one or two and not without a mixer."

Edith had done this before.

Jimmy Ryan and Porteous shifted all the stock up into his spare bedroom. The anti-aircraft guns down in the West End began to sound. Ryan insisted on driving back. His store in Holborn was too precious to leave unattended, especially with so many corrupt auxiliary firemen and ambulance drivers around...not to mention the coppers...

Edith Bell decided she wasn't going to the church crypt and she and Porteous spent most of the night in the cellar sitting on boxes sampling what there was to drink, apart from the gin, that is.

He left just before six to go and get ready for work up in Cricklewood. The need for aircraft instruments was never going to lessen in the near future.

Following Edith Bell's afternoon visit to her friendly magistrate, Inspector Eric Everard of the Metropolitan Police was ordered to either charge Bell and Porteous or release them from their bail. He released them.

Porteous, Alice Halpin and Nancy Keeling went up to the Bayswater Synagogue for Maruska's funeral. As with Jewish custom, they sat with the closed casket for an hour not long after it had been delivered from the mortuary. Doctor Maruska Bergman was buried in Golders Green Cemetery. The good people of Kensal Town contributed to the costs of the casket and burial plot.

Peter Porteous settled back into his routine of working in the factory, fire-watching and knocking out illicit goods to the good folk of Kensal Town.

Doctor Maruska Bergman gradually faded from his thoughts. Nancy Keeling gave him enough worries as she waded along the murky path of London vice and Charlie 'The Maltese' Maitland...

Chapter 24

1942
Burtonwood USAAF Base, Warrington
Life Changes

Maruska Bergman blended into Southport's Jewish community, blissfully unaware that she was supposedly buried in Golders Green Cemetery. Life in the sleepy coastal resort continued as though what went on in the outside world was of no consequence. She wasn't a great attender at the Arndale Road Synagogue, but she presented herself enough to dispel any doubts from Rabbi Samuelson about her provenance.

Her Saxon bicycle turned out to be a very useful acquisition. During her time off, she cycled around the borough's multiple parks, but her favourite was definitely the Botanic Gardens in Churchtown with its boating lake, museum and the regular Sunday afternoon brass band concerts. Mrs Janowicz, Maruska's employer, was a sprightly eighty-year-old whose family had escaped one of the many pogroms in Eastern Europe. Her husband had been something in the fur business. When he died, he left her with pots of money and no children, much to her regret. She grew to be very fond of the Czechoslovakian doctor who now resided in her large home. Indeed, she made it her aim in life to find Maruska Bergman a suitable husband from one of the available Jewish men in the area.

Maruska was having none of it. She politely turned down any requests from these men who invariably called at the house, dressed in their best suits, clutching a bunch of seasonal flowers. Mrs Janowicz didn't know that Maruska spoke Polish well enough to understand when she was chatting idly on the telephone, which she did for most of the day. Maruska found herself with enough free time to explore the town with its genteel atmosphere. She felt safe enough to dispose of her forged identity card. There didn't appear to be anything resembling the Alien Tribunal Board in the locality. What policemen she encountered were those who had been summoned back from retirement and were anxious not to generate any work. The local police she came across usually tipped their helmets to this attractive, dark-haired female who seemed to go everywhere by bicycle. For the first time in recent years, Maruska Bergman felt safe.

By July 1942, Maruska had been living with Mrs Janowicz for over eighteen months. They had settled into a routine. Maruska rose early and did most of the daily chores before she woke Mrs Janowicz with her early morning tea. After lunch, she would make some excuse to leave the house and go off somewhere if the weather was nice. She rarely wore the boiler suit away from the house. Mrs Janowicz had told her it was unseemly for a person of Maruska's standing to be taken for a simple factory girl, and she must dress appropriately when out and about.

About eleven one morning, Maruska and Mrs Janowicz were sitting in the large kitchen drinking their mid-morning tea when the front doorbell sounded. Maruska went to answer it, hoping it wasn't one of Mrs Janowicz' suitors. Maruska had been cleaning, so she was dressed in her boiler suit. She opened the door to be greeted by a tall and rather handsome USA army captain holding his hat anxiously in both hands.

Instinctively, she brushed back her hair, which was supposed to be tucked into one of her turban-type scarfs. She blushed, embarrassed to be seen like this. She looked across to see a jeep with a driver parked up on the stone drive.

He spoke, "Ma'am, I'm looking for Doctor Maruska Bergman."

Maruska's heart thumped wildly in her chest, "Yes, yes," she stammered, "How can I help you?"

The captain's drawl was definitely southern, "Ma'am, I need a word with Doctor Bergman. Is she at home?"

Maruska was about to tell him she wasn't when a loud voice called out from behind her, "Maruska, for goodness' sake, child, where are your manners? Show the gentleman in."

Maruska felt an arm on hers as she was pulled away from the door.

"Do come in, won't you?"

The officer nodded to the old lady, "Why, thank you, Ma'am. I promise I won't keep you long. My driver is waiting."

Mrs Janowitcz smiled, "You can take as long as you want, can't he, Maruska? We have nothing planned for the day."

She smiled sweetly at the officer and led him into the front room which was rarely used, except for the occasional Bridge session when Mrs Janowicz' cronies arrived for an afternoon's gossip and game.

"Go and fetch the gentleman some fresh tea, Maruska. I'm sure he would like some refreshment."

He sat down, looking suitably embarrassed. Mrs Janowicz gave him a rapid interrogation...

Maruska had tidied herself up whilst she was in the kitchen, wishing she had put on a brassiere earlier in the day. He stood up when she returned carrying a tray.

Mrs Janowicz prodded him, "Go on, Captain Dreyfus, I'm sure Doctor Bergman would love to know why you are here."

He swallowed and turned to the now seated Maruska, "Ma'am, sorry, I mean Doctor Bergman, my name is Meir Dreyfus, Doctor Meir Dreyfus of the 55th Field Hospital based at Burtonwood Airbase in Warrington. Do you know where that is?"

Mrs Janowicz interrupted, "Don't worry, child, it is a little industrial town about an hour away."

Captain Dreyfus looked at the old woman who smiled meekly and sipped her tea, "Doctor Bergman, we need your help."

Maruska looked at him with her big brown eyes, "I'm-I'm not sure how I can help," she stammered.

"Ma'am, we are short of doctors, and we're expecting an evacuation plane later this afternoon of severely injured soldiers. They were on a training exercise somewhere in the South when there was an explosion. We've got about twenty coming in, and we don't have enough doctors to cover all the other sick patients already in the hospital."

Maruska looked at him, "I'm sorry, Captain, but I'm not registered to practise here in England. The General Medical Council has still not approved my registration."

Captain Dreyfus looked at her, "Are you a qualified doctor?"

She nodded.

"Where did you train?"

"Vienna, I'm a refugee."

"Yes, Doctor Hedges speaks very highly of you."

Maruska looked at Mrs Janowicz who shook her head and raised her eyebrows as if to say she knew nothing about it.

The Captain went on, "Look, do you have anything to say you are a doctor?"

Maruska looked at him, "Yes, I have my certificates."

"Go and fetch them, child," interjected Mrs Janowicz. Maruska glared at her.

He examined them carefully, "All right, Ma'am. My colonel has instructed me to bring you back, if you are willing. Once you are on the base, it's technically the USA. We have different procedures for registering doctors. You can be granted a temporary licence, all legal and above board. The colonel will sort out any niceties later once we have cleared the emergency, but we must hurry. The transport is due in about three hours."

Ten minutes later, Doctor Maruska Bergman found herself in the back of a USA Army jeep hurtling through the countryside clutching a bag that contained her precious certificates, still dressed in her boiler suit much to the amusement of Mrs Janowicz who waved her off from the front doorstep before she rushed off to telephone her friends with the news.

The airbase was huge. She didn't know how many personnel were stationed there, but there seemed to be thousands. She wondered why the black soldiers were kept to a different part of the base. It seemed to her that the USA had taken over this part of sleepy northwest England.

Colonel Steven Price looked at Maruska Bergman's papers and said, "You'll do. I will sort out the paperwork later."

He shouted, "Lauren! Doctor Bergman needs some more appropriate clothing."

A tall, thin female corporal rushed in, saluted and ushered Maruska out.

As they walked over to the stores, Maruska could hear the roar of heavy planes as they took off and landed on the huge runway in the distance.

The corporal shouted in her ear, "Don't worry, Ma'am, you'll soon get used to it. My quarters are right at the end of the runway and I sleep like a baby."

Maruska Bergman exited from the stores about thirty minutes later, clutching a paper bag containing her boiler suit and headscarf. She was dressed in army fatigues complete with boots and a hastily knocked up name badge which proudly stated 'Captain Doctor Maruska Bergman, 55th Field Hospital,' and an uncomfortable army issue brassiere.

Meir Dreyfus was waiting for her in the entrance to the hospital. He smiled and led her into a side room with glass windows. He pointed to a rack, "Everything you'll need is there, just help yourself."

She selected a stethoscope and a few other items that she was able to stow in her white coat. He led her onto the ward and introduced her to a senior nurse.

He asked her, "Have you done much trauma medicine?"

She shook her head, "Only on rotation, I'm actually a paediatrician."

He laughed, "That's good because most of the patients here are just grown up kids. Nurse Carey will make sure you don't kill anyone."

Maruska blushed.

He looked at his watch, "I have to go. If we need you later, one of the orderlies will bring you over. Trauma reception is in another building."

With that, he was gone...

Maruska went about her work. Most of the patients were routine, nothing that taxed her. Nurse Carey chatted with her as they went about their business. The nurse was impressed with how the male patients reacted to this pretty doctor. Any signs of rustiness in Maruska soon disappeared as she administered injections, listened to hearts and wrote up charts. She almost forgot about her situation until later in the afternoon when all hell let loose. The transport had landed; there were more critical patients than expected. Maruska was taken over to the building, where even Colonel Steven Price was dressed in a white coat.

She donned a surgical mask and gown as he beckoned her over. The place was mad busy with each patient being attended to by a nurse. Other doctors were working on even more critical casualties. Already, two hadn't made the evacuation trip. Maruska had seen similar emergencies in Vienna following a factory fire.

Colonel Price called her over, "Captain, I need your assistance. We've got a bleeder here. I have to open him up to get at the artery. I could do with an extra pair of hands."

Maruska had done limited surgery, but she managed with the experienced hand of the colonel by her side. It took about five hours to get some semblance of order to the unit. Maruska stitched up several deep wounds and prepared patients with third degree burns for transport to Manchester and the Burns Unit. She knew from experience that many of them would not make it, succumbing to infections later, but at least they were pain-free by the time they were moved.

The medical staff sat in a restroom drinking strong coffee with the storm having passed for the moment. One or two of them had actually dozed off. It was well into the night. Maruska felt her eyes closing. She hadn't eaten all day. Her tummy rumbled. The phone rang at the end of the room. A nurse picked it up and looked over at Maruska.

"Doctor Bergman, you are wanted on the general ward..."

It was nearly lunchtime the next day when the driver saluted Maruska when he returned her to Southport. She was still dressed in her army uniform. She clutched the brown paper bag with her boiler suit. The boots hurt her feet. The army issue bra dug into her skin. Mrs Janowicz smiled at her,

"My, don't you look so pretty in that uniform? How was Captain Dreyfus? Did you get a chance to talk to him?"

Maruska smiled at her as she pushed past her and trudged upstairs to take a long soak in the bath. She lay in the hot water, closed her eyes and fell asleep.

Over the next few months, Meir Dreyfus called at the house several times at Mrs Janowicz' invitation. Maruska allowed him to take her to afternoon tea and a walk along a windy Promenade. She clutched at his arm as the breeze made her shiver. She even allowed him to kiss her on the cheek. When he indicated that he wanted more, she pushed him away. What she didn't need was another relationship. She still dreamed of Peter Porteous and how they used to make love. Sometimes, she felt bad about what had happened, but she knew that the net had been closing in on her double life.

The same driver came for her once or twice a week at the beginning and then three or four times, usually at night. She became a respected part of the team. She was technically classed as a volunteer. The usual background checks were held in abeyance as the war in Europe intensified. Colonel Steven Price often asked for her in the operating theatre. The nurses became a little jealous of this rather attractive newcomer, who seemed to get all the male attention.

The tide of the war turned in June 1944 when the Allies invaded Europe through Normandy in France. By this time, there were over one and a half million USA troops stationed in Britain. Maruska saw many of them pass through Burtonwood Air Base, which eventually became one of the busiest with planes taking off and landing throughout the day.

At this point, Maruska was more or less full time at the base. She was given some sleeping quarters, but she much preferred to return to her home. Mrs Janowicz was disappointed to learn that Meir Dreyfus had been transferred to active service somewhere in Europe. Occasionally, he had even escorted the old lady to the Synagogue even though it was not generally part of her everyday life, but it was something to bring the young Texan to the house. Maruska showed little interest.

The threat of invasion had diminished significantly, but air raids were still happening. The Germans had tried to knock out the docks in Liverpool because the port was vital to the trans-Atlantic trade. It was late one evening on the trauma ward when there was a commotion. Maruska was at the nurses' station when the double doors burst open and two burly British Red Cap military police arrived with an orderly pushing a trolley upon which a German aircrew member was lying. Maruska went over to attend to him. His uniform was torn. It looked as though he had descended through the upper branches of a tree. He had deep gashes and lacerations over his body, and possibly a broken shoulder.

The Red Caps saluted Maruska, "Ma'am, one Jerry flyer for you. Bailed out of a Heinkel and landed in an old oak tree near Widnes. His two mates are already detained. This fellow looks like he could do with some medical attention."

Maruska smiled, "He certainly does, Corporal. We'll deal with him."

"Sorry, Ma'am, but we've got instructions not to leave him and to bring him back as soon as you've patched him up."

Maruska looked at one of the nurses who shook her head, "This young man is not going anywhere tonight."

It was a couple of hours before they finished working on the Unteroffizier. The orthopaedic surgeon reset his shoulder and Maruska tended to the other wounds. She shot him full of morphine to ease his pain. He kept crying out for his mother in German. The young lad was only in his early twenties.

The Red Caps soon got bored and, realising that the mess had real coffee, they soon disappeared. Maruska sat with the German as he lay in a bed in a side room. He woke about three in the morning just as Maruska was going to return to her quarters for a few hours sleep. She gave him some water. He looked at her and spoke in German,

"Where am I?"

She placed her hands on his arm and responded, "You are safe, although it looks as though you've had a lucky escape."

It took him a few seconds to realise that Maruska was speaking German; his eyes opened wide, "Who are you?"

Maruska pointed to her official name tag, "What's your name?"

He sat back and breathed out, "Xavier Dien, Captain. Thank you for helping me. Will I be okay?"

Maruska nodded, "Yes. It will take some time for you to get full use of your shoulder, but you'll be fine. You'll have a few scars from the cuts. I've put in over twenty sutures, but it won't detract from your good looks. You'll soon have the ladies swooning over you."

He looked at her, "Where are you from?"

She put a finger to her lips, "Speak quietly; I'm from Bohemia in what you Germans now call the Sudetenland via Vienna."

He smiled, "Ah, now I recognise the accent. What are you doing here?"

She stood up, "I'm a Jew, Xavier. What was I supposed to do when your leader is intent on slaughtering my race."

He looked down, embarrassed. He didn't want to get involved with this. Like many young Germans of his generation, they knew what was happening was wrong but did little about it for fear of their own personal safety.

Maruska softened, "What is your job?"

"I'm a radio operator. We weren't bombing. It was just a reconnaissance flight."

"It doesn't matter. You are the enemy. You should see what happened to London. I was there in 1940. You destroyed my home and killed someone I loved."

He looked away, "The war is lost."

Maruska took his hand, "No, Xavier, the war is won. Just think, when you leave here you will go to an internment camp and spend the rest of the war in safety. Then you can return to Germany a hero, having made a contribution. You are now safe from any more threat."

He nodded, she asked him about his family. They spent the next hour talking about his life. He was from Bonn and was about to go to university to study engineering when he was called up for service. She told him she knew a little about radios, and he nodded. He decided it was better not to ask about her family.

He asked, "What did you have to do to escape?"

She stood up and smiled as one of the nurses came looking for her, "That's for another time, Xavier."

She took a few days off. When she came back, the young man had been taken away to sit out the rest of the war in relative peace and quiet, with three square meals a day and no one shooting at him.

In early 1945 as snow carpeted the north of England, Colonel Steven Price summoned Maruska to a meeting. With casualties coming in from mainland Europe, the hospital was exceptionally busy. Those who could be patched up were given some rest and recuperation and sent back to their units. There were many whose lives would be forever changed.

She knocked on Price's door and entered. He stood up, "Have you not learnt to salute a superior officer yet, Captain?"

Maruska froze and then she saw a broad smile on his face; he burst out laughing, "I thought that would get you, Maruska, please sit down."

He opened a wooden cigarette box and offered one to her. She declined. He lit it and sat back, inhaling the smoke deep into his lungs. His fingers played with a sheet of closely typed paper.

"I have a new assignment for you, if you would consider it. They are organising troopships to return the severely wounded to their families in America. These transport carriers will need qualified medical staff to accompany the soldiers. As it would be unreasonable of us to ask you to go to the front lines, we thought you might like to think about it. It would mean about a month away from Britain." He paused, "On the other hand, it could be what you've been looking for."

He stopped to let that sink in.

She stared ahead, "I have family in New York, sir. We have all agreed to meet up there after the war. Europe is no place for us Jews right now."

He nodded, "I guessed you might say that."

"But sir, I have no papers but those given to me when I first arrived."

"Don't worry. You'll travel on a military identity card. No immigration officer will query an army captain. We'll give you a full military kit, so leave your civilian attire at home. You wouldn't be allowed to wear it on board anyway. I'll also provide you with sufficient references for both the New York Health Authorities and Immigration Services, should you decide to spend a little more time there. There are ships coming and going every week. Take a little time in New York. See what there is to see. Look up your family. You can always come back if things don't work out, but this war will soon end. The Nazis are beaten. We won't be here much longer. I could make a few enquiries about your position being regularised, but you would have to go into training and there would be further background checks..."

There was an electric pause before he continued, "And I'm not sure if that would be beneficial all round."

Maruska looked down trying her best not to look guilty, "Can I think about it, Colonel?"

He shook his head, "No, Maruska, this is a one time offer. If you don't take the opportunity now, it could be years before the USA authorities even begin to think about accepting refugees." He paused, before he added, "Especially those who speak fluent German..."

She swallowed, and then stood up, "When is the next transport, sir?"

Mrs Janowicz cried when she was told the news. Maruska had to move onto the base full-time until the ship sailed from Liverpool.

Three weeks later, on a cold February morning, Maruska Bergman stood on the deck and watched as the ship sailed past the Statue of Liberty.

Chapter 25

Vienna
November 1945
Interviews

Giles Deeprose, otherwise known as Mr Brown of Ashford Detention Centre in Kent, was not amused. He sat with his back pressed up hard against the side of the Douglas C54 Skymaster cargo plane. He had been sitting in this boneshaker for nearly four hours; he was decidedly fed up. Not only was he cold, but also the constant dripping of condensation from the roof had thoroughly soaked his clothes. The noise had been deafening. In the absence of anything better, he had torn up a silk handkerchief and stuffed little balls into his ears. The transport plane was packed with American troops, who, used to this indignity, looked upon the trip as an opportunity to catch up with much-needed sleep, play cards and read in what little light there was.

At least, there was no chance of being intercepted by some hostile enemy aircraft. Well, the Russians hadn't yet declared war on the western Allied Powers. Giles Deeprose belonged to MI5 and as such was sworn to protect Britain from internal threats. MI6 did the foreign stuff; couldn't they find someone in that branch to come out to this ruined city?

Apparently, no, according to his boss Dorothy Smith of some anonymous department in Whitehall. He was one of her top interrogators, so he would just go where he was told. There were plenty of ex-Nazis to 'interview' and he could just jolly well go and help out. Besides, she told him, he might just enjoy it.

The plane landed with an almighty thump on the temporary landing strip, somewhere to the west of the ruined city. The Soviet Army had taken part of the city, and the Allied bombers had destroyed what was left of the west. The place was in ruins with the Soviets occupying much of the east with France, Britain and the United States, the rest. There was a shared international sector in the centre. He had been told only to venture in the Soviet Sector with permission.

It was pouring with rain when he got off the plane, and it was pitch black. He soon realised this was just a flat patch of grass that had been reinforced to take the weight of the planes as they landed. He was easy to spot as he was the only civilian on the flight. He was approached in the dark by a young private,

"Sir, Captain Deeprose?"

He hated these military titles. If he had wanted to don a uniform and shoot the enemy, he would have done so. He preferred his Saville Row suits.

He looked at the boy who couldn't have been more than twenty years old, "Yes, who the bloody hell did you think it would be?"

The private looked embarrassed. Deeprose caught himself, "Look, sorry about that. It's been a long flight."

The private picked up his kit bag and asked Deeprose to follow him.

He asked, "Where are we going, Private...Sorry, what's your name?"

"Lubach, sir, but everyone calls me Jake."

"Well, Private Jake, where are you taking me?"

"You have accommodation in District 13 near the Lanzinger Tiergarten. I'll take you over to headquarters first thing tomorrow morning."

The soldier tossed Deeprose's kitbag into the back of the jeep and climbed in. At least the jeep had a soft top that only leaked a little...

The next morning, Dorothy Smith greeted him as he entered her office. The room was small but functional. A welcoming blaze burned in the hearth. She stood with her back to the fire,

"Ah, Giles, I trust you found your quarters comfortable?"

He glared at her, "You know, Ma'am, this trip is not exactly in my job description?"

"Oh, do sit down, Giles, and stop being such a prima donna. There's important work to be done here. There's a dozen or so German officers downstairs, and at least half of them are wanted Nazis. Two of them are definitely SS, and we think one of them is Gestapo. I want the bastards, and there's no one better to seek out a wrong 'un like you."

He sat down as she thrust a cup of ersatz coffee in his hand. He sipped, grimaced and sighed,

"Okay, okay. Let me see the files."

She pushed over three manila files. He looked at her, "I thought you said there were twelve?"

"There are, but the Yanks are helping out and these will do for starters."

He raised his eyebrows and his face betrayed the hint of a smile, "What about the Russians?"

She snorted, "They don't bother to interrogate them. They extract confessions and then shoot them."

"Hmm, that's one way of keeping down the costs, can't we do the same?"

She laughed, "If only; British standards of decency and all that. Which is why so many of the bastards did everything they could to surrender to us rather than face the wrath of the Russkies."

He picked up the first file and opened it. There was a picture of a German SS officer looking arrogantly into the camera, resplendent in his uniform and medals. He flicked through the file, "Hmm, a major, I see."

"Yes, a Sturmbannfürer. Nasty piece of work, by all accounts. The French want him for taking part in the massacre in Oradour-sur-Glane in June 1944. He was a commander in the SS Panzer Division that slaughtered over six hundred locals. We picked him up in a Wehrmacht private's uniform. Claims he's just a foot soldier obeying orders."

Deeprose stood up scraping his chair, "Okay, the sooner I get confessions, the sooner I can go home." Dorothy Smith smiled.

"That's the spirit, Giles, onwards and upwards and think of all those expenses you can claim."

Giles Deeprose had plenty of money already. He didn't even need his salary. He looked at her...

The German looked nervous as Giles Deeprose entered the room. He was dishevelled, unshaven and dirty. A duty Red Cap corporal stood with his arms behind his back and legs slightly apart, against the door, rigid, never taking his eyes off the prisoner.

Deeprose tossed the file onto the battered table together with his gold topped fountain pen and a sheaf of notepaper onto which he had written copious notes in neat writing, the product of an expensive private education.

He spoke in fluent German, "Right Sturmbannfürer, let's stop pissing about, shall we?"

The major swallowed nervously, Deeprose's accent was untraceable but impeccable, he would have to be careful here if he wanted to save his neck.

He affected a Bavarian accent,

"Sorry, sir, my name is Karl Bauer. I'm from Stuttgart. I'm a private in the Wehrmacht."

Deeprose sighed; it might take a bit of time... "No you're not. You are Friedrich Schmidt, Sturmbannfürer of the 2nd SS Panzer Division, Das Reich." He paused to let that sink in and then went on, "You know, the Division that slaughtered all those innocent French citizens in Oradour-sur-Glane in June 1944."

Deeprose shook his head, "What happened that day? Did your boss wake up with a hangover?"

The prisoner swallowed loudly.

Deeprose sighed and continued, "Okay, Friedrich, tell me about your childhood..."

Eight hours later, Giles Deeprose had a confession. He asked so many questions that Schmidt eventually tied himself up in knots. It didn't help that Deeprose refused him a toilet break. The Red Cap guard was changed four times. Deeprose just kept badgering away until the man broke down.

He picked up the file as Schmidt sobbed on the table with his head down as urine trickled down his legs and exited the room. Dorothy Smith was waiting for him.

He looked at her, "Send a clerk in to get a full confession and then let the French know they can have him. I'm going home for the day..."

Smith patted him on the back as he went past her, "Well done, Giles, only a dozen or so more to go..."

Private Lubach was waiting for him in the lobby of the requisitioned hotel. He saluted smartly. Deeprose asked, "Have you been here all day, Jake?"

"Yes, sir, I've been told to stay with you."

"Well, Jake, take me to a bar that serves a decent G&T."

"Sir?"

"I need a bloody drink to wash the taste of that Nazi out of my mouth."

"Sir, I've been instructed to take you straight back to your quarters."

"Bugger that, Jake, just do as you are told, that's all."

Private Lubach swallowed, "Sir, there's a bar in the international zone that is stocked by the Yanks. It's normally out of bounds to British officers."

"Good, that sounds like my kind of place. Come on, laddie, and don't spare the horses..."

Deeprose sank three gin and tonics before he allowed Private 'Jake' Lubach to take him home. The French guards at the checkpoint waved him through, smiling at Private Lubach.

It went on for nearly two weeks. Deeprose extracted confessions from all but one of the prisoners. He was convinced that the remaining one was who he said he was, and therefore completely innocent. Smith instructed the relieved man to be returned to the prisoner of war camp some twenty miles away to await discharge processing.

By this time, Deeprose was a regular in the bar in the Hotel Wagner in the International Zone. He was looking forward to his early flight to Biggin Hill, London the next day. He was seriously considering taking up the offer of tenure at his Alma Marta, Trinity Hall, Oxford. At least they wouldn't ask him to soil his hands dealing with war criminals.

The Hotel Wagner was particularly empty that evening. He sat in a corner sipping his drink, reading a two-day-old copy of the London Times when a man in a dark suit sat down opposite him. Deeprose glanced up.

"Can I help you?"

The man spoke in heavily accented English, "Maybe, English, we can help each other."

Deeprose sighed; he knew by the accent that the man opposite was a member of the Soviet Union's security services, the NKVD.

Deeprose folded his paper, "What are you? Major? Colonel? Either way, I don't care. If you want to speak to me, go through official channels and wait at least a month for an acknowledgement."

The Russian held out his hand, "Alexy Petrov. I have some information for you."

Deeprose ignored the hand and sipped his drink, "Look, Alexy, or whatever your name is, you know I can't speak with you. Don't you have someone on MI6 you can drink with?"

He smiled, "Yes, of course, but they don't have what you have."

Deeprose sighed; he knew he should have finished his drink, got up and left, but his naturally inquisitive nature kept him there.

"What have I got that you want?"

Petrov threw down a large envelope, "Take a look whilst I get you another drink."

He stood up and went to the bar. Deeprose picked up the envelope as though it might have exploded in his face. He shook out the contents. Immediately, he recognised the photograph.

Petrov came back and put down two glasses of Vodka; "Here's a real drink for you."

"Alexy, this is one of our files. Where did you get this?"

"Of course it is, English, where else would I get this information?"

Petrov picked up the photograph, "Paul Koch, my bosses want him for the murder of three hundred Jews in a small village in Ukraine during Operation Barbarossa."

Deeprose raised his eyes, "I thought you Russians weren't bothered about Jews."

"Well, we are about these. It's called making a statement. You can't just walk into the Soviet Union and kill three hundred of its citizens and expect to get away with it."

"He's already been processed. He made no attempt to hide his identity. Seems as though he thinks it's his duty to hold up his hands. He's going to be sent for trial and then I suppose, Pierrepoint will have his day."

"Ah, yes Albert Pierrepoint, your chief executioner. He's been busy up in northern Germany, so I hear. The thing is, English, we want him for trial."

Deeprose put down his drink, "Why? Dead is dead, after all."

"My bosses want to take him back to the village and shoot him in front of what's left of the people."

Deeprose nodded, "Well, there's nothing I can do about it." He stood up to leave, "Make an official request through official circles. Nice to have met you, Alexy."

"Wait a minute, English. We have something you might just like."

"I doubt it, Alexy, I'm on the early morning flight to London first thing tomorrow."

The Russian produced another envelope, "Sit down, English. Have a look at this."

Against his better judgement, Giles Deeprose sat down. He opened the envelope and a picture of a pretty woman fell onto the table. He shrugged his shoulders, "Who's this?" he asked.

"Wehrmacht Auxiliary Jutta Meyer of the Abwehr"

"What did she do? Attempt to poison Uncle Joe Stalin?"

Petrov roared with laughter, "That's a good one, English, I must remember that." He paused and then said, "Does the name Maruska Bergman ring any bells?"

Of course it did; Maruska Bergman was the one that got away. Alexy Petrov tossed a picture of Maruska Bergman on the table.

For the first time in the conversation, Giles Deeprose was almost lost for words.

"She's dead, Alexy. Buried in Golders Green Cemetery, as far as I can recall."

Petrov smiled, "Ah, but is she? You buried the burnt and unrecognisable remains of a female."

"Case closed. What's it got to do with me?"

"Ah, English, she beat you, didn't she? Listen for a minute. This attractive lady was Bergman's radio operator in Hamburg in 1940. She was working here with the Abwehr when we picked her up."

"Has she committed any crimes?"

"Not as far as we know."

"Then release the poor girl. We have no proof that Bergman was a spy."

Petrov smiled, "Not so fast, English, she's singing like, how do you say, a budgerigar?"

"Canary, Alexy, canary. One sings like a canary. What is she singing about?"

"Oh, this and that. She seems to know a lot about Western Intelligence. It looks like our Jutta was an even better listener than radio operator. She appears to have been invisible when her officers were speaking around her. She claims that just before the end of April, some senior Abwehr personnel were speaking with their opposite numbers in the Office of Strategic Services."

"The OSS? Well, Alexy, I'm suitably impressed."

"Yes, it seems deals were done under the table for some Germans to be taken to the USA for their knowledge."

"You wouldn't be thinking about certain rocket scientists, would you?"

Petrov smiled again, "My, English, you do know a lot more than you let on. Anyway, would you be interested in having a word with Jutta?"

"For what purpose, Alexy?"

"For your peace of mind, English and then you can go and take up the offer at your posh college in Oxford..."

Deeprose thought for a few moments, "I'll have to run it by my boss, if you don't mind."

The Russian sipped his drink and waved the file, "Already did, old boy. Where do you think I got this?"

Chapter 26

Vienna
November 1945
Confusion

Private Jake Lubach was nervous. He wasn't supposed to let Giles Deeprose out of his sight, yet the Captain had gone off with some shady-looking Russian. The captain had told him to go home; he would make his own way back...

He sat in the back of a commandeered Volkswagen Kübelwagen. Alexy Petrov sat up front with a uniformed driver who smelled like his body hadn't seen water for a couple of weeks. Petrov insisted on smoking some foul-smelling cigarettes. They gabbled away in Russian. Deeprose was relieved when the wagon pulled up in front of a partially damaged building that was once an office of the city council.

Jutta Meyer was indeed an attractive lady in her mid twenties, but a month or so of imprisonment by the Russians had knocked the stuffing out of her. Her face was gaunt, with deep, dark circles under her eyes. Her Abwehr uniform of a skirt and blouse appeared to be the only clothes she had. They hung off her emaciated body. They were dirty and creased, as though she had slept in them. She didn't look anything like the photo Alexy Petrov had shown him earlier. Deeprose was shocked. He would try to help this woman if he could. As far as he knew, she hadn't committed any crimes, just served her country.

Petrov sat down, indicating Deeprose to do the same. He pushed over a file and spoke quietly, "She's all yours, English."

Deeprose spoke in German, "Miss Meyer, my name is Giles Deeprose. I work for the British, and I'm going to see if I can help you."

She looked away, "Unless you can stop these pigs from raping me, you are wasting your time?"

Deeprose looked over at the passive Petrov who showed no signs of emotion. This is not how the British do things.

"Look, I promise I'll do my best, if you'll excuse me for a moment." He turned to Petrov and spoke rapidly in Russian.

"What in God's name have you done to her, Petrov? Have you never heard of the Geneva Convention?"

He shrugged his shoulders; "The men have a little fun with her, what's wrong with that?"

"Jesus, Petrov. Do you want your Nazi or what?"

"Calm down, English, we'll both get what we want. Just do your job."

Deeprose turned to Jutta Meyer and showed her Maruska Bergman's photograph, "Do you know this person, Jutta?" He was back in German

The Abwehr employee spoke quietly, "Yes, she was a good radio transmitter."

"How do you know this, Jutta?"

"I read her file. When the office was quiet, I did lots of filing."

"What was your job in Hamburg?"

"I was assigned three operators, all in Britain. The only one that functioned was this one." She pointed at Maruska.

Deeprose reached over and took her hand, "Tell me what you know, and I'll get you out of here if I have to kill every one of these animals."

Petrov snorted, "They picked up Maruska Bergman in Vienna just after the Anschluss in May 1938."

"Who picked her up, Jutta?"

"The Gestapo. She was working in the University Hospital as a doctor, but she was a Jew. She was destined for the death camps but they used her mother and father against her."

"What do you mean?"

"They already had their eyes on the Sudetenland, so they had targeted her whole family. They promised Bergman that they would all be safe if she worked for them."

Deeprose sat back; Maruska Bergman did get away from him after all, "Go on," he urged.

"They trained her in Switzerland, in Zurich, I understand. She was very bright, spoke several languages and was a fast learner." She looked up into the room, wistfully, "She had a beautiful touch on the key. It used to send shivers down my spine when she broadcast."

"What did she send?"

"At first, nothing very useful. Then we got some good information on the Spitfire dispersal factories in Southampton. Towards the end, she sent information on train movements from one of your stations. I cannot remember which one."

"Paddington, Jutta. She lived next to it."

There was a pause as Petrov lit another one of his foul-smelling cigarettes.

"Who ran the cell, Jutta?"

"The wife of an Ustaše commander. I don't know her real name, but she was given the code name of Freda. She was a sleeper in London for over a year."

"Who else was in the cell?"

"A Portuguese diplomat, a British Fascist and a member of the Irish Republican Army."

Petrov pushed over a piece of paper with the names of Berlina Candido, Charles Wilson and Mícheál Conlan.

Deeprose examined the paper; he asked her? "What happened to these?"

"All dead."

Petrov smiled, "Bergman killed them all, including the woman known as Freda. If you don't believe me, check with your police when you get back. Wilson and Conlan were stabbed, Candido was electrocuted in her bath and Freda was smothered whilst intoxicated. It seems that Doctor Bergman was not opposed to taking lives when she should have been saving them."

"It's called self-preservation, Alexy."

The Russian shrugged his shoulders.

He turned back to the German, "What happened to Bergman, Jutta?"

"She stopped broadcasting in late December 1940 at the height of the bombing. We found out later that her home had been destroyed."

Deeprose nodded, "Yes, she's buried in a London Cemetery."

Petrov chuckled, "No, she's not..."

Deeprose's eyes opened wide, "What do you mean?"

"You buried a woman, but it wasn't Bergman. Tell him Jutta."

"She checked into a hotel in Liverpool a few days later..."

"How do you know this?" Deeprose was shocked.

"There were more agents in Britain than your organisation would care to admit. Help me get out of here, and I'll be glad to give you as much information as I can, but I can't stay another night in this hellhole."

Petrov stood up, "Come on, English, time for negotiation."

Jutta Meyer reached out to Deeprose and pleaded. There were tears in her eyes, "Don't leave me, sir, the pigs take me two at a time..."

Deeprose looked down at her, "Don't worry, I'll get you out."

Petrov looked directly at Deeprose in an outside room, "You want her, we want Koch."

"I-I don't know if that's possible, Alexy."

He shrugged his shoulders; "You know, the men draw lots to see who would have their turns with her. It's true what she says, there's so many of them that they take her two at a time."

"Jesus, Petrov, is there not a trace of humanity in you?"

Petrov snarled back, "These animals are responsible for the deaths of over twenty million Soviet citizens, English. How many did your trifling little country lose?"

Deeprose turned on his heels, "Get me back to my HQ, Petrov, and I'll see what I can do but, by Christ, if one of your men touches her before I can sort something out, I'll personally hunt you down and kill you like a dog."

Petrov burst out laughing, "That's the spirit, English. I knew there was something in you."

An hour later, Giles Deeprose burst into Dorothy Smith's office. It was nearly ten in the evening. She didn't look up,

"How did it go with Alexy, Giles?"

"What do you mean, 'How did it go?'"

"Did you do a deal with him?"

"What? Deal with that animal?"

She finally looked up and sighed, "You really aren't cut out for the sharp end of this work, are you Giles? Needs must. I want this woman at all costs. She has information on spies that we missed during the war. For all we know, there could be hundreds of the buggers assimilated into society, and I want them before they do some real damage. I don't care about Bergman or the people she's supposed to have murdered. They took their chances when they signed up. As far as I'm concerned, they got what they deserved. It saved the British taxpayer the costs of their trials and executions. The hangman Pierrepoint's already making his pension from stringing up the bastards."

Giles Deeprose sat down, the wind had been taken from his sales; "What about Paul Koch? If they get him, they'll torture him looking for any local sympathisers and then publicly execute him."

Smith shrugged her shoulders; "He's already a dead man, Giles. Who cares?"

Deeprose was shocked at the callousness. She continued, "I've already traded her to the Yanks and John Porter wants a go at her about the codes they used. He doesn't like loose ends."

"What do the Yanks want with her?"

"Who knows what the OSS are after? Probably more information on the scientists they are ferreting away to the USA. They want them before the Russkies get hold of them."

"Where's Paul Koch now?"

"Downstairs, comatose in the back of an ambulance. He thinks he's being taken to an American prison to await trial in Nuremburg, Germany. I can't be seen to be involved with something like this. You know, diplomatic niceties and all that. Go with the truck and bring Fräulein Meyer back, and then get a good night's sleep. I want you on that plane tomorrow evening."

"I thought I was going first thing?"

"It's full. Anyway I thought you might like to do a bit of sightseeing before you left..."

Back in the Soviet Sector, Petrov slapped him on the back, "See, English, I knew you could do it. Now you don't need to kill me in a later life."

Jutta Meyer clung onto him all the way back. As she was leaving the back of the ambulance, she whispered in his ear, "Get your Russian pig of a friend to take you to the University Hospital..."

Before he had time to question her, she was swept away by two female guards.

He left her at the entrance to the Hotel HQ. Dorothy Smith waved at him as she took the girl.

Giles Deeprose tossed and turned throughout the night, 'What did Jutta Meyer mean?' He finally dropped off just before dawn, but Private Jake Lubach awakened him soon after.

"Sir, sorry to bother you, but there's a Russian Major downstairs who wants to speak with you."

Deeprose shook his head, "Jesus, Jake, don't you ever sleep?"

"I will, sir, once I put you on a plane later today."

Deeprose smiled, "What does the Russian want?"

"Dunno, sir, something about a trip to the University?"

Deeprose was washed and dressed in about ten minutes. He climbed into the back of the Kübelwagen. The aroma from Petov's foul tobacco mixed with the smell from the driver made him gag.

"Where are we going, Alexy."

"Oh, just a little trip to see Doctor Bergman's work colleagues, well, one at least."

"Why would I want to do that, Alexy?"

"Because, English, you don't like loose ends."

The University Hospital was badly damaged, but one of the wings was still functioning. The Russians had taken it over and press-ganged the staff into offering what care they could, given the general shortage of medical supplies. The patients were all long-term wounded Russian soldiers awaiting transport back to the Motherland before they could be corrupted by exposure to the decadent west.

He followed Petrov up three flights of broken stairs that had their wooden railings removed, presumably to use as firewood as the oil-fired boilers were out of order. The Russian led him into an office and then through to what looked like a large records room. A middle-aged and rather attractive woman was sat writing at a desk. She was well-presented and looked as though she had access to make-up and clothes that others in Vienna did not. She looked up and spoke in German,

"Major Petrov, what can I do for you? You seem to be making a habit of coming here."

"Only when I want some information, Frau Hoffman, this is Captain Deeprose. He's interested in Doctor Lisle Weiss."

She looked at Deeprose, "You, the Americans, and I presume the Brits as well?"

Petrov looked at Deeprose, "Frau Hoffman has been a hospital administrator since long before the war. If you want to know anything about the staff and students here, she's the one to ask."

Deeprose looked at Petrov, "Lisle Weiss, who is this, Alexy?"

"Patience, English, all will be soon revealed. You'd better sit down to hear this. Go on, Frau Hoffman, tell the good captain what you told me and start at the beginning."

The woman put down her pen and sighed, "Oh really, Alexy, how many times must I repeat this story?"

"Last time, Klara, I promise; cross my heart and hope to die, as the Captain English here would say." He smirked.

She smiled coyly at the flirting Russian. Deeprose had to give it him; he had all the tricks.

She took a deep breath, "Lisle Weiss, came to us as a fresh-faced student in the early Thirties to study from the Sudetenland. She was the top student on her course. She excelled at nearly everything. She was popular with both students and medical staff alike. She had a succession of boyfriends and girlfriends. She had everyone eating out of her hands."

Deeprose raised his eyebrows, "She had girlfriends as well?"

She shook her head, "Oh my dear boy, it was the fashion before the Nazis turned up. Men are pretty useless, you know."

Petrov laughed, "Go on, Klara, get to the interesting bit."

"Weiss qualified and went back to Prague, where she had her first job. I believe her father, a country doctor, had some influence even though the authorities there were reluctant to train females, which is why she came here in the first place."

"Weiss got engaged to a young doctor from Munich who was working here. He was a raving Nazi, but she was swept away by him. Of course, the bugger turned a blind eye to the fact that she was a Jew. She could have done so much better." Hoffman shook her head.

"Anyway, I wasn't surprised to see Lisle back here on a course. She was supposed to be doing something in paediatrics, but her records show she hardly ever attended. She seemed to spend more time with her Nazi friend. She kept disappearing on leave to Germany with him."

Deeprose interrupted, "What about her course?"

"Well, that's it. She kept passing with flying colours. There was nothing her professors could do. She would just bat her big eyes at them, and they melted in her hands. She is, however, a very good doctor. Well, she disappeared just after the Anschluss and we never saw her again."

She sat back and folded her arms. Deeprose looked at Alexy Petrov, "What's this woman got to do with me?"

He smiled and said, "Ask, Klara about Maruska Bergman."

Deeprose looked at the German woman expectantly.

She went on, "Bergman? The Nazis took her off to one of their brothels in Bavaria. It seems they had uses for Jewesses after all. She was also a good doctor; a bit like Weiss. In fact, Weiss's boyfriend dropped Bergman to go with Weiss. Bergman was rounded up with the rest of the unfortunate Jews of Vienna. The professional Jews thought they would be immune from persecution. I mean, only the

Nazis would want to remove half of your intelligentsia, especially doctors? Stupid idiots. There was a shortage of medical staff after that."

Deeprose looked confused, "Do you have a picture of Bergman?"

She opened a file and passed over a photo of a woman who was definitely not whom Deeprose thought was Maruska Bergman. The face was rounder and the hair was much lighter and shorter. The female was a beauty in her own right, but not up to the standards of the woman he thought was Bergman. He could see why the Nazis would take her to a brothel.

Alexy Petrov slowly pushed over a photo. It was the photo that Deeprose thought was Maruska Bergman, he said,

"Who is this, Klara?"

She smiled, "You know who that is Alexy, it's Lisle Weiss..."

A naked Klara Hoffman lay in bed later that night as a very confused and chastened Giles Deeprose was suffering the indignity of yet another uncomfortable flight back to London. She prodded the sleeping figure of Alexy Petrov as he slept next to her.

"Alexy! Alexy! Why did you make me lie to your English?"

Petrov slowly turned over as Hoffman sat up and reached for one of the Russian's cigarettes. She lit it and breathed out the smoke.

He looked up at his Austrian lover, "Part of the game, Klara. It sows confusion in the British Secret Services. We got one over on them."

"To what purpose?"

He reached over, took the burning cigarette and shrugged, "It tells English and his bosses that we know more than they do. It's all about peddling misinformation."

"What about that reference request for Maruska Bergman from the hospital authorities in New York? Doesn't he deserve to know about that?"

His face was down in the pillow, "That's for another time, Klara, and besides, he'd had enough bad news for the day…"

He snorted, rolled over and went back to sleep…

Chapter 27

New York
August 1947
Giles Deeprose

The man in the dark suit stood opposite the Lennox Hill Hospital on East 77th Street. The heat and humidity were oppressive. He would have taken off his jacket if he could, but his white shirt was soaked in sweat. He would get the suit laundered and pressed back at his hotel later in the day. He loosened his tie as yet another ambulance pulled up in front of the trauma unit. He watched as the crew went about their business efficiently and with care for the sick patient.

The man had been on his observation post for nearly three days, yet he had still not seen his target. Perhaps the Embassy had got things wrong? The under-secretary had assured him that this was where the object of his attentions was located.

The little Italian delicatessen two doors along had a few window tables where he could sit for hours on end pretending to read a newspaper. He marvelled at the amount and variety of sweet and savoury pastries that were on sale together with real coffee. In London, everything was rationed. Residents of Britain's capital city could only dream of such luxuries. The large fan over the table kept the air moving and provided some relief.

The under-secretary at the Embassy was rapidly running out of patience. Yes, he would certainly offer one of MI5's most celebrated officers, albeit now retired, the courtesy of assistance, but this was getting ridiculous. Didn't Captain Deeprose realise that he had other duties with which to attend? It had taken the under-secretary and his meagre staff, four days to search New York's hospitals for a Lisle Weiss, and then they came up with nothing. Lisle Weiss certainly wasn't employed anywhere in the New York heath system.

Deeprose was beginning to think that his journey was wasted. His notes from Ashford confirmed that Lisle Weiss had told him she had a brother in New York, which was also where her mother had lived. So, the city had to be where she would go, or so he thought. He could have been sitting in his college in Oxford preparing the paper that was due to be presented in early October. His department was relying on it as it could perhaps generate some additional funding from one of the wealthy benefactors, so he'd better not mess it up...

Giles Deeprose was sat in the lobby of his hotel one evening, sipping a pre-dinner Martini after one of his fruitless days. An olive sat forlornly in the middle of the drink, skewered on what appeared to be a wooden toothpick. Deeprose couldn't see the point of it; he'd never really appreciated the Mediterranean fruit...He was trying to do the crossword in the New York Times. He felt the table move as two fresh drinks were plonked down in front of him. He looked up to see a man dressed in a dark suit, wearing what appeared to be an old Harrovian tie. Deeprose looked upon him with a measure of disdain. He'd always thought that if one has to constantly remind the world that one attended Harrow Public School, there was something sadly lacking in his character...

His uninvited guest spoke, "Giles, old boy, I've been meaning to catch up with you."

The accent was refined and definitely upper middle class in origin.

Deeprose eyed the man, "I'm sorry, have we been introduced?"

The man smiled at him, "Oh, I beg your pardon, how rude of me." He proffered his hand, "Cosmo Atherton. I'm something on the sixth floor."

Deeprose ignored the hand, "What can I do for you, Cosmo Atherton of the sixth floor?"

The Embassy sixth floor contained what the British Government euphemistically called 'Cultural Attaches' but in reality hosted the desks of various spooks and intelligence officers of MI6.

"You've been looking for Lisle Weiss."

Deeprose sipped his drink, "Is that a question or a statement?"

Atherton narrowed his eyes, "Come on, old boy, play nicely. I've come here to tell you that you are wasting your time."

Deeprose sighed and sat back, "Care to elaborate, old boy?" He exaggerated the last two words as a parody.

"Lisle Weiss died in Ravensbrück Concentration Camp after she was taken from a brothel in Munich in March 1945 just before the Soviet Army liberated the camp. So, Captain Deeprose, there is little point in you looking for her."

Deeprose disguised his surprise. Years of interrogating spies and Nazis had served him well. His look was deadpan.

"How do you know this, Atherton?"

Atherton sipped his drink, "Ah, well that would be telling, old boy, wouldn't it? Stop looking for a dead person and look for Maruska Bergman, whom, I might add, is not buried in some Jewish plot in Golders Green Cemetery." Atherton stood up, "Nice to have had this little chat with you, Giles. Do what you have to with the lovely Doctor Maruska but remember, she has the full protection of the United States; she isn't going anywhere."

For the first time in the meeting, Deeprose's face betrayed his feelings. He felt himself flush up. Atherton leaned into the seated man, "Oh, by the way, Alexy Petrov sends his warmest regards." He let that sink in, "I'm sure that paper on the perilous nature of post-war British economics that's sitting on your desk in Trinity Hall, could do with some of your attention..."

Deeprose watched as the man arrogantly walked off, mission accomplished.

The under-secretary's staff at the Embassy found Doctor Maruska Bergman in less than an hour...

That was three days ago. Deeprose had been observing the hospital entrance since then. He was running out of time; his ship was due to leave for Southampton in two days' time. He needed to move on with his life.

He sipped the third coffee of the morning when he saw a beautiful woman exit from the hospital. She was dressed in a bright yellow dress, carrying a patent leather handbag. She wore a pair of pristine white cotton gloves. The modest heel on her black court shoes accentuated the curves on her bare legs. Her long, luxuriant black hair was immaculately coiffured. It was tied back. She had on a pair of dark sunglasses and looked to the entire world as a minor film star.

Deeprose nearly spilled the coffee. He tossed a dollar bill on the table and walked out into the midday, oppressive heat. The blast of hot air almost took away his breath. The woman walked up Third Avenue and turned left towards Central Park. Deeprose kept a reasonable distance behind her. The yellow dress was easily visible. He watched as admiring men turned towards her after they had walked past.

She crossed into the park and passed the Metropolitan Museum of Art. She walked up to the Lake and onto one of the winding paths in what is known as the Ramble. Deeprose had to hurry as he was loosing sight of her in the trees and bushes. He turned onto one path, but she was nowhere to be seen. He quickly spun around, but he had lost her. He was annoyed with himself, but he was an interrogator, not a field operative.

He stood with his hands on his hips trying to decide which way he would walk. He felt the blunt instrument in the small of his back.

"Are you looking for me, Mr Brown?"

He attempted to turn, but the object pressed firmly into his back, "Not just yet. If you make a sudden move, my little snub-nosed Smith and Wesson will make a rather nasty hole in your back."

He began to raise his hands, She hissed, "Lower your arms, Mr Brown. Don't make it so obvious. It's a few years since I've done this. This is America, everyone has a gun..."

He stood there for a minute, wondering if this really had been such a good idea.

Maruska Bergman smiled, "I'm going to put my weapon back in my bag. If you make a scene, it will suddenly reappear and blow off your head."

Giles Deeprose swallowed, "Okay, Doctor Bergman, you're in charge."

"Good, good. Now would you care to tell me your real name we can have a civilised conversation?"

He looked at her, "Giles Deeprose."

She smiled, "Would you like some homemade lemon iced tea? My maid is really good at making it."

He nodded as she put an arm through his, "Come on, my home is a short walk away from here. I've had enough of the sun for one day."

The large brownstone house was on West 85th Street. Maruska Bergman went up the steps and beckoned Deeprose to follow. She extracted some keys and turned the front door lock. Deeprose looked up at the four-storey house with a basement.

He asked, "Do you have an apartment here?"

"No, Giles, I own the whole house."

She went inside and called out, "Louisa! We have a guest for refreshments."

A black female appeared from the rear of the floor, smoothing down the apron on her uniform. She bowed slightly, "Good afternoon, Doctor Bergman."

Maruska Bergman kicked off her shoes and peeled off the gloves. She tossed them onto the stand next to the front door, "Could you pour some iced tea and bring it into the drawing room?"

Louisa nodded, "Certainly, Doctor Bergman. Will we have an extra guest for dinner?"

Before Deeprose had time to answer, Maruska said, "Of course, Louisa, I'm sure Captain Deeprose would love to sample some of your home cooking. You can set the table for three. Please show him into the drawing room. I'll be back in a few minutes."

The maid led Deeprose into the drawing room that was situated at the back of the house. She disappeared to make the refreshments. Deeprose looked over the neat garden. The room was expensively but tastefully furnished. He wandered over to the grand piano, upon which were placed several photographs. He picked them up one by one and examined them. There were a few old sepia pictures of what looked like Maruska's mother and father sitting rather formally. In one, all three of the children were posed stiffly between their parents. He thought he could just make out a rather young Maruska.

He picked up one that was placed behind the others as though it was meant to be partially hidden. His eyes opened wide when he saw Maruska Bergman dressed in the USA army uniform of a captain of the 55th Field Hospital based in Burtonwood, Warrington in Britain. He breathed in, trying to get his head around that.

The door opened. Maruska Bergman walked in wearing a pair of beige, high-wasted slacks, complete with a silk blouse. She was in bare feet as she walked along the highly polished floorboards. She sat on the sofa and tucked her legs under her feet.

She said, "Please sit down, Giles. The Americans said that eventually, curiosity would get the better of you." She smiled as

Louisa brought in a tray of iced lemon tea, complete with some cut glass tumblers. She poured out the drinks and handed one to Deeprose. She turned to Maruska,

"If it's all right, Ma'am, I'll get on with the dinner. The gardener is due this afternoon, but Lord knows how he'll be able to work in this heat." The accent was southern.

"Give him lots of your iced tea, Louisa..."

The maid smiled at her employer as she went out through the door.

Maruska turned to Deeprose, "Take off your jacket, Giles. You'll be much more comfortable. These brownstones are cool in the summer and warm in the winter."

He removed his jacket and placed it next to him.

She said, "I've been watching you ever since you arrived in front of the hospital. I had to talk to the Americans before I would let you approach me."

He nodded at the army picture, "I see you have friends in high places, Captain Bergman."

She chuckled, "The rank is purely honorary for the time being, I can assure you, but, nevertheless, very useful."

She looked at him, "Why are you here, Giles?"

He sipped the drink; it was surprisingly refreshing, "You are a loose end, Maruska. You beat me once, and then the Russians did the same. You are the only one that got away from me."

Maruska raised her eyebrows, "I didn't beat you, Giles. You did a good job. Together with your colleagues, you got to me in the end. If it hadn't been for the Americans, either the Nazis or the British would have caught me."

"What's the connection with the Americans?"

She shrugged her shoulders, "I helped out at the airbase."

He snorted, "You must have done a lot more than simply helping out."

"No matter. They expressed their gratitude in a variety of ways."

There was a pause; she said, "Ask me what you want. I promise to be as truthful as I can. I have nothing to hide any more. There's little you or your British Government can do about it."

He went over to the piano and picked up the family photo, "Is this your family?"

She stared into the distance and nodded.

He asked, "Did any of them survive?"

She shook her head, "They are all dead. My mother and father, together with my eldest brother David and his family, died in Theresienstadt. It is not definite, but I understand they all contracted typhus sometime in 1942. The camp and ghetto were rife with it."

"You had a brother in New York."

She nodded, "Yes, Lukas. He was killed on Omaha Beach during the Normandy landings in 1944. He has a grave in Colleville-sur-Mer but I have never seen it; I will one day. The photographs came from my sister-in-law. She had no need of them when she remarried and moved to Texas."

Deeprose was silent for a minute, "So, you are the only one to survive?"

She nodded. He said, "Tell me what happened, and I'll try to recall if Klara Hoffman was telling the truth."

Maruska smiled, "There's a name I haven't heard of in a few years. She was the self-appointed queen of the University Hospital. She was always nagging me about non-attendance at courses."

"It seems you always passed, anyway."

Maruska chuckled, "Yes, I was a bit lucky with that one."

"Hoffman got you confused with Lisle Weiss."

Maruska shook her head, "No, Giles, her Russian boyfriend played you. But have no concerns, when her Russian protector grew tired of her, he sent her to East Berlin. I'm told she works in the archives in the Embassy on Unter Den Linden. Married a junior diplomat, I understand, but never to be seen again in the West. She knows where all the bodies are buried."

Deeprose smiled, he hadn't heard that expression for some time, he said, "I understand that Lisle Weiss died in Ravensbrück?"

Maruska stared ahead again, "Yes, she was a good friend."

Deeprose interjected, "You took her Nazi boyfriend."

"No, Giles. He wanted a wife of good Aryan stock for breeding. It was never going to work out for her or me. I seduced him so I could use him. He set me up with the Abwehr after they took my parents."

"Did you have a choice?"

She sighed, "Well, yes, we all had a choice. It was either cooperate or suffer some gruesome death in one of the camps. I chose to live on the off chance that my family would survive."

"What happened to the Nazi?"

"Killed at Stallingrad. Best place for him."

Deeprose's thoughts were all over the place, "Who is buried in Golders Green?"

"Shira Adelman of Star Street, Paddington. She was wearing my clothes when the bomb hit the house."

"Boiler suit with brass buttons..."

She smiled, "Yes, I miss that old overall. When I wore it, no one saw me. It was as though I was invisible."

"Did you kill her husband?"

The question remained unanswered as Maruska stared ahead.

She thought and said, "If I did, he deserved it. He was a wife beater."

"What about the members of your cell?"

Maruska shrugged her shoulders and stood up. She went to the large French windows and looked out at the African American gardener who was toiling under the hot sun. He could hear Louisa chatting to him.

"What about Berlina Candido, Charles Wilson and Mícheál Conlan?"

"They presented a threat."

"Candido was a junior diplomat."

"She attempted to undermine me."

He raised his eyebrows, "And Wilson and Conlan?"

"I did you all a favour."

He smiled at that, "And the woman known as Freda, your handler?"

"Ustaše; worse than the Nazis. She's partly responsible for some of the terrible bomb damage in the East End of London."

He joined her at the window. He sighed, "I can't argue with that."

The gardener looked up at the window and waved. Maruska waved back.

She said, "You know Burtonwood was segregated, even the hospital?"

"They still are, Maruska. They even built a separate quartering patch away from the camp for their black soldiers."

She shook her head, "I used to go over there from time to time to help out, but my bosses frowned on it. They never had enough medical staff. These were good, honest folk who were willing to give up their lives for their country and this is how they were treated." She paused, "I suppose it's because I'm a Jew that I can empathise with them."

Deeprose sat back down and poured himself another glass of iced tea. "Tell me about Ashford, Maruska."

She turned, "Horrible place, Giles; you don't know the half of it. It was a struggle to survive it. I nearly gave myself up, but the consequences were too serious."

"We didn't hang the women, Maruska."

"No, but the Nazis would have killed my parents once they found out."

He spoke quietly, "We now know what those books were used for."

She smiled again, "Yes, simple but effective. I had to memorise the coding rota to know which books to use for each transmission, "

"You did a good job. Where are the books now?"

"They were destroyed in the bombing of the house, anyway, I have no wish to be reminded of them. I remember you surprised me when you spoke in Czech."

He smiled, "I give off the impression that I know more than I actually do." There was a lengthy silence, "Tell me about your boyfriend, Peter Porteous."

She was wistful, "That's my one regret apart from the wasted lives. We were told never to fall in love, and I'm afraid I did." She paused and then asked, "What is he up to now?"

Deeprose shrugged, "As far as I know, he's still in Kensal Town up to his nefarious activities, but that's a police matter and I really have no idea."

Maruska smiled, "He'll never change, but he has a warm heart. He took good care of me and his other ladies."

Deeprose stood up, "What about this, Maruska, where did this house come from? Even as a doctor, you wouldn't earn enough to purchase a house this size in Manhattan."

"I carried a small fortune in diamonds."

"What? We searched you and took apart what little property you had. You were carrying nothing."

Maruska smiled, she said, "Wait there, Giles, I've something to show you."

She returned about three minutes later. He heard her bare feet on the wooden stairs. She took his arm and dropped the little silk bag into the palm of his hand, "I put the down payment on this house with the contents of this little bag."

He shook his head, "I-I-don't understand." He examined the bag with the silk drawstring.

"I carried this bag in me for over four years. I kind of missed it when I bought the house and had no more need of it."

He looked blank; she said, "Do you want me to demonstrate?" She moved her hand towards her groin.

He put his hands over his eyes, "Jesus, how could the girls have missed that?"

"They were too busy staring at our nakedness to bother searching our body cavities properly."

"Where did the gems come from?"

"My Nazi boyfriend stole them off a Jew. He found them in a burnt-out shop in Munich. The Abwehr taught us how to use the cavity for secreting objects, but they definitely weren't thinking about diamonds. That silk bag is official Abwehr issue."

He shook his head and closed his eyes, "So, how did you get to this position?"

"Simple, really. My boss in Burtonwood was a colonel. He asked me to accompany a troopship to New York with injured soldiers who needed to be invalided home. We lost many on the voyage. They were only boys, most of them. When I landed, Immigration paid me no heed. I just waved my military identity card and walked through. I was in full uniform. I had a letter of recommendation to the New York Health Board, and they placed me in a veterans' hospital in Brooklyn. They eventually wrote to Klara Hoffman for a reference when the war ended. She provided a really good one. After all, no one could complain about my medical skills. The Health Board required me to attend a conversion course, and I graduated from there some time ago. I now have full state registration. I'm now a qualified resident trauma doctor."

"What about your citizenship?"

"Dunno, really. I was told to attend a service at one of the town halls one morning, raised my right hand and swore allegiance to the flag of the United States of America."

"Did they not check your background?"

"I don't know, but soon after, I was approached by the OSS. They wanted information on my Abwehr handlers."

"So they knew you had a dubious background?"

She shrugged her shoulders, "I think your Russian friend told them."

"Who, Alexy Petrov?"

She nodded, "Anyway, they were too embarrassed to admit that they had a possible German agent working on Burtonwood Airbase." She smiled...

"Did your colonel know?"

"He certainly had his suspicions, but he was a kind man and a very good doctor. He recognised my skills and I thank him for that. I think if I had stayed in Britain I wouldn't be here today. There were many more Abwehr agents in Britain than your organisation would care to admit. One of them would have got me especially as I'm a Jew."

He nodded, "The official line is that most were caught. It would have been bad for morale if the general public thought there were German spies operating with impunity. I suppose one day the truth will come out; it usually does."

Their conversation was halted when the doorbell sounded. Maruska offered a polite "Excuse me," and went to the hallway. Deeprose shook his head, but at least he was getting answers. He stopped...he could hear German being spoken in the hallway.

The drawing room door opened, Maruska led in a good-looking female, probably a little younger than herself,

"Giles, I have someone here who would like to speak with you..."

His eyes opened wide. Standing before him was Jutta Meyer.

Jutta walked up to him; she spoke in accented English, "Mr Deeprose; I finally get the opportunity to thank you personally."

Giles Deeprose was an articulate fellow who prided himself on his ability to make sense of the most senseless situations. This time he was almost stumped for words as Jutta Meyer threw her arms around the Englishman and hugged him tightly.

She stood back and grabbed hold of his hands, "I owe you my life, Mr Deeprose. If you hadn't come back for me that very same day, I had planned to kill myself. I had managed to get a piece of sharp glass. I was going to slash my wrists."

He finally spoke as Louisa entered carrying a tray of drinks. The maid smiled as she looked at the two of them. Maruska stood back.

"I-I-I wouldn't have recognised you Frau Meyer, you look completely different."

Jutta smiled, "Yes, I wasn't exactly at my best when you last saw me. It must have taken me three refills of bath water to scrub those pigs off my skin. Your boss, I don't know her name, was very kind. She allowed me to rest for nearly a week before she handed me over to the Americans."

"Dorothy Smith, Miss Meyer, that was her name. Her gentle appearance belied her true nature. She was as callous as the rest when she needed to be."

"Call me Jutta."

"And you must call me Giles."

Maruska spoke, "Time for an apéritif, Giles, I have some good gin that I'm sure you will appreciate."

They sat down. He noticed how close Jutta Meyer and Maruska Bergman sat together on the sofa. He asked, "What happened to you, Jutta?"

"In early 1941, I was in Hamburg at the height of the bombing of Britain. We had a dozen or so agents operating. They could collect information, but it was becoming increasingly difficult to transmit. The British authorities were getting good at tracking down the transmissions at source. Their equipment was getting more and more precise."

Maruska poured the drinks.

"When Hitler turned towards the East, they moved me to Berlin to listen to our agents there. By this time, Maruska had disappeared, but I knew she was still alive. We tracked her to Liverpool but lost her from there. It was only much later that I learned she was working at an American Airbase." She smiled at Maruska and sipped her drink,

"When Berlin was getting bombed, the Abwehr decided to clear out. They attempted to destroy what they could, even though most operatives had not committed any war crimes. I was never a member of the Nazi Party, so I had nothing to fear. I just did my job. They sent me to Vienna to monitor the Russian advance. I just didn't get out quickly enough before those animals got me." She stared ahead, "I was too honest. When they found out I was in the Abwehr, I got passed from one unit to the other. It was that pig Petrov who decided they could trade me for that SS Major."

"Sturmbannführer Paul Koch." Deeprose smiled, "The Russians got a bad deal with him. Koch managed to kill himself before they got him on the plane to Moscow. There was hell to pay over that."

Jutta Meyer sighed, "The Americans took me to Germany and interrogated me for over a month. They didn't mistreat me and there was decent food. I had more trouble from the Nazi women who were detained with me because I wasn't in the Party."

Deeprose spoke, "They were after information on the rocket scientists."

She nodded, "I had seen the files in Berlin. Thank God the Russians didn't know I had this information otherwise I would never have got out."

He asked, "How were you able to get this information in the first place? The rocket programme had nothing to do with the Abwehr."

"We had a department that kept files on all these men. Hitler didn't want anyone who could be suspect, working on the programme. After hostilities ended in April 1945, there was a tug of war between the Russians and the Americans to get hold of these scientists."

Deeprose sighed, "Yes, the Americans got the top prize, Wernher von Braun."

Juttas Meyer laughed, "Along with about one thousand other technicians and scientists. We had files on them all. Von Braun was a Nazi and a member of the SS despite his protestations. Something that the Americans have conveniently forgotten."

There was a pause, Deeprose asked, "So, how did you end up here?"

She shrugged her shoulders, "I just asked to be moved. I claimed my life was in danger from these Nazis. The next thing I knew was that I was on a repatriation ship to New York. Because I have some technical knowledge they put me to work for an electrical company that is developing machines that can do mathematical problems."

Deeprose nodded, "Hmm, I've heard about them. They were working on them at Bletchley Park."

Jutta nodded, "The Company I work for has government contracts. They sponsored me for my citizenship. I have an apartment in Brooklyn. I'm not returning to Germany."

"And meeting up with Maruska?"

Jutta looked at Maruska and smiled, "The OSS. Every now and again, they ask me about individual Germans who are trying to immigrate to the USA as part of background checks. Some I remember, others I don't, but I know which organisations are problematical. One day, out of curiosity, I asked if they had any information on Maruska. I just wondered what had happened to her.

An officer left her file on his desk one day and went for a break. You can imagine my surprise when I discovered she was living so close to me. I had never met her, but I had a deep connection with her through her touch on the radio."

Deeprose nodded, "It's often the way. Plausible deniability."

Maruska stood up, "Come on, let's go and eat..."

About midnight, as Giles Deeprose slept the sleep of the righteous in his hotel after several nightcaps, a naked Maruska Bergman lay on her stomach on the bed in the grand room on the first floor of her house. She was playing with the diamond ring on her finger. A soft nightlight cast off a gentle glow. An equally naked Jutta Meyer lay face down next to her, turning the pages of a technical manual from her company that was propped up on one of the pillows. The large ceiling fan was wafting a cool breeze on their bodies.

She looked over at Maruska, "Do you think Giles was satisfied?"

Maruska glanced at her, "I think so, I'm glad that he finally knows the truth."

Jutta replied, "Yes, he deserves to know it. I liked him in Vienna, and I like him now. He's nice."

Maruska snorted, "His gentle nature masks his true character. He must have sent at least a dozen spies to the hangman, not counting the Nazis after the war." She reached over and traced the tips of her fingers along the contours of Jutta Meyer's back from her shoulders to the base of her spine.

Jutta sighed, "Stop that, Maruska, you know what it does to me. You're on the early shift at the hospital tomorrow."

Maruska licked her lips. Her fingers danced on the bare skin. Jutta Meyer closed her eyes and let out a deep sigh. The technical manual slipped to the floor...

Chapter 28

London
August 1941
The Stocking Strangler

It had been eight months since Peter Porteous had stood by Maruska Bergman's freshly dug grave in the Jewish part of Golders Green Cemetery. He had been back twice to place fresh flowers. The cemetery was beginning to become neglected. Once or twice, he brushed away litter from the plot. Rabbi Levy had managed to get an inscription in Hebrew carved into the simple headstone. He had no idea what it said.

Porteous was permanently tired. Smiths in Cricklewood demanded more and more of his time, and there never seemed to be a let up from his fire-watching tasks. Occasionally, he was placed on black-out duties, which essentially meant he would walk around a regular beat shouting at residents to shut out the lights.

Jimmy Ryan and he had replenished the stock destroyed in the bombing of Bosworth Road. The ruins of his old home and those around it on Bosworth Road, lay cordoned off with police tape, although it didn't seem to prevent local children from scavenging what metal they could, to be sold in the scrapyard at the top of Kensal Road for pennies.

Items in demand were getting harder to obtain as the war took its toll on supply chains. His regular customers were more intent on acquiring enough food to eat rather than forking out for a pair of expensive nylon or the increasingly rare silk stockings. Ryan was gradually moving into tinned food, most of which had been liberated from some military store somewhere in Hertfordshire. The supervisor, an overweight sergeant never destined for active service, was sufficiently clever enough to fiddle the inventory so that his crimes wouldn't be discovered.

One evening in late August, Porteous left the girls in Smiths slightly early; he needed some sleep. Alice Halpin was more than able to cajole and encourage the ladies to meet their daily targets, unless one of the unreliable pressing machines gave up the ghost again.

The early evening was muggy and balmy; a typical British summer, with two hot days and a thunderstorm. As he pushed his bicycle out of the yard and onto the high road, the skies were darkening. He felt the first drops of rain before he had reached the end of the Broadway. He pedalled along Shoot Up Hill and turned into Mill Lane. By the time he reached Nancy Keeling's house, he was soaking wet. He turned the key in the front door and pushed it open, wheeling the dripping bike over the pristine tiles.

Nancy appeared at the kitchen door with her arms folded, "I hope you're going to mop that up, Porteous, I've been on my knees for hours scrubbing those tiles." She was wearing one of Maruska's boiler suits and a turban headscarf.

He looked up, trying to flick the wet hair from his eyes, "Bloody British weather..."

Nancy sat on the end of the old roll-top bath and soaped Porteous' back. There was a pile of wet clothes on the floor. He spoke quietly,

"Alice's friend, the one who works in the typing pool for the police, says that Shira is now officially a suspect in her husband's death."

Nancy snorted and shook her head, "That's not Shira's style. As has been said before, she would have just plunged a blade into his heart, sat down with a bottle of gin and waited for the police."

Porteous laughed, "Yeah, I suppose you're correct. Alice said that they even considered the possibility of the Stocking Strangler."

"Nah, he only takes women so he can defile them after death. What use is an old man to that pervert?"

"Hmm, that's what I thought, although the stocking is certainly interesting. It could be Shira, but if you think about it, she would have had nowhere to go."

Nancy poured some water over his hair, "She would have ended up at your place, no doubt."

She felt him nod, "What would you have done?"

"Taken her to the police. There's plenty of people who would testify that the old bastard knocked her about on a regular basis. She's turned up more than once at the Bayswater Synagogue with black eyes. Maruska told me of at least one time."

Nancy sighed, "I'm not sure the courts would take that as an excuse. They've hanged women for less at the Old Bailey."

She slapped his back, "Come on, shove over; that's the last of the hot water, and I'm working tonight. We need to cook dinner."

She threw off her old boiler suit and clambered into the bath which wasn't really big enough for both of them...

They were in the kitchen eating a stew of indeterminate identity with boiled, mashed turnips, there being no potatoes in the shops recently, when the door knocked loudly.

Porteous looked at Nancy, she said, "Get that for me, Porteous, it'll be Mifty."

She stood up, "I'll just fix my face."

Porteous sighed, "Tell him you can't work tonight."

She shook her head, "Party down in Mayfair. Charlie has booked loads of girls. There should be good money." She paused then raised her voice, "Now, don't start, Porteous, we've had this conversation too many times to mention."

She disappeared up the stairs as Porteous reluctantly opened the door to be greeted by one of Charlie Maitland's bruisers. The Wolsey Hornet in which he had arrived, sat on the road outside the house with the engine still running. Michael 'Mifty' Mitchell sneered at Porteous,

"Peter Porteous, what are you doing here?"

Porteous looked at the battered face of the retired bare-knuckle fairground boxer. His nose looked like it had been broken too many times to count. His baldhead glistened in the summer heat. He was about five feet three and about as wide as he was tall. His black woollen suit strained to keep the man's bulk in check. Folds of flesh bulged out over his collar. Mifty Mitchell had a set of large rings on four of the fingers on his right hand. These rings had torn many a rival's face. Porteous knew not to mess with Mitchell.

"Just eating, Mifty, that's all."

Mitchell pushed his way past Porteous into the hall, "Where's that tart of yours?" He leaned on the banister, "Nancy! Get your backside down here now. I've got two other girls to pick up!"

Porteous stood back against the wall. Mitchell got in his face, "I hear you and that runt, Jimmy Ryan, have been doing good business. I'd watch it, if I was you, 'cos Charlie's thinking of making you two chancers business partners. He's already spoken to Elphicke." He laughed out loud and tapped Porteous on the cheek. "Insignificant, that's what yer are."

Porteous looked down at the man and turned his face away. Mitchell straightened up his suit and cleared his throat, "Charlie will want to see you two soon. When he calls, don't keep him waiting. Now fuck off!"

Nancy Keeling appeared at the top of the stairs, "Mifty! Leave him alone. He's nothing to you."

Mitchell stepped back, smiling, "Yeah. I suppose you're right, he's nothing..."

Nancy clipped down the wooden stairs and got in between Porteous and Mitchell. She put her arms around Porteous' neck, reached up and kissed him on the lips, "I'll see you later."

Mitchell took Nancy's arm and pulled her out of the door, "Get in the Hornet."

He turned to Porteous, "Don't wait up for her..." He burst out laughing.

Porteous tidied the kitchen and then left for home on his bicycle. Mifty Mitchell would get his sooner or later...

Nancy Keeling was sat on the lap of a minor aristocrat in the upstairs dining room of a private club in Marlborough Place, overlooking St James' Park. There were about thirty men, all dressed formally in dinner jackets. Charlie Maitland had provided all the ladies for the night, who magically appeared after the waitresses had cleared away the remnants of a five-course meal. Nancy was vainly trying to stop the man from putting his hand up her skirt. She leaned into the man and whispered in his ear,

"You pay to touch."

He laughed, reached into his pocket and withdrew a five-pound note, "How much touching can I get for this?"

Nancy smiled and took the note. She stood up, smoothed down her dress and said, "I'll just go and freshen up..."

The man knocked back his brandy, banged the glass on the table and shouted for a refill. Mifty Mitchell looked over at Nancy and nodded imperceptibly. Nancy managed to get into the ladies' toilet, pushing off other drunken, amorous males in the process.

She stood at the mirrors trying to refresh her make-up. She looked over as a young female exited from a cubicle and joined her at the sinks.

Nancy looked at the girl. She was far too young to be in this occupation.

She enquired, "Are you okay?"

The girl half smiled, "I'm not used to so many men."

Nancy looked at her in the mirror, "I've not seen you before."

"I'm new. One of Charlie's boys picked me up in Wardour Street. I didn't know you had to be one of his girls before you could work."

Nancy shook her head, "The Maltese bastard controls all the girls here but don't worry, we've all made that mistake at the beginning and been punished for it."

The girl said defiantly, "I'm not staying!"

Nancy shrugged her shoulders, "It's only just getting started. There's plenty of money to be made even after you've paid the rent." She reached into her purse, "Look, I've just got five pounds from one of the toffs. He's so drunk he won't be able to get it up."

The girl put her leg up the bench, raised her yellow dress and began adjusting her stockings.

Nancy shook her head, "I wouldn't wear those at the moment. You've heard of the Stocking Strangler?"

The girl snorted, "I can look after myself." She opened her purse and took out a little flick knife that had seen better days. "I'm going to go up to Camden Town. There are plenty of servicemen up there looking for company."

Nancy raised her eyebrows, "Look, what's your name? Stay with me. I'm sure I can get you a nice man for the evening, especially as you are much younger than me."

"Maple, that's my name, as in syrup, but thanks for the offer. I can't stand these people. They think they own the world."

Nancy sighed, "They do, actually. If you are going to leave, go out through the kitchen at the back. With all that chaos in there, the minders won't miss you until it's too late."

"Have you got a day job?"

Maple was at the door, "Yeah, I'm a clerk in Holborn. Thanks again, but I'm off."

With that, she was gone...

About the same time as Nancy was having her brief conversation with the female called Maple, Gordon Cummins, having borrowed one pound from his wife in Southwark, got off the bus in Camden Town and headed for the first hostelry that was still open. He was smartly dressed in his blue Flight Sergeant's Royal Air Force uniform. He was anonymous. There were thousands of service personnel thronging the pubs and bars of London, desperate for some relief from the war.

He was hoping to get a few drinks down him and pick up a pretty young thing before the early warning sirens announced the arrival of the nightly air raids. The Camden Road Arms, opposite the Underground Station, was busy. He walked in to be met with a cacophony of noise and an atmosphere of stale beer and sweat. The place was teeming with men from all three services. There were probably as many ladies as the men, all dressed in their best finery even though it was a Tuesday evening. He pushed his way to the bar and managed to persuade the buxom barmaid to serve him two drinks. He made his way over to the sidewall as a slightly out of tune piano sounded out from across the room. He couldn't see who was playing the instrument because a bunch of soldiers crowded around, each clutching their pints and singing along.

Cummins placed one of the drinks on the ledge next to an overflowing ashtray and looked to see if there was a decent young thing that might like to spend some time with him later in the evening. He had told his wife after his fleeting visit that he had to return to his unit in Regent's Park, as he was on duty first thing in the morning. The night was all his.

The young girl in the yellow dress caught his eye; she smiled coyly and then turned away. Ten minutes later, the two of them were deep in conversation. He had managed to acquire her a small gin and tonic that she sipped delicately as though she wasn't a hardened drinker. The female looked at Cummins; he wasn't bad looking, and he had already showed her a one-pound note.

They left the pub just before nine. The air raid warnings would certainly go off in the next hour or so. German bomber pilots didn't like flying in daylight. It was all right in the winter months, but in the long days of summer, you were asking for a greeting from one of the Hurricane fighters over the green fields of Kent as you approached the capital.

She put her arm through his as they walked down Camden High Street. She had suggested that they walk into Regent's Park to conduct their business. She had taken clients to one particular spot before and, as the weather was fine, this would be perfect. The railings had long since been taken away for the war effort; they wouldn't need to enter through one of the gates. They passed a row of bombed out houses on Hampstead Road at the rear of Euston Station.

Cummins suggested they find a place in one of them. The woman was a little unsure. She preferred the open space of the park. At least, she could cry out if there were any problems; there were always other courting couples nearby. The night was falling quickly. He gently pulled her into the ruins. The front of the house was gone, but the rear still appeared to have at least two floors intact.

He pushed on a door. It was sticking in the warped frame, but he managed to get it open. A dirty mattress lay in the middle of the floor. She said,

"I'm not lying on that."

He smiled and took off his RAF jacket. He swept away some of the brick dust with his hand and then laid the garment on the mattress. She was still hesitant, but a pound is still a pound, when all said and done.

"Can I see the money, first?" She asked.

He dug deep into his pocket and produced the folded up note. She took it quickly and put it in her handbag.

He began unbuttoning his trousers as he lay on the makeshift bed, "Come on, let's see what I get for my money."

She put down her bag and began to unbutton her thin, cotton dress. She let it fall open. He licked his lips at the sight of the woman dressed in a cream-coloured brassiere and matching French knickers, under which he could see the outline of her suspender belt. He grabbed at her. She backed away,

"Wait a second, I don't want my underwear torn. This is my best set."

She deftly removed the knickers. He said, "Leave the stockings on."

She looked at him, "It will cost you if you rip them." He shrugged his shoulders.

She got on top of him. At first, he was gentle. She looked at his face in the pale light of the moon. His eyes were closed; it wasn't a bad life, really. He'd be done in a few minutes. The money would do nicely until her wages came at the end of the week. No need to worry about being pawed up by some rich toffs up in Mayfair.

He flipped her on her back. His weight pressed against her. She began to protest. She got a sharp slap by the way of a rebuke. He began to turn her over.

"No! No! I don't do that?"

He thumped the back of her head. She saw stars. He pressed her head down on the mattress and lifted up her buttocks. He couldn't penetrate her. The more he tried, the more his erection began to subside. He hit her again.

Two days later, workmen discovered Maple Churchyard's semi-naked body in the back room of the bombed-out house. She had been strangled with her own camiknickers. She was missing one stocking. The contents of her handbag were strewn over the dirty floorboards; the cash was missing...

Nancy Keeling cried off from her job for the next week, as did many of the other ladies. Charlie Maitland was not amused.

She stayed at Peter Porteous' with Mifty Mitchell not daring to cross over the Ha'penny Steps to seek out either of them...

Author's notes

The Ha'penny Steps trilogy is a work of fiction.

Research for this series commenced several years ago. Having written books about contemporary London fiction, I had always been fascinated about the area of London in which I lived and worked. I was as a young teacher in Kensal Town and I became even more interested in this area that is steeped in working class history.

I went back to Kensal Town in 2021 only to find the original Ha'penny Steps bridge over the canal had been demolished by the local authority and replaced by a modern, easy access crossing. The picture of the original bridge that adorns the covers of all three parts of the trilogy has been taken and modified from a series of photographs on Pinterest. I am also indebted to local librarians and historians who have been helpful in finding pictures of the area pre-demolition, and the original Steps.

It was whilst watching the black and white film "The Blue Lamp" of 1950 that my imagination was finally stirred into life. The film has a few shots of the original buildings and tenements on Kensal Road and Bosworth Road and the original Ha'penny Steps. There are little, if any of these buildings left. The Roman Catholic Church on the corner of Hazelwood Crescent and Bosworth Road, The Church of Our Lady of the Holy Souls, remains in all its glory. I do not know if the crypt was actually used as an air-raid shelter during the height of the Blitz but please allow me some artistic licence.

The Catholic primary school at the bottom of East Row still exists. It was opposite this school that Porteous moved after his home on Bosworth Road was demolished by the parachute land mine in Part 1 of the series. I do not know if there were ever any houses there, as I can find no existing pictures of the road. Most of the original properties were demolished as part of The Royal Borough of Kensington and Chelsea's slum clearance programme post- war. Many suffered bomb damage owing to their close proximity to the major railway lines that ran into Paddington Station.

The 1951, Ordinance Survey map number 51/28 SW, which I acquired from the National Library of Scotland, is the closest I could find to an actual representation of the complete area but even this shows some of the bomb damage that was noticeable in The Blue Lamp. The area between Bosworth Road and East Row is now completely taken up by the open recreational space, the delightfully named Emslie Horniman's Pleasance. Mr Horniman, a wealthy politician, donated the land and funds upon which the park was created in 1911. The park was extensively renovated in the 1990s.

Kensal Town is sometimes referred to as Kensal New Town and should not be confused with Kensal Rise which is about two or three kilometres to the north up Kilburn Lane and into Chamberlayne Road. Kensal Rise was formerly in the Borough of Willesden, now Brent.

From the earliest records, it can be seen that Kensal Town was unique in its own way. Bordered by the Grand Union Canal and the Harrow Road on the North Eastern side (over which the Ha'penny Steps crossed) and the major railways lines into Paddington Station to the South West, it is easy to see how the area became isolated even more so before the Steps were constructed. It was an essentially working class area often occupied by the Irish labourers who helped construct both the railway line and before that, the canal. Sanitary conditions were poor with several families sharing one toilet. Criminality was rife throughout the area facilitated by the abundance of public houses, some of which still exist to this day. The construction of a public washhouse in Wedlake Street points to the complete absence of bathing facilities in most of the houses.

Victorian newspapers often record the prevalence of dog fighting upon which there was a thriving betting industry.

What is known is that the police rarely crossed the Steps except in pairs, and preferably mob-handed.

Wartime German Spies in Britain

Churchill had become convinced that what he called Fifth Columnists or German spies, were operating in Britain by the time he became prime minister in May 1940. He simply could not accept that the Germany's rapid victories across much of Europe were down to superior firepower and military tactics. He believed that the Germans must have had local support from these fifth columnists. He enacted the Treachery Act by the end of the month to deal explicitly with foreign agents as Britain's treason laws could only be applied to British subjects. Between 1940 and 1946 twenty spies and saboteurs were prosecuted in secret under the Treachery Act. Nineteen of these were hanged. The Ministry of Information would have supressed any news of these trials. One spy was tried under courts martial regulations, convicted and taken to the indoor firing range at the Tower of London where he was tied to a chair and shot by a detachment of Scots Guards.

Officially, MI5 claim that only one Abwehr agent operated in Britain at the height of the war and that he killed himself to evade capture. Unofficially, it will never be known how many German agents there actually were. What is known is that the Luftwaffe had detailed information of their targets, including in Southampton after the dispersal following the bombing of the Supermarine Factory in Woolaston where the Spitfire was being constructed. (More of this in Book 3 of the trilogy.) This information must have come from agents acting on the ground. MI5 also claim that when enemy agents were identified they would do their best to turn them so as to supply false information back to Germany. Sometimes it was do this or face the hangman.

There is also evidence that the Nazis used blackmail and other methods to pressurise citizens into working for them. Maruska's story is entirely plausible in the light of this.

Immediately prior to the war as the Nazis over ran Europe, many refugees arrived in Britain especially from Austria, Germany and Czechoslovakia. The authorities did their best to weed out possible spies from the thousands who arrived on British shores at reception centres. The character of Giles Deeprose is loosely based on Lieutenant Colonel Oresto Pinto who is reckoned to have interviewed over thirty thousand refugees during the period of the war as part of his work for MI5. It is claimed he actually identified eight spies masquerading as genuine refugees.

Acknowledgements

I read widely around the subject of the London Blitz, including some good fiction that highlighted the work of the Auxiliary Fire Brigade and the Auxiliary Ambulance Service. I have nothing but praise and gratitude for the men and women who regularly risked their lives during heavy bombing.

No Cake, No Jam: Hardship and Happiness in Wartime London by Constantine Fitzgibbon gives a detailed picture of life at the time for the less well off.

Ambulance Girls: A Gritty Wartime Saga set in the London Blitz by Deborah Burrows gives the reader a no holds barred account of life as an ambulance girl.

The Blitz: The Story of the Blitz in London by Constantine Fitzgibbon, gives a thorough and very comprehensive account of the bombing and its impact upon London's residents.

Between Silk and Cyanide: A Code Maker's War 1941-1945 by Leo Marks. Marks was *Chef du Code* for the Special Operations Executive, (SOE) and gives a detailed account of agents' codes and code breaking.

The staff at RAF Burtonwood Heritage Centre in Warrington, including John Cotterill, who patiently answered my questions.

Cover by Tatiana Vila, Vila Designs. www.viladesign.net

Of course, I greatly acknowledge the part played in *Wikipedia* in my writing. The on-line encyclopaedia is my go-to place not only for initial facts but also to check references. I contribute regularly to the cause. If you use the service, please consider making a donation.

Most importantly, I would like to thank my old college buddy, Ken Nevitt, who willingly reads my early drafts and then corrects my historical inaccuracies. His attention to detail is breath-taking...He picks up even the most insignificant factual errors. He did the final edit on all three of the books. Thank you, Ken! In addition, my former colleague Chris Hotham read the early drafts and gave me good feedback.

It goes without saying I couldn't undertake these works without the lovely Anaclette who is not only my biggest critic but also my biggest supporter. She tells me in no uncertain terms where I have gone wrong...

We have done our very best to eliminate any errors either factual or typographical.

If you find any, please contact, phoneme52@yahoo.com

CR Spencer. July 2024

Other books by CR Spencer

The Penance Trilogy Penance: Disruption
   Penance: Keeping Busy
   Penance: Absolution
   An Unlikely Killer
   The Opener
   The Closer

All available from Amazon worldwide and Smashwords for Kindle, iBooks, Kobo and Barnes and Noble in all formats.

For a preview for Book 2 of the Ha'penny Steps, Nancy's Story, read on….

The Ha'penny Steps. Part 2; Nancy's Story.

Prologue Part 1
December 1937
London
Nancy Keeling

It was late. Peter Porteous sat in a window seat of the small café on the corner of Wardour Street and Brewer Street in Soho. He was sipping a cup of lukewarm tea. His chest was bothering him; he wasn't sure if he was going to get a full-on asthma attack. He had been visiting Jimmy Ryan in Holborn, who had been trying to persuade him to take some illicit goods back up to Kensal Town. These goods had apparently fallen off the back of a lorry in docklands...

Porteous was not entirely convinced that the good residents of Kensal Town would be that interested in men's shirts, socks and trousers...Now, if Ryan was offering good-quality hosiery or lingerie, that would be an entirely different kettle of fish...Porteous was very hesitant but Dennis Elphicke, the man who controlled all the stolen and black market goods in East London, wanted a return on the clothing and Ryan and Porteous would just have to get on with it, wouldn't they?

He looked out at the garishly lit street. The pavements were busy with couples exiting from some show or single men seeking out female company, if they were lucky. Every ten yards or so, on Brewer Street, a lady stood offering her wares with impunity. The so-called King of Soho, Charlie Maitland, had the franchise and with it came the Metropolitan Police, at a suitable price, of course.

Porteous looked at the row of ladies. Some were barely out of their teenage years. Some were on the wrong side of forty, but they all had one thing in common, the desire to earn quick money, despite the drawbacks.

Porteous looked for the minders. He could see them standing in shop doorways sucking on cheap tobacco and looking very furtive. A punter would be given the once over as he negotiated with his chosen lady. The female would look over as she pointed out her keeper. This let the client know that there would be consequences if there were any funny business. Porteous smiled to himself. There were several ladies of the night in Kensal Town who were good customers of his.

Some of these females came up to the West End to ply their trade. Some of them worked out of King's Cross, or the back of Paddington Station. His good friend, Edith Bell, the landlady of the White Horse Public House on Kensal Road, was not really a prostitute. It was just something she did from time to time when the takings in the pub were a little low. Porteous smiled at the thought. Edith could certainly handle herself when requested. Although the licence was in her husband's name, he hadn't been seen in Kensal Town for a number of years. Edith had a way of persuading her friendly magistrate to renew the licence; the rooms at the back of the courthouse were secluded enough for that purpose...

He sipped his tea and stared at the humanity spread out in front of him. He picked up the evening paper. The front page was full of doom and gloom about the impending chaos in Europe. Britain and France had signed away the Sudetenland to Hitler and his Germans. There were grumblings about the amount of appeasement being lavished on the dictator. He flicked over the pages and glanced at the stories. One in particular caught his attention, that of increasing shortages in the shops. Porteous raised his eyebrows. Shortages meant an upturn in trade for him and Jimmy Ryan... He smiled...

He was startled when the door burst open. He looked up to see a dark-haired female in her early twenties standing still and breathing heavily as though she had been running. A voice cried out from behind the counter,

"Oi! I don't want no trouble in 'ere. Do yer 'ear me?"

The female looked over at the proprietress and nodded, "It's okay; just a little misunderstanding, that's all."

"Well, take yer misunderstanding and bugger off..."

Porteous could see a commotion outside. One of the minders had crossed the street and was engaged in a conversation with one of the working girls; she pointed a finger at the café.

Porteous raised his eyebrows and pushed out the chair opposite him,

"You'd better sit down." He looked at the café proprietress, "Two more teas, Mable, please."

Mable sighed, "It's on you, Porteous. If there's any damage, you're payin' fer it..."

Porteous looked up at the young woman, "Sit down and take off your coat, quickly. What's your name?"

The female sat down, pulling off her coat, "Nancy, Nancy Keeling."

Porteous smiled, "Well, Nancy Keeling, you've been sat here with me for the last hour. Isn't that right, Mable?"

The proprietress swore loudly as she poured two more teas and brought them over to the table. Several other occupants looked up from their refreshments and then looked down...

The door opened noisily. Porteous looked up to see one of Charlie Maitland's minders.

Mable called out, "If yer comin' in, then shut the bloody door. Otherwise, bugger off. Yer disturbing me customers."

The minder sneered at the woman, "Shut up, Mable. Mind yer Ps and Qs. Did you see a tart come in here? She was wearin' a beige coat?"

Porteous pushed the coat further under the table.

Mable raised her voice, "Do yer see any tarts in ere? This is a respectable establishment. Ah pays me dues to Charlie like everybody else, so clear off!"

The minder walked slowly over to the counter, "A tom was plying her trade in Old Compton Street. She's not one of ours. If you see her, tell her she's gonna have her pretty little face smashed in."

He slapped his hand on the glass counter making the whole unit shake and wagged his finger in her face. "If I find she's been in 'ere, you're in deep shit."

Mable rolled her eyes, "Yeah, and if you or one of your thugs lays a hand on me or me place, Charlie will chop yer fingers off..."

The thug snorted and blew the proprietress a kiss. She swore loudly at him. As he turned, his eyes landed on Porteous and Nancy Keeling. He looked at the couple. He walked slowly up to the table. Porteous sipped at his tea. Nancy stared straight ahead...

The thug leaned into Porteous, "What are you doin' up here, Porteous?"

Porteous blew away some steam from the hot tea, "Just a bit of business, that's all."

The thug nodded his head at Nancy, "Who's yer lady friend?"

Porteous put down his cup, "That's my cousin, Nancy. I was showing her the sights."

The thug stared at Nancy, "You wasn't just in Old Compton Street, was yer?"

Nancy Keeling smiled sweetly, "No, I've been with Porteous all day. We may have walked down Old Compton Street, but that was hours ago."

The thug straightened up and looked at Porteous, "You'd better watch yerself, Porteous. Charlie's bin asking questions about yer business. If I were you, I'd stick to that shithole yer call Kensal Town. You aint grand enough to play with the big boys."

Porteous stared at him, "Be sure to give Charlie my best regards."

The door opened. A rough voice called out, "Mifty; she's been seen at the other end of Wardour Street..."

Michael 'Mifty' Mitchell smirked, at Porteous, "I'll catch up with you soon enough, Porteous and yer'll get what's comin' to you, wiv interest..."

Porteous sipped his tea and stared at the bald ex-fairground fighter.

Mifty Mitchell rushed out of the door, grabbing his mate as he pushed past.

The silenced café collectively breathed a sigh of relief.

Mable spoke loudly, "Porteous! Take yer friend out the back door, now! And yer owe me one and sixpence for the refreshments..."

Porteous gripped Nancy Keeling by the arm and pulled her up as she tried to retrieve her coat from under the table, "Come on, Nancy, let's not push our luck..."

Mable ushered them behind the counter and shoved them through a door into a rather grubby kitchen and out into a backyard. She slid across the bolts on the high gate at the end of the yard that led into a dark alley. She said,

"Follow the alley down to Berwick Street and then yer on yer own."

She looked at Porteous, "Yer a pain in the arse, Porteous. Take yer lady friend and put her right." She smiled at him as she closed the gate and slid the bolts back into place.

Porteous grabbed Nancy Keeling and hurried her along the alley that was littered with evidence of recent sexual activity and out into the throng in Berwick Street. He felt her pull him back.

"It's all right, Porteous, I'll find my own way home now."

"Look behind you, Nancy. Look over the road. Maitland's boys are everywhere." He paused and then asked, "Where's home? At least I can see you there."

"I'm staying in a hostel near Russell Square."

Porteous shrugged his shoulders, "Okay, let's go there, then."

"I'm perfectly capable of finding my own way, thank you."

She pulled away from him as he shrugged his shoulders.

He smiled at her, "Look, Nancy, I mean you no harm, but if you think you can just come down to Soho and stand on a street corner without Charlie Maitland's permission, you don't understand how things work here."

Nancy Keeling looked down, embarrassed.

Porteous continued, "Mifty Mitchell will give you a right slap when he catches up with you and if you encroach on his territory again, he will catch up with you."

Nancy pouted, "I'm just trying to earn a few bob to send home to my mum and sister, that's all."

She began to leave.

He said, "There are lots of easier ways of doing it."

She shrugged her shoulders, "What's it to do with you, anyway?"

"Absolutely nothing, Nancy...take care..." He began to walk away.

Nancy looked around her into the thronging crowds. She had no idea who was who. Men stared at her; one man licked his lips as he approached her. Her heart began to beat quickly. A woman pushed past her, muttering audibly,

"Out of the way, whore..."

A female out on her own at this time of night in Soho could only be one kind of woman...

Porteous was about ten yards away from her. She ran quickly. He turned as he felt her arm in his. He allowed himself a little smirk...

She gushed breathlessly, "Porteous, you can walk me home, if you like."

He nodded as he stared ahead. They began to chat as they walked.

"What are you doing here, Nancy?" he asked, more in hope than expectation

She answered quietly, "I told you; trying to earn some quick money to send home to my mum and sister."

Porteous looked at her as they reached a very crowded Oxford Street.

"As I said, there are plenty of ways to earn money; you don't have to do what you are trying to do."

She looked down and clutched at him even more tightly, "My mum's in trouble."

"What kind of trouble?"

"Money; what other kind can there be? If I don't get her some money by the end of the week, she's going to be evicted."

Porteous raised his eyebrows, "How much?"

"Over ten pounds."

"That's a lot of money, Nancy."

She stared ahead, "I know..."

They were almost at Tottenham Court Road. He pointed at the Crown Public House, "There's just enough time to get a drink, and you can tell me all about it."

She didn't object as he led her over the road. The public bar was crowded and very smoky. He led her into a quieter area where the beer was a penny dearer. He pushed past several servicemen still in their army uniforms, clearly enjoying a night out before King and country called upon them. A Royal Air Force sergeant leered at her; she flushed up.

He plonked two gin and tonics on the little table; she began to talk.

They were ushered out of the pub just after eleven-fifteen. By this time he had learned all he needed to know about Nancy Keeling, and that she certainly had no idea of what life was like as a working girl in central London.

They stood outside the imposing four-storey house on Bedford Way, just along from the British Museum. The gin had loosened her tongue.

He said, "Look, if you are determined to follow your chosen line of work, you are going to need help. There are a couple of girls where I live who work for Charlie Maitland. It might be better if you speak with them first instead of freelancing on the streets of Soho."

She nodded, "You might be right." She stared up at the building. "I'd better leave you here. I'm supposed to be home by midnight before they lock the door."

She reached up and pecked him on the cheek, "Thanks, Porteous. How do I contact you?"

"The White Horse on Kensal Road. Look up the telephone number and ask for the landlady, Edith Bell. She knows a little of your business. She will get a message to me." He looked at the tall, extremely good-looking woman.

"In the meantime, keep off the streets. There's plenty of other work to be had…"

She smiled at him and went up the stone steps. When she reached the top, she turned but, Porteous had already disappeared into the night.

The night bell sounded as she opened the heavy-wooden door. She stood in the dimly lit and rather grand entrance hall that had somehow lost its charm over the years. The mosaic floor tiles were cracked and showing signs of a hasty repair. A wooden booth with a glass window had been created to the right. A rather stern looking woman with reading glasses perched on the end of her nose glared at her.

The woman rapped on the glass. Nancy looked up. The woman beckoned her over.

"Miss Keeling, you've been here for four days. You know the rules. Have you managed to secure employment yet?"

Nancy looked down, "Not yet Miss Ledston, but I've had a number of interviews. I'm just waiting to be contacted." She paused, "Have there been any messages for me?"

Ledston cleared her throat and turned to a numbered board behind her with little slots. "You are in 501; there's nothing for you. Your rent is due on Friday. Do you have the means to pay it?"

Nancy nodded, "I'm sure I'll have something sorted by the end of the week."

Ledston summoned her even closer, "I have to tell you that one of the other residents saw you on Old Compton Street; was that you?"

Nancy swallowed nervously, "It-it's possible, Miss. I met my cousin, and we walked all over the West End."

"Cousin? You didn't say you had a cousin living in London."

"Yes-yes. He lives in a place called Kensal Town over in West London."

Miss Ledston narrowed her eyes, "I hope you haven't been working on the streets, Miss Keeling. The trustees of this hostel take a very dim view of such behaviour. This establishment is for respectable-working ladies seeking to establish themselves in London, and not a sleeping house for common prostitutes. Do you understand?"

Nancy nodded and looked down, "Of course, Miss Ledston. I'll have employment in the next few days."

Ledston opened the wooden door to her little cubicle rattling a bunch of keys, "Now, if you'll excuse me, Miss Keeling, it's time I locked the doors. Good night…"

Nancy Keeling trudged wearily up five flights of stairs. Her room, for what it was, was situated at the end of a dimly lit corridor. She inserted a key into the old lock and opened the door. She immediately felt the cold, with the heating having been turned off a few hours earlier. She closed the door behind her and slid across the bolt. The room was barely ten feet by six. A single bed was on one wall, with a sink and a battered wardrobe on the other. The bed linen was threadbare. She had taken to throwing her only coat over the bed to keep warm.

The toilet was back down the corridor. If the ladies wanted a bath, they had to seek a key from whoever was on duty in the entrance hall. Residents needed to purchase a token to insert into the slot meter to acquire hot water. Rooms had a supply of lukewarm water that was sufficient for guests to give themselves an all-over wash standing in a basin. For the privilege of residing in this establishment, Nancy paid nineteen shillings and six pence a week.

Nancy threw off her coat and sat on the end of her bed. She could hear two of the girls chatting in the room next door through the thinly-partitioned walls. Her neighbours hadn't spoken to her since she had moved in the previous weekend, not that she was bothered anyway. Her local vicar in Mulbarton on the outskirts of Norwich had arranged the accommodation for her.

She kicked off her shoes. Porteous was nice and didn't seem to want to take advantage of her, but that was for another day…

She woke about eight the next morning. Noise from the other residents would have wakened the dead as they busied themselves for a day in their 'regular' jobs. Nancy pulled the pillow over her head…

The cafeteria was virtually empty by the time she got down there. Two assistants were making desultory efforts to clean up. She stood over the tea urn and poured some tea. She sat down, picked up a battered newspaper and skimmed through the advertisements for the job vacancies. There was plenty of work to be had, ranging from shop assistants to typists and even switchboard operators in the local telephone exchange. Unfortunately, none of them would give her sufficient money to stop her mother and sister being evicted by the end of the week. There was only one thing to do...She made her way to the payphone in the reception area and made the call...

The Ha'penny Steps. Part 2; Nancy's Story, is now available.